THE IDOLS OF THE CAVE

THE IDOLS OF THE CAVE

Frederic Prokosch

MODERN
TIMES

The Idols of the Cave are the idols of the individual man. For every one (besides the errors common to human nature in general) has a cave or den of his own, which refracts and discolours the light of nature. ... So that the spirit of man is in fact a thing variable and full of perturbation, and governed as it were by chance.

BACON, *Novum Organum*

CONTENTS

EDITORIAL PREFACE

Reading Gore Vidal's collection of essays, *United States,* nearly twenty years ago, I came across a portrait of a writer of whom I had never heard: Frederic Prokosch. The portrait sparked my interest and I went on to read several of Prokosch's novels, starting with the faux travelogue that made him famous, *The Asiatics.* I wrote to Vidal asking where I could learn more about this forgotten author. He replied that everything he has to say about Prokosch was there in that essay. But I had my doubts. One always has doubts regarding Prokosch.

The conventional story of Prokosch is the familiar one of the shooting star. None of the novels or books of poetry he wrote came close to the popularity of *The Asiatics.* None was as praised by the great and the good as that book had been. His reputation, mainly as an adroit fantasy writer and stylist, is obscure.

So Prokosch was in life. He said that he was, and always would be, unknowable. This is the little that is known: Frederic "Fritz" Prokosch grew up in Wisconsin, Texas, Illinois, Pennsylvania, and Europe as the son of an Austrian father and an American mother. His father was a linguist, his mother was a pianist. Prokosch earned his own PhD with a thesis on Chaucerian apocrypha. Then the chronology blurs. He became an expatriate, mostly in Europe, eventually settling in the south of France, where he lived until his death in 1989.

One or two other details about him stand out. Prokosch loved maps. And he had a competitive streak: He was a fierce player of squash and tennis. Recognition probably meant something to him. He wrote to famous writers and poets. He sent them gifts-special editions of their work, which he had printed, lines of his own poetry, and sometimes photographs of himself.

He had a certain idea of ambition. But he had also had, and lost, fame. He liked to live well but was not, as far as one can tell, a fortune hunter. Prokosch relished solitude and considered it to be a source of freedom, yet he wrote to be read. Nearly all his novels feature a seeker, a quest, and a didactic philosophical tone that, as he has suggested, wields ambiguity as a weapon of truth. What did he seek? What did he need?

Prokosch's fame arrived on the eve of the Second World War, but the war was not good to him. One of the war's casualties, it is said, was the spiritual journey. There had already been one lost generation after the last war. Nobody wanted to read about another one. To be lost twice over meant not being, or appearing to be, lost at all. This unsympathetic trend did not serve Prokosch.

Another reason that Prokosch fell out of fashion was his talent for crafting scenes. The magical locales in *The Asiatics,* and New York City in *The Idols of the Cave,* are his protagonists. They speak, feel, and act more vividly—and perhaps, with the war in mind, more violently—than any of his human characters. Adopting the cocktail party lingo that one might have heard spoken in *The Idols of the Cave,* it would be fair to say that Prokosch's writing juxtaposes impressionistic characters with expressionistic settings. This juxtaposition did not suit postwar audiences.

Yet Prokosch was a formidable mimic with a fine ear. His characters may be slight and falsifying, and his prose sometimes purple, but his scenes are remarkable. His precise sense of place in this novel also extended to time. New York during WWII was filled with odd European exiles, but they eventually left, and the city, following textbook film noir, resumed being a place of mystery where people hear their names whispered in the shadows.

The Idols of the Cave is more of a study than a story. It is a study of fear, uncertainty, doubt, apprehension, and betrayal-lined with brittle attraction. What is its source and its import? A well-informed outsider's perverted sense of superiority; a small captivation and a strange taste in the mouth; a dampened sensitivity of an adult who spent his days as a child keeping his feet away from fallen leaves so as not to hurt their imaginary feelings; a wish to escape to a place that is simpler, more direct, purer, maybe more perfect.

Here, too, you hear the sort of rarefied mimicry found in the memoir he wrote late in life, *Voices,* filled with conversations conducted and overheard, which were, most likely, as reinvented as the pitch-perfect scenes in *The Asiatics.* Prokosch has been called an elusive solipsist. His scenes, characters, and even his plots hint at existing elsewhere, as if his writing were a roman-à-clef that dare not speak its name because to do so would be a betrayal of Prokosch's own imagination and integrity. Hence the concept of the idol, deriving from Bacon, which acts in aid of a parable presumably more intricate and genuine than a refractive masquerade: It suggests a moral failing, a layered perfidy, an aspirational conceit, and, at the same time, an ameliorative remaking of the self. Although for what purpose?

Gore Vidal has provided a clue. In his essay, he tells the story of Prokosch's visit to New York when the two went to a party with some local academics.

> Naturally they regarded Prokosch with contempt. They knew that he had once been famous ... but they had forgotten why. ... A great deal was said about poetry ... Prokosch was entirely ignored. But he listened politely as the uses of poetry in general and of the classics in particular were brought into question. Extreme positions were taken. Finally, one poet-teacher pulled the chain, as it were, on all of Western civilization:The classics, as such, were totally irrelevant. For a moment, there was a blessed silence. Then Prokosch began to recite in Latin a passage from Virgil; and the room grew very cold and still. "It's Dante," a full professor whispered to a full wife. ... When Prokosch had finished, he said mildly, "Those lines are carved in marble in the gardens of the Villa Borghese at Rome. I used to look at them every day and I'd think, that is what poetry is, something that can be carved in marble, something that can still be beautiful to read after so many centuries."

Prokosch had great expectations for *The Idols of the Cave.* He had just switched publishers and imagined that the novel would bring a rebirth of both his craft and his career. At the time, he was also working on translations of works by Euripides, Hölderin, Labé, and Michelangelo, so it is fair to say that with *Idols* he aimed to solidify his reputation as a writer's writer—to achieve a note of worth, or to conserve what was left of it, though again by inference and suggestion, and so by the tendency to perform the role of the literary trickster. But *The Idols of the Cave* is a melancholy book. It is, like its author, in search of a vital second act. We now know that it never came for Frederic Prokosch. Or perhaps it has not come yet.

—Kenneth Weisbrode

PART ONE: 1941

1

A SHADOW fell; there was a sense of catastrophe. A sudden rustle sprang through the park, and the deep green air began to quiver.

Then the clouds exploded. It was like an eclipse. A curtain of rain was hurled over the Plaza, and a great tree of lightning shot forth above Harlem. The peaks of Fifth Avenue grew momentous and shadowy, like some huge volcanic structure caught in a cloud of ashes.

The city, for once, looked curiously helpless; at the disposal of an energy more immense than its own. Along the streets there was a kind of exuberant frenzy: hats blown away, umbrellas colliding, a cascade of apples rolling across the pavement.

It poured with great violence for about fifteen minutes. Then, as suddenly as it had begun, it ceased. The clouds thinned and parted; the sky grew radiant. A fresh, electrical fragrance flowed through the park. The umbrellas vanished, the pigeons reappeared, and the traffic went hissing down the wet black asphalt.

A taxi whose panes were still streaming with raindrops came to a halt with a weary squeal, in front of the Devonshire Hotel. A boy in green gabardine languidly approached, and reached into the car for the luggage. There were three large bags, rather battered and worn, covered with labels from Bordeaux, Barcelona and Lisbon.

The room clerk gazed stonily at the newcomer. "You cabled? ... I'll see, sir. What is the full name? ... Jonathan Ely; just a moment, sir. ... Yes. We have a reservation. Boy, please! Room 2317. ... Yes, it has a private bath. ... Of course. You're very welcome, sir."

Jonathan waited for several minutes in the enormous lobby. Streams of guests—elderly ladies, nervous foreigners, British officers—were drifting among the marble columns. A sound of dance music rose from the cocktail lounge. The maze of tall mirrors and fluorescent lights cast a nervous glitter through the hall; there was a sense of confusion and overexcitement.

The bellboy came strolling up with the bags. Jonathan stepped into one of a long row of elevators, and a moment later he felt himself floating noiselessly skyward. He closed his eyes. The sense of unreality grew; it acted upon him like a narcotic.

He arrived in his room on the twenty-third floor. The bellboy deposited the luggage, turned on the light in the bathroom, and paused significantly. He took his tip and departed.

Jonathan sat down in the armchair and looked around. It was an arid little room, all in yellow and brown, with a chenille coverlet on the bed and two small etchings on the wall. There was a hard expressionless look about the furniture.

A sense of bleakness, of desolation, swept over him. He took off his coat and stepped to the window. The broad autumnal sea of Central Park shone below, rippling northward between two tremendous aisles of stone. The storm had cleared the air; the city shone with a strong amber luster.

One by one he singled out the familiar towers. The sun was setting, and only the peaks of the Pierre and the Sherry-Netherland still wore a fiery crest. The façades of Fifth Avenue rose sharply against the sky with their finely modulated whites, grays, and browns. Every detail of the scene was a stroke of human artifice: nowhere was it touched with humanity. It was a sight he had seen innumerable times in the past; but now, seen freshly, it rose before him with a spectacular oddity.

He sat down again in his armchair, leafed absent-mindedly through the phone book, and finally picked up the telephone. First of all he called up his cousin, Quincy Potter.

The maid answered the phone. "Mr. Potter is at the club, sir. We're expecting him home in time for dinner."

Jonathan called the Yale Club. Mr. Potter, they explained, was still on the squash courts. Presently a brisk, emphatic voice came from the other end of the wire.

"Who is this, please?"

"Is that you, Quincy? This is Jonathan! I'm here in the Devonshire. ... "

"Jonathan! By God, it's good to hear your voice again! You just arrived from Lisbon?"

"My boat landed at noon. It took four hours to go through all the nuisance. ... "

"Well, come to dinner tonight, old fellow! I'll call up right away and tell Delia." Quincy's voice was sharp and breathless. "You've never met Delia? No, we were married after you left, of course. Well, seven o'clock, then? I've got to dash back to the court now. See you later, old boy!"

Jonathan opened his bags and began to hang up his suits, laid his shirts in the dresser, and placed his toilet articles on the white glass shelf in the bathroom. He undressed, took a bath, shaved, and stepped into a gray flannel suit.

He looked at himself in the full-length mirror. He was a sturdy young man of middle height, with bright dark eyes and short black hair; there was a thin, rather unusual streak of white hair across the center. His face was still very brown from the sun, and his features had a rough but modest and appealing, an unmistakably American look: his expression was hesitant and searching; there was only a hint, carefully hidden, of intensity.

He sat down again beside the telephone. He tried to call several of his friends; all were out. He tried to reach his old uncle, Mr. Mannering, and then his aunt, Mrs. Westover; both, as it happened, were out of town for the week end. Finally he called an old Yale friend of his, Horace Hayden.

"Jonathan, well, well," said Horace in his high, effusive voice. "The wanderer is home again! And how was Europe? You really must have had some shattering experiences! ... By the way, can you come to the ballet with me tonight? ... Marvelous. Meet me in front of the Met. Eight-thirty, on the dot. *Au revoir!*"

Jonathan sat motionless in his chair for several minutes. It was growing darker. A touch of coolness crossed the room, and the light from the bathroom door grew sharper. A radio was playing in the adjoining chamber.

He found his muscles growing tense. His nerves were suddenly on the alert. Something was wrong: an effect of the light, perhaps. A faintly unpleasant aroma. An undertone, a fugitive little staccato.

But it was more than that. He rose, opened his window, and leaned out.

Night was falling. A plum-colored mist filled the park. The lights along Fifth Avenue were beginning to shine. A block to the right lay the twilight elegance of the Plaza; two blocks to the left, the feverish sparkle of Columbus Circle. Far below rolled the traffic, wave upon wave, flinging its shattered streams through the neighboring gorges. It sobbed, it stuttered, it moaned like a cataract. There was no trace, none whatever, of human will or control; nothing that he could see but an endless thrust of metal.

But then, quite imperceptibly, a trace of life appeared—a few wayward fringes along Central Park South. They were human beings; so it appeared; it struck him with a kind of pathos. They looked like tiny chessmen, tiny figures in white or black mysteriously creeping over a great checkered pattern. They wandered past the lamplight, listened, hesitated, glanced about: a policeman, two Negroes, two sailors in white. And at last a quick chill of elation swept over him. The darkness below was like a pool, a well of experience which awaited him. He felt like a diver poised on the brink of a new element. The past had suddenly withered; below lay the present, crisp, transparent. And around it, in dark little eddies, swirled the future.

2

IT WAS seven o'clock exactly, when Jonathan arrived at Quincy Potter's house on Sixty-third Street.

He instantly recognized the old butler, Sturgis, who opened the door for him. "Good evening, Mr. Ely." He surveyed Jonathan with an air of ruthless scrutiny, and raised his brows. "So you're back from Europe? It has left you in remarkably good health, sir, if I may say so."

Sturgis was a cadaverous man with huge red ears and a mournful bearing. He took Jonathan's hat and opened the door into the drawing room; then he murmured, with a sigh:

"Mr. Potter will be down directly, sir. ... "

"He's been well, I trust?" said Jonathan.

"I believe, sir," remarked Sturgis, "that you'll find he's hardly changed." He coughed equivocally and withdrew.

The long dark drawing room was precisely as Jonathan had last seen it, not quite five years ago. Indeed, it seemed scarcely to have been touched for a generation. It was like an album of old photographs: everything blurred and slightly yellowed. Four Renaissance chairs stood at the farther end of the room, among the towering mahogany bookshelves. Faded sets of Whittier, Longfellow, and Lowell stood gathering dust, tier upon tier. A rosewood console stood between two french windows, which opened upon a tiny garden. There was a round-arched fireplace of black marble; on the mantel stood an ormolu clock, whose hands still pointed, as they had five years before, at a quarter to five. Two white porcelain poodles stood on either side of the clock. In the corner stood a grand piano with immense, fluted legs; an album of Brahms waltzes stood opened above the keyboard.

But more suggestive than the effect of these disconsolate objects was the scent of the room, and the interplay of light and shadow. There was a smell of old plush, old books, decaying leather; all helping to create a kind of posthumous tyranny, a limbo of anachronisms. The evening light, fading as it slipped through the curtains, crouched like a prisoner in a distant corner.

There was a light rustle in the hallway, and the sound of a girl's voice:

"Oh, good evening! Are you Jonathan?"

Jonathan turned. A blond girl in a sky-blue dress had entered the room, and was walking slowly toward him.

"Yes," said Jonathan, "yes, I am!"

"Do forgive us! We're always late," she murmured apologetically. "It's dreadful, isn't it?"

Her voice, face, and figure were still immersed in shadow: there was, for an instant, the illusion of a creature floating through the depths of a pool.

"Dreadful?" said Jonathan very gently. "Why, no! Not at all. ... Are you Delia?"

She nodded, with a touch of embarrassment, and gazed past him into the garden. She stood beside him and drew the curtains gently to one side.

He watched her with a gathering incredulity. It seemed quite unbelievable that this was Quincy's wife. The evening light drew a fine russet thread across her profile.

"Were you looking at the garden?" she inquired rather thoughtfully. "It's a dear little garden, isn't it?...I water the flowers every day. On sunny days I sit there and read."

"Really? How delightful!" said Jonathan, watching her with amazement. "And what do you read?"

"Oh"—she moved her hand in a vague gesture toward the bookshelves—"everything! I'm trying to be systematic. Last year I read Harrison Ainsworth. This year I'm doing Louisa Alcott. Next year, perhaps, I'll come to Jane Austen."

"And you'll go straight through the alphabet?"

"Certainly!" said Delia cheerfully. "Why not?"

"You'll be quite an old lady," said Jonathan, smiling, "when you reach Emile Zola."

"Oh, perhaps!" said Delia patiently. "But I don't mind, really!"

"You are very ambitious," said Jonathan, with admiration.

She turned and looked at him, a little startled. "Ambitious? Well, I never thought of that....I really don't have anything else to do, you know!"

She let the curtain fall back, with a little sigh, and walked slowly toward the piano. "Quincy has talked of you so often," she murmured. "He said you were very clever, in a quiet sort of way!" She was looking at him with curiosity, then suddenly blushed. "I thought you'd be rather thin, and very dull. Like a schoolteacher. But you aren't, are you?"

She paused in front of the piano, looked down with a smile, and drew her fingers soundlessly along the keyboard.

"No," said Jonathan in hardly more than a whisper, "I'm not....not quite a schoolteacher. But I'm afraid," he added sadly, "that I'm really rather..."

The sentence remained unfinished; she was gazing at him attentively. And again, for only a moment, she seemed imperceptibly to recede; her beauty deepened, darkened, dissolved.

There were footsteps on the stairway, and a moment later Jonathan saw his cousin Quincy stalk into the room.

"Well, well, here's our cousin Jonathan at last! It's great to see you, old man. We thought you'd never get back! God, Europe must be a desperate place these days. . . . "

Quincy's face was glossy, like pink china, from the bath and the exercise. He looked extremely, almost disconcertingly cheerful. He was taller than Jonathan, sharply featured, broad-hipped. Nothing in him had changed, except for a hint of fat under the jaw, and a slightly ominous withdrawal of the hair. He was only thirty-three; but Jonathan felt, with a certain shock, that for all his boyishness of manner, Quincy was in essence already middle-aged.

"You've met Delia, of course," he continued in his loud, breezy voice. "She's been eager to see you. Wondering what you'd be like. Haven't you, Delia? . . . I've been telling her what a splendid fellow you are! So don't disappoint her!" His teeth shone in a flat, affable smile.

He looked toward the table, with an air of satisfaction. "Ah, here are the cocktails. Well, Sturgis, what have you got for us today? Did you get hold of some of that undrinkable gin again? You'll have a martini, won't you, Jonathan?"

Jonathan nodded vaguely; he hardly heard what Quincy was saying. A gentle agitation was working on his senses.

He turned, with a sudden access of shyness, to Delia. "Do you come from New York"—he hesitated slightly—"Delia?"

"Oh, I'm afraid not," said Delia cautiously. "I'm from Philadelphia; I never laid eyes on New York till I married!"

"Do you like it?" He coughed faintly. "New York, I mean? The life? The people?"

She smiled faintly, with a puzzled air. "Like it? Well, you know, I haven't really seen much of it.... I always heard it was such a wicked, adventurous city." She gazed wistfully through the window. "But you see, we live rather quietly. Quincy feels it's more dignified. I read, I play the piano. That's just what I did in Philadelphia. So, you see, I hardly notice the difference!"

She had returned to the window; again she drew aside the curtain. A brief gleam of light was flung across the room, like a knife, and hung quivering on the opposite wall.

Then the darkness grew firm. Sturgis crossed the hall and turned on the light.

Quincy was standing beside the table, where Sturgis had placed a bowl of ice, together with the gin and vermouth bottles. He measured the ingredients with zealous precision, then stirred them up in a green glass pitcher. He touched the glasses very lightly, to see whether they had been properly chilled. Then he poured out the drinks and squeezed the peel of a lemon above each glass. He smiled placidly and allowed the vapor to settle. "I think they're best this way," he stated, in the tones of an expert. "Here, try it. You like it? ... Well, Jonathan, old man, here's to your return to New York!"

The remaining two guests arrived at this moment: Mrs. Mannering, who was the second wife of Jonathan's uncle, a tall and resolute woman with blue-gray hair; and Wilfred Silliman, a flourishing bachelor in his fifties.

They both greeted Jonathan with a crisp, casual air; he might have been away five days instead of five years.

"My dear," said Mrs. Mannering, gazing stonily past him, "I don't see how you stood it so long! I really don't!"

"Europe," sighed Wilfred Silliman, fluttering his hands in alarm. "It's all a ghastly nightmare. When I think of the years I've spent there ... in London, Paris, Antibes ... "

"Well, they've brought it on themselves," said Mrs. Mannering caustically. "Let us hope," she added with emphasis, "that it will teach those idiots a lesson."

"Oh, Pauline," cried Wilfred, "you're really too, too disciplinarian, my dear!"

Sturgis appeared at the door at that point, and morosely announced that dinner was ready.

3

THE dinner began, rather conservatively, with a cream of celery soup, passed quietly on to roast lamb with mint jelly, and ended, sedately, with vanilla ice cream and chocolate sauce. Quincy had ordered, in view of the occasion, that a bottle of burgundy be opened. Delia requested Sturgis to serve the coffee at the table instead of in the drawing room.

"Should we open, do you suppose, a bottle of Napoleon brandy?" suggested Quincy, with a twinkle in his pale gray eyes. "To celebrate our cousin Jonathan's return from the land of the lost?" He leaned over one of the candles to light his cigar.

Delia turned gravely to look at Jonathan. "Would that please you, Jonathan? Do you like Napoleon brandy?"

"We always have time," said Wilfred Silliman ceremoniously, "for a drop of Napoleon brandy. ... You're off to the ballet, my boy?"

Jonathan nodded. "Yes. I haven't seen the ballet for years."

"It's a delicious program tonight," put in Wilfred. "Kirillova's dancing. You've seen her before, of course?"

"I'm afraid not," said Jonathan. "I'm very ignorant about the ballet."

"Tch, tch! You've missed a great artist, my lad. Kirillova is glorious! Absolutely heavenly!"

"Well now," said Mrs. Mannering, with a cool, inquisitorial air, "do tell us about your adventures, my dear. You left France right after the outbreak? And then two whole years in Spain and Portugal! What on earth were you doing? In those peculiar countries?"

"Oh, painting. Traveling about. Sketching," said Jonathan vaguely. "Cathedrals and castles and monasteries."

"Oh yes, of course, you're planning to be an architect. ... Well, I just wonder, will there be any cathedrals left in Europe after this war?" Mrs. Mannering sighed, and gazed at her long scarlet fingernails.

"Don't, don't, my dear!" pleaded Wilfred. "I feel faint at the mere thought of a bomb dropping on Chartres, or Siena ... "

"Weren't you nervous, my dear? Over there?" demanded Mrs. Mannering.

"Nervous?" said Jonathan. "No. Not in the least."

"Weren't you homesick?" inquired Delia solemnly.

"Homesick?" Jonathan paused. "I think not; no, not really."

Sturgis was leaning, over, with an air of cynicism, to pour the brandy into pear-shaped glasses. Wilfred held his glass tenderly in both hands, raised his brows, closed his eyes, and inhaled the fragrance. He nodded astutely. Mrs. Mannering lit a cigarette and stared disparagingly at the ceiling. Quincy was smiling affably, as always, and Delia listened quietly with lowered eyes. She was drawing her finger lightly around the rim of the brandy glass.

For several moments no one spoke. Four candles were burning on the table, and cast a mellow light on the bowl of asters in the center. The stealthy light of the flames shone in the brandy glasses and the silver cutlery. The dark walls and the ceiling retired into shadow. The old family portraits—the Potters, the

15

Mannerings—took on a misty, saturnine look; they seemed to be crouching behind the dinner guests, spying on them from a state of perpetual ambush.

And for a moment Jonathan had a curious impression of things left unuttered, of a subtle atavism about to operate; of, perhaps, a veiled conspiracy between the house and the ancestors, between the walls, the knives and glasses, the family portraits, and the guests. Wilfred sipped tenderly at the brandy glass, Quincy puffed at his cigar. Mrs. Mannering drew her scarlet finger tips slowly across her neck.

Delia sat in silence, submissive, isolated. One of the flames leaped suddenly; her lips and eyes grew brilliant; her hair seemed to be, for an instant, aflame.

The silence hovered over the dinner table a moment longer. Mrs. Mannering crushed her cigarette and sighed.

"And what," she inquired wearily, "do you suppose is going to happen now? Will there be a compromise peace? Or will Europe insist on being utterly destroyed?"

"I think," declared Quincy, "we should keep out of the sordid mess. We can't snatch Europe's chestnuts out of the fire, again and again!"

"True, true," murmured Wilfred sadly. "But, my dear, I simply shudder at the thought of my beloved England being brought to her knees by those dreadful barbarians. ... " He ran his hand softly over his wavy gray hair.

Jonathan glanced at his watch and rose, with an air of apology. "Please forgive me! It's very rude of me, I'm afraid."

"Oh, you'd better hurry!" said Delia, with a worried look. "You mustn't be late, Jonathan!" There was a flash of affection in her voice. Jonathan pressed her warm, firm hand.

Mrs. Mannering smiled a little frostily. Wilfred waved his fingers limply. "It would be too ghastly, really, if you missed Kirillova! Do rush, my dear boy."

Quincy took him by the arm and accompanied him to the door, with an air of cousinly affection. "Well, be good!" he shouted merrily, as he stood by the door. "And be careful! New York City has its dangers, too, you know!"

Jonathan laughed. "Don't be afraid!"

He ran down the steps and hailed a taxi.

4

HORACE HAYDEN was waiting impatiently in front of the theater. He was standing under the marquee, wearing a green tweed jacket and gray flannel slacks; there was no mistaking his bulging eyes and round, apprehensive face.

He seized Jonathan's hand and muttered breathlessly: "Really, I thought you'd never come! You're madly late, you know. I'd rather die than miss *Lilac Garden!* Come, let's rush. ... "

They darted through the empty foyer and crept down the dark aisle toward their seats, which were on the extreme left, very near the orchestra. Horace Hayden whispered an apology: "They're the only ones I could get, I'm afraid! The ballet's frightfully popular these days. ... "

The opening number was well under way. The backdrop revealed a darkened garden overflowing with lilac. There were three characters on the stage, in costumes of the 1830s, gliding about with yearning gestures to an accompaniment of music by Chausson.

Jonathan had seen very little ballet; he knew nothing whatever of its finer points. It all seemed rather feverish, a little pointless, and utterly artificial.

A new character appeared on the stage, a slight, black-haired woman in a long white dress.

"It's Kirillova!" whispered Horace Hayden, in tones of awe.

Kirillova moved across the stage, extended her arms, turned her head. The gestures were extremely plain, her face was quite expressionless. Jonathan saw nothing stirring or impressive in her presence. He felt rather disappointed.

The music continued; the plot progressed. Jonathan now understood that it was a tale of frustrated love, in which four people were involved; and that all four were making poignant gestures and heroic sacrifices.

But he remained unimpressed, until he noticed that Horace Hayden had grown pale with admiration. He began to watch a little more closely.

And gradually, as the pattern of the dance gained intensity, something of its hidden meaning finally reached him. He felt stirred at last; he began to see in Kirillova's barren movements a sudden, electrical loveliness.

Little by little an obscure feeling in him grew more distinct; a feeling that he was being initiated into some half-remembered world, a world continually unreal and yet, in some disturbing way, more real than any he had known. It was a sense of life abnormally sharpened and accelerated and yet, somehow, abnormally dimmed. He had felt it ever since his arrival that morning; and he now saw it curiously reflected in the ballet dancers.

They seemed to be wearing masks. Their faces looked petrified and inhuman. Their gestures and passions seemed governed by an influence beyond their control. They moved slowly across the stage, caught in a hypnotic spell, enthralled by all the delicate refinements of a ritual. Love had lost its co-ordinating power; it was an opiate, a ceremony. And what emerged from this exquisite quartet, whose every posture was flawlessly harmonized, was nothing but a desperate solitude.

The curtain fell and the audience applauded wildly. Kirillova appeared for her calls, bowed daintily several times, and slipped away again. The two friends strolled to the bar for a drink.

"Wonderful, isn't she?" said Horace fervently, placing his elbow on the bar. "The subtlety! The precision! She's absolutely on a level with Pavlova, I'm convinced. These old names become a legend, you know; one tends to overrate them.

"By the way," he went on, sipping his drink, "I hope you're free after the show? We've been asked to a small party. I think you might be amused. Chiefly painters and writers. Some of the ballet dancers are coming too, I suspect."

Jonathan glanced at Horace with curiosity. Horace had shed entirely his Yale manners and attitudes; a perceptible lisp had appeared in his voice, a studied languor had crept into his gestures. He had turned, it was evident, into a fashionable bohemian.

They returned to their seats for the second number. This was *The Three-Cornered Hat;* Horace sighed with pleasure at Picasso's backdrop, and vigorously applauded Massine's impersonation. The third number was *Aurora's Wedding,* with music by Tchaikovsky. This Jonathan enjoyed for its unaffected pageantry, but it left Horace relatively cool.

"Look," he murmured, "that's José Valdez doing the adagio. He's a newcomer. Very promising... And that's Lydia Ivanova over there on the right. You see the one I mean? I think she's coming to the party, by the way."

Valdez was a sinuous young man with very white teeth, who did a series of spectacular leaps across the stage. Ivanova was a slim, crisply built dancer, with curly brown hair and sharply defined features.

Jonathan watched her for a minute or two. There was a Russian flavor in her little face, with its firm, clean line of the chin and prominent cheekbones. She was charming, but not in the least brilliant. Then he caught sight of another dancer at the opposite end of the stage, with a blond Grecian head, who struck him as exquisite.

"Who is that?" he whispered to Horace.

"The blonde? That's Natalia Petrova," said Horace eagerly. "She's considered the real beauty of the company. You'll be seeing her tonight, too, I imagine."

Horace rose promptly when the performance was over. He refused to wait for the curtain calls.

"Come," he whispered anxiously. "Let's grab a cab, before the rush. ... We'll go straight to Peter Sebastian's flat down in the Village."

They called a taxi, and Horace gave an address on Tenth Street. "I do hope you'll be amused," he repeated somewhat wistfully. He looked at Jonathan with sudden affection. "Well, what was it like over there? You must tell me all about it, sometime. I'm dying to hear! Was it terribly depressing?"

The taxi followed the plunge of traffic down Broadway, and finally entered the dimmer regions of Greenwich Village.

5

JONATHAN followed Horace up three gloomy flights of stairs. A huge man with a thick black beard caught sight of them through the open door and wandered out to greet them.

"Do come in! The party's a sickening failure," he muttered. "So this is your friend who's just arrived from Europe? ... Things are pretty bad over there, eh? Well, he won't find them much better over here, I'm afraid." He regarded Jonathan with a clinical air.

Horace introduced this melancholy person as their host, Peter Sebastian. Sebastian must have been almost six and a half feet tall. His bones were enormous, and he was putting on fat. Everything about him was immense except his eyes, which were pink, defiant, and almost invisible. He wore a red shirt with an open collar and tight-fitting, oil-stained dungarees.

Jonathan had a small cup of reddish liquid thrust casually into his hand. He smelled it, and detected a faint scent of grenadine. He felt himself surrounded by a tangle of disillusioned voices, strangely dressed bodies, and apathetic faces.

He noticed a half-finished portrait on one wall, and wandered over to look at it closely. Immediately Sebastian, flattered by his interest, came sauntering wearily to his side.

"It's absolutely no good," he said, shrugging his shoulders. "It refuses to come to life. It's dead as a doornail. ... It's no use, quite frankly, in trying to paint decently nowadays. There's nothing worth painting. The human race is decaying. ... "

It was a portrait of a young woman, apparently, though the features were rather difficult to distinguish. There was a violently colored background of black, red, and yellow. The manner was a mingling of Rouault and Modigliani.

"It's very ... emphatic," said Jonathan discreetly. "Who is it?"

"Lydia Ivanova, the dancer." Sebastian smiled rather ambiguously. "She's been sitting for this portrait for months. But it's no use; I'll never be able to finish it. To finish anything, nowadays, is to distort reality. ... " He wandered back toward the door to greet a new group of guests.

A literary conversation had begun beside Jonathan. Three people were sitting on the floor, engaged in a cynical discourse on poetry. One of these was Horace Hayden, another was a small, bald character with thick glasses, the third was a huge, aggressive woman with very short hair.

"It's no use pretending," said the large woman disdainfully, "that poetry can bring you or me salvation. No, no. The era for these easy panaceas is past!"

"Then," said the bald little man, "you see nothing but darkness ahead for the creative artist?"

The large woman snarled faintly. "Creative artist? Don't be ludicrous! There is no such thing, in our society, as a creative artist! We're all hacks; why not face it? Art for us is just a masquerade!"

Jonathan, as he listened, grew a little puzzled. He had been at a similar type of party once, some five or six years ago; and then there had been a very obstinate, impassioned series of arguments, concerning the social responsibilities of the writer, and so on. Something unusual, he felt, must have happened in the meantime.

"Have you read Marsden's new book of poems?" inquired Horace, peering rather anxiously at the large, grim woman. Hubert Marsden was a young Englishman whose work was enjoying a certain vogue in advanced circles.

"Marsden?" The woman shot a patronizing look at Horace. "Just another of those Oxford dilettanti. Caught in his own neurotic tangle. Just another lost soul. There's no hope for him, I'm afraid. ..."

A group of guests had just arrived. Horace rose, with a look of relief, and greeted them effusively.

"Natalia! Lydia! José!" he squealed, and kissed the two girls tenderly on their cheeks.

Jonathan was introduced to the newcomers, who were all three dancers. He vaguely recognized the dark, languorous youth and one of the women; but it was the third, the overpowering blonde with the striking profile, dressed in bright vermilion, who instantly caught his eye.

"Go and talk to Natalia," whispered Horace, with a crafty wink. "I can see she's your type. She has a weakness for Yale men, too, I've noticed."

Jonathan found himself standing next to Natalia by the open window. A fragrance of rain-drenched autumn shrubbery rose from the courtyard, and mingled with the scent of violets which clung to Natalia.

"I hope you didn't go to that silly ballet tonight," said Natalia gently.

"Yes, I did," said Jonathan eagerly. "I thought it was splendid!"

"It was a revolting program," said Natalia, smiling enigmatically. "Don't you think?"

"I rather liked it," said Jonathan tactfully. "Of course, I know nothing at all about the ballet."

"Well," said Natalia firmly, in her deep rich voice, "those dreary, moth-eaten ballets, like *Aurora* or *Sylphides*, are quite out of date, you know. We're all sick to death of them. They're kept in the repertoire merely to please the old ballerinas."

Jonathan finished his drink, and found another immediately thrust into his hand.

"The audience seemed very enthusiastic," he observed.

"Oh, they always are," said Natalia with contempt. "American audiences are imbecile."

"Are you Russian?" asked Jonathan, in a sympathetic tone.

"Ukrainian," said the dancer wearily. She placed her fingers on her bright blond hair, which was wound in a braid across the top of her head.

She smiled suddenly at Jonathan. Her face grew luminous and arrogant, her lips parted, and her eyes shone with a fiery, undisguised challenge.

But at that moment Sebastian descended on them, and ushered Natalia toward a group of newcomers. The studio was packed with guests at this point, but instead of an air of exuberance and gaiety, there was an unmistakable atmosphere of ennui. An aura of fatigue had already replaced the first brief flush of speculation.

Jonathan looked down at the narrow courtyard. The trees looked dim and dejected. He was beginning to feel the effect of Peter Sebastian's punch.

He noticed that a slender girl was standing beside him; it was the other dancer, the little brunette, Lydia Ivanova.

"You look melancholy," she murmured. "Do you feel melancholy?"

"Oh no," said Jonathan. "Not melancholy, precisely. A little puzzled, that's all."

"Puzzled?" She raised her brows. "Why puzzled, my dear?"

Jonathan glanced wistfully across the room; he was looking for Natalia. She had mysteriously vanished.

"I've just come back from Europe," he replied. "It seems a bit odd here. A bit confusing."

"Odd. Confusing. Yes. I understand," said Lydia rather sadly. "Are you American?"

Jonathan nodded rather curtly. "Don't I look American?"

He looked at her again. She was wearing a dress of clinging green crepe. A scent of honeysuckle hung about her.

"Well," said Lydia, "your face is American. Your eyes are American. Your mouth and chin are American. But still, somehow ... "

"Yes?"

She smiled non-committally. "Your attitude isn't quite American, I can't help feeling."

"Well," admitted Jonathan, "my father was English, or rather Welsh. But my mother is American."

"You live with her?" asked Lydia discreetly.

"Oh no; she's been living in London. Ever since my father died."

"Ah! Your father died. How sad," said Lydia, with sympathy. "He was an artist, of course?"

"Not exactly," said Jonathan. "He was a diplomat."

"It comes to the same thing," said Lydia serenely. "How old are you, my dear?"

"Twenty-seven," said Jonathan. He was beginning to like Lydia. She had a low, suggestive voice, and there was a mischievous luster in her great brown eyes. A small dark mole clung to the side of her chin.

Jonathan peered at his watch. It was half-past one. He looked around the room, somewhat guiltily. Several of the guests were leaving; Horace had disappeared. Valdez, the dancer, was doing a strip tease. Sebastian, the host, lay sprawled on the couch. A sense of disintegration had crept into the gathering.

"Come," whispered Lydia. "The party's breaking up. Don't you think we'd better go?"

He looked at her calm little face with surprise. She was gazing innocently into his eyes. There was, it occurred to him, no resemblance whatever between her and the swift, glittering dancer he had seen on the stage. Or almost none; the rich chestnut curls he recognized, and the clear, slavonic line of the chin. That was all. She was not really beautiful.

She took him gravely by the arm, and they slipped together through the doorway. No one seemed to notice them. Jonathan felt a rush of expectancy pass through him as they wandered, arm in arm, down the dark crimson stairway.

6

IT WAS beginning to rain again. They waited in the doorway for several minutes, looking up and down the street. There was no trace of a taxi, and the busses seemed to have stopped running along the avenue.

"Come," said Lydia, with sudden determination. "It's rather dreary here, don't you think?"

She took his arm, and they darted through the rain for a block and a half. They arrived at a desolate little brownstone house. It was quite unlit, and appeared uninhabited. A smell of wet plaster, sawdust, and garlic greeted them as they opened the front door.

"Some rather lurid people have just moved in," Lydia explained. "A Hungarian sculptor and his wife, with their pet kangaroo. And a Negro boy friend." She sighed apologetically. They climbed a creaking staircase, paused at a door while Lydia inserted the key, and cautiously entered. She turned on the light.

The room was extremely narrow, with a single window which looked upon Tenth Street. There were bits of luggage strewn about, labeled with tags from Omaha, Quebec, Guadalajara, and a yellow slip of paper with the words: "The New Ballet Company."

On one wall hung a well-known Van Gogh reproduction: a sullen young man in a blue hat and a yellow coat. Beside it hung a small Matisse etching of an odalisque. On the other wall hung numerous photographs of Lydia, all of them in ballet poses. There was a mingled scent of talcum powder, coffee grounds, and rubbing alcohol.

"It's a sweet little room, don't you think?" said Lydia cheerfully. "Small but cozy. Do forgive all this mess; it looks like a nomad's tent, doesn't it?"

She looked at him briskly. "Here, take off your coat; it's dripping with rain! You'll catch pneumonia, if you're not careful!" She vanished in the bathroom and reappeared five minutes later in a peach-colored dressing robe. "Well, now we can relax a bit," she declared, gently but firmly.

She sat down on the studio couch, and he sat in his shirt sleeves on the open window sill. It was very silent in this part of town; he could hear the clandestine whisper of rain, and the sound of distant footsteps on a neighboring street.

"Were you born in America, Miss Ivanova?" inquired Jonathan carefully. "There's hardly a trace of accent. . . . "

"Well," said Lydia, running her fingers through her chestnut curls, "I've lived here for seven years. Do call me Lydia, by the way. We might as well be cozy, don't you think? Fokine discovered me in Paris when I was sixteen; he brought me to New York when I was seventeen. . . . So you see, I'm not a stranger here!" She smiled, rather slyly.

"That makes you twenty-four," said Jonathan thoughtfully. "You look younger than twenty-four."

"Thank you, my dear," she said, with a sigh. She touched, rather thoughtfully, the little mole on her chin.

"Where were you born, Lydia?"

"In Cracow. Have you ever heard of Cracow?"

"Oh, certainly. It's in Poland."

"You are very clever, my dear. You have culture, I can see."

"You prefer America to Poland?"

"Oh, I adore America! May I call you Jonathan? Yes? Well, I simply worship America, Jonathan. Sometimes, perhaps, I feel a trifle uneasy."

"Uneasy?"

"Yes. You see, America is much too big. Too many people. Too much money ... Tell me," she said slowly, rising and regarding her face in the mirror, "you rather like Natalia, don't you?"

Jonathan hesitated. "Well," he murmured, "she's very handsome, of course."

"Is she your type?" demanded Lydia, staring coldly into the mirror.

Jonathan didn't know quite what to say. "Oh, it all depends; in a way ... "

"You're blushing," she observed teasingly. His face was reflected in the mirror behind her own. "You are an innocent boy, I think, Jonathan!"

Jonathan smiled feebly in reply. "Well," he stammered, "I've just come back from Europe, you see. ... "

"Ah well," murmured Lydia, "you'll soon get used to things over here. America's changing, you know. Things are growing pretty feverish. I can't imagine," she added casually, "where it's all going to end. Something weird is going to happen. Something thoroughly sinister. Wait and see!"

She returned to the couch and sat down. "Are you interested in painting?" she inquired, running her fingers across the velvet coverlet. He had been looking at the Van Gogh.

Jonathan nodded. "Oh yes. I am. Very much!"

"Whom do you like? Braque? Picasso?" She gazed vaguely across the room.

"I'm afraid I'm rather dull," confessed Jonathan. "I like Velásquez. And Vermeer."

"Oh," murmured Lydia, raising her brows. "Well, last year I had a weakness for Matisse. I can't bear to look at him now. I've taken a sudden fancy to Modigliani. ... Do you like music too?"

"Well," said Jonathan wistfully, "I'm very fond of Mozart and Schubert."

Lydia was lighting a cigarette. Her fingers trembled slightly. She seemed nervous, preoccupied. "Well," she said, "one's tastes become rather jaded in the ballet, somehow; I can still stand Bach and Handel, but that's about all. Béla Bartók and Hindemith are the only two I really care for." She puffed at her cigarette, and smiled rather hazily.

She rose and placed a record on a small electric phonograph beside the dresser. The music began; it was Handel's *Alcina Suite.*

Lydia turned around and gazed at him intently: it was as though a curtain had been drawn aside. Jonathan felt the atmosphere in the room swiftly heightening. It grew deft and mysterious. Some occult pattern was coming into play; a magical ceremony was beginning. Lydia stood poised before him, her back reflected in the mirror, the lamplight shining on her fingers and toes, her face adroitly drawn into shadow. She looked like a masked dancer about to spring into motion. The little room seemed transformed, and her eyes looked tense and electrical. Her slender figure looked almost queenly in its arrogance and grace. Jonathan scarcely knew what he was doing. He rose and moved toward her, as though guided by a hidden magnet; he drew her to him without a word.

Slowly he covered her warm, opening lips with his own. Her eyes closed, her head fell back, and her body yielded to a hidden fury. It was like the body of a sacrificial victim.

7

HE AWOKE very early in the morning; he felt the warmth and weight of her body in his arms. He could hear the raindrops pass the open window with a faint, incessant sigh.

He turned to look at her face. Only a sheet lay lightly over their bare, interlacing bodies. He drew himself up on his elbow and bent silently over her.

Her face lay sideways on the pillow, framed in a tangled mass of curls. The features were indistinct, and seemed to float in the deep blue haze of the room. Only the parted lips and the long dark eyelashes stood out clearly and expressively. He could see her body stir in the even rhythm of her breath. He leaned closer; her warmth rose toward him. He recognized the scent of her skin. His lips drew closer still, and touched her brow, her cheek, her neck.

A powerful protective instinct was arising in him. She looked utterly helpless there, in the half-light of early morning; helpless, innocent, and contented as a freshly nursed child. Her right hand lay curled under her breast; the left lay extended on the pillow. She opened her eyes and peered at him dreamily. Her curling eyelashes seemed reluctant to part. Her eyes looked almost black now, in the slowly gathering light; her moist curls clung to her forehead, and her whole body, as it slowly opened to his embrace, seemed tender, fragrant, and budding with sleep.

"What time is it, darling?" Her whispering voice groped for the words, a little hoarsely.

"Not yet six."

"Darling." She sighed.

"Darling," he said very softly.

With surprising strength she placed her arms around him and drew him upon her, and yielded her mouth to his.

He fell asleep again; but the mood continued in his dreams. A pearly twilight accompanied him through vista after vista. A long dark corridor opened upon a garden. Pale shapes passed through the avenues of green, hands extended, garments clinging. They seemed about to join in a passionate embrace; but a curtain of glass fell between them, and their arms hung frozen in the air. The garden rose, dilated, spread great veins of stone and metal; it became a giant city. The air of love was tinged with hysteria.

The dream grew more and more intense; his search grew increasingly poignant and painful. And then it all subsided in a rush of darkness.

It was almost eleven when he awoke again. He saw Lydia standing in front of the mirror, quite naked, arranging the curls on her head, and scrutinizing the faint blue shadows in her face.

She saw him lying awake; she turned and smiled, and suppressed a whimsical yawn. "How ghastly," she murmured. "It's ten to eleven. I was to appear for rehearsal at half-past ten. ... What time did we finally go to sleep, dear?"

"Three, perhaps," said Jonathan thoughtfully. "Or perhaps half-past."

"Mercy." She sighed. "I'm afraid I drank too much; that sordid punch of Peter Sebastian's. Did I do anything appalling?"

"Not," said Jonathan cautiously, "that I recall."

"Well, I hope not. Sometimes, you know, I seem to forget myself a little." Her voice grew faintly ironical. "Did you sleep well, dear? ... You kept muttering in your sleep. You kept calling for someone. In a rather desperate sort of way."

"Calling for someone?"

"So it seemed. A woman's name ... I may be wrong." She yawned again, and placed two fingers in front of her mouth. Her manner had grown distinctly cool.

She moved to the window and looked out. The sun was shining brightly. He now, for the first time, saw her body clearly: it was exquisite. The sunlight drew a rosy edge along her shoulders and thighs. Every line was miraculously pure. The proportions were those of an ancient Diana—supple, resilient; they suggested the spring and speed of a huntress.

She began to dress. He rose too, and she watched him with a mischievous smile as he drew the sheet from his body, and sat for a moment, naked and upright, on the bed. He bent down and reached for his socks. One he found; the other was missing. She watched him playfully as he knelt on the floor and groped under the bed.

Then he rose to dress; he felt bewildered, ecstatic.

"What weird little underdrawers," she murmured, picking them up from the chair. "Where on earth did you get them?" She looked for the label. "Barcelona. Well, well."

He reached for them, but she snatched them away. She held them hidden behind her back, and cast a wicked smile at him. He took her by the wrists and drew her closer, tenderly.

"Don't," she whispered. "Don't, Jonathan. Please. Please let me go."

He rose, warm with yearning, and was about to put his arms around her; but she slipped from his grasp. "No, no," she said. "Please. Not now."

And she smiled reproachfully. "You do look rather crude, darling. Rather silly. Like an amorous faun, or something of the sort ... "

She slipped into a violet dress, and drew the zipper along the side. "Come, dear, we'll have to rush. God knows what that fiend Sevastopoulos will say. ... "

Five minutes later they were walking down the street toward Fifth Avenue. Lydia reached the corner just in time to leap into a bus. She climbed the stairway to the open deck on top, and he stood and watched her as the bus rolled up the avenue.

She waved her hand, twice, smiling; then she vanished from sight. And instantly he felt that the whole night was a mirage, that he had never seen her, that she did not exist.

8

HE CONTINUED to stand for several minutes on the corner of Tenth Street and Fifth Avenue. He felt that he had entered a bewildering new world.

He had been in New York less than a day; yet already he had drifted through layer upon layer of its quivering organism. He looked up the sun-striped abyss of Fifth Avenue, and knew he had never seen it quite like this; quite so opulently lit, quite so subtle and immediate. It was a city like no other in the world. Its visual effect was unique: a volcanic mass of angles washed by a hard and spacious sea light. It was a universe of its own, with its own weird system of desires.

He turned and strolled across Washington Square. The autumn leaves were bright and burnished. Here, in the little red brick houses which hung on the brink of the avenue, like flowers on the edge of a precipice, there still lay scattered vestiges of a gentler, more decorous past. But they were mementos only; the vitality had gone. His aunt, Mrs. Westover, had lived here twenty years ago, and he remembered how he had played in the park as a boy, with his nurse and poodle and rubber ball. In those days an air of authority still lingered in the red façades. But now no longer; they exhaled the meek, tolerated fragrance of a museum.

He sat down on the edge of the fountain. Memories of his childhood began to drift past him. He saw his mother again, in her green lace dress, playing upon the great black piano beside the window. He saw his old uncle Winthrop among his Chinese jades, and his old aunt Lucy pouring tea beside her trophies; recollections that were brittle and pale, like the wings of a moth. They had left with him nothing vital, nothing firm or secure.

He rose again and walked slowly up Fifth Avenue. The peaceful little houses, with their hints of a vanished life, gave way to the mountainous ugliness of the apartments. Their expressive old faces yielded to a vast anonymity. An irresistible economic tyranny had crept, like a glacier, over the sense of human character. Yet, for some mysterious reason, it was not entirely depressing. What was lost had been impermanent; destined to be lost. And somehow, into that faceless immensity, a strand of human happiness had been woven. Scarcely more than a hope, an afterthought; but still, it was there.

A taxi paused beside him and he entered; he returned to his hotel, shaved, put on a fresh blue shirt and a knitted tie, and went out again into the dazzling autumn weather.

He felt abnormally brisk and alive. The air was like a sea breeze, bright and leaping. He found himself imperceptibly quickening his stride; he found it almost impossible to saunter or linger. Every muscle in his body was on the alert. Every object looked brilliantly sharpened, accelerated.

He paused in front of several shopwindows, trying to quiet his nerves. But the things he saw—books, shoes, bits of porcelain—all sparkled and quivered in the bright, new current of his love.

He felt that he was gliding through the air without touching the ground, and that he could, if he wished, leap over the Empire State Building. He felt uncannily free of his body; except for a sudden pang, now and again, when a glimpse of the previous night shot through his consciousness and set his flesh tingling.

He turned in at Rockefeller Plaza and walked along the promenade. Six bronze water statues, three male, three female, were shining in the sunlight among freshly placed asters. Everything began to echo with a more intimate meaning—the flowing water, the bronze bodies, the blossoming flowers, the leaping sunlight: all suggested the firm, responsive rhythm of Lydia's body.

Every handsome woman he passed, through resemblance or contrast, carried his thoughts immediately back to Lydia's own beauty. Every shopwindow was filled with objects which brought her suddenly closer: a pair of slippers that might suit her, a pigskin valise, a small Van Gogh.

The whole city seemed but a tremendous receptacle for her presence; all conspiring to heighten her magic, to cast a new light on her. The whole city seemed touched with her own sexual splendor; and his recollection of her, in turn, was tinged with the city's hard, electrical glitter.

He leaned over the parapet which surrounded the sunken plaza. People were already having lunch under the green umbrellas. A waiter hurried past with a row of cocktails on a tray.

He heard his name called; he turned.

"Pierre!"

"Well, I thought it was you, Jonathan. ... Lost in thought, as usual!"

A tall young man in a pin-striped suit, blond, smooth, vivacious, took Jonathan's hand affectionately in his own.

9

JONATHAN and Pierre strolled down the stairs to the sunken terrace. They found an outdoor table behind a small potted hedge, near the gilded Prometheus with his great, rushing waterfall. Pierre laid his hat on an empty chair, ordered a vermouth, and began to talk.

His curls were a little moist above the forehead; his face looked flushed and exuberant. He was a slender, sparkling fellow; there was a mingling of adventure and ambition in his fine gray eyes.

Pierre Maillard was a young French painter. Jonathan had met him at Fontainebleau and had, at the beginning, found him vain, mannered, and arrogant. But Pierre's vitality and charm soon won him over: they became, first casual companions, then sudden and inseparable friends. They went skiing together in the French Alps in the winter, and did water colors in Provence in the summer. Soon after the outbreak of war they had separated. Pierre had been sent to Tunisia, Jonathan went to Spain. A year later they met in Barcelona. France had fallen, and Pierre was heading for the Americas. Again they parted when Pierre sailed for Rio de Janeiro; and this was the last Jonathan had heard of him.

"Well, how long have you been here?" asked Jonathan. "I thought you were still in Brazil!"

"I've been here almost a month. I've been looking for a studio. And for company! And you?"

"I arrived yesterday," replied Jonathan. "I've been here only a single night. ... "

The waiter came up and took their order for lunch. Pierre asked for the wine list, and ordered a bottle of claret.

"What a city this is!" he exclaimed, raising his eyes to the great rectangular cliffs of Radio City.

"Do you like it? Really like it?"

"Like it? It's overwhelming! One's whole sense of proportion is uprooted. ... One grows used to it, I suppose. But have you noticed how curious the people look? Watch them. There is something rather odd about them all. ... What is it?"

Jonathan gazed at the crowd passing above them. "There are too many, of course," he said gently. "And they walk too quickly."

"Not only that!" said Pierre. "Look again. It could never be France or England. It could never be Italy or Spain. It's the women! They are the roosters over here. They wear the spurs and the brilliant plumage. See how they walk! Like prima donnas, like petty tyrants, with all their furs and jewels and Schiaparelli gowns. ... And then look at the men, in their mousy gray colors, scurrying humbly about like so many little hens. Something is wrong. There's no real passion between the sexes—I can feel it! The women despise the men; the men are terrified of the women. Why is it? Where will it end?"

"Then you don't," suggested Jonathan, "intend to fall in love over here?"

"Certainly not. Not even in the American manner," declared Pierre. "Not even for a week. Not even at a distance!"

"You think we are unfaithful?"

"Call it restless," said Pierre. "Call it hopelessly idealistic. Call it self-indulgent. Call it immature; call it anything you wish."

"Yes," said Jonathan thoughtfully. "One can call it anything one wishes, I suppose."

"And as for love itself," said Pierre, "you won't find it; it begins to wither, like a camellia, the instant you expose it to the air of New York."

Jonathan said nothing; he drew his thumb across the tablecloth.

Pierre shot a look of tender, teasing familiarity at him. "What has happened to you, Jonathan?" he whispered. "Anything new? Anything exciting?"

"Oh no," said Jonathan rather sheepishly. "Nothing really ... Not yet ... "

Something was troubling Jonathan obscurely. He was extremely happy to see Pierre, but this pleasure disturbed, and seemed incompatible with a deeper, richer, more absorbing joy which had just been disclosed to him.

Their lunch arrived, a fine shrimp omelet, and they felt more at ease. They began to talk again of their plans and ambitions. They had often sat together like this in the cafés of Paris and Barcelona, speculating about the passers-by, elaborating their vision of the world. Jonathan felt the past returning, and New York began to assume a new aspect, more convivial and human, and faintly European.

Above them rose the barren precipice of Rockefeller Center, and behind them sounded the cataract of Prometheus. Jonathan felt that they were sitting, not in a city of mortal men, but in the presence of some vast geological phenomenon. Yet Pierre's shrewd and witty company made it seem, somehow, like Montparnasse or the Rue Royale.

They sat in silence for several minutes, sipping their claret and feeling the autumn sunlight on their hands.

They were about to leave when Jonathan caught sight of a tall, middle-aged woman passing among the tables. She was beautifully dressed in a powder-blue suit and a bright blue hat, with a silver fox over her shoulders. It was his aunt, Mrs. Mannering. She looked tremendously smart. She had, apparently, just been lunching with some friends.

He rose and called to her; she stopped and smiled in her dry, casual way, and cast a rapid look at Pierre, who had also risen. Jonathan introduced them, with an ill-defined sense of uneasiness.

"Isn't it a perfectly heavenly day, Jonathan? I see you're already making yourself quite at home here. I've just been having lunch with Mimi Suarez and Kitty de Montfleury. You remember Kitty, don't you? ... By the way, my dear, would you like to come out to Wyndham Park on Sunday? If the weather is fine?"

"I should love to," said Jonathan pleasantly. "I'm very eager to see Uncle Winthrop again!"

"Quincy is coming too," said Mrs. Mannering. A touch of calculation had entered her voice. "And dear old Wilfred Silliman. And your aunt Lucy, of course. We'll be having a bit of tennis, if it doesn't rain. The court's in splendid shape. ... Do you play tennis, Monsieur Maillard?"

Pierre smiled handsomely and nodded.

"Oh, do come out too, then, won't you? We'll need a fourth for doubles!" And she began to explain to them both, painstakingly, about the Sunday trains to Long Island.

Then she said, "Well, I must be off. Time flies! It's almost three. I'm meeting Estelle Webber at the St. Regis at four, and I have to do a bit of shopping first. Good-by, my dear. We'll see you both on Sunday. ... "

And she hurried away in her firm, athletic stride. Pierre caught Jonathan's eye; and they both began to smile, somewhat guiltily.

10

JONATHAN sat in the train and watched the fierce, unmitigated squalor of Queens move past him.

He kept thinking of Lydia. His body longed for her continually; but a touch of precaution clung to his mind. He knew that a crucial part of her being still lay concealed from him. What he had seen of her was only an emerging fragment, like the tip of an iceberg. Underneath, he suspected, played the perilous and secret currents. By some subtle process of association, she had become linked in his mind with a flavor peculiar to the city itself; a kind of continual, self-absorbed agitation. He kept wondering about her past; he kept brooding about her future. She seemed poised, vertiginously, on the thread of the present.

And he felt that in himself, as well, an invisible opiate had begun to operate; his mind, here in the city, was working less clearly; his eyes saw less sharply; his values were growing, already, somewhat stultified. The hard, feline sexuality of the city, embodied in Lydia, was diluting his energies, his senses.

He leaned back in his seat and watched the horrifying suburbs move past. And gradually, as New York faded behind him, a kind of detachment intervened. The countryside appeared. He drew a breath of relief.

The trip took just under an hour. A chauffeur met him at the station and drove him slowly through the village, and then more swiftly past a series of autumn-tinted fields and copses. He watched the curves of green roll past, and smelled the sweet dry clover, and felt the lazy, caressing tempo of the countryside. They passed a golf course, a race track, and several estates—long pale houses momentarily visible behind their walls and hedges.

Presently they turned in through a big iron gateway, surmounted by heraldic lions and bearing a small inscription: "Wyndham Park." The house rose at the end of a maple-edged drive.

It was an elaborate structure, built in the first decade of the century, and more or less in the style of Queen Anne, with stray touches of French rococo and a hint of the Italianate. The interior, however, was largely American. Jonathan had not visited the house for seven years; but he remembered a portrait of Martin Van Buren in the drawing room, and two large Audubon prints in the bedroom. He also remembered the plates from which he had eaten long ago, stamped with some dubiously ancestral coat of arms. He remembered very faintly Mr. Mannering's great library, where guests were only rarely allowed to set foot. He remembered, more clearly, the tennis court with the red pavilion, and the striped umbrellas upon the lawn.

The chauffeur dropped him at the door and he wandered down the path to the tennis court.

Through the overhanging elms he could see the players darting to and fro. Their clean white shapes flashed through the sloping sunlight. A red-and-white umbrella was standing in front of the pavilion. Foaming clouds were passing indolently overhead, and the air was scented with the keen, delightful spices of fall.

Now he recognized the tennis players; they were playing a mixed double. Pierre, to Jonathan's surprise, had arrived by an earlier train. He and Mrs. Mannering were playing against

Quincy Potter and Wilfred Silliman. Delia, it appeared, had decided not to come. A disconcerting conjecture passed through Jonathan's mind.

He noticed, as he approached the pavilion, a small gray shape under the umbrella. It was his aunt, Mrs. Westover.

She turned and saw him, and extended her gaunt little arms. "Here he is!" she cried briskly. "What a big boy he's grown to be! How long is it since I've seen him? Six years? Seven years? My favorite nephew, I used to call him!" She drew him to the seat beside her. Her eyes grew narrow with a kind of matriarchal appraisal.

"He has the broad Mannering forehead," she stated cheerfully; "and the Mannering cheekbones; signs of a solid character! But those bright black eyes—I'm afraid you got those from your dear departed father.... Come, kiss me, my boy. There, there. Mercy me..."

Mrs. Westover was very tiny, very old, and amazingly lively. Over fifty years had passed since Mr. Westover's death, eleven months after their marriage. But the fearless green eyes and the resolute, uncompromising voice had bridged the interval undimmed. She wore a dress of oyster-gray crepe with lace cuffs, and a long lace shawl. Her hair seemed to be of lace, and her skin of crepe, with a pattern of large, half-obliterated freckles.

Jonathan greeted the tennis players politely. Mrs. Westover placed her trembling hand on his arm. "You've seen my trophies? They've been placed in the pavilion."

Jonathan turned; he could see a row of silver cups on a shelf above the little oak bar.

"I used to be quite a champion, you know! I was famous at the old Newport casino for my undercut service. But dear, dear; that was centuries ago. I won my last cup in 1915. Tennis was a very different proposition in those days. Much more genteel, altogether more ladylike. ... " She sighed nostalgically. "I shall never forget playing at Wimbledon, one year, against the invincible Mrs. Lambert-Chambers. Queen Mary was in the royal box, with her mauve parasol. She always adored lawn tennis, you know. I was quite overcome with nerves; I could hardly hit the ball. ... " She glanced at Jonathan with her playful, weather-beaten eyes.

An elderly butler arrived with a tray of tall drinks. For Mrs. Westover he brought a small black pot of tea and a slice of melba toast.

The players changed courts. Mrs. Mannering and Pierre had just won the first set. Mrs. Mannering invited Jonathan to take her place, but he discreetly refused.

Wilfred played a crisp and fastidious game, with his feet close together and moving in small, rapid steps. He never smiled; he took his game very seriously. He was wearing white flannels cut high and full, in the English fashion; and a lemon-colored pullover, with a flannel scarf around his neck.

"Oh, well calculated!" he would shout, in his Oxford accent. "Beautifully played, old chap! Jolly good service!"

Quincy's game was as loose and ungainly as Wilfred's was prim and ceremonious. He swung his racket in great, vigorous parabolas; most of his shots flew straight into the net. He wore old gray shorts and a battered Yale blazer. His pink head, a trifle bald, was shining with moisture.

Pierre was incomparably the best player of the four, and the only one who played with a natural ease. Mrs. Mannering's game was prosaic and steady; she was, quite obviously, determined to win.

Mrs. Westover sipped her tea and turned again to Jonathan.

"How is your mother, dear boy? Still in England? When is she coming? Goodness, it's been months and months since I last heard from Grace. ... She was always a naughty, neglectful sister, I'm afraid. ... Dear, dear."

She leaned over and whispered in Jonathan's ear. "That's your friend, is it, that French boy? He plays quite agreeably, I must say. He has style. ... But he's much too good-looking, my dear! No man should be that good-looking!"

An exciting rally was taking place. Quincy was at the net, with Pierre directly facing him, while both Wilfred and Mrs. Mannering were lobbing industriously from the back of the court. Finally Pierre took a low lob and smashed it vigorously past Quincy, so that the ball bounced over the backstop, landing in a bed of chrysanthemums.

"Bravo!" cried Mrs. Westover, and clapped her little hands. Then she whispered again to Jonathan: "Still, you know, I'd like to see Quincy beat that cocky young Apollo!"

The match was now in its third and deciding set. Jonathan rose to retrieve the ball from the flower bed, and then began to wander toward the shore. The lawn lay smooth and amber-hued in the evening sun. A group of elms immediately below him, spreading toward the top like a fan, shielded the lawn from the dull horizon of the Sound; but through their curving boughs he could see the blue-gray stripe of water and, like a handkerchief waving good-by, the distant flicker of a small white sail.

He felt a gathering unreality in himself, a sense of seclusion and utter stillness. His impulse toward life lay trapped in the city; locked in a small dark room, and in the memory of a slender body. Yet he felt, somehow, that the room and the body were illusory. It was this sea-calmed stillness, this dying light, which were real.

Jonathan strolled back across the lawn toward the tennis court. But the players had left, and he wandered up the path toward the house. The air had grown moist; a fog was rising from the Sound.

11

HE HAD only fifteen minutes to change into a dinner jacket; a black tie for dinner was obligatory in Wyndham Park. When he came down the stairway he saw the guests already assembled in the oak-paneled hall, which flickered with the cherry-colored light of burning logs. A footman was passing a tray of cocktails.

The tennis players looked transfigured and decorous in their dinner clothes. Their faces were bright and ruddy, the cocktail glasses sparkled in their hands. Just as Jonathan joined them he saw his uncle, old Mr. Mannering, limping in from the library.

"Good evening, my boy," he said, without a smile, taking his nephew's hand crisply in his own. "So you're back. It's high time. How was Europe?"

But he did not wait for a reply. He looked dourly at Quincy. "Well, where's Delia today? Why didn't you bring her along?"

"Delia's up in Tarrytown today," said Quincy cheerfully. "Visiting the Van Lenneps."

"Oh yes," put in Wilfred, "dear old Cornelia van Lennep's having a birthday party. I was asked too, but, well, you know ... "

"Have you met Delia yet?" said Mrs. Mannering softly, turning to Pierre.

"No, I think not," said Pierre politely.

"Pity," said Mr. Mannering grimly. "You've missed something. She's a real American beauty. ... Well, how was the tennis?"

"Splendid," said Mrs. Mannering brightly. "We had some perfectly lovely rallies."

Mr. Mannering was, at first sight, a twisted and sour-faced old man. But beneath this harsh, pecuniary air lay a kind of way-ward simplicity. His heartless gray eyes would suddenly take on a look of surprising innocence; his small, irritable mouth would fall into lines of repression and wounded susceptibility. His gifts, one felt, had been somehow distorted. The optimism, the enter-prise had gone astray.

He strolled in front of the fire and stared at it dourly. His withered face grew orange-colored, and the firelight played upon his pince-nez.

"Tennis. It's all nonsense," he muttered. "I don't believe in these games. Used to play myself, but it gave me lum-bago. . . . Still, I was pretty good at it. Wasn't I, Lucy?" He turned with an air of challenge to Mrs. Westover.

"Good, but not good enough," she answered brightly. "Your backhand was an absolute scandal, my dear."

He pinched her arm with a brusque, fraternal affection, hardly distinguishable from fury, and stared back at the fire. There was a brief silence.

"Monsieur Maillard played beautifully," said Mrs. Mannering suddenly, in a rather odd tone of voice. There was a slanting light in her eyes.

Jonathan felt at that moment that a new flavor had entered the room. It seemed suddenly alert. The flaming logs were the only source of light; their vivid red glow drew a tremulous mask over each face. Mrs. Westover looked tiny and malicious, Wilfred abnormally swollen and ornate, Quincy pink and rather hol-low, Mr. Mannering reddish, a little apelike. Mrs. Mannering, with her glass in one hand and the other resting lightly on her forehead, looked unnaturally flushed; her eyes looked bright and tense. Only Pierre seemed calm and aloof, smiling in his casual, ironical manner.

"Well, who won the match?" demanded Mr. Mannering rather querulously.

"We did," said Mrs. Mannering gently; "Monsieur Maillard and I. Just barely; we were rather lucky toward the end, as a matter of fact."

Mr. Mannering turned and cast a stony gaze upon Pierre. "I didn't know," he muttered slowly, "that the French knew how to play a winning game."

There was a painful hush. Mrs. Mannering's face assumed a sudden rigidity.

"Look at those roses!" exclaimed Wilfred Silliman, to ease the tension. "Aren't they absolutely gorgeous?"

An enormous jar of yellow roses stood on the long black table; the blossoms were washed in the hovering brightness from the logs. Mrs. Mannering leaned over and thoughtfully rearranged them, drawing them out, one by one, with her long white fingers.

Pierre turned and looked at a cabinet full of old bits of pottery, blue and iridescent under the light which shone behind the glass.

"I picked them up in Persia," said Mr. Mannering rather defiantly. "Thirty years ago. I was digging for oil."

"They are superb," said Pierre. "You have excellent taste, Mr. Mannering."

Mr. Mannering's eyes grew mild and mellow. His voice took on a conciliatory tone. "I've been collecting things all my life," he murmured. "I started with cigar bands. Then I went on to postage stamps. But as I grew older ... Well, one begins to look

for other things in life. I turned to ... old and beautiful things."
He hesitated. He seemed about to say something more; but he
remained silent.

The butler appeared and announced that dinner was served.

12

DINNER passed in a series of bleak, brittle snatches of talk.

"I love France," declared Mrs. Westover, turning to Pierre. "I last visited your lovely country in 1909. But I expect it hasn't really changed much since I saw it; Europe changes so slowly, thank the Lord. We used to stay at Aixles-Bains, my sister Grace and I. Then we joined Aunt Theodora in Nice, which was considered rather a daring place to visit, what with the gambling rooms and such. After that we went to Italy. I shall never forget Pisa. Frankly, we have nothing quite like that over here. But we have our advantages!" Her voice rang with pride, and her eyes shone triumphantly as she looked into Pierre's calm, intelligent face. "I'm a very old lady. I've had time to weigh these matters. Ruined castles and Romanesque cathedrals, my young man, are all very well. But there are other things than cultural monuments!"

Mr. Mannering had sat through dinner in silence. He turned his small, dyspeptic face on Mrs. Westover. "Cultural monuments?" he snapped. "Don't talk nonsense, Lucy. What do you know about culture? There's no such thing as culture, nowadays!"

"New York is overflowing with culture, if you know where to look," said Mrs. Mannering. "Next week, for example, they're opening a brilliant exhibition at the Modern Museum."

"Boston," put in Wilfred Silliman, "is the only place where one can still find traces of the old *douceur de vivre*. Don't you agree, Lucy?"

"Well," said Mrs. Westover, "back in the days when I used to visit with Aunt Celia, who had a house on Rittenhouse Square, I felt that Philadelphia was very alert. But I hear it's fallen sadly behind Boston, and even Chicago."

"There's an island of culture down in Richmond," said Quincy Potter. "And I've been hearing good things about Nashville and Cincinnati. The love of culture is spreading, definitely. New museums, new orchestras ... "

"The price of first editions has gone up steadily," admitted Mr. Mannering. "Hard cash—that's the only dependable way of measuring public taste."

"And then the terrific new vogue of the ballet," said Wilfred. "You can hardly get a seat at the Metropolitan, my dear."

Jonathan was listening carefully. He had a fleeting impression that Wilfred was trying to catch his eye. And he began to feel that underneath this banal interchange of prejudices, an astute and treacherous little game was being played.

"Yes," continued Wilfred, "they're doing some delicious new things. Kirillova is more dazzling than ever this year. She simply takes your breath away in *Giselle*. And there's a fine group of younger dancers. That fellow Valdez, for example. And this brilliant new girl, Lydia Ivanova ... "

Mrs. Mannering turned to Pierre. "Have you seen much of America, Monsieur Maillard?"

"Not yet, unfortunately," said Pierre. "But I hope to see more of it, before long!" He paused a moment, thoughtfully. Then he said: "Which, may I ask, is considered the loveliest city in America?"

"Oh, you should go to New Orleans!" cried Quincy. "You'll find the real French atmosphere!"

"Well, if it's the Old World elegance you want," said Wilfred in mellow tones, "you can't do better than Boston."

"There's no place to touch Newport," declared Mrs. Westover staunchly. "For sheer local color. For a sense of the past."

"Why not New York?" observed Jonathan, who had been listening in silence.

"New York?" sneered Mr. Mannering. "They've ruined New York!"

"Ruined it?" inquired Jonathan innocently.

"They don't belong here. They've cheapened it. They've vulgarized it," said Mr. Mannering bitterly.

"Who has vulgarized it?" said Wilfred blandly. Mrs. Mannering was looking with concern across the dinner table; she cast a nervous glance at Pierre.

"Who?" shouted Mr. Mannering. "Those damned foreigners! Those dirty refugees from Europe!"

A hush fell over the table. Mrs. Mannering's face fell into a series of painful angles.

"After all," she said hastily, "one can hardly blame them, nowadays."

"And then," said Wilfred, with tact, "they add a touch of color, you know."

No one was looking at Pierre, who seemed not to have heard.

"Well," said Mrs. Mannering discreetly, as she rose, "I think we'd better have our coffee in the other room. . . . Could you bring the coffee and the benedictine to the living room, Avery?"

13

THEY finished their coffee in front of the fire; then Mr. Mannering led Jonathan into the library.

It was an oval-shaped room, with a curve of high arched windows confronting the door. At one end stood a huge mahogany desk littered with silver inkstands, pen racks, and paperweights. At the other stood a single enormous chair, upholstered in crimson leather. It was an imposing room, but a little too contrived. An indirect light shone on the rows of leather. Small statuettes of jade and agate, adroitly lit from below, were placed at intervals along the shelves. An atmosphere of ritual pervaded the room; it resembled a place for worship, a shrine.

Jonathan was impressed with the brilliant bindings and elaborate slipcases. On the walls he noticed several finely framed manuscripts: a letter from Swinburne, a poem by Austin Dobson, a note from Keats to Fanny Brawne.

"I began," said the old man, "to collect books fifteen years ago, my boy. I was already fifty-five but I felt that something was missing from my life." His tone grew mild and confidential; a pale, diffused light appeared in his eyes. "I had all the money I wanted. I owned a yacht. I had been a golf champion. I had traveled around the world. I was a member of Skull and Bones. But I kept on searching for something else. Call it romance ... Well, when I was a child someone once gave me a copy of *Alice in*

Wonderland. One day, almost fifty years later, I discovered that it was a first edition. And worth, mind you, a good twelve hundred dollars. Well, that's how my collection started!"

He gazed at Jonathan with an air of triumph.

And then he rambled on, plucking one book after another from the shelf with trembling hands. His tastes were those of a schoolboy. He liked books entirely for reasons of caprice; because they were set in a locality he knew, or touched some memory of his childhood, or because the hero's name was that of a friend, or because he had once met the author.

"Here's a fine *Lorna Doone,*" he said, drawing out a green morocco case. "I paid ninety dollars for it. Now it's worth a thousand. And this is *Vanity Fair* in the original parts. One of my real treasures! Worth five thousand if it's worth a cent. I don't go so much for poetry, as a rule, but here's *A Shropshire Lad,* printed in 1896. That's the year I left college. I remember reading it way back then. It's the only poetry that ever brought tears to my eyes. Perhaps I'm sentimental. It's worth three hundred or so; not one of my real jewels. Like this one." He drew out a copy of *Adonais,* in a resplendent black leather case. "This is one of my triumphs," he stated proudly. "I've never dared open the book. It's worth a solid four thousand! I picked it up on the Quai Voltaire for seven francs. I read it, I remember, when I was a sophomore; something about 'the white radiance of eternity.' Splendid, but I prefer Housman.... Here's *The Last Days of Pompeii.* The first novel I ever read. And *East Lynne.* Believe it or not, it's worth a good eight hundred dollars. That's *The Sign of the Four,* in the yellow case; I have all of Conan Doyle. *Sherlock Holmes* is one of the monuments of English prose. And here's the *Confessions of an Opium Eater.* Have you ever smoked opium? I did once, out in Shanghai.... Well, here's *Walden*. A bit on the quiet side. But a tremendous bargain; I picked it up for a dollar in Newburyport one summer. The bookseller had no idea what it was, of course.... This is a mint copy of *Leaves of Grass*. I don't care for free verse as a rule. People try, from time to time, to sell me some of this new-fangled literature. Queer stuff like *Ulysses* and *The Waste Land*. No, thank you. They're just fads. I know a sound investment when I see it. There is such a thing as inflation, you know, in rare books as in all other things!" He smiled at Jonathan with an air of cunning.

"And," he added softly, "the fine thing, you know, about collecting first editions is that you kill two birds with one stone. You satisfy your gambling instinct and your love of literature as well!"

He glanced around the room proudly, and with a look of intense, almost sensual possessiveness. He paused by a shelf of Dickens, and ran his finger tips tenderly along the red morocco spines. He peered suddenly at Jonathan: there was a strangely repellent light in his eyes—a mingling of greed, sentimentality, and frustration. Then he turned out the lights again and they rejoined the others in the drawing room, where the fire was crumbling into ashes.

Quincy was kneeling on the floor, blowing at the embers with a pair of bellows. Wilfred and Mrs. Westover were playing checkers. Mrs. Mannering and Pierre were sitting on a couch, leafing through an album of photographs.

"This one was taken in Cannes," Mrs. Mannering was saying, "on the Carlton beach. That's Kitty de Montfleury on the left, with the Pekinese. And that's Wilfred, of course, with the polka-dotted trunks, next to that Austrian boy. He looks positively like Tarzan...."

She looked up brightly when Jonathan entered. "Ah, here you are at last! Have you seen enough books? Would you care for a rubber of bridge?" Her eyes were glittering; her face looked transformed and alert, almost feminine.

14

SEVERAL days later Mrs. Mannering drove into town to have lunch with two elderly friends of hers, the Misses Wilmerding, at their brownstone house on Seventieth Street. Afterward she went to do a bit of shopping, visited the hairdresser, and attended the opening of an exhibition.

This exhibition was composed of recent works by three refugee painters: a German, Otto Baum, a Belgian, Duchêne, and a Pole, Karnilowski. All three were very much in vogue that particular season. The surrealists admired Baum. The abstractionists preferred Duchêne. Those who desired, so to speak, an agonized utterance from war-torn Europe, extolled the work of Karnilowski.

The museum was a bright, airy building, lined with strips of chromium, glass, and cool-colored tiles. But a peculiar irritation clung to Mrs. Mannering. She had an attack of migraine; she felt antagonistic and weary. And the pictures, which before she had succeeded in admiring, today seemed curiously nonsensical. There was an air of absurdity about the crowd of visitors; about their clothes, their gestures, and indeed their mere presence.

"I'm not well," she reflected. "I must go to bed early. ..."

She was standing in front of a portrait entitled *Metaphysical Repose,* when Horace Hayden entered the room. Quincy had once brought Horace out to Wyndham, to inspect the first editions.

He came darting through the crowd when he caught sight of Mrs. Mannering, his eyes bulging, sweat pouring from his brow.

"Thrilling, aren't they?" he shouted, gesturing toward the paintings.

Mrs. Mannering smiled non-committally. "By the way," she murmured, "you're a friend of Jonathan's, aren't you? He's back, you know."

"Oh yes," exclaimed Horace, "he phoned me the minute he landed. He's a great friend of mine. Splendid fellow. Genuine. Unassuming. I'm devoted to Jonathan. ... "

"He's a nice boy," said Mrs. Mannering, nodding faintly. "Rather vague, perhaps. A bit impractical, and a trifle naïve, of course."

She paused a moment; then she added, "I do hope he doesn't get himself involved with the wrong sort. ... You haven't heard anything, by the way, about his knowing a young Russian dancer? Wilfred dropped a hint the other day. ... "

Horace Hayden looked thoughtful. "Russian dancer? Oh, I doubt it! I'm sure that's not Jonathan's type of thing. ... "

"A friend of his came out last Sunday," Mrs. Mannering continued, with an air of absorption. "A Frenchman. Maillard. A rather odd young man. Have you met him, by any chance?"

Horace seemed to blush momentarily. "No, I think not. ... Not that I know of." There was a brief, rather embarrassed pause.

"Well, what do you think of the Baums?" said Horace enthusiastically. "Really exciting, aren't they? Crudely painted, full of irritating colors. But God, the man has talent!" He wiped his brow.

He walked on beside her. "There, look at that one, for example. *Osmosis of a Nun,* it's called. Say what you will, it has something. And this one: *Reveries of an Amoeba*. Maybe it's cheap, maybe it's neurotic. But all the same there's genius in it!"

They walked on to the Karnilowskis. They were largely studies of massacred bodies, severed heads and smoking ruins.

Horace Hayden gazed at them with feeling. "You know," he reflected, in bitter tones, "one can't help feeling a certain indignation. Europe full of suffering and bloodshed, and here are the dowagers of New York looking at it all through their lorgnettes! Look at Mrs. van Twillingen, for instance, over there by the window. What's she doing here? And I think I see Lady Webber in the next room, if I'm not mistaken. That kind of frippery must go. Their world is as dead as the dodo. ... Oh, look, there's Baum himself!"

Otto Baum was standing in the middle of a group of whispering admirers, looking timorous and perplexed. He was a dim little man with white hair which stood out like a marmoset's. He had developed a new technique, which gave his paintings the appearance of scenes under water; the figures appeared to be overgrown with barnacles and moss.

In the next room they saw Duchêne. He was a Belgian émigré with a huge nose and tiny blue eyes. His paintings were not unlike linoleum patterns; but if one looked closely one could see faint lines wriggling across the canvas, like microscopic eels. These may, to be sure, have been merely cracks in the paint. The admirers of Duchêne thought Otto Baum theatrical and insincere.

In the third room they came across Karnilowski, surrounded by a group of small, noisy people. He was a Pole by birth who had lived in Paris most of his life. He had begun by painting in the South Sea manner of Gauguin, then switched over to Braque, and more recently had taken up social revolt, subtly mingled with surrealism. He did paintings of destruction, such as one entitled *Czestochowa, 1939,* in a manner full of delicate browns, yellows, and reds, suggestive of autumn leaves.

It all seemed suddenly unbearable to Mrs. Mannering; the group of pallid eccentrics, the elderly matrons, the gesturing expatriates, against this hysterical background of paintings. Her headache had grown worse; her temples were throbbing with the persistence of a metronome.

Lady Webber entered the room and caught sight of Mrs. Mannering.

"Pauline! Where have you been? You look devastating today! What is it, Mainbocher?"

"No," said Mrs. Mannering, smiling vividly, "you know I always swear by Molyneux. But this is just an old rag. I've had it for years."

"It's your figure then. You'd look chic in a burlap sack, I'm convinced of it. Speaking of burlap sacks, my dear, guess whom I met on Fifty-seventh Street this afternoon."

"I couldn't, Estelle."

"Laura Carter, looking a dream. I hear she's having a new passion."

"Really! I can't bear it! Who is it, my dear?"

"Oh, someone in the Brazilian Embassy—Lopez, Gomez, something of the sort. He has a terrific mustache, I'm told. Well, anyway, we stopped to look at Baba's new exhibition. It's too divine. Much better than the atrocities you see here. Do you know what Laura said? 'I prefer Marie Laurencin,' she said. I positively blushed. She's turning into an absolute period piece, poor angel. It's like Amy van Twillingen the other day when I asked for her favorite opera. Out she popped with it. *Pagliacci!* I hope I managed to keep a straight face. I expected *Lohengrin,* or at least *Carmen.* But no. *Pagliacci!* Isn't it too, too delicious?" She went into peals of laughter.

"Well, I'm rather old-fashioned myself," she continued, "but all the same ... "

"Tut, tut," interrupted Mrs. Mannering. "You old-fashioned, Estelle!"

"Yes, I am," insisted Lady Webber. "I'm really perfectly humdrum in my tastes. I used to enjoy French novels, I'll admit—Gide, Cocteau, that sort of thing. But really, with Europe on the brink of disintegration ... No, the French are too soft. France is rotting away. I'll never want to see Paris again, believe me, Pauline."

She took Mrs. Mannering softly by the arm. "What are you doing now, dear? Come across to the St. Regis with me; we'll have just a wee little drink together."

15

LADY WEBBER was an American by birth. She had come from a town in Nebraska, gifted with a native ambition and cunning, and a certain crude but insistent sense for the refinements of life. Eventually she became the fashion editor of a well-known journal, which sent her to Paris every spring to attend the openings of Lanvin, Patou, and Poiret. There, some thirty years before, and already a woman of forty, she had met and married a cheerful, bibulous peer, Lord Webber. Since then she had dwelt, in accordance with the mysterious migratory instincts of a certain set, in a house in the Faubourg St.-Germain, a villa in Fontainebleau, a château above Juan-les-Pins, a Saracen castle below Leghorn, a small *Schloss* outside Salzburg, a *palazzo* in Venice, a *châtelet* near Saint-Moritz, and a hacienda in Mexico.

She was now on the brink of eighty; and so small, so brittle, that she looked, as she entered a room, like an exquisitely coifed marionette. Her arms and head moved in delicate jerks, as though maneuvered by strings; movements which had only the most fortuitous bearing on the conversation, and assumed the broken, recondite pattern of a Nô-dance. She wore very short skirts; her legs were still quite shapely. She was growing, of late, disconcertingly coquettish.

"And how is your husband, dear?" she inquired, as the waiter brought them their drinks. They were sitting side by side on a green plush banquette. "How is his heart? Any better? ... Of course, he's so much older than you, Pauline. It's a crime. No, darling, don't pretend it isn't. Years ago Cecil and I agreed to be absolutely independent; to separate for six months every year, religiously. It's more discreet. Love can't last forever, you know. We both like a bit of liberty. I've left him back in Santa Barbara.... Why don't you do something, Pauline?"

"Do what, Estelle?" said Mrs. Mannering nervously. "I'm terribly busy as it is."

"You know what I mean." Lady Webber fixed her with a hard, sloping gaze.

"No, I don't, Estelle." She noticed that her voice was trembling.

Lady Webber lit a cigarette with her crepe-skinned hand.

Mrs. Mannering's nervous headache seemed to come to a peak. She unexpectedly caught sight of herself and Lady Webber in a mirror across the room: Lady Webber in a lime-colored dress with coral-red stripes, she herself in a simple beige suit. Lady Webber was wearing a flat black hat with a red feather; it was like a costume for a *bal masque*. There was something indefinably macabre in the sight.

Lady Webber's tiny hands kept fluttering nervously through the air.

"You don't mind my being frank, do you? You look dreadful, Pauline. Those lines in your face are catching up with you." Her voice had grown intimate and strangely harsh.

Mrs. Mannering's face remained calm. "One learns not to mind," she said lightly.

"Have you learned not to mind?"

"Oh, Estelle, do be sensible."

"Very well, I'll be sensible. You know what's wrong. Do I need to tell you? Winthrop was never the thing for you; you know it as well as I. Why not face it? Before it's too late."

"Before it's too late?" repeated Mrs. Mannering, with a bitter smile.

"Exactly," whispered Lady Webber. "You're still handsome, Pauline. Be practical. You need a lover. ... "

They ordered another drink, and then a third. Twenty minutes later Lady Webber rose.

"Good-by, my child. Do call me up. I'm staying at the Waldorf this time. Don't forget!"

Mrs. Mannering strolled into the powder room, and glanced at herself in the mirror. The taffeta-cushioned room was empty. She sat down and lit a cigarette; she felt a little dizzy.

And she thought of her past; of her days at Vassar; of her premature and passionless marriage; of the meaningless succession of bridge parties, tennis matches, country week ends, committee meetings, visits to the hairdresser, struggles with the servants, and wasted opportunities.

She remembered a handsome young man in a restaurant, three years ago, who had sent her a provocative little note by the waiter. She thought of Dr. Wainwright, who had loved her for fifteen years, so he insisted, but whose tone of late had been growing a shade academic. She recalled a dark young Frenchman in Juan-les-Pins just before the war, who had tried to kiss her one day as they drove back from a tennis match.

She looked again at her face in the mirror. A warm apricot light fell over her features. She drew her cheeks upward with her finger tips; she raised her eyebrows. She smiled very slowly, showing her teeth. She began to feel something very close to terror.

She strolled over to the phone booth and called Pierre Maillard.

16

PIERRE was sitting on the balcony behind his studio. The view gave out on a row of small, walled-in gardens. Each had its own little flavor, brisk and concentrated, like a capsule. One was crude and rustic, overflowing with honeysuckle. One was ultra-modern, full of glass and chromium. One was filled with Italian statuettes. One was Chinese, with a small pagoda.

Pierre was, all in all, an unusually fortunate young man. Both of his parents had died when he was still a boy, but he had come under the benevolent protection of an elderly friend of his father's, a certain Baron Legué, who had sent him to the Lycée and then to Trinity College, Cambridge. It was under his influence that Pierre had gone to Fontainebleau to study painting, for which he revealed a strong natural talent. He spoke English with a very faint accent, dressed smartly, danced excellently, and had a charming manner. He had a native self-regard and self-assurance; he knew by instinct precisely how to play his cards. He was blond and stalwart, and had a low, fine voice. Men found him a bit smooth, but virile and vigorous; women found him beautiful and conceited, but forgave him. There was a continual smile on his lips and a bright, ironical sparkle in his eyes. He had always been uncannily lucky. He had never, even for a single day, been really unhappy.

When he first arrived in New York he felt a little lost and disconcerted. The city was too swiftly moving and impersonal; no one welcomed him, no one, it seemed, so much as noticed him. But he retained his sparkling smile. Within a fortnight he discovered several bars and cafés that appealed to him, and had made, in his own way, several erotic conquests. Within a month he had found a well-located studio, had made friends with several influential dealers, and had agreeably impressed certain of the more conspicuous social figures.

He often sat on his small green balcony at dusk, when the light in the studio was too dim for work. He would watch the sun disappear from the shrubs in the small French garden next door. Sometimes he would hear piano music gliding through the windows below; a Chopin mazurka, perhaps, or a piece by Debussy. And sometimes a girl with smooth blond hair would step across the flagstones, recline in a chaise longue, and read a book, or a letter. He never really saw her clearly, but he had the impression that she might be lovely and he wondered, rather dreamily, how he might contrive to meet her. Once, in the long clear light of the afternoon, he saw her sitting there in a blue dressing gown, apparently unwell. A Negro maid in a bright red turban appeared with a pot of tea on a silver tray. The array of bright colors—red, green, black, and silver—seemed unusually charming and suggestive, as though the scene were not a small garden in New York but a late eighteenth-century vignette set, perhaps, in Martinique.

And there were times, as he sat here, when a sense of dereliction came over him. The little French, Italian, and Chinese gardens, bathed in the hard American light, looked pitifully unconvincing. And he felt that he himself, like the Renaissance statuettes and the toy pagoda, did not quite belong here, had lost something of his authenticity.

He was sitting on the balcony, listening to the music from the house next door, when the telephone rang.

He rose and answered. "Yes, it's Pierre Maillard. ... Who? ... Oh yes! How good of you to call. ... No, I'm doing nothing at all. ... Yes, by all means, do come; you have the address?"

He walked slowly across the room, and looked instinctively at his face in the mirror. He straightened his tie and ran a comb through his curly hair.

He sighed, half bored, half flattered and amused, and lit a cigarette. Then he sat down on the cushioned window sill to wait for Mrs. Mannering.

17

MRS. MANNERING looked pleasantly calm and businesslike as she entered the studio. Pierre also noticed that she looked amazingly smart, and a trifle younger than usual.

"You must think I'm dreadfully rude."

"Not in the least, Mrs. Mannering."

"Well, it's rather unforgivable of me to drop in at this hour; but frankly, I'm up against it. I've been told to arrange a luncheon—one of those wearisome things, you know. To help rescue French professors, or something of the sort. I need names for the committee. There it is. I thought of you."

"I feel very much flattered."

"Please don't. It's all too dreadfully tiresome. Do you mind?" She placed a cigarette in her mouth, and he leaned over to light it for her; he grew aware of a faint, bitter fragrance; he cast an inquisitive glance at her face.

Mrs. Mannering was by nature far from beautiful. But she had learned with great exactitude how to present herself. She knew just how to wear her hair, with its becoming streak of gray, to frame her face most auspiciously; how to tint her lips to match the color of her gown; how to dress, smile, walk, talk, shrug her shoulders, raise her eyebrows, and light a cigarette. She had made the most of her advantages.

She was very tall for a woman, and her bearing was casual, faintly masculine. Her features were lean and large; her mouth was rather broad, her chin strong and square, her voice low and competent. The attitudes of Vassar, of the bridge table, of the tennis court and the committee meeting lay amalgamated in her cool, determined stare.

"It must be strange for you," she said quietly.

"Strange?" said Pierre. "Why?"

"In New York. All alone."

"I feel quite contented, I must say."

"Do you find people tiresome?"

"Not at all. Quite the contrary."

"I mean rude. Ill-bred. I feel too awful, by the way, about Winthrop the other evening; it was really unpardonable."

There was a certain tension in her voice, in the way she held her cigarette. Pierre noticed this instantly; he was on the alert.

"I've spent quite a lot of time in France myself," she continued. Her voice was growing swifter and less restrained. "I went to a school near Aix-les-Bains for a year, just before I went to Vassar. I've spent two summers in Cannes, and one in Deauville. I absolutely adore France. . . . But, frankly, I've never seen a Frenchman I trusted. Don't be angry, please!"

"Perhaps," said Pierre discreetly, "you haven't seen the real France. One doesn't meet the real Frenchmen at the beaches and casinos."

"The French are too clever," said Mrs. Mannering, closing her eyes a little. "They quarrel constantly. Their relationships are too perverse, too angular. . . . You are different, I feel. You look trustworthy, straightforward."

"Thank you," said Pierre, without expression.

"I began to wonder about you that first day we met. You interest me, rather. Won't you tell me about your painting?" She opened her eyes very wide.

"Could I give you a glass of sherry?" Pierre inquired.

She nodded vaguely and went on: "I thought of speaking to Howard Prendergast about you. He's at the Modern Museum, you know. He might be able to help you a little. ... "

She rose, with the glass in her hand, and stepped upon the balcony. It was almost seven; the gardens lay in shadow. Pierre noticed that the sound of the piano had ceased.

"I wonder," murmured Mrs. Mannering. "What do you think of American women?"

Pierre smiled equivocally.

"Oh, I know what you're going to say," she added swiftly. "That we're very natural and uninhibited. That we dress well. That we have nice legs. All Frenchmen say the same thing." She turned and looked at him appraisingly.

Pierre returned her gaze. They were standing side by side, their hands resting lightly on the iron railing. It was almost dark.

"You're a great friend," she murmured, "of Jonathan's, aren't you?"

"I met him at Fontainebleau," stated Pierre, with restraint.

"He's an odd boy," murmured Mrs. Mannering. "Rather immature, I can't help thinking."

"A dreamer, perhaps," said Pierre cautiously.

"And bewildered, I suppose," said Mrs. Mannering. "Like so many young Americans. He needs to see a bit more of the world. ... "

She paused a moment. Then she added softly:

"He's devoted to you, isn't he?" She raised the cigarette to her lips; its hovering gleam shone in the dusk.

"We are friends; we have the same interests," said Pierre with serenity.

"You're a strange young man," said Mrs. Mannering, after a pause. "I don't quite understand you."

Pierre detected a new note in her voice, a touch of insinuation.

"Strange?" he said, with deliberation. "In what way?"

"I don't quite know. You seem so ... indifferent." She looked suddenly into his eyes. "Do you ... care for women?"

She paused, her lips remained parted; her face, in the evening light, looked ruthless and predatory.

Pierre drew a deep, decisive breath; he accepted the challenge. "I'm human," he said, in a low, ironical tone. "My tastes are—well, not unusual."

He turned around and faced her. He reached out and took her empty sherry glass, and allowed his hand to rest lightly on hers.

"You needn't be afraid of me," said Mrs. Mannering softly. She smiled at him with her gray, hard eyes. Her teeth shone faintly; her voice was trembling a little.

"I am not afraid of you," he said, and took her hand in his own.

18

THAT same night, a hot, windless night, Jonathan called for Lydia at the stage entrance, instead of waiting for her as usual in the little bar on Fortieth Street. Just a week had passed since he first had met her; he had seen her every night since his Sunday at Wyndham Park.

The porter, a surly Irishman with a pock-pitted face, demanded to see his pass. Jonathan felt a little sheepish, and was about to turn away.

At that moment Valdez, the young Cuban dancer, came strolling down the corridor. He was naked to the waist; he had a huge, silky brown chest, like a swimmer's. "Come in, Jonathan!" he cried, in his fine low voice. "Do you remember me?

"Look here, O'Hara," he added brusquely, turning to the porter, "this is a friend of Lochwitzky's. He works for the press. Let him in."

The porter shrugged his shoulders and returned to his evening paper.

Jonathan entered and found himself trapped in a tangle of ropes, cases, and stage properties, which were being dragged about by the grumbling stagehands.

"This way," said Valdez pleasantly, taking him by the hand. "You're looking for Lydia, I suppose?"

Jonathan nodded. "Yes, I am." He added cautiously: "You danced very well tonight. Congratulations!"

Valdez had appeared in *The Afternoon of a Faun* earlier in the evening. He grinned; the purple streaks on his face grew thin and sharp. "You liked me? How nice!"

Three girls from the *corps de ballet* were rushing past on their way to the dressing rooms. The program had ended with *Les Sylphides*. They seemed to be floating in white tulle; white butterfly wings were quivering on their backs. They looked inquisitively at Jonathan with their huge, heavily shadowed eyes.

Valdez led him straight across the stage, which was filled with the smell of dust and burlap.

Natalia darted past at that moment. Jonathan scarcely recognized her; her eyes were vast and sloping, her face was streaming with sweat. She smiled briefly at Jonathan and disappeared in the corridor.

"Some night when you're free," said Valdez swiftly, "why don't we get together, you and I?"

Jonathan hesitated; he felt himself blushing. "Well, yes, of course, if you'd like. ... "

Valdez looked at him with a swift, audacious intimacy. His hand felt warm and firm. Then his face broadened into a candid, disarming smile; his white teeth shone.

"Lydia, you know," he began in a whisper, "is a bit odd in some ways. There's a thing or two you ought to know. Why don't you come to my dressing room? We can have a little talk. ... "

At that moment Lydia emerged from the opposite side. She was already dressed in her street clothes. She wore a trim little suit of deep green, with a big silver fish pinned across the front, slightly on one side. Her hair was a tangle of dark brown locks.

She took Jonathan's hand quite casually, without any sign of welcome. They walked back to the street and stepped into a taxi.

Jonathan drew her to him in the darkness, and kissed her on the mouth without a word. She yielded for a moment; then her body grew tense and drew away.

"Did José Valdez say anything to you?" she suddenly demanded.

"Nothing of consequence. Why?"

She glanced at him darkly. "Did I see him holding your hand, or was it my imagination?"

"Yes, he was taking me to your room," said Jonathan, blushing for some ill-defined reason. "He was merely being helpful."

"Don't let him get hold of you," she said crisply. "He looks like a Greek god, but he's a swine ... and a dreadful liar."

"Don't worry," said Jonathan rather thoughtfully.

"He keeps getting into the most indecent scrapes," she whispered. "Sevastopoulos is on the verge of firing him."

"Let's not talk about Valdez," said Jonathan, placing his arm over her shoulder. "Let's talk about you."

"Me?" Her voice grew rather cautious. "I'm afraid there's nothing, darling, to talk about!"

She laid her hand in his lap rather dreamily; she drew her fingers across the fabric. For a moment they were silent; Jonathan grew tender and responsive. She smiled and drew her hand away. "Naughty, naughty," she whispered.

They arrived at Lydia's little flat in Greenwich Village, and paused on the street before entering. The night was still and breathless. And here, in this part of the city, Jonathan felt for the first time the hush of intimacy, the predominant human touch, the lull of whispers and seclusion. The tempo of life had fallen to a murmur. The rest of the city continued to rumble, like a distant ocean, far to the north.

He drew her to him under the street lamp. She pressed her firm cool lips to his, and held them there for a long time. He opened his eyes again, and saw the light shine hard and blue in her curls.

"Darling," she whispered, with a teasing smile. "Do be patient.... Come, let's hurry."

They crept upstairs and entered her room. Lydia lit two candles, and Jonathan felt a flush of unexpected delight.

She had set a bridge table in front of the couch, and on it a cool supper lay neatly arranged. Two yellow bowls of jellied madrilene stood side by side. There was a bottle of California wine, a tray of muffins and a dish of olives. On the bookcase lay two deviled crabs and a mound of potato salad, two pear tarts, two coffee cups, and two silver triangles of Camembert.

They sat down and began to eat by the warm, intimate glow of the candles. Jonathan felt uncannily happy.

"Do you like it?" whispered Lydia.

He nodded twice; then he leaned over and kissed her.

"I thought I'd have a little surprise for you," she said, in her low, caressing voice.

"It's a lovely surprise," said Jonathan. "You don't need to surprise me, though, darling."

She placed her hand tenderly on his knee. "Well, I did my best.... I'm rather stupid about these things, I'm afraid. I've never even been to school; did you know that? I don't know a thing about arithmetic, chemistry, and all that type of thing." She placed a spoonful of consommé in her mouth, meditatively.

"Still, you've lived," suggested Jonathan. "You've learned other things. In other ways."

"Don't insinuate, please, darling. . . . Really, sometimes you can be rather cruel!"

"I merely meant," added Jonathan hastily, "that you understand people. You are a judge of character. You've been taught in the great world, instead of the schoolhouse!"

"Oh, now you sound like a country parson, or something! No, but seriously. You should teach me a few things. A bit of history. A bit of literature."

She rose to heat the coffee, and wistfully placed the cheese and crackers on the table.

"Well, you know quite a lot about music," said Jonathan. "Don't you?"

"Oh, music." She shrugged her shoulders. "After all, what is music?"

"And painting too. You were very clever about Gauguin the other day at the museum."

"Oh, but that isn't culture, dear. That's merely a smattering. Merely chi-chi . . . " She touched the little mole on her chin, rather dreamily, with her finger tip. "No, really, I'd love to be able to talk about Giotto—is that how you pronounce it?—and Charlemagne, and Chinese vases. I feel on awfully thin ice when I begin to talk about things like that. . . . For example, I don't even know who Julius Caesar was, exactly. He was a Roman, I suppose? Did he write books?"

"Very well. Let us begin with Julius Caesar," said Jonathan, as she sat down beside him and began to sip her coffee.

"Yes." She nodded. "Well now, tell me, was Julius Caesar really—you know—just a trifle peculiar?" She looked at him mischievously.

"I shouldn't be surprised," said Jonathan. He put down his cup. "Well, that's the end of lesson one."

And he felt his arms irresistibly drawn to her body. He leaned over and reached for her lips; and she leaned back, closed her eyes with a wicked smile, and let her fingers trail on the floor. The warm yellow candlelight fell on her chin and neck, while her face slid into shadow.

"Wait. Wait," she whispered. "Not yet, darling."

And she held both his hands in her own.

A little later he watched her silently as she took off her clothes. Then, as always, her movements were swift, decisive, and graceful. She moved across the floor in her ballet dancer's gait, with the legs firm and straight and the toes pointed outward. She stood naked before a mirror, and posed *en arabesque;* the candlelight drew slow, golden lines across her back, leaving the front of her body mirrored in shadows.

Two ballet dancers stood poised in front of him: one luminous and fleshly, with her back turned to him, hard and slender as a boy's; the other a mere shadow, blue and insubstantial, in which the femininity of face, breast, and thigh floated like ornaments. Jonathan felt his bewilderment and desire intermingle, suddenly fuse. He felt that he, too, was being drawn into the pattern of the dance.

She did an *entrechat,* and finally faced him. The light flickered across her firm little breasts. He rose; she smiled and nodded; and he drew her to him. Her body yielded and she whispered, "Yes, darling. Now. Now."

He lay beside her, with her head beneath his. One of the candles had died; the other was dying.

The lovely thing in her head was the eyes. She had a beautifully shaped head, with fine chestnut-colored hair which spun itself into a glossy mass of curls. Her cheekbones were high and broad, her chin sharp and a little treacherous. Her lips were sensual, almost Negroid. But her eyes were so wonderfully expressive, so direct, so poignant, so full of cunning and vitality, that her whole being seemed continually lit; and she seemed to be what she never was: a beautiful woman.

The second candle began to quiver; then it leaped and died.

As he lay beside her in the darkness he felt that time was coming to a halt. The glow of the city hung diffused beyond the window; the long white curtains stirred intermittently. He felt that they were floating on a warm and limitless sea. The roar of the waves was very distant, and the present moment seemed complete. The future and the past spread calmly on either side. The undercurrent of fear had vanished, and the flicker of guilt had died away.

Lydia opened her eyes and turned to him in the darkness.

"I can't sleep, Jonathan. I can feel you thinking. ... What are you thinking?"

"Thinking of you, Lydia. And the rest of the world."

"Think only of me. Don't think of the rest of the world."

"All right, my darling. I'll think only of you."

"Think only of me," she whispered, "and I'll always let you love me."

She drew him upon her with sudden passion. "Like this," she whispered. "Always like this."

And even while she slept, her arms still reached out for him and her face retained its blind, obsessive look. Even in her dreams, it seemed, the touch of horror hung, very lightly, upon her.

19

THE following evening, while Jonathan was talcing a bath in his hotel, the telephone rang. He leaped out of the tub.

"What are you doing, darling?"

"It's you, Lydia! ... Well, I'm taking a bath, as it happens."

"Oh. ... Do get dressed, won't you, like an angel, and come over to the theater right away?"

"I'm afraid I can't at the moment, Lydia."

There was a tense silence at the other end of the wire.

"You see, I promised to meet a friend of mine for dinner. ... "

"And you can't come to the performance?" Lydia inquired in a slow, caressing tone.

"Not tonight, I'm afraid," said Jonathan apologetically. He had flung a towel over his shoulders; the drops of water were rolling down his body.

There was a pause. "I'm doing *Petrouchka* tonight, you know."

"Oh, you are?" said Jonathan brightly. "I'll be very sorry to miss that!"

"You needn't miss it, dear."

"But I'll have to meet Pierre ... "

She interrupted him: "Oh, it's Pierre now, is it? Who, may I ask, is Pierre? ... Well, never mind. I'll call up Peter Sebastian. I happen to have an extra ticket."

A small pool of water had gathered at his feet. A faint warm breeze was passing through the room. He began, unaccountably, to shiver.

"I'm very sorry, Lydia."

Her voice sounded lighthearted and casual. "Oh, never mind. Some other time, perhaps."

"Could I come and see you afterward?"

"No, please don't inconvenience yourself. I'm sure Pierre would be upset if you go rushing off...."

"Please be reasonable, Lydia."

"Reasonable?" Her voice suddenly rose to a tremulous high pitch. "Am I being unreasonable? Is it unreasonable to..." She paused. For several moments neither of them spoke. Then he heard a faint sigh and the dull click of the receiver.

No weapon is so effective, Jonathan learned, in the hands of someone who is loved, as silence. For a week Lydia did not telephone him. He left messages at the theater, at her flat, at the ballet school; she did not call back. He wrote her two brief notes. She left them unanswered.

Jonathan was free to imagine anything he chose. Perhaps she was miserable; perhaps she had found another lover; perhaps she was sick; perhaps she was dying. He felt, in turn, remorse, apprehension, anger, and a desperate jealousy. His love was feeding feverishly on uncertainty and absence.

And he wondered, at times, why he had fallen in love with Lydia. She wasn't really beautiful; she wasn't even in his style, really. There were moments when he felt that he might have fallen in love with anyone at all; that his love for Lydia was a flight from some more insoluble longing; that the fascination of Lydia was an aura, a kind of distillation of the city, and his submission to Lydia was a symbolical act of obedience to the city's own hypnotic power.

He lived, for a week, in a state of continual suspense. Each time that the telephone rang he leaped from his chair; each time there was a knock on the door he felt a sudden tremor of hope. He saw Quincy once or twice at the Yale Club; he lunched with Pierre once or twice, and had drinks one night with Horace Hayden. Once he played squash with his friend Charlie Holliday, in whose architectural firm he hoped to get a job in a fortnight.

Once he ran into Delia, in the lounge of the Ritz; for a moment he did not recognize her, and was stunned with her beauty. Then she looked at him and smiled. It was a moment he never forgot; it gave him the sensation of being suddenly transported to another climate, a benignant, sunny land where his nature felt at peace. A disturbing set of emotions began to stir in him, as he spoke to her: he instantly repressed them. They parted casually.

He visited the little galleries on Fifty-seventh Street, and looked at the Braques, the Dufys, the Pissarros. He wrote a long, affectionate letter to his mother in London; he paid several visits to the Metropolitan Museum; he started reading *War and Peace;* and he went to an afternoon concert at Carnegie Hall. But he carefully kept his evenings free, in the perpetual hope that Lydia might call him.

Finally, one Thursday afternoon, he reached her by phone at the theater.

"Lydia?"

"Yes? Who is it? ... Oh, Jonathan." Her voice sounded amiable and unconcerned.

"I thought I'd call. Are you still alive?"

"Oh!" She laughed gaily. "In the best of health, my dear!"

"Tell me, Lydia. What are you doing tonight?"

"Tonight? ... Oh, I have a harrowing schedule tonight. I'm in all three numbers. *Romeo, Fancy Free,* and *Aurora.* I'm going straight to bed afterward."

"What about tomorrow?"

"Tomorrow? ... Let's see ... Wait a minute ... No, tomorrow I'm having supper with Sevastopoulos."

"Well, I just thought I'd call. Are you going to the party on Saturday?"

"You mean the one at the Sherry-Netherland? That Indian prince—what's his name?"

"Prince Sharavaji."

"I thought I might. Did he ask you too?"

"Yes, he did. May I take you?"

"I promised Natalia and Peter Sebastian to go with them. I'm dreadfully sorry."

"Well, have a good time," said Jonathan in a calm, despondent tone.

"Oh, never fear!" she said cheerfully. "I'll see you Saturday then? At Prince ... I've forgotten his name again!"

"Prince Sharavaji."

"Prince Sharavaji. I simply don't see how those Orientals keep their names straight. Well, good-by, dear!"

"Good-by, Lydia."

There was a click. Jonathan saw, as he hung up the receiver, that his hand was trembling with excitement.

20

PRINCE SHARAVAJI was the son of the Maharajah of Badrapur. He was rather notorious; he owned a yellow Rolls coupé, a suite at the Sherry-Netherland, and a spectacular collection of cuff links, gloves, and golden cigarette cases.

He had been in Paris when the war broke out; and had traveled swiftly to Biarritz, then to San Sebastian, then to Seville. It was in Seville that he had met Jonathan, one day, in the bar of the Andalucia Palace. From Seville he took a small American boat to New York. Ever since his arrival in New York he had been living at the Sherry-Netherland, in somewhat eccentric splendor, except for a trip or two to Florida, and an amorous excursion to Taos.

He was a homely little man with an egg-shaped head and a frail, fidgeting body. His arms and legs moved like an insect's— in rigid, desultory spasms. His skin was faintly bluish and iridescent. Only his eyes were impressive; they were large and limpid, and absolutely black. He wore a huge golden bracelet, studded with sapphires.

Jonathan was the first guest to arrive. Prince Sharavaji was delighted to see him, cried softly, and clapped his dark little hands with joy.

"Ah, my long-lost friend!" he exclaimed. "So you are safe at last! From the agonies of Europe! I was terribly worried about you, Jonathan. ... " He had been at Balliol for a year, and spoke with an Oxford accent.

"Well," said Jonathan conscientiously, "it wasn't so bad, really. I felt quite safe there. I didn't starve. I felt rather happy, to tell the truth."

"Happy!" cried the little prince. "Who can be happy nowadays? Have you no sympathy for the world's miseries, you cruel man?"

Jonathan smiled involuntarily. "Oh, I do, definitely! But then, sometimes I feel so well, I can't help thinking life is worth living. In spite of the world's miseries ... "

"Oh, Jonathan," sighed the prince, placing a finger daintily on his chin and regarding his guest reproachfully, "you are an animal, I am afraid. A clever, friendly, good-looking animal, without a soul. Like all Americans!

"I long desperately for Paris," he continued nostalgically. "And for Rome and Monte Carlo. The great monuments of the old world. You see, my dear Jonathan, I am really a child of Western civilization, at heart. ... And now it is falling into ruins. Cannes, Venice, Salzburg—they'll be nothing but rubble! Capri, Biarritz—will we ever see them again?" He spoke with a kind of fluttering, birdlike accent.

He drew Jonathan into the library and triumphantly showed him some recent purchases. They included several pieces of Dresden china, an old harp, a Chippendale mirror, and two small paintings.

"What do you think of them, quite frankly?" inquired the prince, looking at the paintings with a sly, professional air. "I bought them at a wonderful bargain. The dealer didn't realize their value, poor man. They seemed rather expensive, I must say, until I realized what they were. The one on the right is a

Boucher; the other is a Fragonard. I'm practically certain of it. There's no signature, of course, but I see a certain something in the color, the brush stroke ... " He screwed his eyes together cunningly, his little brown fingers danced through the air.

"People know nothing about these finer points in New York. They are really barbarians, when it comes to the subtleties of culture. Still, it is a great place for bargains, if you know where to look. I suppose, between you and me, this dealer never even heard of Fragonard! ... Well, what do you think of them, Jonathan, my dear? Quite frankly?"

Jonathan felt a little shy. The pictures were painfully mediocre.

"They show," he said tactfully, "that you have a real enthusiasm for art. You know what you like. You have a mind of your own."

"Yes," the prince admitted with a happy smile, "I have come to worship art. Art is to me what sex is to some of my friends. I think of it morning, noon, and night. I spend a fortune on it. I go down on my knees to it. I suffer for it. I lose sleep over it. It is a mania, my dear Jonathan!"

"But a very fine, sensitive mania," said Jonathan flatteringly.

"Ah, thank you, my dear," said Prince Sharavaji, with deep contentment.

"I used to be a very sad person, Jonathan," he continued, after a thoughtful pause. "Very pessimistic, very dreamy. I was born, I think, to be a philosopher. But what is there to do, nowadays, for a philosopher? No, no." He waved his forefinger and shook his head. "Life has become too cynical. Too materialistic. Too nervous. I sometimes try to meditate a little, after breakfast. But no, the phone rings all day long. People ask me to lunch, ask me to cocktails, ask me to the ballet. ... It is a sociable whirl!"

He shrugged his shoulders helplessly. "So I have become a lover of art. ... Do you feel, Jonathan, that it is a suitable role for me?" He smiled appealingly.

"I am sure of it," replied Jonathan rather awkwardly. "With your feeling for ... glamour."

"Glamour. Yes. Exactly," said Prince Sharavaji with a sigh.

"I am so glad you could come tonight, Jonathan," the prince continued, in a more practical tone. "I think you'll enjoy it. There'll be some rather choice guests." His black eyes twinkled. "Some real beauties. For every taste! ... Do you prefer brunettes or blondes, Jonathan?" He placed his forefinger on his chin demurely.

Jonathan hesitated. "Well, it all depends," he murmured thoughtfully. "I am like you, perhaps. I like ... surprises."

The prince's voice grew rather mischievous. "I hear, from my spies, that you are quite a connoisseur of the ballet. Is it true?" He wagged his finger. "Well, I've asked a few of them for tonight. The great Kirillova is coming. So are some of the younger girls. ... And there'll be a little surprise or two. You'll see!" His voice was trembling with expectation.

At that moment a group of guests arrived, and he followed Jonathan into the drawing room.

21

IT WAS not far from midnight, and the drawing room was almost full, when Lydia finally arrived.

A strange assortment of guests was sitting, standing, leaning against the window sills, and crouching on the floor. Several were listening to a man with red hair who was playing the piano. Others were standing in moody isolation. The rest were chatting and waiting for the door to the dining room to open.

Lydia arrived, not with Sebastian, but with two other women, one of them robust and blond, the other dark and thin. Jonathan recognized neither of them. Lydia smiled at him casually across the room, but did not come to join him.

His heart sank. She looked sparkling, happy, and intensely desirable. She was wearing a long, clinging dress of dark blue silk; and, for the first time, a pair of crescent-shaped silver earrings which he had given her. She had contrived to give herself an air of fragility, of distinction.

Jonathan knew only three or four of the other guests. He recognized a friend of Pierre's, a Frenchman named Maxim de la Tour, sitting in a corner. Horace Hayden had arrived, and stood near the piano, talking to Natalia, who had just arrived with Sebastian. Jonathan himself had cautiously put on a black dinner jacket, but Horace was wearing a tweed suit with a magenta bow tie. Sebastian, as usual, wore a dark shirt with an open collar.

Natalia looked superb in a gown of deep red taffeta, with a row of huge golden bracelets flickering on her arm.

Presently Sebastian came up to him. "Where is our host?" he inquired rather defiantly, his tiny black eyes flashing. "Has he been taken ill, or something?"

Jonathan looked around; Prince Sharavaji had vanished.

"Oh, he's in the dining room," chirped a tall lady beside him. "Arranging the table. It's a special ceremony with him. ... *C'est une petite manie avec lui, vous savez,*" she added in atrocious French, assuming that they both understood her. *"Alors,"* she said, taking Sebastian by the arm and leading him away. "Now tell me about yourself, *mon cher.* What have you been up to? I've been hearing strange tales. ... "

Jonathan was left alone. But only for a moment; Valdez, the Cuban dancer, came up and greeted him. Jonathan found himself constantly glancing at Lydia, who was deep in conversation, it appeared, with a young ensign.

Valdez put his hand on Jonathan's shoulder. His teeth and his eyes were sparkling with mischief; he seemed a little drunk. "Hello, good-looking!" he announced with a wink. "Where have you been hiding? Are you afraid of me?"

A young Russian, extremely tall and emaciated, appeared with two elderly ladies in tow: Princess Volkoff and Princess Kubinsky, Valdez explained, in somewhat skeptical tones. One of them was hideous, hilarious, and old; the other, a frail and mousy person, retired into a corner where she remained throughout the evening.

At that moment the doors of the dining room were drawn open. Prince Sharavaji appeared with outspread arms, in an oriental robe of green brocade embroidered in gold. There was a momentary hush. The candles behind him flickered.

"Please!" he squealed, with an air of joy. "Gentlemen! Ladies! The delicacies are served!"

He clapped his hands and two butlers appeared, one with a cold roast turkey, the other with a Virginia ham. Tremendous bowls of salad and urns of hot hors d'oeuvres lined the table. The guests began to flood the dining room, and there was a tinkle of china and cutlery. Presently they returned to the drawing room with their plates and glasses filled.

Princess Kubinsky now attached herself to the handsome young ensign. She was whispering merrily in his ear, while he listened with a childlike smile, gazing past her at Lydia. Lydia was talking to Natalia at the farther end of the room, and returned the ensign's gaze. Jonathan felt a stab of pain, too confused and inchoate to be jealousy.

And all the glitter and gaiety of the party appeared to grow muted. The tinkle of the glasses and forks, the interplay of nods and glances had faded into a backdrop against which stirred, with an exquisite precision, the most trivial of Lydia's movements. Every time she stirred a finger or opened her lips, a flash of light seemed to play about her, obscuring all the other guests. Jonathan felt his whole body aching with suspense.

Natalia rose and wandered over to Jonathan. "You look lonely," she said, with solicitude. "Come. Let me introduce you to the great Kirillova." And she led him over to the dark, thin creature who had arrived with Lydia.

Kirillova nodded, smiled, and seemed paralyzed with shyness. She was wearing a gown of black crepe, severe and unadorned. Jonathan remembered how she had appeared on the stage—diaphanous and floating. She now looked almost ugly. The lines of her face were sharp with strain, and her eyes held a flat, expressionless glitter. But there was something about her that he instantly liked: the air of coolness and utter detachment, which lay behind her shyness.

The tall thin Russian now approached them with his friend, the Princess Kubinsky. He bowed to Natalia and Kirillova.

"Princess Kubinsky has asked to meet you.... Madame Kirillova, Princess Kubinsky.... And this is Natalia Petrova. Princess Kubinsky."

Natalia hurriedly introduced Jonathan to both of them. They glanced at him indulgently and then turned to Kirillova.

"Princess Kubinsky is a tremendous admirer of your dancing," whispered the young Russian.

"Of your profile as well," put in Princess Kubinsky, with a slight leer.

Kirillova's face broke into a painful smile. "Thank you," she said thinly.

"I also admire this other young lady's art," said the princess, turning massively toward Natalia. "I saw her in *Giselle.* It was transcendent! It was epical!"

Horace Hayden came up and joined the group. Natalia greeted him with a regal air. She turned slowly and expertly, casting the full glory of her gaze upon him, and extended her bracelet-covered arms. She possessed, to the highest degree, the kind of beauty called classic; a beauty superbly tall and untroubled, with tremendous onyx eyes that shone like jewels in a medallion.

But Jonathan ceased watching her. His eyes returned to Lydia, whose dark blue shape was circulating among a group of young men in the dining room. The nervous intensity of his longing filled the room with a kind of fever. She turned and glanced at him, for an instant, and laid her hand playfully on the ensign's shoulder. He was about to cross the room in her direction.

But at that very moment Prince Sharavaji rose majestically in the doorway, climbed upon the piano bench, and clapped his hands three times.

He announced in exuberant tones: "Gentlemen, ladies, please! A surprise for you!"

He waved his hands a little, as a kind of warning, and climbed down from the bench. He stepped dramatically to one side, made a sweeping bow, and cried out: "Madame Argentinita! Madame Pilar Lopez!"

The two sisters advanced, like birds of prey. A young Spaniard had begun strumming on a guitar. The dance began, to the dizzy click of the castanets. There was a predatory swirl of bright red skirts. A breathless silence filled the room; a mingling of exhilaration and alarm. Soon the dance was over; a second followed, then a third. The young Spaniard had begun to sing, and his slow flamenco voice, combined with the spectacular staccato of the dance, produced an oddly desolate effect.

The food had been removed from the long table in the dining room, which was now covered with countless bottles and glasses, silver buckets of ice, and shell-shaped bowls of sugared fruits. The guests were distributing themselves among the neighboring rooms, strategically. Some would slip away, vanish, and return fifteen minutes later with a bright and casual, or perhaps a faintly languishing appearance.

Jonathan looked around for Lydia; she had disappeared. The guests had discreetly begun to leave.

He sat down on a window sill and leaned out into the night. The park lay far below, blue, impenetrable, like the sea. Small shadows were advancing and retiring, like ripples, along the borders of the avenue. The whole city seemed unusually grand and suggestive at this moment. There were almost no lights, but an exhalation of light rose, like a hot breath, from the western distances. A searchlight was piercing the low-lying clouds, which hung in oceanic masses.

A low call, like a tremendous sob, rose from the sea of shrubbery. It was, Jonathan realized, the roar of a lion in the zoo. The whole night seemed to tremble, to grow alive in reply. And suddenly the buildings looked intensely frail and ephemeral—a vaporous chain of structures washed by a hidden glow, a kind of jungle mist, about to dissolve.

"You look worried, my dear," someone whispered. He turned; it was Natalia. "You look as though the world were coming to an end!"

He stared past her sullenly. "I was looking at the park," he said. "Well, sometimes," he added, "I feel sure that it's only a question of hours."

"A question of hours, my dear?"

"Until the world explodes. Bursts into fire. Dissolves into vapor." There was a pause.

"You were thinking of someone?" Her voice was very gentle.

He looked at her and nodded. Her beauty floated about her like an ambience, a perfume.

"I understand," she said very gently. "I think I know what is wrong."

"Has she left?" whispered Jonathan.

"I think so. Yes. I'm sure. ... Come, we'd better be going too, my dear. It's time to leave."

She placed her gold-encircled arm on his, and led him slowly to the door. A fragrance of lilac rose from her shoulders; there was something reassuring in the touch of her cool, calm hand.

22

JONATHAN took Natalia to her hotel and was about to drive on when she said:

"Why don't you come in, Jonathan? And have a drink with me? We'll talk about Lydia. Perhaps I'll be able to give you a bit of advice. ... " She smiled in a friendly, confidential manner.

She lived in a small, rather intimate type of hotel, the Picardy, which overlooked Fifty-seventh Street. A myopic little man at the desk nodded to her rather disapprovingly as they passed.

The black elevator boy smiled familiarly and said: "How are you, Miss Pitrovy? It's pretty hot tonight, ain't it? ... Well, it looks like we'll get snarled up in this war, I guess!"

"Oh, I suppose so," said Natalia, with a sigh. "This dreary old war—what a bore it is!"

Her room was bright and agreeable, and far tidier than Lydia's. A low mirror-topped table stood in front of a huge couch upholstered in lemon. There was a Daumier lithograph on the wall, and an etching of Notre Dame.

"Let me mix you a drink," she said cheerfully. "What about a gin and tonic?" She spoke English with a playful Slavonic accent, and a faint, rather appealing lisp.

Jonathan was hardly listening. He nodded absent-mindedly. "She's an odd, elusive kind of girl," he suddenly declared. "Like an elf. A will-o'-the-wisp."

He drew his hand across his forehead; it was throbbing feverishly. It occurred to him that he had been drinking a bit too much.

"Personally," observed Natalia, "I wouldn't call her a will-o'-the-wisp, exactly." She placed their drinks on the mirror-topped table, and sat down beside him. "There've been times, I'm afraid, when she's been anything but elusive." She lowered her eyes deploringly.

"What do you mean, Natalia?"

"She is not, I'm afraid, quite what you think, my dear Jonathan."

Jonathan paused. "I don't," he said quietly, "expect her to be a saint. She's had affairs; she didn't deny it. I knew it. I accepted it."

"Oh," said Natalia, "you are innocent, Jonathan! You are like a little lamb!"

Jonathan looked at her with his brows wrinkled and his hands pressed painfully together.

"Affairs!" Natalia continued, in an amused yet sympathetic tone. "Who cares about affairs? We've all had affairs by the dozen! It is the thing to do in New York. People are shocked and disgusted if you don't. ... But oh, with Lydia it is a much less simple matter, my dear Jonathan, than just having affairs."

"Yes?" said Jonathan, with a sullen ache in his heart. "What is it, then?"

"What we do to others," replied Natalia ambiguously. "What we do to ourselves, Jonathan."

"I don't quite understand you, Natalia."

"Well, my dear, I have known women who led the life of Messalina, and yet had hearts as white as snow. But Lydia. Well, remember that I warned you!"

"But of what?" whispered Jonathan a little hoarsely. He felt an ardent impulse to defend Lydia, which conflicted with his painful yearning to learn more about her. "She seems," he said tentatively, "such a child, sometimes. Such a babe in the woods."

"Nonsense," said Natalia brutally. "She is an old, old woman."

"She is wise beyond her years, of course," admitted Jonathan.

Natalia gazed at him with a certain pity. "Lydia's heart, my dear Jonathan, is a Gordian knot. Don't try to untangle it. You'll never succeed! I know her pretty well. I am devoted to Lydia, as a matter of fact. I always take her side when the other girls begin to gossip. ... They all absolutely loathe her, you know."

Jonathan walked slowly to the window and looked into the night: he felt that he had entered a psychological realm as alien, as enigmatic as the Gobi Desert.

"But perhaps you could help me, a little," he began slowly, walking back from the window and sitting beside her. "You could give me some advice, at least, Natalia. Perhaps she's furious at me. ... "

Natalia smiled compassionately. "Furious? Don't be silly, my dear. It's all happened before, over and over. People fall in love with her all the time. Every age, sex, and color. God knows why! She's not beautiful. But once they've been in bed with her, it seems, they find her rather fascinating. ... "

Jonathan felt faintly dizzy. The room seemed suddenly very hot. "Does she," he began hoarsely, "does she—really go to bed with every age, sex, and color?"

"Oh, good heavens," said Natalia, raising her brows, "don't take me so literally, Jonathan! No, what I meant is simply that Lydia is—well, you know—rather broad-minded. Distinctly tolerant." She stirred around her ice cube, with a look of penetration.

The more they spoke of Lydia, the more misty and contradictory her image became, and the more intense his yearning.

"I think of nothing but her," he said hoarsely. "Of no one but her. She draws my thoughts like a magnet. She fills the city like a ... perfume."

Natalia shook her head slowly. "My poor child," she said patiently. "You will certainly burn your fingers on her! It's a crime, it really is!"

She was looking at him with her tranquil and luminous eyes. She looked lovely; incomparably more lovely than Lydia.

At that moment the telephone rang. Natalia turned her head and stared at it with apprehension. It rang again, impatiently, and then a third and a fourth time—a shrill, infuriated little squeal.

"Hadn't you better answer?" said Jonathan.

Natalia sat motionless. "No," she whispered. "Better not. ... I think I know who it is."

Jonathan looked at her with a flush of excitement. "Do you think ... "

"It's Peter Sebastian," she stated, shrugging her shoulders. "I am sure of it. How revolting of Peter to call at this hour!" She glanced at her watch somewhat furtively. Jonathan saw that it was after three.

"Do you think he knows I'm here?" said Jonathan, with a tingle of guilt.

"Of course he does," said Natalia blandly. "He was standing in the lobby when we left the Sherry-Netherland together. Didn't you see him?" She shrugged her shoulders again. "Well, never mind ... Here, let me get you another drink, my dear."

She was about to rise when someone knocked at the door.

Natalia sat absolutely immobile. Then she gazed meaning-fully at Jonathan and slowly placed her forefinger to her lips.

There was another knock; a very light one.

Natalia said nothing, and placed her hand lightly on Jonathan's shoulder, as though to keep him under control.

There was a third, almost inaudible knock, then silence. Jonathan imagined he could hear faint footsteps vanishing down the hall.

Finally Natalia said softly: "Really, I can't think what has gotten into Peter lately. He's been growing positively morbid. ... "

She rose, listened at the door a moment, then wandered across the room to mix another drink.

Jonathan felt his body streaming with heat. "Do you mind," he said modestly, "if I take off my coat, Natalia?"

"Certainly not, dear. Go right ahead."

"Thank you." Jonathan rose and took off his black coat. He noticed that his shirt was drenched in sweat.

"Look here," said Natalia, in firm, competent tones. "I've been watching you, Jonathan. You have a fine, clean character. You have a sensitive soul. You're by no means an idiot. But, well, you haven't been around in New York quite enough. Someday you'll learn about Lydia. It's not for me to say. ... Remember, my dear Jonathan, all I want is to help you!"

She sighed vaguely. She seemed a little restless. She rose and dropped another cube of ice into his drink; then she drew down the Venetian blinds, with a sigh, and disappeared briefly in the bathroom.

When she returned Jonathan noticed a pronounced scent of eau de cologne. He looked at her with sudden curiosity.

She stood before him in her burgundy gown, one hand on her hip, the other on the back of her neck. Her pale hair lay heaped in a coil on the top of her head. Her bracelets were glistening. She was gazing at him gravely with her deep onyx eyes; he felt the strong, firm rush of her beauty.

"You are a funny boy," she said. "I like you. You are sweet, Jonathan."

She gazed dreamily toward the window.

Jonathan rose. "I think I'd better be going, Natalia," he said. "I . . . I feel rather queer."

Natalia behaved very gracefully. She regarded him with solicitude. "Would an aspirin help?" she inquired softly.

"No, thanks," said Jonathan; "it's just that I need a bit of sleep, I suppose." Everything in the room looked abnormally bright and magnified.

She helped him on with his coat and straightened his black tic. "There," she murmured. "You won't think," she added, with a sudden magnificent smile, "that I've been meddlesome, my dear?"

"No, no," said Jonathan eagerly. He leaned forward and was about to kiss her. Then he turned to the door and said: "Thank you, Natalia."

"Good night, my dear child!"

23

THE streets were altogether silent and deserted. An air of limbo shrouded the buildings; the windows and doorways looked blind and hollow.

It was a short five minutes' walk to his own hotel. He passed only a single person on Fifty-seventh Street—an old man who was wearing, in spite of the heat, a long black coat, and who stared at Jonathan with a kind of senile ferocity.

When he arrived at his hotel the night porter called after him, through the empty lobby: "Mr. Ely? Just a moment, sir."

Jonathan turned back. "There's a package for you, sir," said the porter, with bleary eyes, and handed him a small brown parcel.

"When did this arrive?"

"A young lady left it here, I believe, sir. Fifteen or twenty minutes ago."

Jonathan opened the parcel. It contained a blue silk handkerchief, a leather-bound copy of *Alice in Wonderland*, and two crescent-shaped earrings.

Enclosed was a note hastily scrawled in pencil:

JONATHAN:

I never want to see you again. It has been a terrible experience. I am tired of being hurt. How could you go with that poisonous woman? I feel utterly sick when I think of it. Here are the things you gave me. Don't ever try to see me again. I loved you so, so desperately. God have mercy on you. L.

Jonathan stood by the door of the lobby and stared into the street. His hands were trembling; his face was wet and feverish. For several minutes he was incapable of moving, of thinking, of making any kind of decision. He felt a strangling sensation in his throat.

He rushed into the street and looked for a taxi. He ran for two blocks, and finally found one parked on the corner of Fifty-sixth Street. He leaped in and, in a breathless, unnatural voice, gave the driver Lydia's address in Greenwich Village.

The cab went speeding down the smooth dark regions of Fifth Avenue. The buildings looked wild and derelict, a row of huge machinery heaped like debris on an empty battlefield. Even the human vestiges—a lonely walker, a white dress in a window—had a forlorn, anachronistic air. The stillness was not that of sleep and repose, but that of extinction, obliteration.

It was already growing hazy and gray when he arrived. He raced up the ramshackle stairs with a pounding heart, and rang the bell. An unbroken silence filled the house. It was as though he had entered a ruin. There was only the whisper of tiny insects, perhaps, or crumbling plaster. He rang a second time; but he heard only the sound of his own breathing. He pressed his ear against the door. Not a sound was to be heard. He peered through the keyhole: there was nothing but blackness.

Then, as he tried the doorknob, to his surprise the door opened. He stole into the silent room, expecting some desperate, some electrical revelation. But a moment later, though he still saw nothing, he knew that the room was empty.

He struck a match. The couch lay smooth and unruffled. Three half-empty glasses caught a splinter of light, and the Van Gogh postman stared at him with his sullen blue eyes.

He caught sight, as he turned, of his own face in the mirror, brightened by the flicker of the match. He was shocked by the hollow setting of his eyes, and their hot and unfamiliar glitter. There was something tubercular in the flush of the face.

The flame bit at his finger tips, and he threw the match on the floor. He walked slowly to the window. There was no one outside. A gray, swampy shimmer was creeping along Tenth Street.

Slowly he drew off his clothes. His legs were quivering, his whole body was aching with nervous exhaustion.

And as he sat on the couch, with his clothes cast on the floor around him, he felt the full flavor of desolation fill the room. He felt that he had been infected by a kind of creeping paralysis, a vicious malady peculiar to New York: a sense of hollowness and instability so acute that even the walls seemed impregnated with it. The whole desperate spiral of promiscuity and self-indulgence, of sexual fever, of physical deterioration, was but an elaborate symptom of it. Nothing was certain, nothing was safe, and the very beating of his heart seemed charged with treachery.

At last he lay down and buried his face in the pillow, from which the sweet delicate scent of Lydia's hair rose to his lips.

24

BUT he could not fall asleep. He saw the first haze of light beginning to filter through the blinds, and he heard the early tinkle of the milk bottles below. The sparrows began to twitter in the stunted trees. The low, protracted hiss of distant traffic had begun.

He heard the sound of water dripping: it was the tap in the bathroom. There was something a bit insane in the stealthy rhythm of the drops. They sounded like footsteps climbing an interminable stairway.

A bell started ringing. He sprang from the bed and listened. It rang again; it was on the floor below, apparently.

He looked at his watch. It was almost seven.

He rose and tiptoed to the window, and peered past the blinds. Perhaps she was wandering down the street at that very moment? But what if she weren't alone? Perhaps Sebastian was with her? Or perhaps she had spent the whole night at Sebastian's? He felt miserable and unsettled to a point which bordered on delirium.

And his love began to encroach upon his mind still further, swelling, dilating on the rush of suspicions that came upon him with the early morning light.

The street outside looked like a street of the dead. The houses were shabby and monstrous, each with its little pots of flowers, its faded curtains, its socks hung out to dry. But it was no longer merely the monotony of a gray city street; it was the landscape of degeneration and defeat.

He went back to bed and fell into a desultory slumber. He was utterly exhausted; yet he felt, as he fell asleep, that his body was gradually hardening with desire. He felt that the sheets in which he lay were touched, ever so faintly, with the fragrance and sensuality of her body.

He awoke just in time to hear the sound of footsteps coming up the stairs. Quickly he looked at his watch. The room was noticeably lighter; it was already twenty past nine. Long ribbons of sunlight were slipping through the blinds.

He lay still in bed, the sheet drawn loosely over him. His heart had begun to beat uncontrollably. He heard the click of the doorknob and then the flat, deliberate sound of a door being opened.

Then the door was closed again. Without turning his head he could see, very dimly, the dark, slender shadow beside the door.

He realized that she had not yet seen him.

She took two or three casual steps toward the center of the room. Then she halted and stood motionless; he knew that she had seen him.

As he turned his head to look at her she continued on her way, walked past the bed without glancing at him, and quietly opened the door of the wardrobe. He saw her reach among the row of brightly patterned dresses that hung from the metal hangers.

She looked pale and grave. She was still in her dark blue dress, and he could not help noticing that the silver earrings were gone. He recognized the glossy mass of curls on her head, and the slope of her neck, and the resolute, peculiarly graceful posture of her body.

A stab of longing, such as he had never felt before, then suddenly shook him from head to foot.

She drew a light summer coat from the hanger, placed it over her arm, closed the door of the wardrobe, and walked impassively back to the door. She gave no sign whatever of having seen him.

He heard the door open, her feet cross the threshold, and then the door casually close again.

And at that instant something burst within him; his entire body was flooded with panic. He felt that she was gliding from his arms forever.

He sprang naked from the bed, ran to the door, and flung it open. He caught sight of her slender blue shape a flight below. It turned slowly, descended, and disappeared a moment later.

He called after her: "Lydia!" But she did not turn around. He heard her footsteps moving quietly down the second stairway. He called her name again; there was no reply. He strode across the landing to the head of the stairs, and called her name a third time, in a voice so weird and vibrant that he felt a shock when he heard it; it sounded like the voice of a madman.

The sound of her footsteps died away. He paused for a moment, with his hands on the wooden railing, then turned back into the room. He walked swiftly to the window and flung open the blinds. He looked down at the sidewalk, leaning out as far as he could, and fixed his gaze upon the entrance to the house.

But he noticed no one either entering or leaving. He glanced up and down the street for a sign of her blue dress. But he saw only strangers meandering to and fro. A piercing ache shot through his forehead, like an ice-cold needle, from temple to temple. She had passed from his grasp; he felt, with a horrible dullness of perception, that he would never see her again. The soft morning breeze passed through his hair and over his arms.

He stared for a long time, hoping without hope that he still might catch some glimpse of her in the distance. The minutes passed. The sense of the irrevocable came over him. His eyes grew dim; he was about to burst into sobs.

At that moment he felt two arms enclose his body, ever so gently. He felt the soft, tender touch of a head against his back.

"Jonathan," she whispered very faintly.

A rush of sweetness poured through him, washing away at a stroke all the hours of misery and desolation. It was like returning home from a prison; the air began to glitter.

He drew her to him and covered her face with kisses. He felt the hidden magic of her body rise to greet him, and then dissolve in his arms, with a look of love.

At last he said: "Oh, Lydia ... I've been waiting here for hours." He had much more to say, but no longer a need to say it. The feeling of her warm, resilient body in his arms drained all the meaning from his words.

She looked past his head with a kind of deep, dark gravity. "It's been terrible, Jonathan. ... You'll never know how terrible."

He nodded. "Yes," he murmured, and kissed her again. "Yes, darling. Now it's over. We're together once more."

She sighed. "I couldn't believe it," she whispered. "I stood in Fifty-seventh Street for two whole hours, watching the light in her room. I kept phoning. I beat at the door. Once I saw you at the window. ... Oh, Jonathan, it hurt horribly, it still hurts. I still can't quite believe it."

"I thought of no one but you," he said. "You know it, Lydia."

She looked at him wearily and shook her head; she closed her eyes for a moment.

"I didn't even touch her," he said in a hoarse, urgent voice. "You know it, Lydia. I wanted no one but you."

He drew back her head and kissed her neck, eyes, and forehead. The dark blue silk of her dress slipped through his fingers, like a tiny cascade.

She drew away; she lowered her glance, and looked at his warm, excited body. A subtle smile appeared on her face. But only for an instant. It was followed by a gaze of mute reproach, and this in turn by a look of listless sadness.

He drew her to him again. "I can't help it," he whispered.

She sighed a little. "I had hoped your love was ... a bit more spiritual, Jonathan."

He picked her up in his arms and carried her to the couch; and she smiled again as he crouched on his knees beside her—a quick, incomprehensible smile of triumph.

25

AT TWO o'clock they left her flat and took a taxi to Central Park. Jonathan stopped at his hotel, quickly changed into a suit of gray flannel, and rejoined her a few minutes later. They got out at the Zoo and strolled to the cafeteria terrace.

They ate a shrimp salad and drank beer from the cool brown bottles. The warm autumn day hung ripe and fragrant on the city. Lydia had changed into light lime-colored slacks, and wore a blue Norwegian pull-over with a row of reindeer across the chest. Her figure was firm and slender at the hips; she looked like a child as she leaned back and yawned. Then she plucked an aster from the flower box, tucked it in her hair, and gazed dreamily at the sea lions.

Jonathan found himself tingling with happiness. The whole city seemed wonderfully carefree, idyllic. A little blond boy was playing a mouth organ. Two lovers were holding hands at the next table. A French governess was scolding a tiny girl in pink. A British lieutenant was flirting with a young Filipino.

Everything grew equal and harmonious in the dappled sunlight. Nothing seemed evil. Everyone looked kind and lovable. It was as though the world had been freshly scrubbed and polished.

Lydia lit a cigarette, and said: "Let's look at the wild animals, darling, shall we?"

They began with the cage immediately below the cafeteria. A small black sign, lettered in gold, read: "Hippopotamus amphibius. Hab. Africa. Rose and Schlemil." Rose and Schlemil, separated by a galvanized metal fence, were lying as close together as they could; their nostrils were touching rather pathetically. Their small raw ears were raised attentively and their tiny, insidious eyes moved to and fro. They looked unspeakably gross; but there was a glint of sentimentality in their eyes.

"If our bodies looked like our souls," asserted Lydia, "some of us would look exactly like Rose and Schlemil, I'm afraid."

"And Rose and Schlemil," agreed Jonathan, "might look like flamingos, perhaps, or gazelles."

She drew her fingers through her bright brown curls and paused near by to look at the raccoons: "Procyon lotor, Hab. North America." Three furry cushions, with black masks across their eyes, were grasping the bars of their cage with tiny blue hands. They were pleading for peanuts, with a kind of melancholy optimism. Suddenly all three ran back into their house with an affectionate air.

"They seem to prefer threesomes," said Lydia primly. "The little beasts."

They stepped around the corner to look at the giraffe. The sign read: "Giraffa camelopardis. Hab. Kenya, Africa." There were only two. They seemed mournfully aware of their own oddity. They looked down at Jonathan with a coquettish air, batted their eyelids, then grew suddenly haughty and walked off in a mincing gait, waggling their behinds. There was a rarefied look about them, in conspicuous contrast to the hippopotamuses. But they were not without a certain *outré* elegance.

Lydia observed them with a sympathetic look, and placed two fingers on her cheek. "I wish all queer people," she sighed, "could learn to be so dignified about it!"

They strolled on. They passed the red deer, five of them in a cage, shy, lightly spotted animals, with a tawny pattern on their haunches. They moved with long yearning necks and brittle, intensely nervous legs. One was a male with his horns in velvet. He was clumsily raising his hind leg to scratch his ear. Jonathan was reminded, for a moment, of a wood in Maine long ago, where he had once seen a buck and a doe leap over a stream.

And a strange little fit of yearning swept over him; a sudden desire to escape from the city. The shade of the pines and larches, the hum of the saw and the ax's echo, the moss agate of the lake shining through the summer evening—all sprang before him like a mirage, and perished immediately. They wandered on, from cage to cage.

When they passed the Peruvian llama Lydia whispered, "I declare, it looks exactly like Simonova doing a curtain call. ... Really, you know, New York is growing more and more like a jungle. We dress up like leopards and foxes: and some of us are beginning to act like them too!"

They looked at the yak, "Poephagus grunniens, Hab. Tibet." He appeared still to be shrouded in his Himalayan origin. He lay quietly munching, and rolled his coal-black eyes, which were limpid and passive to the point of hypnosis. There was a wart on his nose, and his long Tibetan fur was matted with the soot of the city.

Lydia grew meditative. She seemed about to make a comment, but refrained. An odd gleam of sympathy appeared in her eyes; a hint of recognition.

They crossed to the house of the great cats, and beheld the lion.

Instantly the world of the animals fell into its true perspective. The lion began to roar, and the lioness returned his roar.

The sound was like a great door opening into the wilderness. The lion watched Lydia with his clear and mighty eyes. There was something unutterably tender in his look. The blazing irises narrowed and then widened again, like finely latticed blinds; there was a deep majestical quivering, a flicker of infinitude. All his fury came to a peak in the intensity of his gaze; his terrible strength flowed forth into a golden sweetness. And the true nature of passion seemed suddenly revealed to Jonathan.

26

THEY came upon Natalia, Valdez, and Sheila Snow in front of the polar bears. All three were obviously in the best of spirits. Lydia greeted them with a casual air. Natalia looked fresh and unconcerned, as though nothing had occurred. Only Valdez seemed alert, and cast a speculative glance from one to the other.

All five climbed the path, crossed the drive, and entered the Mall. They came into a meadow where some little boys were playing football. The afternoon light was rich and sherry-colored, and a delightful autumn spice lay sprinkled on the foliage. Valdez began to leap through the air; he was famous for his leap in *Le Spectre de la Rose*. Sheila did a pirouette, and Natalia posed in a magnificent arabesque.

They strolled between a broad double row of benches and past an open, semicircular theater. Then they walked down a stairway and entered a cool dark tunnel which burrowed beneath a road. The walls of the tunnel were chalked with primitive inscriptions, such as "Beatrice L. loves Sidney K." and "Every sailor loves Central Park." Odd little stains and indentations covered the walls; there was something lascivious in the atmosphere. Through the end of the tunnel, surrounded by crisp, curling foliage, they could see the glittering spray of a fountain playing. Beyond lay a lake covered with brightly colored rowboats.

They continued on their way and reached a small, shadowy copse. They came to a shallow stream, and began to tiptoe across the steppingstones. Valdez gave Natalia a push, and she slipped into the water up to her knees. She squealed, and began to splash handfuls of water at Valdez. Then she took off her ballet slippers, and walked merrily through the grass on her bare feet.

They came to a strip of lawn and lay down in the brittle grass. Valdez took out his pencil and began drawing on the edge of a magazine. He drew a ship, then a stork, then the Empire State Building. In each picture he managed to suggest certain embarrassing resemblances. Sheila blushed and looked away. Natalia murmured, "Shame on you, José!"

Lydia tore off a corner of the page and scribbled some words on it, with a preoccupied air. She folded the paper and passed it furtively to Jonathan.

"Don't let the others see it!" she whispered.

Valdez tried to snatch it from her.

Lydia cried, "Quick, Jonathan!"

Jonathan plucked the paper from her fingers, turned aside, and unfolded it. It read: "Lydia I. loves Jonathan E." He slipped it silently into his pocket.

He reached out and placed his hand on Lydia's, very tenderly, with the elated sense of a lover acknowledged. She peered at him through her lashes, and blew a little kiss at him.

"Look at Jonathan!" cried Valdez, pointing rather lewdly. "He's bubbling over with passion! He's really in love, poor boy!"

"Hush, hush," said Natalia. Sheila glanced tactfully at the sky. Jonathan blushed and crossed his legs demurely.

"I wish we had some poetry to read," remarked Natalia dreamily. "I feel terribly poetic.... Do you know any poems by heart, Jonathan?"

"I'm afraid not," murmured Jonathan.

"I know one or two," declared Valdez, with a leer. He recited a limerick about a young man from Bombay.

Natalia sighed. "Oh dear, we've all heard that one so often. Can't you be more original? What about you, Sheila?"

Sheila proceeded virtuously to recite some lines from *Hiawatha*.

"Ugh," said Natalia, with disgust. "That's even worse than the Bombay poem.... Let's write something ourselves. Something clean but cheerful."

"I used to write poems in high school," observed Sheila, with a blush. "I was the class poet."

"Well, then," said Natalia challengingly, passing her the pencil, "let's see what you can do!"

"Yes," said Valdez, winking at Lydia, "perhaps you're another Sappho in disguise!"

Sheila wrinkled her brow and bit the pencil with concentration. Finally she read the following lines aloud in a trembling voice:

> *"I love the pretty autumn trees,*
> *The clouds so bright and fair,*
> *I love the little birds and bees*
> *That flutter through the air!"*

Natalia groaned faintly. "I'm afraid, my dear, you're not exactly one of the *avant-garde*. ... No, what we want is something gay. Something spicy."

"Gay? Spicy?" said Valdez. "Here. Wait just a minute. I'll dash off something for you." He took the paper and pencil in his hand, and after several minutes produced the following quatrain:

> *"I dote on Lydia's curly head,*
> *And Sheila's shining eyes,*
> *But when it comes to fun in bed,*
> *Natalia wins the prize!"*

There was an outcry. Natalia leaped upon Valdez and began to tear his hair. "You're a fine one to talk!" she cried, with indignation. Her Russian accent grew more pronounced. "Just wait, you little pansy, till I write a poem about you!"

She snatched the pencil from Valdez's hand and began scribbling away, with a furious glitter in her eyes. Sheila lit a cigarette discreetly, and Valdez sat watching with a wicked smile.

Lydia took Jonathan by the hand, very gently.

"They'll go from bad to worse, I'm afraid," she whispered. "Come, darling. Let's take a stroll through the trees."

27

THEY walked hand in hand beneath the locusts and sycamores, and came to a sudden curve in the brook.

Two large willows were standing here, forming a screen. Jonathan took Lydia by the arms, drew her close, and kissed her passionately. He held her like this for a long time, motionless, pressing her body more and more tightly to his. He felt, as she grew almost liquid in his arms, that his passion was flowing over into her, filling her, purifying her, and making her entirely his own.

At last he let her go. She gazed at him meltingly. "That was lovely," she whispered. "Really lovely, darling."

"I've never in my life been so happy," he said gently.

They sat down on a log near the edge of the water.

He laid his head on her lap; she ran her fingers slowly through his hair.

"Your hair is like a savage's," she whispered. "So straight and thick except for that weird little white streak down the middle. ... How did you ever get that, darling?"

"I don't know. I always had it," said Jonathan apologetically.

"It makes you look a little older. And yet a little younger, too," she murmured. "I noticed it the first minute I saw you. It made me ... " She hesitated. "It made me want to take care of you, darling."

She drew her fingers softly across his cheeks. "Yes. You look just like an Indian," she said in a low, teasing voice. "Your skin is so dark. And your broad high cheekbones. And your brown, watchful eyes. And your voice. Low and cautious ... Did you have a Cherokee grandfather, darling?"

"Perhaps," said Jonathan, smiling. "Who knows?"

"You walk like an Indian too, I've noticed. On the balls of your feet. As though you were creeping through a jungle!"

The sun-gilded motes of the autumn evening flowed past them. Tiny grains and threads and summery tufts of silk were floating over the stream. A water spider was skillfully skipping against the current. There was a smell of slow, peaceful decomposition.

Lydia was leaning silently, rather intently, over the grass.

"What on earth are you doing, Lydia?"

"Nothing. Just looking for a four-leafed clover."

"You don't need good luck, Lydia."

"Oh, I don't? Wait and see!"

She glanced at him with a solemn expression. There was a brief silence.

"Do you ever look into the future, Lydia?"

She shrugged her shoulders. "What do you mean, dear?"

"Well, do you wonder what will happen to you in five years? Or in ten or twenty years?"

She glanced at him again. There was a touch of defiance in her eyes, a slight hint of antagonism. But only for a moment. She laughed lightly.

"I have my career, you know! I'm going to be a really great ballerina! Not strictly traditional, like Kirillova; a bit more experimental, if you know what I mean. And then, when I'm old, I'll write my memoirs. I'll make millions of dollars. ... And we'll travel together, won't we? I want you to take me to Paris, Genoa, Venice—all the places you love. And if they're all in ruins, well, never mind, we'll go to Cairo or Calcutta. ... We'll learn to grow old gracefully. Maybe you'll have a beard, like a professor. I'll be stout and matronly. We'll be terribly dignified and rather humdrum. ... " She sighed wistfully. "It will be so cozy, darling."

Then she asked softly: "Are you going to start work soon, Jonathan?"

"Week after next," said Jonathan. "I talked with Charlie Holliday on Saturday."

"I'm sure you'll be brilliant, darling. With your imagination. Your background."

She returned to her search for a four-leafed clover. "How do you feel about it all?" she murmured, peering closely at the grass. "Being with me like this?"

Jonathan looked at her blankly. "Being with you? How do you mean?"

"Oh, it's a new kind of atmosphere for you. My type of friends, I mean—dancing girls, dancing boys. Natalia's such a whore. And Valdez, well, you know. And Sheila's Brooklyn accent. How do you feel about them, dear?"

"I find them charming," said Jonathan. "They really enjoy life. ... They're natural and spontaneous, at any rate."

"Do they shock you a little? They don't belong to the four hundred, exactly. Valdez wouldn't look quite right in the Yale Club, I'm sure. They're, well, a bit crude."

"Maybe that's what I like."

"You're just saying that to please me. Be honest, now." She leaned over the stream and dipped her forefinger in the water. She looked like a mischievous boy, pouting a little, in her light green trousers and dark blue pull-over.

"I am honest. I like them. Why shouldn't I like them?"

"Do you like Sheila?" she inquired.

Jonathan nodded judiciously.

"Do you like Valdez?" she asked softly.

"Well, he's friendly. He's gay."

"He certainly is," said Lydia cuttingly.

"And they're all so fresh and honest. There isn't a speck of hypocrisy in them."

Lydia sighed a little. "Tell me the truth, Jonathan." Her voice had changed. "Do you really like Natalia?"

She was leaning over the stream, switching the water with a willow twig. A leafy pattern of light fell through the foliage on her head; on her face shone the quivering reflection of the sunlit water. She looked, at that moment, amazingly fresh and lovely.

"Yes," said Jonathan quietly. "Natalia has been very..." He hesitated. "Well, very cordial."

Lydia continued to gaze at the water. She ran her hand across her cheek, and thoughtfully touched the little mole on her chin. Then she turned and looked at him with a hard, flat look.

"A woman never forgets those things, you know. It cuts into her like a knife. I feel I can never trust you again!"

Jonathan looked at her with bewilderment. "You know you can trust me, Lydia. I've never lied to you."

She drew a deep breath. "Oh, Jonathan, I was so wretched last night. I was so insanely jealous. Do try to understand. It's because I really love you, I guess...." She shook her head sadly. "Men are strange. I suppose you just couldn't help going to bed with Natalia."

Jonathan said nothing; he felt genuinely shocked.

"I suppose," she murmured sadly, "I'll have to learn not to mind. It's hard, but I'll try."

"I never touched Natalia," said Jonathan hoarsely. He felt guilty and uneasy, without quite knowing why.

Lydia continued to look at him with tolerant reproach. "Perhaps not," she sighed. "But I've felt uneasy ever since that first night, when you muttered someone's name in your sleep. ... "

"Someone's name?"

She nodded. "A strange woman's. It hurt desperately, darling. Really."

Jonathan felt a pang of curiosity.

"I'll try not to be jealous," she said gently. "When you're with me I feel safe. I feel sure of you. But when you're away ... "

And he felt that a treacherous undercurrent was already troubling their relationship. He felt the flush and leap of his joy beginning to crumble. Somewhere, hidden from the eye, lurked an element of decay.

"Lydia," he cried fervently, "we must trust one another! No matter what happens, we must never lie!" He sat up and held her firmly. "Let us promise that we'll never lie!"

She lowered her eyes. She looked rather tired. "Yes. I promise. ... And you?"

"I promise, Lydia!"

He looked at her carefully, trying to penetrate her mind. He watched her lips, her lowered eyes. She looked suddenly like a stranger. She had changed, since a week ago; something odd had happened to her. She looked, perhaps, a little harder, and a little less beautiful.

Yet he felt still more firmly bound to her than before. He felt that he could never cease loving and desiring her.

28

JONATHAN, on his way home from dinner with Horace Hayden the following night, was walking past Pierre's flat on Sixty-third Street.

He looked at his watch; it was a quarter to eleven. It was still too early to call for Lydia at the theater. He felt an impulse to talk to Pierre, and to hear his healthy, ironical voice. He found the front door open, entered, and ran the elevator to the floor where Pierre had his studio.

He rang twice at Pierre's door. Then he knocked. There was no answer. He was about to leave; absent-mindedly he tried the doorknob. The door, caught in a sudden gust of wind, swung open.

The studio was dark and rather cold. A window was open and a current of air crossed the room. All he could see was a dim assembly of angles: tables, frames, easels, and canvases, shrouded in the glimmer that fell through the skylight.

He groped for a light but found none. Then gradually his eyes grew used to the darkness. He walked cautiously across the deep, uncarpeted room. There was a broad low window sill, covered with cushions; and beside it the door that gave on the balcony. He hesitated, then stepped into the starlit darkness. Here and there a window was softly lit, and touched with a warm, sequestered tranquillity. In one a woman in a red robe was combing her hair; in another an old man was sitting, puffing at his pipe.

Below lay the row of silent, indistinguishable gardens. On one of them shone a light, and from it rose the sound of a piano: someone was playing a Schubert impromptu. The music ceased. A pale, slender figure appeared in the garden. With a sudden thrill of recognition Jonathan saw that it was Delia. She stood quietly and looked at the sky for several minutes: it seemed she was looking directly at him. Then she disappeared again, and once more Jonathan heard the sound of the piano—this time a strange little piece by Scriabin.

He stepped back into the room, and closed the door behind him. Slowly he walked to the nearest easel and struck a match. Only a few dark strokes had been laid on the canvas. There seemed to be an obelisk rising from a plateau, and two small tents, or possibly mosques, faintly visible in the distance. There were no colors as yet, except a touch of blue in the sky, and a tentative stroke of crimson across the land.

He felt vaguely guilty, as though he were reading another man's letter, or watching him through a keyhole. And he realized how little he really knew of Pierre's true nature.

He turned to another painting, which was leaning against the wall. He struck a second match: it was a Negro nude. At that moment he heard the sound of footsteps in the hallway.

The door opened and an instant later a yellow light flooded the room.

"Jonathan! My God, I was worried for a moment. What are you doing here?"

"I stopped by to see whether you were in. You weren't. So I've been waiting!"

"In the darkness. Well, well. Were you meditating? ... Have a drink!"

Pierre looked unnaturally bright and nervous. He stole a covert look at Jonathan as he poured the whisky into a glass; a rapid, speculative glance. Jonathan caught it, but could not quite divine its meaning.

"My cousin Quincy lives next door to you," said Jonathan casually. "Did you know that?"

"Your cousin Quincy ... Ah, the tennis player. So he lives next door?" Pierre smiled and brought Jonathan his drink. "There's no ice. You don't mind?"

They sat down on the window sill and began to talk. Pierre was wearing a dinner jacket with a carnation in his buttonhole; he looked exceedingly trim and healthy. His face had a noticeable glow of sun tan.

"It's a bit cool," he said, with a sidelong glance. "Shall we have a fire?"

He slipped off his black coat and knelt down in front of the fireplace. Skillfully he built a structure of twigs and pine logs, and soon the flames began to ripple.

He placed a corduroy cushion on the floor and sat down in front of the fire. The flames drew their flicker over his blond curly head. He undid his black tie and opened his collar; he stared at the crackling twigs, and began to smile reminiscently.

"Do you remember, Jonathan, how we used to sit like this? In our ski boots? In Mégève?"

Jonathan nodded. "It was much easier to feel cozy in Mégève, wasn't it, Pierre?"

"I felt very close to you in those days," said Pierre, no longer smiling. "Much closer than to any woman."

Jonathan looked at Pierre with curiosity. He smiled. "You've been wicked, have you, Pierre?"

Pierre frowned. His face grew troubled and preoccupied. He reached over and placed his hand on Jonathan's knee.

Their eyes met; a strange electrical flicker, a look of sudden intensity leaped to Pierre's eyes. And suddenly Jonathan felt that he was in the presence of a stranger. He realized that Pierre had changed in some profound sexual sense. And the relation between them suddenly altered, took on depth and complexity.

Pierre seemed to blush; he turned his head and looked away. He gazed intently at the fire, which had blossomed into a labyrinth of golden petals. Small drops of sweat had appeared on his face, and the nervous light played on his cheeks. And for the first time Jonathan detected something faintly unpleasant in his face; a touch of cruelty perhaps; a hint of a hidden personality. For the first time he noticed the striking dichotomy in Pierre's face—the left side grave and loyal, ambitious, resolute, the right side narcissistic, sensual, unscrupulous.

"Well, let's not change too much," said Pierre, looking at Jonathan with a shining smile. "Let's ... remain honest, at any rate."

The tension between them was suddenly released; the spark was extinguished. The easy, rather impersonal atmosphere was restored.

"Well, what's been happening to you lately?" said Jonathan casually, running his thumb along the edge of the glass. "What do you think of Americans, these days?"

Pierre leaned back his head and stared at the ceiling. "I still feel puzzled. More than ever!"

"You don't understand us? Why not?"

Pierre shrugged his shoulders. "God knows. Americans are so simple, so spontaneous. Europeans are so torn and twisted. Yet in Europe I could find my way. Here, I don't know why, I feel lost in a wilderness!"

He smiled, rather absent-mindedly, and flicked the ash from his cigarette. Then he turned again to Jonathan, with a sudden flush of excitement.

"You are developing a new race here, Jonathan! Look carefully at the youngsters. Their parents could still pass as Europeans. But not the young ones! America has entered their bones! Look at them; tall, loose-jointed bodies, high cheekbones, square jaws, heavy chins, sloping eyes, something languid in the voice and movements. A distinct touch of the Oriental. Very handsome, but very strange. What is it? The climate? The soil? The spirit?" He closed his eyes with the effort of formulating an idea. "You've turned your back on Europe; you're coming of age. And you find yourself caught between Europe and Asia. The border of individualism. The flavor of anonymity. It's a little frightening, you know!"

"Yes," said Jonathan, in a strange, low tone. "New York is a dream. Everything, even love, becomes a form of somnambulism."

Pierre looked at Jonathan sharply, through half-closed eyes. "You've changed after all," he said; then he added softly, "Have you fallen in love?"

Jonathan remained silent. His sense of ease and warmth had vanished. The image of Lydia rose irresistibly within him, filling his body and his mind. He felt an immediate yearning to talk to Pierre about her; to tell him everything, to pour out his heart. But it was impossible. The subtle residue in his relation to Pierre lingered on; he felt shy.

Then he said: "And you, Pierre?"

Pierre blushed; he smiled uneasily. "I've been a fool," he said.

"A fool? I've never known you to be a fool, Pierre."

Pierre looked at his watch and rose. He began to undress. "Worse than a fool, perhaps," he said, with a jocular air of guilt. "One gets entangled. Willy-nilly. . . . I've been a weakling." He slipped off his shirt and crouched before the logs. The tiny curls on his body, faintly moist, began to glitter.

Then he said, as Jonathan rose to go: "I've been having a small affair lately."

Jonathan paused beside the door. He looked at Pierre's fine, ruddy head; he felt troubled and somehow melancholy. "A small affair? Yes? With whom?"

"With your aunt, Mrs. Mannering."

29

PIERRE had made love to Mrs. Mannering largely out of bravado. He had accepted her challenge, so to speak, out of a mingling of vanity, boredom, and opportunism.

But she wanted a grand passion. She showered him with presents. She sent him a leather-bound set of Henry James, a small water color by Constantin Guys, and a set of ivory hair brushes with engraved initials.

At first he felt grateful, then embarrassed, then ashamed. Then he began to take it all for granted.

She took him to dinner at Voisin's or the Colony; or else, on certain evenings, to a place where they could dance.

Both Pierre and Mrs. Mannering were excellent dancers. He began to enjoy these glittering evenings. They tried El Morocco and Monte Carlo; then they tried the Cotillion Room in the Pierre, and the Persian Room in the Plaza. He always wore his dinner jacket, and he noticed that Mrs. Mannering began to dress magnificently, in clinging gowns of subtly hued crepes and taffetas, with pearls and sapphires shining on her skin and exquisite furs cast over her shoulders.

He used to meet her in the St. Regis, where she usually stayed, at seven o'clock. They would order two daiquiris sent to her room. He would tell her a bit of gossip, and kiss her blithely once or twice; then, toward eight, they would merrily start off for dinner. He paid for it the first time, the second, and the third.

Then she said: "You can't afford this, dear. Why not be practical?" And she slipped him a twenty-dollar bill when the check arrived.

This humiliated him too, but at the same time he enjoyed it. It gave him a sense of sexual irresponsibility, of luxury, which was novel and exhilarating.

She tried to help him. "New York is a labyrinth," she explained one night, as they sipped their crème de menthe. "You'll be lost, my dear Pierre, if you're not careful. You have enemies already. You're too good-looking, for one thing. And the French, right now, aren't frightfully popular. ... Still, I think you'll go far if you play your cards properly, dear."

She looked at him shrewdly. He nodded. "I should be discreet, I suppose."

"Use your charm, dear. But don't get involved." Her voice was low and commanding. "Be careful whom you're seen with. The arts, here in New York, are simply riddled with ... well, degenerates. If you once get into the wrong set, you'll never get out of it. ... Making a career as a painter, you know, isn't all beer and skittles."

"I'm sure of it," murmured Pierre.

She raised the green, ice-filled liquid to her lips. "I think I can help you a little, my dear. I can't help feeling that you're rather ambitious. I'll take you around to meet some of my friends. There's Henrietta Clyde, for instance. She knows all the curators. And Laura Carter. She adores having her portrait done. And Lady Temperly, of course. You'll meet loads of celebrities at her teas. And Estelle Webber; though, frankly, I don't suppose she'd be much use. ... "

"Won't people begin to talk?" inquired Pierre discreetly.

"Talk? Talk?" Mrs. Mannering laughed a bit nervously. "They always talk, no matter what you do! And after all, gossip is really a kind of compliment, you know. A bit of talk won't do us any harm. ... " A note of defiance had entered her voice.

Pierre listened politely. "The main thing for me is to paint," he observed, after a moment.

"Oh, of course," she said. "Certainly. The main thing is to paint. ... But don't be so naïve as to imagine, my dear, that anyone gets ahead in New York on mere merit!"

They sat in silence for several minutes. Pierre lit a cigarette. He watched the smoke ascend from the tip in two sinuous, expanding spirals.

Then Mrs. Mannering said: "Have you seen Jonathan lately?" Her eyes were lowered.

"He dropped in," said Pierre, "one night about a week ago."

"I hear he's having quite an affair," said Mrs. Mannering, gazing with interest at the chandelier.

"Yes?"

"With a dreadful little ballet dancer. Popova. Nonova. Something of the sort."

Pierre kept his gaze fixed on the coiling strands of smoke.

"I hear she's rather attractive," said Mrs. Mannering lightly. "But, well, not exactly what you'd call a stay-at-home. A bit of a harlot, I understand."

Pierre raised the cigarette to his lips, paused, then crushed it slowly in the copper tray.

"You've never met her?" said Mrs. Mannering.

"No," said Pierre. "I've never met her."

He glanced at Mrs. Mannering. Her graying hair was carefully waved. A large sapphire was shining in her ear, and a thick pearl necklace clung to her neck. She was wearing a dress of dark green crepe, heavily embroidered down the front in silver. She looked immensely sure of herself.

"Well," she sighed, "it's rather stupid of Jonathan, really. He's such a clean, sweet, simplehearted person. Not an Apollo like you, but still, very attractive in his dark, wholesome way. I hate to see him heading for trouble. He always seemed so sober. Still, that's always the type that is bowled over, they say." She gazed at her tapering, blood-colored fingernails.

"It's strange, isn't it?" she murmured presently. "You can never really be sure about people. You study them day after day. You think you know them from tip to toe. But they always end up, sooner or later, by surprising you. ... " She allowed a puff of smoke to drift through her nostrils.

The lights in the room were lowered as two Spanish dancers appeared on the floor. The music began, and a steel-blue light was hurled on the spinning couple. Mrs. Mannering's profile was turned; she was unaware of being watched. A feathery strand of light, swift as mercury, passed over her features. And suddenly he saw what had been hidden before—a kind of sterile angularity in the whole structure of the face, a hint almost of anguish in the shrewd, cool composure.

She turned and caught his eye. The waiter was approaching with the check.

Mrs. Mannering opened her bag and slipped a twenty-dollar bill under Pierre's coffee cup.

But Pierre ignored it. He took out his wallet and paid the check, which came to slightly over eighteen dollars.

Mrs. Mannering raised her brows very slightly. "You look strange, Pierre. What's the matter?"

"Nothing at all," said Pierre calmly.

They rose, made their way through the overcrowded room, paused in the entry for their coats, and ordered a taxi.

"Aren't you well, darling?" she whispered as they drove up Fifth Avenue.

He turned and faced her in the darkness. "I wish you'd leave me alone," he said quite calmly.

Mrs. Mannering's face grew very pale. Her eyes grew faintly glazed; at first with disbelief, then with confusion, then with rage.

She leaned over and spoke to the taxi driver. "Please drop me at the St. Regis," she said, in a trembling voice.

They said nothing more, and when they arrived she got out without a word, slamming the taxi door behind her. Pierre continued on his way with a mingling of relief and apprehension.

30

PIERRE was sauntering along Madison Avenue the following afternoon, peering with dejection into the brightly lit windows.

It was a moist November day, windless and oppressive. Autumn was drawing to a close. New York was shedding its glamour. The exhilaration in the streets, the rush of leaves in the park, the dramatic autumn sunsets, the sense of spaciousness and tension, all were being absorbed into a thick, damp gloom.

He stopped to look at a set of old English silverware. Then he paused in front of a Meissen figurine, a strip of imported tweed, and an album of Berlioz recordings. He felt a vague chill; he knew that he was catching a cold. He drew out a handkerchief to blow his nose.

At that moment he saw, reflected in the shopwindow, a withered but dandified figure at his side.

He turned around. A light of recognition appeared in both faces.

"Legué!"

"Pierre!"

It was Baron Legué, an old friend of his father's and a well-known art collector in Paris before the war. He had been Pierre's guardian and patron for a number of years, after the death of his parents.

"When did you arrive?"

"A week ago. I heard you were here. I tried to reach you. Impossible."

Baron Legué was a small, frail, overcivilized man with eyes that were constantly watering. His face was pitifully ugly, covered with unhealthy creases and purple stains. He seemed to be suffering from some malignant disease. Only his voice had remained exquisite; clear and melodious as a bell.

They strolled together toward Fifty-ninth Street.

"Well, where have you been?" said Pierre. "Since I last saw you?"

"Everywhere," replied the baron gloomily. "Everywhere. Spain, Morocco, Algiers ... "

"You left right after the fall of Paris?"

"I was staying in my place near Chinon," he said. "The Germans took it over one day. They used my best linen and silver. They broke my eighteenth-century wineglasses. After a week I couldn't stand it; I ran away."

They wandered slowly down the street. The elderly exile began to talk of his home, in his low, cool voice. It sounded as though he were reciting a poem. "I think of it day and night. The Loire flowing past. The smell of the wet trees and the ponds. The creaking gate into the pasture ... I want only one thing. To return and hear the gate creaking. To smell the pond and hear the frogs. I hope that I ... " He paused.

"You'll find it the way you left it," said Pierre, touched by some hint of intensity in the old man. "You'll be back there in two years. Or less. I'm sure of it."

"I'm not well, you know," said the baron quietly.

Pierre turned and looked at the sick, grief-ravaged face. He felt curiously at peace in the baron's presence. It was his flawless tact, his courtesy, his voice; but it was more than that. A sense of consummate self-knowledge radiated from his neat little person. He spoke as though nothing in the world could surprise him. His features looked intensely dissipated—eyes, eyelids, lips, forehead, each cracked and burrowed like old ivory by years of uninterrupted indulgence. It was as though, having lived through every kind of evil, he had finally purged himself of its power, and now, at last, could look at the world with true composure.

Pierre felt a wave of affection for the old, decaying gentleman, who seemed as helpless as a child and yet so curiously invulnerable.

They turned left on Fifty-ninth Street.

"I wonder," the baron said presently, "whether life has always been like this. Look. What do you see? Nothing but a staggering façade. We spend our lives in concealment; our real nature remains buried. No one, no one is allowed even a glimpse of it. We ourselves least of all! Instead, we create a kind of rag doll, which we call by our name. A hodge-podge of imitations, customs, accidents, vanities, God knows what odds and ends; and that we imagine to be our soul."

"Perhaps it is," said Pierre gently.

"Perhaps," said the baron sadly. "Still, sometimes, in a café, in a train, in my bed, I suddenly catch sight of this frightful little doll. And I wonder who it can be. And I wonder what has happened in the meantime to my real, my buried self. Is it gone for good?" He drew his lips into a dry little smile.

Pierre had grown very thoughtful. "I'm beginning to worry too," he said. "I used to be so sure of everything. Of my talent. Of my integrity. But now ... " He paused. "Well, perhaps it's the war."

"Sometimes," observed the baron, placing his finger tips together in a characteristic gesture, "sometimes this war appears to me as the true modern symbol. So icy cold, so impersonal. So frightfully ingenious and so utterly insane. A bit of cool common sense—and the world would have been saved. Or am I wrong? Probably I am." He sighed and shrugged his shoulders.

"Perhaps, after all," he said, "we're still a horde of Hottentots. Each one squatting in his own little cave. Beating his own little drum. In the middle of a jungle." He coughed. "Well, enough of that. Let's be practical. Do you like New York?"

Pierre remained silent and thoughtful.

The baron turned and looked at him with his wise, watery eyes. "You're discontented here, my boy?" His voice was low and intimate.

Pierre was a bit startled. "Well, dissatisfied, a little."

"With yourself?"

Pierre hesitated, and blushed; then he nodded. "Possibly."

"Well," said the baron, "that's a good sign, at any rate." He placed his hand on Pierre's shoulder; he paused; then he whispered: "New York is like a cobra, my boy. It strikes when you're not looking!"

They had reached the Plaza.

"What are you doing now?" inquired the baron. "Are you busy?"

"Nothing at all," said Pierre, after a moment's hesitation. "I was on my way back to the studio."

"You've been painting?" The baron smiled rather teasingly.

"I've been trying!" Pierre smiled back. "Now and then ... In my spare moments!"

The baron nodded, and looked at Pierre with his old, cherry-colored eyes, in which a light of deep affection had appeared. "Yes, I know," he murmured. "It is so tempting, here in New

York. ... They are all so good-looking. And so available. And so clever. ... "

He grew serious again. "Come to tea with me at Lady Temperly's. She'll be delighted to have you. A most unusual woman. I used to see quite a bit of her in Florence."

He took Pierre by the elbow. They strolled up the steps into the Plaza.

31

NEW YORK, after the fall of France, had begun to acquire a certain hothouse flavor. Scattered specimens of European culture had been culled from the brink of the catastrophe, as it were, and hastily transplanted to a firmer, breezier climate. Thousands of refugees filled the city; every type, every nationality. Some were luckless and impoverished; others arrived with bags of jewelry, furs, and works of art. Some were humble and unknown; others were distinguished artists, poets, and philosophers. And others, again, bore the great names of Europe—Hapsburg, Bourbon-Parma, Talleyrand, Richelieu. Some had come as fugitives from countries invaded by the Germans. Others had come to find peace of mind, perhaps, or profit. Some were planning to return with the peace. Others had settled down to stay. But for all of them New York was the funnel through which, at some point, they were forced to pass; perhaps to remain there, perhaps to drift on to Brooklyn, Bryn Mawr, or Santa Barbara.

In small nooks and crannies the whole length of Manhattan these uprooted plants continued an artificial survival. Cheap restaurants sprang up for the Greeks, the Czechs, the Yugoslavs. Special shops were opened where one could speak Dutch, or Danish, or Polish. Little periodicals appeared where one could read the lyrics of the French underground, or heroic tales from occupied Norway. Theaters were opened where one could see

Les Femmes savantes or *Goetz von Berlichingen.* Certain of the cafés acquired a vividly continental flavor. Certain hotels began serving Parisian croissants or Danish rolls for breakfast. Strange ladies with unusual clothes and bearded gentlemen with portfolios began to frequent the open-air cafeteria in the park; and Central Park, in certain stretches, took on a fleeting resemblance to the Hofgarten or the Bois de Boulogne.

And by some subtle process of amalgamation, the very landscape seemed to change; slowly, imperceptibly transformed by foreign presences. One could see them sitting on benches under the maple trees, reading Schiller or Baudelaire; or strolling down a path at midnight with a dachshund on the leash; gesticulating in the cocktail bars in French, or Viennese; or peering in the galleries at Botticelli and Breughel. Their unfamiliar habits lay sprinkled, like a spice, on the smooth American scene. The city began to look a little mellower, a little older.

But it was in private homes that most of these nomads found security. One could discover small flats on various side streets, some frugal, some luxurious, where the flavor of Brussels or Amsterdam was recaptured intact. One could see it in the books, the pictures, the crockery, above all in that indefinable air in a room which derives from mental habits; one could feel, so to speak, the presence of alien ancestors. Even the smells from the kitchen had a transatlantic whiff—a scent of sauerkraut, possibly, or a touch of garlic.

Certain domiciles, however, had a more distinguished air. The Baroness Landau, who had lived in Paris, filled her rooms with French engravings and sets of Proust and Saint-Simon. Madame de Klopf, a wealthy Dutchwoman, hung a Ruysdael in the library and did the bathroom in delicately patterned delft tiles. The Marchese Guidotti displayed a Piranesi print, a vellum-bound set of D'Annunzio, and an ivory replica of the Leaning Tower of Pisa.

Lady Temperly's suite in the Plaza was specifically English. The furniture was Chippendale. There was an apple-cheeked Romney in the hall. Three Rowlandson prints and a view of Tintern Abbey appeared in the bedroom. In the drawing room hung an Augustus John, and, as a rare concession, a tiny Félicien Rops. Jane Austen, Trollope, and Disraeli lined the bookshelves. A rosewood tea caddy stood on the mantel, and on the table lay scattered old copies of the *Tatler* and the London *Times*.

32

THERE were six or eight people sitting around a low coffee table; all were engaged in a single, well-maneuvered conversation. Pierre was introduced to Lady Temperly.

She was a tall, frail woman in her seventies, with an excessively nervous manner. Her face seemed unnaturally drawn and faintly translucent. She wore a pink flowered dress, strangely dowdy and ill-suited to the season. Her voice was sharp and arrogant; her manner was tense and capricious.

"Sit down over there, please, my dear Baron. Next to Lady Brooke. Move over a bit, Pamela. There. You'll have milk in your tea? Both of you? ... We were talking about poetry. You've met Madame Nikolaides, of course? She has done some beautifully chiseled translations from Mallarmé. Tell us about them, won't you, my dear?"

"Oh, they're nothing at all: just little exercises," said Madame Nikolaides, a tall, monastic lady in black. "I did them years and years ago."

"Won't you recite one of them to us?" said Lady Temperly. Her eyes lit up dreamily; she smiled softly. "How does it go— the one I like so well? *Brise Marine,* I think it's called. I met him once in the Rue de Rome; he was such a miraculous *raconteur!*"

"I was reading Tennyson this morning," observed Basil Hume, a lean, red-haired Englishman with an aquiline nose. Lady

Temperly looked at him sharply. "Your word about Mallarmé reminded me; chiseled. Such grace, and polish! Such metrical clarity! That's why they detest him, nowadays. ... " He spoke in acid tones, leaned back his head and surveyed the ceiling.

"My mother," said Lady Temperly, stirring her tea, "was quite a friend of Lord Tennyson's, I recall. He used to call on us when I was a child. He had, if you wish, a certain overliquidity of style. But he was a craftsman; a real craftsman. Don't you agree, Dr. Cavanaugh?"

Dr. Cavanaugh was an Irishman in his fifties, with a shrewd, convivial face. "A splendid technician! Splendid! Splendid!" he agreed, rounding his lips with relish, and was about to continue when Lady Temperly interrupted him.

"Still, he was a rather preposterous man, I seem to remember. Full of melancholy airs; and quite absurdly pompous. Today, I suppose, one would call him neurasthenic."

"All great poets were slightly insane," put in Dr. Cavanaugh, with a leer. "Now Yeats, for example ... "

"Don't speak to me of Mr. Yeats!" cried Lady Temperly. "He was intolerably rude! A boor, to be quite frank about it. And far from brilliant company at the dinner table. Say what you will, one can judge a man's work only when one has listened to his conversation. Now Mr. Wilde was always magnificent at dinner. He may have had his whimsicalities, but civilized people ignore such things. He had wit. He had facility. That's what matters!" Her voice floated through the room lightly, musically, and with supreme assurance.

She sat on a couch in front of the low octagonal table, where a small blue flame was burning under the silver pot; and from here she led the conversation like an orchestra conductor, governing its tone, controlling its pace, and nipping all digression on the fringes. No field, as Pierre discovered, did she feel beyond her. She felt no hesitation in challenging a musician on some reference to a Beethoven sonata, or a classical scholar on a verse from Sophocles, or an ambassador on a point in diplomatic etiquette.

Pierre watched her with curiosity. There was an air of continual expectation in her manner, which was gradually imparted to the entire gathering. They all listened, with a kind of awe, for some final, all-illuminating pronouncement. They stirred their cups and sipped their tea, like participants in a ritual.

At this moment a tall, elderly British naval officer entered the room.

"Ah, this is Commander Forbes," cried Lady Temperly with joy, and introduced him perfunctorily. "Sit down over here, Derek. ... Commander Forbes has just arrived from Cairo. How was it, Derek? Have you anything bizarre to tell us? Never mind, you must be exhausted. After all those odalisques and camels ... Have a cup of tea, dear." And she poured him a cup. Whenever someone new arrived in the drawing room, there was a cursory shifting of chairs and rearrangement of places. Perhaps Lady Temperly would introduce the newcomer individually; or she might merely greet him with a wave of the hand and say: "Well, I think you know most of us, don't you, dear? Do sit down. You'll have milk in your tea?"

The conversation continued. "By the way," said Lady Brooke, a tiny woman with enormous, melancholy eyes, "did you know that Willy Belgrave is back in town?"

"I didn't even know he had left!" said Lady Temperly rather irritably. "Willy's movements are growing more and more clandestine. How long was he gone?"

"Only for a few days, my dear. He went to Washington. Kitty de Montfleury met him at the Brazilian Embassy. She was suffering agonies from hay fever when I saw her last, poor darling."

"Hay fever!" cried Baron Legué, who had been sitting very quietly. "At this season! Impossible."

"It's the latest thing," explained Lady Brooke. "Everyone is developing hay fever this year; it's very fashionable. Something to do with nerves, or sex."

"Oh, Pamela," sighed Lady Temperly, putting down her tea-cup, "do let's try to keep away from sex today. ... Will you have one of these cheese biscuits, Dr. Cavanaugh? They're quite uneat-able, I'm afraid. ... By the way, did you see Lady Stonington in Cairo, Derek?"

"No, I was actually in Cairo only a day or two," said Commander Forbes, with a well-disciplined air. He looked, in spite of his age, very pink and robust. The smile of perfect health clung to his lips.

"She's been planning to come to New York for months, hasn't she? She's a cousin of Laura Carter's, you know."

"Is Laura Carter coming for tea today?" demanded Basil Hume, with sudden interest.

"It's strange how she's kept her beauty, isn't it?" said Dr. Cavanaugh innocently. "She is still the most dazzling-looking woman in New York."

"You think so?" said Lady Brooke, with irritation. "I thought she looked rather alarming at Mimi Suarez's last night. She dresses like an angel, of course. You've seen the Degas she bought the other day?"

"Degas," said Lady Temperly wearily; "he's a butcher, my dear. Nothing but slabs of pork and veal, dressed up in dirty chiffon. I could never understand his vogue."

The conversation went on in this manner for another ten minutes. It sprang lightly from Degas to Bakst and Diaghileff and on to Tchaikovsky, Fauré, Verlaine. The delicate apparatus of European culture was unfolded, in brittle segments, like an ivory fan.

The evening light fell through the thin lace curtains. A ray of sunlight appeared through the mist, and a brilliant host of high lights fell on the walls and the ladies' dresses. The bookshelves were washed in a honey-colored glow. The teapot began to sparkle. The elderly heads, aged and accentuated by the sudden light of the sun, looked around in surprise. They seemed to be quivering, fading, dissolving in this sudden rush of warmth and color.

"Mercy! Pull down the shade," cried Lady Temperly. "I can't bear the sunlight; it kills the conversation! Please, Basil, my dear ... "

Basil Hume rose and drew the blinds. A hush fell over the gathering, and then in the cool gray darkness the hum of conversation was gradually resumed.

33

THE door opened slowly and another guest appeared. "Ah, here is the Marquis del Puente!" cried Lady Temperly, with an air of triumph. "You've met Lady Brooke? Dr. Cavanaugh? Monsieur Maillard? Do sit down—here on the couch beside me—and have a cup of tea, won't you?"

The Marquis del Puente was a former ambassador, a desiccated man of eighty, with coal-black eyes and exquisite Castilian manners. The bone structure of an extraordinarily fine face was still visible under the withered skin.

"Have you heard from Spain lately, my dear Marquis?" inquired Lady Brooke.

A weary, almost despondent look appeared in the marquis's face. Spain was very unpopular at that point; there were fresh rumors every day; his position was equivocal.

He shrugged his shoulders. "I've heard nothing. Nothing at all," he murmured sadly.

"Well, now, tell us about Spain under the King, my dear," said Lady Temperly gently, as though she were addressing a well-rehearsed child. "You were in the Army?"

There was a brief pause; the old man's eyes began to glitter. Everyone sat in silence, waiting for him to speak. A breath of intensity passed through the room.

"I was an infantry officer," began the marquis rather shyly; "at the Staff College... I wore a blue tunic with red lining, golden epaulets, and bright red trousers."

"You must have broken the ladies' hearts!" said Lady Temperly softly.

"My father," murmured the marquis, "was on the General Staff; he wore a uniform of dark blue with sky-blue lining; he had on a sash of gold and blue, and huge golden epaulets, and a silver helmet." His black eyes shone with pride; a kind of wistful grandeur hung about him.

"How magnificent!" said Lady Temperly. "Tell us about the balls at the Royal Palace, my dear."

"Tall soldiers of the royal bodyguard," continued the old man in his low, yearning voice, "were standing at the landings of the marble staircase. They were armed with ancient halberds. They wore short black beards. There was a sea of epaulets, jewels, helmets, feathers, and fans. We officers had to hold our swords and caps all in our right hand. I still remember how my sword dangled from my little finger. I held the white-gloved hand of my partner between two fingers in my left hand. I was always hoping, I remember, for an invitation to dance with the Queen. She rarely danced with anyone outside the members of the Court and the Diplomatic Corps, of course."

"Did she ever dance with you?" said Lady Temperly.

"No," said the marquis, with deep contentment. "No, no. She never danced with me."

He sighed a little. A brief hush passed through the room. Pierre grew aware of a curious undertone in the gathering, a sense of things perishing, an era irrevocably lost. It was as though Europe, to this superannuated little group, had ceased to exist as a reality, had been absorbed into the fabric of memory; so that the war, with its huge sufferings, scarcely existed; all that existed was the residue of the past, a floating elegiac vapor.

Lady Temperly caught Pierre's eye, and smiled vivaciously. "Do have another cup of tea, won't you, Monsieur Maillard? There. I forget; do you take milk?"

The tinkle of teacups and of elderly voices revived.

The telephone began to ring just as Wilfred Silliman arrived. "Wilfred," said Lady Temperly, with petulance, "see who that is, please."

Wilfred Silliman obeyed. "It's Estelle Webber," he whispered circumspectly, raising his brows. "She's down in the lobby."

Lady Temperly made a grimace. "It's really too much! Must Estelle come and bother us in the afternoon as well as in the evening? Tell her I'm out, please, Wilfred."

"Lady Temperly has just gone out," sighed Wilfred meekly, in the direction of the receiver. He placed it back on the hook with a conspiratorial air. He crossed the room in his prim, matronly gait, and sat down beside Pierre, whom he greeted with a diminutive smile. He sat very straight, his gray hair rising in a crest, like a cockatoo's. He opened his cloisonne case and drew out a cigarette.

"Have you been to the ballet this year, Clarissa?" he inquired, sipping his tea, and pressing his knees close together.

"Ballet? Please don't tell me, Wilfred, that you go to the ballet!"

Wilfred looked sheepish for a moment. "I adore the ballet, my dear! You should see Kirillova," he cried excitedly, his fingers pirouetting lightly. "She is positively sublime. ... And that fellow Valdez—they say he'll be another Nijinsky in a year or two!"

"I hear," put in Lady Temperly, with a suspicious air, "that there are certain oriental princes in town who give parties for ballet dancers"; she turned on Wilfred. "Do you know such persons, Wilfred, by any chance?"

"All arts deserve a helping hand, I can't help feeling," murmured Wilfred, evasively.

"Ah! Be honest," said Lady Temperly, with a mischievous glance. "There are rumors, Wilfred, that you are developing an affair of the heart. Is it true?"

Wilfred blushed and his lips fell into a puckered, fatuous smirk.

"There!" cried Lady Temperly triumphantly. "I suspected it. Wilfred is going to surprise us someday. Another Lovelace, a Lothario, a Casanova. Which is it, my dear?"

Wilfred had only dropped in for a moment or two, as it happened, to leave a volume of French memoirs for Lady Temperly. After he had left, Lady Brooke delicately inquired:

"Who is the lady, Clarissa?"

"Which lady?" said Lady Temperly cautiously.

"Wilfred's lady, of course."

"Oh." A look of inscrutability appeared on Lady Temperly's face. "A certain Miss Brattleborough, Brattlebone, Brattlethwaite. Something of the kind," she observed, in enigmatic tones. "No one knows her, I believe."

"Did you notice how pale he looked?" insisted Lady Brooke. "And he blushed like a schoolgirl!"

"Wilfred has his little *chinoiseries*," said Lady Temperly, as she extinguished the small blue flame. "But he also has his points. He is a romantic, please remember. He lives in a world of fancy."

"Do you suppose," said Basil Hume heartlessly, "that it's all just a bluff? This Brattlebone business? Just a camouflage?"

"Bluff? Camouflage?" cried Lady Temperly, in tones of casual indignation. "Really, Basil. You've turned into a confirmed cynic!"

"Cynic?" muttered Basil Hume. "Only a cynic can find salvation, nowadays, my dear Clarissa. Only a cynic can see things as they are, without heading for lunacy. ... "

There was a moment's silence. Basil Hume, it appeared, was generally disliked.

"What a lovely necklace that is, Clarissa!" observed Madame Nikolaides suddenly.

"Do you like it?" said Lady Temperly. "It's been painted by Van Dyck, you know. In a portrait of an ancestress of mine, Lady Fedden. So it's genuine, at any rate!"

"You were speaking of Degas a while ago," said Baron Legué. "What has happened to your paintings, Lady Temperly? Do you still have your collection intact?"

"Collection, my dear Baron? You are flattering me, I'm afraid! Just a few odds and ends Lord Temperly left behind; that's all I have. He lived in Paris for fifteen years. He knew most of the impressionists personally—Sisley, Monet, Pissarro. He was, I recall, especially fond of Monet. It is Monet that Proust keeps writing about, isn't it, Basil? Those interminable descriptions of seascapes? ... Well, I can't bear Proust. Say what you like, he's a parvenu. I met him once, at Saint-Cloud; there was something dreadfully pretentious and la-di-da about him, I thought." She turned to Lady Brooke. "I've just been rereading Peacock, by the way. Remind me to lend you *Headlong Hall,* Pamela. I've always adored Peacock. He was in love with my grandmother for years; did I ever tell you about that, Dr. Cavanaugh? It was a *grande passion,* by all accounts!"

One would have gathered that Lady Temperly seriously admired no books, no music, no paintings except those produced by men who had dined at her own table, or the table of her ancestors.

Yet she was, in her way, brilliant. Pierre began to observe her more closely. The art of her conversation was like the art of a tennis champion. Her secret lay in the use of surprise, cushioned in a breezy, ambiguous use of words. She contrived never quite to say precisely what she thought. She employed hints, pauses, and intonations as a tennis player uses chops, lobs, and volleys. She often contradicted herself. She constantly exaggerated. What she said was usually superficial, often arrogant, and sometimes patently absurd. Yet, as Pierre continued to listen, the strange and sustained melody of her personality emerged. Behind the petulant staccato of her conversation lay another, far more passionate individual. Her cold blue eyes shone with a kind of desolation through the mask of her face. She had the power of transfiguring, with her electrical vitality, whatever she touched; giving it an airy lightness, and a curious evocative pathos.

Lady Brooke rose to go. She was accompanied by Dr. Cavanaugh.

"Pamela Brooke," observed Lady Temperly after they had gone, "is having a *crise de nerfs.* ... She is the type of woman who is dominated, I fear, by her passions." She rose, stepped to the window, and began to water a pot of red azaleas. "She has a drop or two of Italian blood," she sighed. "It makes her rather unpredictable. ... She is very pretty, don't you think?" She smiled cunningly at Pierre.

"Very," said Pierre. "She has wonderfully fine features. Magnificent eyes."

"Tell me," said Lady Temperly, looking at him with her blue, impenetrable gaze, "do you find American ladies ... satisfactory?" She stressed each of the last three words somewhat equivocally, so that he did not know on which the emphasis was intended to fall. He felt, to his surprise, a little shocked.

"They are marvelous specimens," he observed. "I find them lovely to look at."

"Specimens," murmured Lady Temperly. "I'm afraid that's just what they are! Hothouse figs and nectarines. Wonderful to look at, blooming with health. But when you bite into them ... I wonder? Perhaps they lack, shall we say, flavor?"

It was six o'clock; Pierre and the baron rose and left together. As they departed Lady Temperly said to Pierre, with a sudden smile which made her look like a girl of nineteen, "It was charming of you to come! And do come again, won't you? I'm in every afternoon at teatime. ... And be careful, please, with these lovely hothouse nectarines!"

34

TWO days later Pierre was sitting on his balcony and reading. The shrubs in the rectangular gardens below had been stripped of their leaves. A scent of dying and decaying plants was in the air.

But there was still a momentary warmth in the noonday sun. He sat in a deck chair, wearing a dark blue shirt and a pair of corduroy trousers, and allowed the windless light to fall on his head. Beside him, on the floor of the balcony, stood a glass of milk and a large white sandwich. He was reading *Salammbô*. He had been working at his easel for two steady hours, and now felt satisfied and calm.

He finished his lunch and began to puff at his pipe. He watched a spider crawling along the railing, listened to a bird, and turned another page; he began to feel drowsy. The strains of a Chopin prelude were rising from the drawing room next door.

He closed his eyes. He thought vaguely and agreeably of promising occasions lying ahead. He thought hopefully, in his youthful way, of the time when he would be a man of recognized distinction; when his pictures would create a stir of admiration in the galleries; when he could afford a fine apartment with a splendid library and a glittering bath; when he could watch the waiter bring a check without a furtive pang of anxiety; when he need not feel unduly impressed at Lady Temperly's salon, or nervous at the Baroness Landau's cocktails.

Since his break with Mrs. Mannering, Pierre had spent most of his time alone. Sometimes he felt a wave of intense homesickness for Paris; for the air of Paris, the intellectual temper, for the sound of his language in the streets, above all for the incomparable lights and colors of Paris. But Pierre was given by nature to plans for the future more than to images of the past. He was restless, continually alert. He had an appetite for novelty. And he began to feel, in New York, the presence of a new, spectacular kind of energy, in which he too had a role to play. He felt, down to his finger tips, a yearning for adventure.

Suddenly he heard a voice below calling softly: "Agatha, Agatha!" He looked into the garden next door. A blond girl in a blue robe was standing on the flagstones, beneath a locust tree.

A small yellow cat was clinging to the top of the tree and mewing uneasily. She stretched out her paws, and the bough swayed perilously; the kitten was terrified. The peak of the tree was directly below Pierre's balcony. It was drooping perceptibly with the weight of the little animal.

"Agatha, dear," called the girl in blue, in a pleading tone.

The cat looked at Pierre with a tense, nervous glitter.

Pierre rose, with a sudden impulse of chivalry, and lifted himself over the railing. He reached out as far as he could while grasping the railing with his left hand, and with his right caught hold of a twig. Little by little he drew it closer, until the kitten was only two feet away. She stepped cautiously forward and crawled along Pierre's arm, digging her tiny claws into his flesh.

She clung to his shoulder, flicked her tail lightly, and leaped upon the balcony with an indignant purr.

"How kind of you," called the girl in the garden. "Would you bring her down, please?"

Pierre slipped on a pair of shoes and a tweed coat. He carried the cat downstairs and to the house next door.

The girl was standing in the doorway, waiting. She took the cat from his arms. "Agatha. Naughty child," she whispered in the kitten's ear, reproachfully.

"It's been a nuisance, I'm afraid," she said to Pierre, with a glistening smile. "You were very brave!"

Pierre stood and watched her silently. She was a little younger than he had thought; scarcely more than twenty, it seemed. The light blue collar of her robe curled softly around her golden neck. She looked radiant with health, her skin and hair seemed flooded with sunlight. But it was her eyes that left Pierre almost breathless; they were marvelously fresh and serene, yet their light was electrical.

She drew her bright smooth hair back over her head; then she blushed. "Thank you," she said softly.

Pierre stood tense and expectant on the steps, with his fingers on the iron railing.

At that moment the telephone rang. "Excuse me," she murmured gently, and closed the door with a look of apology.

Pierre returned slowly to his studio. He had never in his life felt quite like this.

He stared for several minutes through the window, lost in a haze of indecision. What was it he really felt? An awakening? A premonition? He hardly knew. His whole past seemed suddenly unreal; his affairs at Oxford, his feelings for Jonathan, his erotic experiments, his wayward ambitions—all appeared as a series of postures concealing some deeper necessity.

He turned around. The studio was almost dark. The easels and canvases were lost in shadow. A warm, protective odor permeated the room—a scent of linseed oil and alcohol mingled with pine.

He crossed the room and looked through the opposite window into the street. The world changed instantaneously; his peace of mind vanished. Lights were appearing everywhere. The city looked like a great caldron, an inexhaustible reservoir of strange new flavors, shapes, and voices.

He turned on the light and looked at his face in the mirror. He saw his face, for the first time, objectively and clearly; he smiled, and ran a black comb slowly through his hair.

Then he turned out the light again and walked downstairs, with a beating heart. The street was dark when he left the house. The autumn night filled the air.

35

JONATHAN was having lunch with Lydia. They were finishing their coffee in a small Hungarian restaurant off Seventh Avenue.

It was their last lunch together. The ballet company was leaving for Montreal the following morning.

"I'm doing *Pillar of Fire* tonight," she said, placing her small warm hand upon his own. "Sheila's role. You must come! It will be the first time I've ever done it. I can't help feeling I'll be better than Sheila. Poor darling, she looks more like a kangaroo than a harlot, in that role. Don't smile like that. I mean it. ... Have you ever seen *Pillar?*"

Just as literary persons speak of *Cyrano* or *Much Ado*, Jonathan found that the dancers had a way of abbreviating their titles to *Spectre*, or *Faun*, or *Pillar*.

"I had a fight with Lochwitzky again," she continued. "I decided to have it all out with him. I believe in being frank, as you know. I asked for a twenty-dollar raise, and, of course, better roles, I'm rather tired, I must say, of filling in with the *corps de ballet*."

The waiter approached with the bill. Jonathan placed two dollars on the table.

"They know perfectly well," continued Lydia, "that I can do *Petrouchka* better than Sheila, and *Lilac Garden* much better than that old ogress Simonova. I'm the only one they can really use for the Rose Adagio in *Aurora*. Louella is simply too ridiculous in that. Janet Bloom hasn't an ounce of talent, even though she's being kept by Sevastopoulos, and as for Myrtle Hemingway, well, she might as well join the Rockettes. Boris told me the other day, as a matter of fact, that I'm next in line for *Giselle,* if Kirillova decides to leave the company. Did you see what that man in the *Times* said about me the other day? Wait another year, darling, and you'll see what I can really do! You'll be surprised!"

She smiled happily, and dropped her cigarette ash in the empty coffee cup.

Then she stared at him with sudden brilliance. "I wish we were alone, darling," she whispered. "I wish you were holding me in your arms. ... "

Jonathan listened with a feeling of fascination. He watched her volatile little face, which years of theatrical make-up had left with a pearly, unnatural gloss. Her lips were thick and petulant, like those of a spoiled child. Her eyelashes were extremely long and shadowy. Her hair was a jungle of thick, resilient curls. Everything in her head, her voice, and her gaze was a challenge. She seemed to live in a state of continual tension; thoughts and actions followed feverishly on one another, guided by whim rather than reason, continually aglow, but with their roots forever hidden. She was like a scene in the middle of a melodrama. The past and future were an enigma. Only the isolated suspense of the present emerged.

Sometimes it occurred to him that, after all, she was far from beautiful. It was her inexhaustible vitality which gave to her face, and her body too, such continual magnetism. Now and then some hint of the past dropped its shadow on her, like a stain.

Some prematurely seeded corruption, he felt, was spreading its roots through her being.

And he found himself, at moments like this, deeply disturbed, and almost hopeless. He was irresistibly drawn to her; yet, again and again, he experienced a chilling shock, like a warning signal.

She was watching him cunningly. "Do I frighten you, darling?" she murmured.

He picked up her hand, which lay curled beside the coffee cup, and pressed it to his lips.

They rose and stepped into the street, and sauntered lazily toward Fifth Avenue.

"Come," suggested Lydia; "let's do something elevating on our last afternoon! Let's forget about these sordid things, like sex, or the ballet. ... Shall we look at some paintings?"

They took a bus to the Frick Museum.

36

THE world appeared to change as they walked through the silent patio. A marble fountain was playing noiselessly in the center, and tropical patterns of fern rose motionless above black, geometrical areas of earth.

Through the doorways they caught sight of the scattered visitors fastidiously circulating and pausing among the Old Masters.

Jonathan glanced at Lydia. Her eyes were shining with expectation. And instantly he too felt a new susceptibility, a flush of eagerness that heightened the effect of the paintings.

They stepped in front of a Renoir; the blossoming sensuality of childhood rose before them. They passed to a Velásquez; and entered the cool, imperturbable shade of common sense. Next to that hung a Cuyp. The world seemed flooded with an evening light. They turned a corner and came upon a small Vermeer. It was like a whispered invitation; there was a sense of hush and secrecy, a miraculous crystal-like seclusion. Near by was a great Bronzino, full of lustrous, finely modulated greens. All the innuendo, the decay of a patrician society, was caught in the boy's face with an architectural precision. At the end of the room hung an overwhelming Rembrandt self-portrait; and Jonathan could feel emerging from it the grave and steady glow, the final maturity which had its roots in human suffering.

They passed from one room to another. There was a dark high chamber brightened by an exquisite Gainsborough. Another was filled with the fragrance of a great Corot. A third, a small paneled room which resembled a library, was warmed by the shrewd, indulgent air of Titian's *Aretino*.

Lydia seemed very solemn, a little later, as they stepped into the street again. Jonathan glanced about with a feeling of bewilderment; he reached out and hailed a cab.

And as they entered the dark, leathery enclosure, he felt his elation float away, like a flake of mist, into the dull gray air of Seventieth Street.

"It's frightening," said Lydia softly, gazing into space, "to think how much we've lost. How empty our lives have become."

Jonathan looked at her with curiosity. There were times, such as this, when she unexpectedly hinted at some broader, more meditative aspect of her character. And he hoped that she might after all be drawing closer to his own ways of feeling.

"Did you enjoy it?" he asked eagerly.

She nodded. "I enjoyed it. And yet," she said reproachfully, "I wish we hadn't come. I feel puzzled. I feel dissatisfied. Why is it?"

He watched her long, restless eyelashes. He felt an intense yearning, at that moment, to bridge the remaining abyss that still divided them, and feel her final reserve melt away.

"Lydia," he said, taking her hand in his, "there is so much, so much in you that could ... " He hesitated.

"Yes?" She stared at him sullenly.

"Lydia," he whispered ardently, "will you ever let me understand you?"

Her face began to melt. She drew his arms around her, and pressed her head against his own, impulsively. He felt her lips clinging to his cheek, like an affectionate child's. And for the first time he felt that, after all, his love was really necessary to her; that she could not bear to be alone; that she was terrified of the possibilities involved in her own nature.

He dropped her at the theater. She leaned over and kissed his forehead lightly as she stepped from the taxi. "You'll be at the station tomorrow morning? On time? You promise?"

He smiled, and held onto her hand. "Can I see you tonight?"

"Tonight?" Her eyes grew grave and pensive. He had the sense of a tiny calculation crossing her mind, quick as lightning. "No, not tonight, darling. I need all the sleep I can get. ... I have a long, hard program ahead of me!"

He nodded, with an indefinable feeling of misgiving. "Then I'll see you tomorrow morning, at the station," he said slowly. There was a brief, uneasy pause.

"Jonathan," she whispered with sudden desperation, "I don't want to lose you! I don't want to lose you!"

She gazed at him a moment longer, and squeezed his hand. Then she disappeared, like a moth, in the crimson corridor of the stage entrance.

37

JONATHAN arrived at Grand Central Station almost an hour before the train was due to leave.

Hundreds of travelers were floating about in the great hall, with the dazed and rather fishlike expression of crowds in a great terminal. Everyone, presumably, had some purpose in being there; yet there was an air of vast, unmitigated aimlessness. A group of sailors was hovering at one gate for a train to Virginia. Their faces were pink and grubby like baby carp; they were still adolescents. Two or three of them were kissing their girls good-by. One, a mere boy, had his mother beside him. Parents were saying good-by to their children, businessmen were rushing along with their brief cases, soldiers were sauntering listlessly through the haze. There was not a flake of clear emotion in the place, which lay diffused under the anonymous, gray-green light of an aquarium.

A group of young people now was gathering in front of the gate marked Quebec. They were like a school of Japanese fantails; their clothes were brightly hued and glossy, and continually wavered, like fins, with a graceful, beckoning motion. Jonathan recognized Simonova, dripping with platinum-colored furs, and Sheila Snow, with a long pink scarf and a big red hatbox. Sheila apparently had found a new beau; a tall Latin American with a waxed mustache stood at her side, holding her hand. Valdez and

Dimitroff now appeared, wearing camel's-hair coats with long, floating belts. They were smiling maliciously, and continually turned to look behind them with gossipy little gestures.

Jonathan was beginning to feel a bit dejected. The tremendous room made his own individual yearning seem terribly frail. He felt his need of Lydia grow hazy and diluted, as the minutes passed and the crowds flowed by. The suspense of his infatuation seemed to dissolve in the gray, omnivorous twilight of the place.

Valdez caught sight of Jonathan: his eyes grew mischievous and alert. "What's the matter, Jonathan? You look a wee bit forlorn. Have you lost Lydia, by any chance? ... Come, let me cheer you up a bit!" His fine white teeth sparkled brightly as he smiled. Jonathan blushed, and looked intently toward the gate.

Sebastian was there, kissing Natalia good-by. And Kirillova had just arrived, looking very smart, with a magnificent fox clinging to her shoulders. She was surrounded by a battalion of white leather bags. Behind her, like a duenna, stood her Russian mother, a funereal person with black feathers in her hat.

At that moment Lydia came strolling casually through the crowd. Jonathan saw her in the distance; he instantly recognized, with a pang, her trim gray suit and resilient gait. Her face was fresh and rosy with the late November air.

She smiled, took both his hands in her own, and placed her head tenderly against his shoulder.

"Where have you been?" she exclaimed. "I've been calling your hotel all morning. No one answered. I was desperate!"

"I've been here almost an hour," said Jonathan, in a low voice. "I was beginning to hope that you'd miss the train!"

"Come," she said. "Let's get away from this horrible crowd." She took him by the arm and drew him toward a long corridor on the left, which was lined with a row of small underground shops.

She held his hand; they paused beside a small bookshop, and she whispered: "You'll remember me, Jonathan, dearest, when I'm gone?"

Jonathan nodded. "I'll think of you every day, every single day, Lydia!"

"And you'll try to be faithful, darling?"

"I'll try," mumbled Jonathan. "If it really matters to you!"

"It would hurt me so desperately," she whispered, "if I thought that ... " She looked at him musingly. A momentary smile appeared in her eyes.

"There is so little I really know about you," she continued, with a slanting look. "Have you been hiding anything from me, I wonder?"

A little stab of uneasiness shot through Jonathan. "Lydia," he said ardently, "do you really need me? Do you trust me?"

"I've suffered a great deal, Jonathan," she quietly observed, as she gazed down the corridor. "More than you can ever know. My family, for example. Dreadful things went on in my family. My father. And my mother as well. It was a dangerous atmosphere for a child."

And she looked at Jonathan with a touch of hostility. "You've been very lucky, Jonathan. You've had an easy time of it. A nice family. A good education. You don't understand poverty or pain. You're a daydreamer. You need to see a bit of ... ugliness." She turned away, dropped his hand, and sighed.

They stood in silence for a moment.

"Yes. Someday," she said slowly, "I feel I shall do something rather terrible. I think I would be quite capable of murder!" Her voice was casual, a little playful; then it grew more serious. "Darling, if I ever saw you falling in love with another woman ... I think I would kill her!"

They began to stroll back toward the row of gates.

"Oh, I hope," observed Lydia, as she watched a group of soldiers passing, "that we don't go to war! I've been noticing something strange in the air. ... I'm sure something horrid is about to happen!"

A porter rushed past with a huge green suitcase on his back; he almost ran headlong into Jonathan. A long whistle began to sound, and then a distant roar. A woman in a mink coat was racing down the corridor with a black, infuriated Pekinese in her arms. There was a sense of culminating panic.

"I love you," Lydia whispered suddenly in a low, hard voice. "I swear it, Jonathan. ... Don't ever forget that. You're all I have!"

And he suddenly saw her in a fresh light. Her little white face, with its stubby nose and puckered lips, looked utterly pathetic. The mystery in her had fallen away, like leaves from a tree. There was something a little bleak, a little barren about her.

"I'll write you faithfully, Lydia," he said softly. "I promise."

Natalia came running toward them. "Lydia! You're mad, darling! You have ten seconds to make the train!"

Lydia hurled herself into Jonathan's arms, kissed his lips, cheek, and neck, and then tore herself away. There were tears in her huge, chestnut-colored eyes. "Good-by!" she cried as she hurried away. "Good-by, Jonathan, my own darling!"

"Good-by!" he called after her. "Good-by, my Lydia! Please try, please try to ... " But his voice died away. She was gone. The gate had closed behind her.

Jonathan wandered back through the gray, seething limbo of the station. He entered Vanderbilt Avenue and strolled toward the Yale Club. The world, as he walked down the street, grew crystal-clear and prosaic.

He looked up at the sky. A small white feather was spiraling lightly past the precipice of the Biltmore. It floated directly toward him. He reached up and tried to catch it. It spun, leaped, quivered, and disappeared.

He found himself breathing deeply again, with an unmistakable sense of lightness and liberation.

38

ONE Sunday early in December, some ten days after Lydia's departure, Jonathan paid a last visit to Wyndham Park. He had suddenly been drafted; he was leaving New York the following week.

He strolled across the lawn for several minutes before entering the house. It was a dreary day, raw, windy, penetrating. The shrubs were completely stripped of their foliage; the twigs clung together, naked and shuddering. A flock of crows flew cawing over the hedges. Fallen leaves covered the ground, drenched in a black, soggy moisture. The tennis net and the striped umbrellas had been folded away. The leafless elms rose, with the fine precision of an etching, against the wavering, watery grays of the sky and the Sound.

Everything looked bleak and defoliated. And Jonathan felt that from him, too, something had been stripped away. The color and warmth, the drive of life, lay unnaturally dimmed.

His love for Lydia, his devotion to Pierre, his regrets for Europe, his hopes for America—all had lost their earlier luster. Crisis and confusion had dulled them. He felt dispirited; he felt aimless and utterly lonely.

He stood for a moment under the naked elms. The twigs stirred and scraped, like twisted bits of wire. There was a look of chronic disease in the landscape. And for the first time in his life he was unsure of his own identity, his value and vigor as a human being. He no longer was sure what he desired from life, from love, from his own unsettled character; he had lost his youthful ambition and self-confidence. He felt, unaccountably, that he had made some fatal error.

He walked slowly back along the barren path.

A fire was blazing in the drawing room when he entered. There was no one in the room except the footman, Avery, who was kneeling on the floor and blowing at the flames with a pair of bellows.

"Mrs. Mannering will be right down, sir," said Avery, rising and wiping his brow. "Mr. Mannering isn't at all well; he's been in bed all day, sir."

Jonathan walked across to the windows. The day was growing darker as he watched, although it was not yet one o'clock. The weather, tinged with an unfamiliar hue, hung paneled in the windows like a row of Japanese prints, with leafless sprays of forsythia stirring against a steel-tinted sky.

There was an abnormal silence in the house. In the distance he heard an intermittent, querulous cough. As he approached the library he began to detect a faint odor of decay.

He turned and saw the firelight dancing brightly, scattering high lights on the Tanagra figurines. A bowl of hothouse roses stood on the long dark table; the petals were washed in the velvety flicker.

He heard the sound of firm, deliberate footsteps coming down the stairway. It was Mrs. Mannering.

"You're looking well, Jonathan. You've been gaining weight, a little, haven't you?"

She spoke in a sharp, aggressive tone which was new to her. There were unfamiliar lines of fatigue around her mouth. Something nervous and painfully angular had come over her.

"A little, maybe," said Jonathan, with an air of apology.

"What a hideous day," she said wearily.

"There's a cold wind blowing," agreed Jonathan.

She stood beside him in front of the fire, stretching her thin pale hands toward the flames. The long, crimson fingernails looked savage and unnatural.

"What are you doing this winter, Jonathan? Architecture? Something of the sort?"

"I've just been drafted. I'm off to camp in five days."

"Oh," said Mrs. Mannering bravely. "I didn't know. Well, it will be good for you. Your architecture will have to wait, that's all. We all have to resign ourselves to certain sacrifices nowadays." The phrases fell from her lips with a dry, perfunctory sound.

"Well," she added, "it's been deadly out here. Absolutely desolate ... Whom have you been seeing recently?" She peered at him with a sidelong look.

"Oh, my usual friends," said Jonathan cautiously.

"Wilfred said he met you at the ballet one night. For just a moment." There was a touch of insinuation in her voice.

"Yes. Sometime ago," admitted Jonathan. He began to wonder what she was leading up to.

"You have a weakness for the ballet?"

"Well," said Jonathan, "it's something new for me. I enjoy it, sometimes." There was a pause.

"You've seen Pierre Maillard lately?" She gazed carefully at her long, thin fingers. And instantly Jonathan felt a tightening in the air; an element of conflict had come into play.

"Not very often," he said casually. "He's been rather busy."

"Busy?"

"Painting, of course. He's an ambitious fellow."

"Ambitious. Yes. Exactly," said Mrs. Mannering slowly.

She spoke with a curious tension in her voice. She was about to say something more when the door opened and two other guests arrived: Wilfred Silliman, of course, and old Mrs. Westover.

A moment later Avery appeared and said that luncheon was served.

39

AN AIR of aimlessness and fatigue hung over the dining-room table.

"I'm dreadfully worried about Winthrop," sighed Mrs. Mannering, stirring her soup. "He's been having these spells."

"Winthrop's no longer young, you know," said Mrs. Westover, in her chirping voice. "And he was always a bit of a hypochondriac."

"He's been fretting about the war," said Mrs. Mannering uneasily. "He grows frantic at the mere thought of our getting involved. And you know how he feels about Roosevelt."

"Well," said Wilfred with authority, "it will all be over soon. You heard the broadcast the other day? The Russians are about to collapse. It's sheer military dilettantism for them to keep on with the struggle."

"We may not like those Nazis," said Mrs. Westover, "but at any rate Germany is a part of Western civilization. I remember Aunt Theodora taking us on a visit to Rothenburg and Dinkelsbühl. They were absolutely adorable. ... The Russians, well, they're Asiatics."

"Still," said Wilfred anxiously, "I'd hate to see those brutal Nazis sitting in Stratford on Avon. We must never, never forsake England, my dear Lucy!"

"Oh, the English," said Mrs. Mannering, in a vitriolic tone; "they're simply playing a game to get us in. And then, when they've robbed us of our last penny, they'll pretend it was they who won the war!"

There was a painful silence. Mrs. Westover pursed her lips. Wilfred sipped thoughtfully at his wineglass. The luncheon, it appeared, was not a success.

"Well, Wilfred, what do you do these days?" said Mrs. Mannering, helping herself to the turkey. "Everything's going downhill. Books, films, the theater: there's nothing but trash!"

"I haven't," declared Mrs. Westover, "read a really civilized novel since Mrs. Wharton died. I can't bear these queer, childish novels about Mississippi and Georgia."

"Quite," observed Wilfred. "I've had to go back to the classics. I've just started rereading *Anna Karenina*. An absolutely ravishing piece of work, I must say!"

"But oh, how outdated it is!" sighed Mrs. Mannering. "All that silly, antiquated fuss about adultery. As though ... "

"There's something undisciplined about those Russian novelists," agreed Mrs. Westover. "They seem to wallow in morbidities. Give me Jane Austen. Or Anthony Trollope."

"Well," sighed Wilfred, "the Russians aren't quite my cup of tea, politically. But they've done some gorgeous things in literature and music. I'd rather die, my dear, than do without Tchekov!"

Mrs. Mannering had grown silent, and stared across the room with thin, bitter eyes. There was a long, depressing pause. The day was swiftly dimming; there was a clatter of dry twigs outside the window.

Jonathan had begun to feel a little troubled. Something seemed to be wrong; some strange, soporific influence had been cast over the luncheon table, like a scent of chloroform. The carnations in the long silver bowl, he noticed, had begun to wilt.

The butler came in as they were finishing their dessert.

"Could we," said Mrs. Mannering indifferently, "have a bit more of that crème bavaroise, Avery?"

Avery nodded. "Yes, ma'am. I think there's a trifle left in the kitchen."

He turned at the door. "I beg your pardon, ma'am."

"Yes, Avery?"

"There's been a bit of news over the radio. The cook just told us. The Chinese dropped some bombs on Honolulu."

"Honolulu," said Mrs. Westover tartly. "That's rather rude of them, isn't it?"

"You're sure they said Chinese?" said Wilfred Silliman, raising his brows.

"That's what the cook said, sir," replied Avery nervously.

"Impudent of them," said Wilfred Silliman. "This will get them into trouble, mark my words!"

"One of those typical Chinese blunders, probably," said Mrs. Westover. "Like the Boxer Rebellion."

"All Orientals are the same," sighed Mrs. Mannering. "Inefficient. You can't trust them. I remember, I had two Filipino servants some years ago ... "

At that moment a red-haired chambermaid appeared at the door; her hands were fluttering with agitation.

"Please, ma'am," she whispered, peering wildly at Mrs. Mannering.

"Yes?"

"It's Mr. Mannering," said the maid. "He's taken funny, ma'am."

Mrs. Mannering turned pale. For a moment she sat frozen. Then she rose from the table and left the room without a word.

40

MR. MANNERING half sat, half lay in his bed. He looked like a mummy, reduced to his smallest conceivable dimensions. He was wearing a crimson dressing gown piped with black silk. A belt of black rope lay curled in his lap; his fingers lay tangled in its coils, inert and purple. His whole person had shrunk, it seemed, into a kind of dreadful anachronism.

Jonathan had noticed a scent of ammonia as he entered the room. The curtains were drawn. Mrs. Westover and Wilfred Silliman were hovering uneasily near the door.

Mr. Mannering had had a stroke; he was dying.

He still looked mischievous and defiant. His eyes peered at the door with a glitter of contempt. His head had become curiously dark, almost maroon-colored. He was bald, but a delicate white fuzz still clung to his scalp, and small silky tufts protruded from his ears. In his eyebrows the hair was still bristling and aggressive.

The bedroom was very dark. In the corner Jonathan could see a small glass cabinet filled with pale Chinese vases.

Mr. Mannering, even now, looked as though he were carrying a secret with him, and were scoring a lucrative victory over the world, and as though death in some way were the final seal on his well-calculated triumph. He looked dark and malevolent in the vast white bed. His eyes rolled heavily in their swollen pouches. Once he coughed, very thinly, and snorted a little. A golden dragon was embroidered on his pajamas; its eyes were glaring savagely across the room.

Mrs. Mannering stood at the foot of the bed, her blue-gray hair exquisitely waved, her face pale and tense.

The old man's eyes were becoming blurred. He opened his mouth, tried to say something, but failed, and closed it again. A nurse had appeared and stood near the bed, ill at ease. When she moved Jonathan could hear the rustle of her starched white dress and the creak of her white shoes. She crossed to the bedside and lit the satin-shaded lamp. It cast a soft yellow light over the dying man, so that his face appeared smiling and somnolent, like that of an oriental deity.

In the recesses of a window Dr. Wainwright, who had just arrived, was talking softly to Wilfred Silliman, who had silently crossed the room. Mrs. Westover slipped through the door with a swift, clandestine rustle, and disappeared in the corridor.

For several minutes no one moved; nothing stirred. There was a crevice in the curtains, and through it Jonathan could see a blade of steel-blue sky, and a wavering network of twigs. The afternoon was darkening rapidly.

Presently Mr. Mannering began to sigh in a hot, wheezing way. He looked from side to side, and his eyes fell on Jonathan. Some buried impulse seemed to rise to the surface. He opened his eyes wide. There was a tiny bubbling, an explosion of the lips. "Please," he muttered; "please, please"; or so it sounded.

He glanced petulantly toward the window. It was too dark for him, it seemed, and he wanted the curtains drawn aside.

He sat suddenly bolt upright. His eyes gazed at the onlookers with a new, appalling clarity.

The nurse rushed to his side. "There, there, lie down, sir. Lie down!"

He lay back. His face grew pitifully resigned for a moment. And then all trace of expression vanished. He was breathing very deeply; the death rattle could be heard. His head looked like the head of a newly born child. It sank deeper into the pillow, then grew utterly immobile.

The doctor looked solemnly at Mrs. Mannering. She took a long, deep breath, raised her fingers to her face, twisted her body around, then walked swiftly from the room.

PART TWO: 1943

41

MRS. ELY sat in her bed beside the window and looked into the night. She was waiting for the arrival of her son, Jonathan.

The streets below lay hushed and secluded, like country lanes in the middle of winter. For the first time the city lay bathed in its natural illumination. Mrs. Ely, as she looked upon Gramercy Park, could study the cold, clear effects of the moon: it produced in the snow floating stains of light and shadow, such as one might find on a deserted hillside or a prairie. The silhouettes of the trees shone pure and metallic, outlined with the fragility of a Breughel winter landscape. One yellow light shone faintly in the distance, in defiance of the dim-out regulations; it looked like a light in the depth of a forest. The spire of a distant church had the look of a village steeple, and the skyscrapers rose into the night, dark and ill-defined, like a vista among the Pyrenees.

This, she reflected, was what the war had achieved; the city lay delivered to the paralysis of nature. All the brilliance, the agitation, the triviality of peace had gone. A majestical stillness had come instead.

She was sitting up in bed, with a small pink table stretched across her knees. She had been writing a letter; the pen was in her hand. The dinner tray, with its empty dishes, had been placed on the bird's-eye maple desk. A fire was burning in the fireplace on her left. The light flickered softly across her face, casting the shadow of her profile, immensely magnified, on the wall beyond.

She had written the following lines to her sister-in-law in London:

My dearest Norah:

I arrived quite safely—you needn't have worried. I've been here six days, waiting for Jonathan to arrive from Texas. He's been in the camp there for almost a year— in the training command of the Air Force, I believe it's called. I can't tell you how I feel—it's three years, Norah, more than three years since I saw him. I'll be seeing him tonight. He'll be wearing a uniform—it makes me feel proud, yet rather ill too. My heart is heavy, dear Norah. I feel so hopelessly lost in New York. I had forgotten what a weird, gray, desolate place it is—and how it hardens people. I feel very, very old here. And very out of date. To tell the truth, I've been rather unwell—I've grown shockingly thin lately. ...

Her pen rested hesitantly on the page; she gazed across the room, with sudden curiosity.

Two photographs of Jonathan were placed on the dresser, one in a small green frame, taken when he was seventeen; the other one more recent, tucked into the frame of the mirror. She looked very slowly from one to the other, studying the change in expression that had come in the interval: a troubled and dream-clouded look, replacing the earlier sparkle and enthusiasm.

And she tried, for the hundredth time, to see the warm, real features; to recover the illusion of life. The eyes were meditative and dark, the eyebrows exceptionally thick and straight:

his father's eyebrows and eyes, unmistakably. But the lips were still boyish, and a little rebellious. There was something alert yet disturbed in the expression; something vigorous yet cautious in the line of the bones. In that she thought she saw the mingling of nationalities—of the old and the young, of the old and the new. She began to smile involuntarily. Her love for her son was uncritical, boundless; her whole nature succumbed to it, was fortified and united by it. And she knew that her life had been rewarding, ultimately, because it had been ceaselessly guided by her love for Jonathan.

On the bed beside her lay a bundle of letters and an old, leather-bound album of photographs. She slowly began to leaf through the album; her hand cast its thin blue shadow on the page. And by a familiar process of consolation, she summoned forth, one by one, a whole retinue of memories. Smiling images of him passed before her mind, familiar portraits ranging from his birth, in Washington, to his farewell in London three weeks before the war.

The room was filled to overflowing with Jonathan's presence; not Jonathan at any single moment, quite, but a composite of all these images and of all he had been to her, as a child, as a boy, and as a man. She felt that he was already in the room beside her; that his warmth was warming her and his strength was strengthening her; not yet and not quite the real, warm-blooded Jonathan, but the magical imagined son who had never left her.

She closed the album and placed it beside the pillow. She closed her eyes; and for an instant she experienced a thing close to terror. All that trembling chain of memories, that endless sequence of love, that rush of anguish and hope: for whom had it been destined? For an image; a specter; an absolute stranger, whose inner life was as inscrutable as the life on Betelgeuse. And the very power of her love, the very wealth of her memories, only shrouded and disguised still more hopelessly the living character.

She opened her eyes again. The room was growing hot; she cast the shawl from her shoulders. Then she picked up the pen and was about to end her letter.

The telephone rang. She answered; her voice shook.

"Oh, Jonathan, is it you, dear? ... What? ... You're downstairs? ... Yes, I'm waiting. ... "

She replaced the receiver on the hook and stared at the door with a look almost haggard in its intensity. Her parted lips had begun to quiver, and the lines in her face had begun to break.

There was a light knock on the door. Then it slowly opened, and in the half-darkness, hesitant, she caught sight of Jonathan.

42

JONATHAN stood for a moment in the doorway. At first he saw only the bright, orange sparkle of the fire. Then he saw his mother, appallingly thin and fragile, gazing at him from the bed with her huge, imploring eyes. He leaned over and kissed her without a word. She pressed her head to his; he could feel her tiny shape, withered with age and illness, as it clung to his own.

He withdrew and looked into her eyes. Her cheeks were flooded and shining. A feeling of overwhelming pity, of guilt, and something close to panic passed through him. He closed his eyes, held her tilted face in his hands, and kissed her again; as he opened his eyes he saw her looking at him with a clear, instantaneous perception.

"My dear boy," she said softly, in her timid, halting way. "My dear, dear child."

He sat down on the bed. She looked at him with a grave, astonished kind of scrutiny. She touched the sleeve of his uniform somewhat uneasily.

"Have I changed, dear?" she whispered. "Do I look much thinner, Jonathan?"

He shook his head and smiled. "You've hardly changed at all, Mother. How long ago was it ... "

"You look wonderfully healthy!" she exclaimed. And her voice grew apprehensive. "Will they keep you there? In Texas? Might they send you abroad?"

"I think not," he said gently.

"Oh, I hope not," she said, and drew his head close again. "I've been worrying constantly. Try, dear, not to let them send you abroad!"

"You've had dinner up in your room, Mother?"

She nodded her head. "I've been in bed all day, I'm afraid. I thought a rest might do me good. The ocean voyage was a bit of a strain." She smiled and drew her thin, cool fingers across his cheek. "We zigzagged. To avoid the submarines. For seventeen days."

"You shouldn't have come!" he exclaimed involuntarily.

"I had to come," she said patiently. A momentary smile crossed her face; and that was succeeded by a look of anxiety. "And now tell me all that you have done, dear boy."

He looked about the room. Everything was muted, subdued. The bright, crackling logs were falling into embers, and their light washed the walls in a rippling glow. It was, for a hotel room, oddly pleasant and intimate. The furniture was of bird's-eye maple, and old prints of the French cathedrals hung on the walls. He recognized, with a little shock, his own youthful photographs on the dresser.

She followed his glance, and smiled rather curiously. "You've changed, my dear."

"You think that I've changed?"

"You look stronger. Firmer. And a little older, dear.... Do you mind?" She glanced, with a solicitous look, at his corporal's uniform. "Have you made friends in the Army? Down there in the South?"

He shrugged his shoulders. "Friends? It's hard to make real friends, I'm afraid, when one knows they'll be leaving the next day, or the day after. ... One has comrades; that's all; one forgets them the moment they go." He paused, and added thoughtfully, "Most of them, anyway."

"You haven't ... " She hesitated. "You haven't had any unpleasantness?"

He was a bit startled. "No, Mother. Why?"

"One worries." She smiled apologetically. "I thought I saw a little shadow in your eyes."

He shook his head slowly; he took and held her cool, nervous hand in his own.

She asked softly: "You're going back to the same camp?"

"For a while, I suppose." His voice was a little impatient. He felt oddly reluctant to talk of his life in the Army; not because it was bleak or aimless, or particularly uncongenial, but because he felt he had not been quite alive, or quite himself there. There was nothing to say, nothing really to tell about. His mental existence had been hazy and sluggish. His emotions, his desires had been furtive and fitful. His relationships, with a single exception, had all been barren and superficial. Far from maturing him in any way, life in the Army had been almost puerile: a long, dull, irresponsible daydream.

Yet he knew, in spite of this, that his mother was right: something in him had subtly, indefinably changed.

She seemed to have guessed his thoughts. "You are healthy, dear. That is the main thing. ... You have a splendid color. Only ... "

"Yes?"

She was gazing at him shyly. "I do hope, Jonathan, my dear, they won't send you overseas!"

He rose, walked to the window, and gazed silently across Gramercy Park. It looked frozen, caught in a trancelike stillness. The moon was passing, cold and serene, through a radiant field of mackerel clouds. The shrubbery lay woven like lace across the snow.

Half an hour later he kissed her tenderly good night. He walked back to his hotel, for over two miles, through the miraculous, moonlit stillness of the city.

43

THE following afternoon Jonathan was strolling along Central Park South. He had called Lydia that morning at her flat; and she had arranged to meet him that same evening in front of the Plaza.

He looked at his watch. It was not quite five; he had three quarters of an hour to spare. He entered the park by a familiar path, climbed down a slope, and paused at the pond.

The sun was setting beyond Central Park West. A last rivulet of light went flowing down the street and dissolved among the frozen shrubbery. The sheets of ice in the pond grew flaming; small crescents of snow began to sparkle, and the long gray walls were transfigured. The distant reaches of Fifth Avenue, oddly flattened in the winter air, seemed little by little to fade and perish. Then swiftly the light began to slide away.

Several skaters were standing at the edge of the pond, but the ice was thin and they clung to the shore. The snow was gray and worn along the edges. Small tufts of sunlight lingered among the shrubs.

And then, as the path narrowed and he passed beneath some trees, a second transformation occurred. But this time quite without drama; nothing seemed to be happening. A paw-shaped cloud was crossing the sky. Softly, imperceptibly, the snow began to fall. An air of mourning covered the scene.

He turned back into the street and strolled toward the Plaza. Christmas was only a week away, and the city had assumed an air of calculated festivity. Here and there in a window hung a wreath of holly, or a twiglet of mistletoe. Here and there, behind a curtain, lurked a small, halfhearted Christmas tree. It was the endless row of shopwindows which had absorbed all the splendor; they flashed and flickered with streams of merchandise. The gentle cheer of Christmas lay drowned in a glittering sea of expenditure.

Twilight arrived. The day was ending early. The city was retiring into a deeper, more characteristic mood. Wintry lights and shadows flowed about the upper reaches of the buildings, like clouds flanking a perilous mountainside. Slowly, as Jonathan watched, the subtleties of contour fell away. Each dark tower stood isolated, like an inaccessible peak, and swarming within like a separate city.

He looked down again at the dark little figures hurrying past. They struck him, suddenly, as consummate replicas; the parasites, the prey of the buildings above. All natural warmth lay frozen, all indolence lay suppressed. They had acquired, under the laws of protective coloration, all the hollowness and hardness and ingenuity of the skyscrapers. Their eyes, as they passed him, looked like sly little crevices; beady with rapacity, incapable of repose. They wove feverishly among the gorges of masonry, uncontrollable swarms feeding on a colossal, lifeless body.

And his mind reverted to Lydia. His entire memory of her lay woven, inextricably, into the pattern of the city. Whatever in the city was magnetic and sparkling she reflected; and the city's fever and isolation lay mirrored in her as well.

Yet, like the city, she was ceaselessly changing. Nothing remained true or characteristic of her for long. What, he wondered, had happened to her since the last time he saw her? She hadn't written for several months; had she found a new lover?

And he felt, under the subtle influence of proximity, that his yearning for her was reviving. He longed to hear her voice again, to touch her restless little hands.

He wandered toward the Plaza. A small dark figure was standing under the marquee. Her back was turned and her face was hidden; but his heart leaped suddenly with recognition. He knew the tilt of the head and the firm, athletic stance.

And there was something else he recognized—a subtle essence, an emanation; the kind of quality that only love, or fear perhaps, can apprehend.

He called out her name, but she didn't seem to hear. Then he called a second time, a little louder: "Lydia!"

44

LYDIA'S CHEEKS, as he kissed her, were cold and firm against his, but her lips were warm and wet and trembling. There was a fragrance of honeysuckle about her.

He closed his eyes and held her closely. The city around them vanished. He felt her warmth and vitality sweep over him once more.

He opened his eyes again and looked at her. She smiled impulsively, blinked a little, and leaned her head on his shoulder.

"There," she said, with a little sigh. "How lovely to feel it again!

"You look wonderful," he said, in a whisper. "Like an angel! A Polish angel!" And he kissed her again, more boldly than before.

"Yes," she said, placing her hands on his shoulders and holding him at arm's length; her eyes were marvelously brilliant. "Yes, it's you! The same desperate little kiss. A boy's kiss! Come, darling." She drew him close again and slid her arm under his. "I'm absolutely perishing with the cold!"

Her face shone like china, rosy smooth above the dark fur collar. She was wearing a cap of black astrakhan, with a silver medallion pinned to the side. Her cheeks were flushed with cold, and her eyes had begun to water; they were sparkling with curiosity and pleasure. She looked like a doll, sweet and trim and compact. A thrilling feeling of anticipation swept over Jonathan.

In an impulse of tenderness he placed his arms around her waist and lifted her from the ground; she gave a little cry; she was light as a cat. He felt her collar against his face, mysteriously soft and fragrant.

"My soldier boy," she purred. "Two little stripes. How sweet! Does that mean you're a colonel?"

Several people were watching them. They were still standing under the marquee. The visitors to the hotel kept brushing them and turning around as they hurried past.

He was about to take her into the Plaza when she said: "No, darling. Please. Let's go to our little place on Fifty-eighth Street!"

Ten minutes later they were sitting at the same table where they had lunched over a year ago. The same checkered cloth was on the table, and the same empty chianti bottle; only the candle, this time, was yellow instead of red. And for the first time he felt a warm, deep sense of security with Lydia.

"You look terribly cute, darling," she said, touching the cuff of his uniform. "The color suits you perfectly. You've had your hair cut much shorter, too. ... Oh, Jonathan, I'm so glad you've shed those European ways!"

Jonathan was a bit startled. "My European ways?"

"Well, there was something a bit dreamy and peculiar about you, dear. Something rather impractical. But now you look like all the other soldiers. Typically American! Clean and boyish!" She placed her hand on his, affectionately.

The waiter leaned over them; they began to order dinner.

He watched her face as she glanced at the menu. The candlelight was playing across her cheeks. She had aged a little; it showed in the stronger, more conspicuous angles of her face. Her chin seemed more maturely modeled, her cheekbones more prominent. The little mole on her chin looked slightly perverse.

Her beauty, perhaps, had lost some of its bloom. But it had deepened, and lay blended with her eyes and her voice; instead of dwelling in the accident of youth it now rose from her nature, from her unique and accumulated experience. Her eyes shone with a hard, penetrating pleasure.

"Tell me," she whispered. "Why did you stop writing to me?"

Jonathan looked at her with surprise. "It was you, Lydia, who stopped writing!"

"Stopped writing? Be sensible, darling. What on earth could I write? There wasn't a thing to say. But you, with all of your military adventures ... " She looked at him mischievously.

Jonathan smiled. "There were no adventures, I'm afraid."

"Now, now," she said teasingly. "Something must have happened, surely. You've changed, I can feel it. You've grown older. You've grown"—she touched his forearm—"a little harder, haven't you?"

"One works pretty hard down there," admitted Jonathan. "One begins to turn into an animal."

"Animal? Well," she said casually, "did you have any love affairs?" She speared an oyster and dipped it in the crimson sauce.

"No," he said, with a darkening look, "I had no love affairs."

She looked at him with a swift, suspicious brightness. For a moment she said nothing. She gazed mildly at the ceiling. Then she said rather meekly:

"Did you think of me often? Did you long for me? Did you need me, Jonathan?"

He reached across the table, took her hand, and pressed it to his lips.

"Yes," he said gently, "I needed you. Often." He added in a low voice: "I need you tonight."

She lowered her eyes and sipped at the red wine. For several minutes they sat in silence; she with her wet lips smiling and the wineglass in her fingers, he watching the candlelight trembling upon her face.

Then he said: "Tell me about yourself now, Lydia. About your dancing. What have you been doing lately?"

She sighed. "Well, nothing much. I've been working like an absolute slave, that's all. But it's been worth it, I suppose. Kirillova is probably leaving the company at the end of the season. Simonova is definitely leaving; she's going over to the Monte Carlo people. There are big roles waiting for me. The princess in *Bluebeard,* for instance...Unless, of course, that skunk Sevastopoulos gives it to Janet Bloom."

She glanced past him for a moment; she seemed a bit preoccupied.

A large black-haired sailor and his girl were rising from the neighboring table. The sailor, as he passed, cast a furtive glance of recognition at Lydia; or so it seemed to Jonathan.

"Does he know you, Lydia?"

"Who, dear?" She raised her brows.

"That husky sailor over there?"

She looked astonished. "Mercy, no. I know no sailors. Why do you ask, darling?"

"Well, he seemed to look at you in a certain way."

"Oh, Jonathan," she said, in a reproachful tone, "please, please! Don't begin to imagine things! That's why I grew so tired of Peter Sebastian. His perpetual suspicions..." She was winding a trail of spaghetti around her fork.

"Nothing," she murmured, with dignity, "is less becoming than jealousy. After all, can I help it, darling, if strange, husky sailors look at me in a certain way?"

She lit a cigarette and gazed at him quietly. A faint smile flickered across her half-closed eyes. She reached under the table and held his hand, placed her fingers around his wrist, and dug her nails into his flesh.

For several minutes they sat in silence. She looked at him with her brilliant, challenging eyes.

He returned her gaze. A rush of memories came over him. And he felt the familiar passion rising in him again.

45

THEY walked slowly down Broadway. He held her arm in his, and continually turned to look at her face. The feverish vitality of the street had brought a new, bright color to her cheeks.

New York was dimmed out, but on Broadway a haze of light still emerged from thousands of doorways. The half-darkness added a tense and mysterious gaiety to the street. It was like a carnival scene, with a dazzling variety of gowns and uniforms passing through the unending stream of faces. And over it all hung the darkness of the war, which gave them an air of anonymity, of masquerade.

There were the Dutch sailors, with black ribbons dangling from their caps; the French with their vermilion pompons and sharp, clever features; the British with their tall caps and squat, plebeian shapes; the Americans with their clinging blues and light, swaggering gait. There was an air of stoicism and solidarity among the foreigners, of horseplay and boyish frivolity among the Americans. But the awareness, the possibility of death had brought the same faraway look to all their faces.

The soldiers and sailors were rolling brightly, like pebbles, through the promiscuous tangle of civilians. Jonathan had forgotten what a fantastic thoroughfare it was. Nothing here seemed surprising. No one looked out of place. All taboos were abolished; all the barriers were obliterated. Every eccentricity of face, dress, desire had been flung into the onrush. A kind of hordelike fatalism pervaded the scene. It had the air of some vast Asiatic migration.

"Doesn't it excite you, dear?" said Lydia, clinging to his arm.

"It's like nothing else in the world," said Jonathan.

He looked at her again. Her eyes were restless and remote. He felt that she was hardly aware of him now.

Suddenly, to his astonishment, Jonathan caught sight of Wilfred Silliman. He was striding with dignity through the thicket of pedestrians, and seemed to brush them aside as though they were undergrowth in a jungle. He was fastidiously dressed as always, in a chesterfield with a velvet collar, gray gloves, and a white silk scarf. He was carrying a cane. Jonathan thought he detected a certain leer in his eyes.

He called Wilfred's name, and reached out to shake his hand.

"Ah, Jonathan!" exclaimed Wilfred, with an instant straightening of the shoulders and a flicker of embarrassment in the eyes. "Gracious! So you're back with us!" His voice was a nervous falsetto. "Mercy me, you do look healthy! And brutally chic in your new uniform. Well, every cloud has a silver lining, they say!" He tittered fatuously.

"How long are you staying in town?" He glanced suspiciously at Lydia.

"Till after New Year's, I hope," replied Jonathan. "If all goes well."

"Well, then I'll be seeing something of you, I hope," said Wilfred indulgently. There was something a bit lurid about the old gentleman tonight. He had taken on a slight touch of Broadway, it appeared. His voice and manner were faintly predatory.

He glanced down the street with sudden interest. "Well, good night, my boy!" he murmured breathlessly. "And *au revoir!*" He hurried away, with a slight wavering of the hips, turning and gliding down Forty-fourth Street.

"Who was that?" inquired Lydia, a moment later, somewhat acidly.

"Mr. Silliman," explained Jonathan. "An old friend of the Mannerings."

Lydia raised her brows a little. "Oh. So he's that type, is he?"

"You mean ... ?"

"You know perfectly well what I mean, Jonathan. ... Why didn't you introduce me?" She stared at him reproachfully.

"Would you have liked me to?"

"Stop pretending, dear. It's not a question of liking. It's just that I can't help wondering why I never meet your friends."

Jonathan felt a pang of guilt. Lydia had touched, he realized, on a rather delicate problem; she would never fit in with the Mannerings and Potters, obviously. If she ever entered that little circle, he felt, there would be a dangerous flicker, an explosion.

"I didn't think you'd be particularly amused," he muttered vaguely.

"I don't suppose I would," she declared. "But they might be, you know. They might find me rather refreshing, all in all."

"I'm quite sure of it," said Jonathan earnestly.

"Tell me," said Lydia rather sadly, "do you really like that kind of world, Jonathan?"

"What kind of world, Lydia?"

"Oh, snobs. Social butterflies. Titled foreigners. The Long Island set. Do you really feel at home in that kind of atmosphere?"

"Well, I hadn't really thought about it," said Jonathan, in a casual tone.

"Don't they seem rather dull?" said Lydia. "Rather ridiculous and unreal?"

He glanced at her again. He began to feel puzzled. She was staring at him with a kind of nervous defiance.

And he saw that she too had become a part of Broadway. She was caught in the stream; she moved brightly with the current.

Thousands of faces flowed past in the mild green haze of the dim-out, young and old, beautiful and hideous—but all had the same ruthless glitter, the same dynamic air of search and struggle. And as he watched, the world of the Potters and Mannerings, the decorous regions of the Ritz and the Plaza, all grew dim and insubstantial; like a small gray mist above a rushing torrent.

He drew Lydia closer; he felt strangely excited. Her own quality seemed mysteriously heightened. She seemed like a subtle distillation of this world, this deeper and richer vein of the city. Something barbaric in her nature, something faintly oriental, was emerging. Her body seemed filled with a new kind of magic.

But she scarcely seemed to notice him. She drew away again. Her eyes passed incessantly over the crowd, watching, absorbing, drinking from its irresistible flood.

He was overwhelmed by a longing to take her in his arms and kiss her. He desired her suddenly in a strange new way; her flesh had taken on the rich, ripe luster of the crowd.

"Come, darling," he whispered. His voice was hot and urgent. "Come ... let's go down to your flat. ... Let me make love to you again. ... "

But she hardly seemed to be listening. They had arrived at Forty-second Street. The crowd was thicker than ever: it was like a maelstrom. Long blue fingers of light were nervously exploring the darkness overhead.

She turned to him with a desperate, pleading look. "Darling," she murmured, "I have a perfectly ghastly headache. Do you mind dreadfully if I leave you? Will you be an angel and forgive me?"

She squeezed his hand, with a sigh, and drew her fingers across her forehead. Her face looked flushed and overexcited. Then she turned and vanished, near the subway entrance, in the devouring swarms of Forty-second Street.

46

JONATHAN stood motionless on the corner for a long time. He felt utterly stunned. The crowd flowed past and around him, north and south, east and west. A piercing wind began to blow down Forty-second Street. The night was growing colder. He felt desperately alone.

At last he turned and walked slowly up Broadway.

A strange new mood was beginning to creep over him. His desires ceased to be focused on the image of Lydia; they lay scattered all around him, dissipated, confused. The crowd drew him closer, swirled perilously about him. He saw the hungry ripple of eyes appraising his own as he passed. He felt suddenly vulnerable; he had entered the zones of danger.

He stepped through a revolving door into a bar near Forty-fourth Street. It was packed, dimly lit, and intensely hot. The tables on the left were lost in a haze of cigarette smoke. A thick, almost impenetrable mass of men surrounded the oblong bar at the right.

He made his way to the edge of the bar and ordered a whisky and soda. All around him he felt the warm, continual thrust of strangers—soldiers, sailors, airmen, in every kind of uniform. A tall naval officer offered to buy him a drink; a drunken young lieutenant tried to catch his eye.

He finished his whisky and made his way back to the revolving door.

And a new, violent yearning for Lydia came over him as he stepped into the wintry street. For several minutes he stood hesitant. He looked at his watch, and was amazed. It was almost midnight. The curfew was beginning to fill the streets.

He found a taxi, and entered without quite knowing where to go. He felt blindly restless. The thought of returning to his hotel was intolerable.

"Well?" muttered the driver. "What will it be?"

"Take me down to Tenth Street," said Jonathan quietly. "You can drop me at the corner of Seventh Avenue."

The taxi moved nervously through the midnight traffic. Jonathan remembered how once before, late at night, he had taken a cab down to Tenth Street. But then the city had been deserted and still. Now it was shrill and swarming. Yet the effect was the same—one of suspense without drama, of activity without a core.

It was after twelve when he stepped from the cab and wandered down Tenth Street. This part of town lay fast asleep. The lights and noise had vanished, and the darkness enclosed him like a tunnel. There was no one in the street, as far as he could see.

He crossed very cautiously, keeping his eye on the doors and windows, and finally stood opposite Lydia's flat. He looked up at her window; it was black and empty.

He stood motionless for several minutes. Then he sat down on a darkened stairway; his hand was clinging to the iron railing.

He kept staring at Lydia's window, waiting for some crucial revelation. The world lay black and frozen, like an Arctic promontory. He felt stripped, exposed to the bitter winds.

And a painful current of reflections began to flow through his mind.

He realized, then, how much the memory of Lydia had sustained him during the months in Texas, where daily existence had been a cactus-ridden limbo; and where the life within had come to resemble the landscape—flat, frameless, utterly monotonous.

And he realized that all this time a deep hunger had been accumulating. The symbol of New York as a vortex of human variety had remained in his mind; and at the center of this vortex, pale and incalculable, shone the image of Lydia.

And now the whole intensity of months of longing burst forth; he was overcome by the force of his misery. He sat on the hard gray stairs, with his hand on the icy railing. His rejection by Lydia appeared in his mind as a rejection by life itself. His misery, he felt, was neither tragic nor significant, but that of denial, of frustration, of solitude.

He heard footsteps down the street and quickly turned his head. A young woman and a soldier, arm in arm, were hurrying down the other side. They paused for a moment directly opposite Jonathan; they seemed to be debating. Then they entered the house.

Jonathan felt a thrill of realization run through his body. The woman was Lydia. He had known it the moment he heard her footsteps.

He sat motionless, in a state of suspense that bordered on nausea. The street seemed to come alive, like a long black serpent. The darkened buildings began to quiver.

Then he saw a light appear in Lydia's window, and shadows moving faintly across the ceiling. He waited breathlessly. But he saw nothing more, and presently the light went out again.

But over the buildings, as he sat there, an orange glow continued to hang; it was like the glow of a crater. It rose and dilated, and he half expected to see a boiling flood of lava suddenly hurled over the roofs.

He found himself shivering violently. His hands were numb with cold, and his whole body seemed paralyzed. He rose with a desperate effort and walked quickly toward Seventh Avenue.

It was almost two o'clock when he finally arrived in his room.

47

PIERRE was having luncheon, the following day, with the famous Mrs. Bellamy Carter. Mrs. Carter was a Francophile: he had met her through Baron Legué. He arrived at the restaurant punctually at a quarter past one. Mrs. Carter had not yet arrived, and Pierre sat down to wait in the rose-colored antechamber which adjoined the bar.

Great numbers of fashionable ladies were arriving, greeting each other with little cries, hugs, and kisses, then drifting gradually into the dining room, from which a predatory murmur was beginning to flow.

Lady Webber appeared, wearing a magnificent mink coat, and with a dachshund on the leash. She deposited her animal and her furs with the cloak girl, and came gliding breezily toward Pierre.

She puckered her lips and looked at him playfully. She hardly knew him; she had obviously forgotten his name.

"You're waiting for Laura too?" she inquired. "She's always late! Even at her own parties. It's too revolting of her, really. Come, my dear, let's have a drink in the bar, just the two of us. ... Oh, here she is. We were just talking about you, Laura darling! Saying what a wicked creature you are. ... "

Mrs. Carter hastened across the room with both arms extended. Pierre felt surrounded by a rush of perfume. Every detail in her sudden entry was the consummate product of fashion—the little cry of surprise, the subtle fragrance, the incomparable furs and the dazzling hat, the sweeping, imperceptible glance of appraisal.

She greeted Pierre with an air of affectionate spontaneity, and kissed Lady Webber tenderly. "Do forgive me for being late! ... Has Gaby Landau come yet? No? Well, let's go in anyway."

She led the way into the dining room. A hush fell on the tables as she floated by; and then, in her wake, came a ripple of whispers.

Mrs. Carter was a unique and vivid figure in New York society. No one disputed that she was still exquisitely beautiful; but no one quite knew her age. Some guessed charitably at forty-two, others insisted, rather harshly, on fifty-seven. Her entire energies over twenty-odd years had been given to the precarious maintenance of this beauty. It had now reached a miraculous point, it appeared, where the onslaughts of age had at last been permanently subdued. A kind of antique luster, a glow of unassailable workmanship, kept shimmering lightly about her person. Her skin had the quality of fine old lacquer. And her manner, too, had a timeless and impersonal, faintly oriental gloss. Yet, in spite of her spectacular prestige in the world of fashion, there was in her manner a constant undertone of anxiety. She was quite aware that she was hated.

She was famous for her incomparable clothes. Today she appeared in a daring suit of solid vermilion, with long silver buttons and a lining of pearl gray—a combination which suggested a brilliantly reckless air, with a touch of the demure. On her head she wore a tam o'shanter with a tall black feather springing from the top, like an exclamation point.

The headwaiter led them to a table for six in the corner. At that moment Baron Legué appeared, escorting a tall, asceticlooking woman with sunken eyes. Mrs. Carter introduced the Baroness Landau.

"There," said Mrs. Carter. "That's five of us. Who's missing? Oh, of course: Basil Hume. Well, never mind.... Have you a menu, Estelle?"

Baron Legué proceeded in tones of exhaustion to recite the dishes. "Smoked trout, smoked salmon, smoked sturgeon, smoked eel ... "

At that point Basil Hume arrived, and sat down in the empty chair between Mrs. Carter and the baroness. He was panting heavily. "I'm terribly sorry," he muttered. "It's impossible to get a taxi these days! It's a perfect nightmare.... "

"There's hardly a place in New York where one can lunch in peace," sighed Mrs. Carter. "The Ritz is too mournful. The Waldorf is like a railway terminal. So I always end by falling back on the Colony."

"There's nothing like those cozy little spots in Paris," said Lady Webber. "Maxim's, Larue's, and the rest. I remember quite vividly once years and years ago—when you were still just a baby, Laura dear—a small supper party given at the Tour d'Argent by the Duke of Spoleto. Pépé we always called him. I was sitting next to Caruso. Dear, dear, how that man could eat! Duse, who was already well on in years, was sitting at the other end of the table, next to D'Annunzio, or possibly the Duc de Guise, I forget which. The conversation was sparkling, as you may imagine. There's nothing I like better, my dear, than a group of brilliant intellects fencing amid the champagne bottles. Those days will never return, I'm afraid!"

There was always something opulent and faintly apocryphal about Lady Webber's anecdotes. But she had the courage to set them so remotely in the past that no one, if only out of vanity, ever dared to challenge her.

Alphonse, the waiter, appeared with the hot dishes, and set a small juicy steak in front of Pierre.

Basil Hume cleared his throat. "You've heard the latest reports? The Russians are going to ask for a separate peace next Tuesday. I always felt, myself, that they weren't to be trusted. At last they're showing themselves in their true colors. At any rate, we'll know where we stand. They're going to divide the booty with the Germans, of course. Turkey and Persia for Russia, Sweden and the Near East for Germany. After all, they both stand to profit, don't they? Considered logically, a Russo-German agreement was quite in the cards. So we needn't feel surprised."

"Where did you hear all this?" demanded Lady Webber skeptically.

"Don't ask questions like that, please, Estelle," said Basil, with fatigue. "My sources happen to be rather confidential."

Pierre glanced around the dining room. Every table was taken, and the place was filled with a continual tinkle and flutter. A rosy light was shining on tall bowls of gladioli, and on the quivering array of hats.

Suddenly Pierre caught his breath. At a small table in a corner he caught sight of Mrs. Mannering, and beside her a blond, extremely beautiful girl in a blue hat. At that moment Mrs. Mannering caught his eye. He felt himself blushing, and turned away; he hadn't seen her since their break many months ago. He felt a flicker of alertness pass through the room.

The waiter was rolling up the dessert table. Lady Webber pointed cautiously to the stewed plums; Pierre hesitated, and finally chose a Napoleon.

He glanced at a group of fashionable ladies at a near-by table. He recognized Mimi Suarez and Kitty de Montfleury. One was eating poached eggs, the other a small tomato salad. They had come to the Colony, it appeared, not entirely for the food.

The conversation at his own table had shifted from Russia to Germany. Lady Webber was having an argument with Basil Hume.

Lady Webber went out of her way to explain that her contempt for the Germans had nothing to do with the war, but sprang from a deep abhorrence of their culture. The worst she could say of the Germans was that Beethoven was a vulgarian, Goethe a pomposity, and the Cologne Cathedral an error of taste.

Basil Hume, on the other hand, took pride in emphasizing his political loathing of the Germans, but at the same time called attention to his cultural tolerance by frequent references to Rilke, who was fashionable that year, and an intimate mention of names like Bach, Bayreuth, and Baden-Baden.

Mrs. Carter kept her mouth discreetly closed; she never mentioned the Germans.

"Let's talk of something we all love," she finally murmured discreetly. "Let's talk of France, for a change."

"Did you know," said Baron Legué, "they've done a ballet of *Le Bourgeois Gentilhomme?* It occurs to me, why don't they do *Les Précieuses Ridicules?* It's so much more suitable, I can't help feeling!" His bloodshot eyes wandered mournfully across the room.

Pierre was hardly listening. He was longing to look again at Mrs. Mannering's table in the corner; finally he looked. She was chatting busily, and the woman beside her was smiling. With a thrill of pleasure Pierre saw that it was the girl who lived next door to him; the lovely blonde who played the piano and whose kitten he had rescued one day.

And the dining room suddenly grew bright and suggestive. The flicker of hats, the tinkle of glasses took on a new, dramatic quality.

Alphonse came to place a flame under the coffeepot on the wagon. After a moment he poured the coffee into small yellow cups.

"Have you been happy here, Estelle?" inquired Mrs. Carter casually. "In New York? I know you always used to abhor the place. . . . "

"Happy?" said Lady Webber. She placed two fingers against her cheek. "New York, my dear girl, isn't a place where one tries to be happy. It's a place for adventure, for glitter and glamour."

"And yet, oddly enough," said the baron, "nothing truly adventurous ever happens here. Only thrills. Diversions. Escapades. Even the love affairs, most of them, are just little explosions of neurasthenia. . . . "

"Quite," said Basil, with a touch of bitterness. "Love in New York is just a word. It's really greed, or loneliness, or boredom, or sheer stupidity, which passes for love here in New York."

"I couldn't agree more," sighed Mrs. Carter. "New York is a hothouse. Sometimes I feel I'm about to stifle. How I long for the Mediterranean!"

"What about you, Gaby dear?" said Lady Webber to the baroness. She smiled wickedly. "You've been here two years. Do you still feel we are barbarians?"

"Barbarians?" said the baroness quietly. She had been gazing intently across the room. "What a strange choice of words! I love barbarians, when it comes to that. I could do very well with a bit of barbarism in New York. A cowboy striding among these tables would be a reassuring sight. . . . "

"Why is it, then, you're unhappy, dear?" said Laura Carter gently.

The old baroness looked very tired. She shrugged her shoulders. "Am I unhappy? Well, I'm homesick. That is all. I've tried to build my own Paris here; I've failed. I feel lonely."

She rose from the table. "By the way," she said with a dry little smile, "don't forget you're coming on Christmas Eve, all of you, please! Can you come too, Monsieur Maillard? ... Splendid. Don't forget!" She cast a sharp, flickering look across the room. "I must remind Mrs. Potter," she murmured, with sudden preoccupation. "I see her sitting over there. She's coming too. She's such an exquisite creature. ..."

She made her way among the tables, smiled, nodded, and spoke briefly to the blond girl beside Mrs. Mannering.

The rest of Mrs. Carter's guests were rising from the table. As Pierre followed them through the restaurant he turned to look at Delia Potter; and at the same moment she also turned her head, their eyes met, and she smiled in recognition. Pierre felt his pulse quickening. The crowded room seemed mysteriously brightened, harmonized, subdued by the smiling loveliness of Delia.

48

DELIA stepped from the taxi and stood for a moment on the broad, crowded sidewalk of Fifth Avenue.

A sharp wintry sparkle filled the air. She felt a little feverish. What she felt, in particular, was that dizzy mingling of light and shadow which characterizes a fever; a sense of elation, of the glamour of existence, coupled with an ominous touch of vertigo. Everything looked brilliant and tempestuous. Yet she felt afraid; she felt something close to panic.

In one shopwindow there was a Christmas tree of cellophane covered with metallic blue stars. In another there was a Santa Claus of rough gray plaster, done in the manner of the late Picasso. In a cosmetic shop next door hung three tapering black angels, with hair of silver and an air of ennui, each holding onto a tall red candle.

She entered a large English leather shop on the corner. The place was a little less crowded than the others. She glanced about for a present for Quincy. She looked at shaving kits in pigskin, alligator belts, morocco frames, and black leather inkwells. Nothing seemed quite suitable for Quincy. Finally she bought a red morocco brief case.

She stepped into the street again and paused in front of a fruit shop. Huge glimmering pears, grapes enormous as plums, rosy peaches and nectarines, pineapples sprinkled with gold dust lay festively tucked in a nest of ferns.

She stepped into a charming little chocolate shop. Gilded rococo mirrors hung all around the walls, and a delicious scent of coffee and confectionery floated through the room. The red-haired girl behind the counter regarded her with a glazed look.

Delia felt exuberant; she stared at the long glass case. There were chocolates in the shape of acorns, seashells, cornucopias, violins.

"One of those boxes, please, with the little golden drawers you pull out," she said. "Yes. That's the kind! Twelve dollars for two pounds? Mercy! Well, I'll take it."

She crossed the street, and a feeling of boundless energy came over her, as though a door were opening and a miraculous flood of light were enfolding her. Something reminded her of her childhood, the wintry fragrance in the air, the atmosphere of Christmas shopping, and a more elusive quality—a kind of wild, rippling spaciousness, a feeling that she could rise and float through the air.

She entered a shop filled with exquisite glassware. She found herself surrounded by a transparent, aqueous light, which made her feel unreal and peculiarly carefree.

"What is happening to me?" she wondered. She felt inexplicably happy.

The glass was shining on every side, like a continual ripple of water. She felt she had entered a grotto under the sea. Everything looked quivering and expectant; the bowls seemed ready to burst into color.

She touched a bottle, vast and spherical, that shone like a pearl. It seemed to stir under her fingers, to grow live and iridescent. There were huge glass candlesticks, glass fruits, glass flowers, glass animals, all hovering under a deep sea-light.

She bought a large glass jar on which a naked diver was engraved—a pearl fisher plunging through a sea of bubbles.

A tall, rather homely girl in black was waiting on her; she was looking at Delia with an air of surprise.

"It's a lovely day!" whispered Delia. "You should go out for a walk, really!"

And such a wave of delight passed through her suddenly that she wanted to fling her arms around the girl, and kiss her on both checks.

But she restrained herself, and said in a dignified tone:

"Mr. Potter has an account here. Could you charge it? ... Quincy Potter. Sixty-third Street. ... Thank you very much."

She stepped through the door. She paused for a moment, blinking at the torrent of sunlight. A moment later, as she turned her head, she caught sight of Jonathan.

49

JONATHAN felt light and a little dizzy as he wandered down Fifth Avenue. His body seemed to be recovering from an acute electrical shock; still dazed, still groping, but filled with a new rush of energy. The brisk December air radiated a sense of expectation. Something fresh was in the air; life lay changed under the dazzling sea-light.

He glanced from side to side at the passing faces. They were bright and flourishing, all of them. His memory of the night before hung in his mind like a swampy haze. There was a momentary stab; a distant flicker; that was all.

An air of Christmas hung over the window displays. The fruits and flowers, the flasks of cologne and the shaving bowls, the lavender pajamas, the sporting prints—all looked unusually bright and festive.

As he crossed Fifty-sixth Street he heard his name called, in a woman's voice. He turned, and saw Delia.

A flash of delight passed through him. He ran up and took her by the hand; she smiled at him happily. "You're back again, Jonathan!"

She was wearing a charming blue hat and a coat of gray fur. She looked radiant, intensely alive. Her blue eyes shone with excitement; her features looked transfigured in the sunlight.

He said: "Delia! I hardly recognized you. . . . You've changed!"

She blushed and said, "Have I? Really?" She was wearing gloves of pearl gray, and two brightly wrapped parcels were dangling from her fingers. He had forgotten how lovely her voice was—how curiously gentle.

Then she said, "You're a soldier now. . . . It seems so odd of you, Jonathan!" She looked at him with a vague, sweet expression. "You haven't seen Quincy yet?"

"I only arrived two days ago. I was going to phone him."

"Do, Jonathan, please! He's in Washington most of the time now. But he'll be back on Friday. . . . He's become very important, you know. Something to do with the Belgian Congo. Dreadfully secret, of course!"

"You've been shopping?"

"Yes. A little." She glanced at her packages. "I had lunch with Pauline Mannering, and then I decided to look around a bit. . . . Isn't it a marvelous day?" A look of secret delight was hovering in her face.

"Well, it's lovely to see you back, my dear!"

Her eyes filled with sudden affection. She rose up on her toes, placed her hands lightly on his shoulders, and kissed his cheek. "Good-by, Cousin Jonathan. Then you'll phone us, won't you?" And she disappeared in the crowd.

He stood quietly in front of the shopwindow for several minutes. The interior of the shop was filled with glass. A cool, airy ripple flowed along the walls. He caught sight of a dark young face, sharpened by the sunlight, vividly reflected in the window.

It was a face vulnerable, hesitant, restless; a face lit by perpetual search. With a shock he saw that it was his own. He turned away again, and stood at Fifty-sixth Street, waiting for the traffic light to change.

He tried to remember Delia's glowing face, feature by feature. But he failed. Something essential, something vital, eluded him. He felt the brief imprint of her lips upon his cheek like a burn. He was conscious of a new rush of exploration in himself, a sense of wonder and incredulity.

The traffic light changed, he crossed the street, and continued down Fifth Avenue. But he no longer noticed the crowd. His mind was filled with the presence of Delia.

And as he continued to think about her, she grew curiously poignant and elusive. Her nature, he could feel, was the utter opposite of Lydia's. Her heart and mind were all in brightness; there were no shadows, no ambiguities. Yet this very fact, paradoxically, placed her under a threat of darkness which had its source, not in her own being, but in some unfathomable force outside her.

He hailed a taxi and rode down to Gramercy Park.

50

THE following morning Jonathan went to visit Pierre in his studio. Pierre was standing in front of his easel, wearing a dark blue shirt, open at the collar, and dark corduroy trousers. The wintry sun shone through the window on his bright, good-looking face. He hadn't yet shaved; his hair was longer and curlier than before. Small bright curls sprouted below his neck, above the open collar.

His face broke into a great, delighted smile when he saw Jonathan. He laid aside his palette and placed his arm around Jonathan's waist in a vigorous gust of affection.

"Well, well!" he cried. "The handsome young corporal is home again! You look wonderfully fit. ... " He ran his fingers affectionately through Jonathan's short hair. "Here! Take off your coat. It's disgustingly hot in here!"

A scent of oil paints rose from Pierre's shirt, and joined the scent of his young body. His exuberance shone upon Jonathan like a ray of sunlight.

"Well, what's been happening to you?" said Jonathan.

Pierre laughed carelessly. "Very little! I've been working. Harder than I've ever worked before. My things are really beginning to improve, at last!" There was a new quality in Pierre's voice—a deliberate resonance.

"Are you planning an exhibition?"

"It depends." Pierre shrugged his shoulders. "Not yet. Next fall perhaps. It all depends." There was a resolute look in his eyes. "And you?"

Jonathan laughed; to be in Pierre's presence seemed suddenly reassuring. "I? I've been working too, down in Texas. Making charts. Planning lavatories."

"Well," said Pierre, "I'm glad the Army is using you in a sensible way. ... I've never seen you look better!" He folded his arms, spread his legs apart, and peered at Jonathan playfully.

Jonathan glanced around the studio. Three or four unframed but completed canvases stood along the walls. Several others were still unfinished. The one still on the easel was the most ambitious. It was an imaginary landscape—a bridge across a torrent, with a tall, indistinct shape in the background; a tower, perhaps, or a lonely cliff. There was a crisp, sharp texture in the brush work, and the colors were extremely brilliant and daring.

"I like this," said Jonathan.

"You do?" said Pierre. He was obviously pleased. "I've been working on it for a fortnight."

"You've changed your style a bit, haven't you?"

"You think so? Possibly. ... I've stopped imitating. I've been discovering my own manner, as they say!"

There was something delightfully fresh and invigorating in Pierre's voice. Jonathan looked at him carefully; he had grown into a cool and determined, very magnetic young man.

"Well," said Pierre, with a teasing air, "I've been hearing romantic tales about you, Jonathan!"

Jonathan walked slowly toward the window; he stood with his back to Pierre. "Yes? Really?"

Pierre laughed. "Something about a fascinating ballerina. Who is madly in love with you. ... Is it true?"

Jonathan drew his finger along the pane; then he sat down on the window seat and stared at the floor.

"There's nothing in it," he muttered gloomily.

"Nothing at all?" said Pierre. "You're sure?"

"It's all over," said Jonathan. "Definitely."

Pierre shook his head with a skeptical air. "All over? No, no, Jonathan." He smiled mischievously. "Those things are never quite over. ... You'll see!"

"Who told you all this?" inquired Jonathan sullenly.

Pierre had picked up his palette and was dipping his brush in the paint. His face had resumed a serious, concentrated air. "Who told me? Some fellow I ran across the other day," he said vaguely. "Some dancer or other."

"A dancer?" said Jonathan. "What was his name?"

Pierre seemed a bit evasive. "Valdez. Something of the sort."

They stood silent for several minutes. Each was engrossed in his own thoughts.

Then Pierre said, in a changed voice: "You've seen your cousins lately? The Potters?"

Jonathan looked up sharply; he had just been thinking of Delia.

"Quincy's in Washington," he said casually. "I met Delia on the street yesterday, for a moment or two."

Pierre glanced at him swiftly. "You did? Was she ... " He hesitated. "Was she wearing a blue hat?"

"Blue hat?" said Jonathan cautiously. "Yes. I think so. Why?"

"I saw her lunching in a restaurant. Sitting with your aunt, Mrs. Mannering." Pierre's voice was uneasily ironical. Then he added calmly: "She's the most beautiful woman I've seen in New York."

"You think so?" said Jonathan. And for some unaccountable reason he began to feel disturbed, embarrassed, and almost hostile toward Pierre.

51

JONATHAN left Pierre's studio shortly before one, and met his mother for lunch down at Gramercy Park. He returned to his hotel at three, and found that Lydia had called. She had left a message: "Meet Miss Ivanova at the Russian Café at six o'clock. Urgent."

He lay down on his bed to rest; he felt suddenly exhausted. He fell fast asleep and when he awoke, the sky outside was rapidly darkening.

He turned on the light and glanced at his watch: it was halfpast five.

For several minutes he sat on his bed, with his chin on his hand, irresolute. He felt that an insidious little challenge had been offered him; an invitation to continue the dance, to prolong the sterile, tantalizing pattern.

He rose, with a vague feeling of curiosity and obligation, put on his coat, and made his way toward Fifty-seventh Street.

The front bar in the Russian Café was almost empty. It was exactly six o'clock. He sat down on a semicircular banquette and ordered a martini.

Through the glass door he could see the wintry weather outside. The air was dark purple and a cold wind was blowing; a scattering of snowflakes was racing, almost horizontally, down the street.

The minutes passed. Now and then the door opened and a newcomer, sprinkled with flakes, would enter in a gust of wind. It was almost half-past six when the door was flung open, with a mingling of merry voices, and five or six young people with bare heads rushed into the bar.

They were ballet dancers, all of them. Jonathan instantly recognized Sheila Snow and Valdez, and behind them Dimitroff and a dark-eyed, slightly older woman who he thought might be Simonova. Sevastopoulos, a young choreographer, entered a moment later, arm in arm with a handsome Jewish girl, Janet Bloom.

They all seemed to recognize Jonathan, and greeted him cheerfully. Valdez and Sheila stopped at his table.

"Well, I see you've become a brigadier general," said Valdez, peering at Jonathan's uniform. "Have they asked your advice about that big invasion?"

"Oh yes," said Jonathan wearily. "I'm designing a tunnel under the Channel." He felt a wave of irritation, and looked instinctively toward the door.

"You're waiting for Lydia, as usual?" inquired Valdez. His strong brown face looked weary and dissipated, and his manner had grown noticeably effeminate.

"She was frightfully upset yesterday," said Sheila, "about something or other." She gazed earnestly at Jonathan with her gentle, stupid eyes.

Valdez seemed to be enjoying some private joke. "Well, don't be too cruel to her!" he said, as they wandered off. "Don't hurt her! She's a very sensitive creature...." He cast a playful smile at Jonathan.

Jonathan felt that he was being slowly drawn back into a treacherous current. He felt a sudden violent distaste for the atmosphere around him. He looked at his watch a third time, and decided to wait no longer. He beckoned to the waiter.

At that moment the door opened again, and Lydia entered the bar.

She walked straight to Jonathan's table, cast off her coat, and sat down beside him. She was wearing her little astrakhan cap with the silver medal. Small flakes of snow were melting on her face and clinging to her eyebrows. There were faint shadows under her eyes.

She sighed. "What sickening weather!"

"You're forty minutes late," said Jonathan, in a quiet tone.

She stared at him defiantly. "Oh, Jonathan, really ... It's hard enough to slave all day for that damned company, without being criticized! I simply can't help it if I'm late. You'll have to be patient, that's all. ... Waiter, please! A martini."

"I was just about to leave," murmured Jonathan, "when you walked through the door."

She turned and looked at him with amazed and sulky eyes. "You were! Well ... " She drew a deep breath. "What on earth has gotten into you, Jonathan? Here we've been separated for ages, and you seem absolutely callous about it all. ... " She drew a small green handkerchief from her bag and wiped the drops from her face; then she opened her vanity case and began to powder her nose and forehead.

"Please, dear," she murmured wearily. "Light a cigarette for me, will you?"

Jonathan drew out a cigarette, lit it, and passed it to her without a word.

She glanced at him suspiciously. "Well? Aren't you glad to see me?"

"Was there," said Jonathan, a little hoarsely, "something urgent you wanted to see me about?"

"Urgent?" Lydia shrugged her shoulders. A note of caution crept into her voice. "Oh, I just wanted to see you. ... "

"Well, I hope," said Jonathan, in measured tones, "that you had a good night's sleep the other night."

She cast a sharp little look at him. Her drink arrived at that moment. She took a sip, puffed at her cigarette, and then gave him a tender smile.

"It was silly of me, wasn't it?" she said dreamily. "I felt too rude for words, leaving you like that; and I felt dreadfully about it afterward. But really, darling, I simply couldn't keep my eyes open another minute. ... You must remember, Jonathan, that a ballet dancer's life is hard, solid labor from morning till night!" Her hand crept under the table and lit gently on Jonathan's knee. She whispered: "You've forgiven me, darling?"

He nodded his head. "Of course," he said lightly. "After all, there wasn't really anything to forgive. Was there?" And, for the first time since he had known her, he stared at her with a cold, hard sarcasm.

She lowered her eyes immediately; her lips began to tremble.

But she remained silent. For several minutes they sat side by side, smoking their cigarettes, looking vaguely across the room.

Jonathan felt a little surprised at his own self-possession. He felt no trace of passion, no regret, no curiosity; nothing except a sense of relief, and an obscure element of pity.

Suddenly she turned and stared at him with a look he had never seen before: a feverish mingling of defiance, bitterness, exhaustion, and something that bordered on despair.

"Listen, Jonathan!" she said in a low, furious voice. "I don't care what you think! You can think anything you wish! I am sick of pretending. I am sick of your silly, adolescent world—your ridiculous background of Mannerings and Sillimans and the rest. I am sick of being a hypocrite! ... Listen, Jonathan. I've done things that would make your hair stand on end. You'd never touch me again if I told you all there is to tell. Very well. You can take it or leave it. ... I'd just as soon never see you again. Your world isn't my world. My world may be dirty, but it's alive. Yours is neat and prim, but it's dead!" Her eyes flashed wildly, and her voice was growing hysterical. "It's no use! We don't fit together! We'll never fit together! Why not face it? ... You're sweet and good, Jonathan, but oh God, you bore me!" She killed her cigarette. She closed her eyes for a moment. He thought she was about to burst into tears; but she controlled herself.

She seized her coat from the banquette, rose, and hurried from the bar without another word.

52

NEW YORK society, in the course of the war, had experienced certain perceptible changes. For one thing, fashionable ladies found it necessary to dress more austerely. Some of them, under one pretext or another, put on a well-tailored uniform. Others dressed with a new, becoming sobriety—a dark suit, a simple turban—suitable to their patriotic activities and the news from the battle front. Even places like the Colony, the Ritz, and Lady Temperly's salon were visibly affected. One could hardly go to these spots without meeting someone who had just returned from Cairo, or the Solomons. Certain figures, such as Basil Hume and Horace Hayden, grew overnight into experts on military strategy and the subtleties of international diplomacy. They would utter gloomy, Cassandra-like prophecies; sinister developments, they murmured, could shortly be expected in Madrid, Moscow, Montevideo.

Not that there weren't certain definite sacrifices involved. Mrs. Carter, for example, was forced to sell her Rolls. Mrs. Van Twillingen gave up her house in Newport, "to help pay the taxes." Mrs. Clyde moved to a slightly smaller apartment, and cut the number of servants from eight to four. Wilfred Silliman gallantly offered his talents to the Office of Strategic Services. Lady Webber gave up her usual winter trip to Palm Beach.

The idea gained ground that certain hotels were infested with spies, who were paid to listen in on Lady Temperly's and Baroness Landau's telephone conversations. There were continual calls and telegrams, in British circles, full of the latest news from "Duff," or "Brendan," or even "Winston." In certain other groups there were moments of unmistakable strain, public feeling against the Franco and Pétain regimes having reached a new emphasis; there was a growing coolness between the ladies who still invited the attaches from Vichy and Madrid, and those who virtuously refused to do so. It was whispered that a "dangerous Fascist element" had filtered into Mrs. Clyde's cocktail parties. Mrs. Carter was reported to have placed the Vichy Ambassador on her right at a big dinner. Everyone, of course, recalled that Lady Webber had once entertained Ribbentrop in her house in London. And there were some who maliciously asserted that the Countess de Montfleury, who came from Minneapolis, had once spent a week end in Goering's hunting lodge in Pomerania.

Foreigners had been growing more and more unpopular, and for a variety of reasons. Because of their self-indulgence, at a time when their own lands were in distress. Because of their arrogance, in a land where pride is not tolerated. Because of their special kind of European avarice, which recoiled from overtipping. Because of their profusion, which made all forms of life more cumbersome and costly. Because of a new kind of American puritanism, born under the stress of war, and tinged, perhaps, with a sense of guilt. But above all because they were foreigners, with manners and principles at variance with what Americans were used to, trusted, and understood. Everything they did seemed vaguely distasteful—their way of kissing the ladies' hands, their way of bickering about prices, their way of arguing with the waiters, their interminable complaints in the shops, their shrill, ecstatic voices, their overtailored clothes, their sleek, pomaded hair, the flowers in their buttonholes, their suavity, their smells, their excitability, their self-pity.

The refugees themselves, in the meanwhile, had fallen into well-defined groups. Some of these circles attained a certain vogue, even a certain power. There was, for instance, the group surrounding Lady Temperly. These were chiefly writers, composers, and titled Englishmen with a leaning to the arts; though noticeably on the genteel, even the octogenarian, side; and, of course, quite inaccessible to the vulgar touch of the society columns.

The Countess Pirelli's circle, generally speaking, was a little more in the public eye. It included figures from the world of the opera, the ballet, the art galleries, the welfare societies. Whenever a new project was launched to raise money for the Poles, or the Dutch, or the Greeks, Countess Pirelli could be depended on to serve on the committee and help, if necessary, in arranging a smart little luncheon at Sherry's.

But it was in the Baroness Landau's drawing room that the most illustrious visitors were to be found. It was here that the diplomats gathered, the journalists, the generals, and even a stray anthropologist or mathematician. Art and music were only infrequently mentioned. Instead, people discussed the future of Europe, Africa, and Asia with an authoritative air, and in alarming tones.

These three circles were contiguous, so to speak, and interpenetrated. There were figures who periodically drifted from one circle to another. The Countess Pirelli sometimes had a Latin-American diplomat or two to lunch. The Baroness Landau occasionally invited a well-known Spanish painter for cocktails. Lady

Temperly once went so far as to have the ballet dancer, Kirillova, for tea.

All three of these circles strove, in their way, for a kind of dignity and power. All three were generally thought to be bright, influential, and distinguished. All three were, in fact, as insubstantial as a nomad's tent, and as anachronistic.

53

THE Baroness Landau was waiting for her guests. She walked slowly from one end of the long, dark drawing room to the other.

It was, she reflected, her thirty-fourth Christmas ball. The previous thirty-three had been held in her chateau in the forest of Compiègne. She was accustomed to hearing her kitchens and pantries full of bustle for a fortnight, and to seeing the trees in her park weighed down with snow. She was also used to providing her guests with bowls of Russian caviar, chocolate pastilles from Vienna, almond cakes from Basel, Sicilian figs, and a band of musicians from the neighboring village, who played old waltzes and French country dances.

This time, instead of seeing her guests arrive in sleighs and coaches, they would appear in the elevator. The food would be served by a caterer on Madison Avenue; and the music would be supplied by a quartet from Fifty-second Street. But she had done her best. She had been fortunate enough to find three especially fine geese, ten bottles of Veuve Clicquot 1934, and some jars of real pâté de foie gras with truffles.

She was a tall, narrow woman, intensely old, white as wax, with deep-set eyes of a cold sea green. Her nose was thin and aquiline, her chin sharp and ruthless, and her fingers were phenomenally long. Once, as a girl, she must have been ugly. But her intelligence and strength of will had accumulated, at last, a kind of beauty. Not the beauty of a woman; rather the beauty of a carving in stone, or metal.

Everything about her—voice, manner, glance—was highly polished but on the brink of collapse. Everything trembled a little; the intensity was giving out. Her whole person, it seemed, had been sprinkled with a fine silver powder.

The guests had been invited for eight-thirty. It was now twenty-five past; and the bell had not yet rung. Taxis, she reflected, were hard to get. Punctuality was a lost art. The last guests would be sure not to arrive before nine.

And suddenly she realized that she wished them not to come at all. Five minutes remained; the prospect of the Christmas guests appalled her. For the first time she wanted, desperately, to spend the night alone. A sense of devouring futility possessed her. She felt, for a moment, on the verge of hysteria: she thought of locking herself in her bedroom, and pretending sudden illness.

She took a deep breath, and wandered back through the drawing room.

She halted at the entrance to the dining room. Gravely she surveyed the sparkling table. It was drawn out, leaf by leaf, to its rare, most festive length. There were thirty-three chairs, and ninety-nine glasses. One guest, the Chilean Ambassadress, had dropped out at the last moment. Twelve silver candlesticks, fluted like Ionic columns, bearing sixty white candles, still unlit, towered above the plates. Six silver pheasants were strolling through a heap of dark red roses.

She turned back into the drawing room; she paused as she entered. Here too the lights were not yet lit. A thin ray from the hallway sprang across the enormous Aubusson. The room seemed petrified and hushed in expectation of the guests. In the distance she heard the footmen tinkling among the cutlery and platters.

The furniture and hangings were lost in shadow, only here and there shone a fragile high light—the gilt of a frame, the glint of a statuette. The chairs were Empire and exquisite; and there was a fine Beauvais armchair depicting the legend of Leda and the swan. A radiant Fantin-Latour hung over the mantel. On one side of it hung a tiny Boudin, on the other a Fragonard water color. A Cousinet nymph and satyr stood on the long walnut table. Crimson rows of La Fontaine and Madame de Sévigné, stamped with a great baronial crest, stood in a niche of shelves in the corner.

She walked slowly to the window, drew aside the curtain, and sat down on the sill. A round marble-top table with gilt legs stood beside her. On it lay a gold-tooled *Almanach de Gotha,* a cigarette tray of red glass, and a bronze statue of Eros.

Her hand moved across the marble and came to rest on the naked boy; she ran her finger tips along his arms and throat. She touched lightly the crisp, unyielding curls on his head. A chill sprang through her hands, and a tremor ran toward her shoulder. She sighed; she looked at the clock. It was eight thirty-five.

And at that moment the doorbell rang, lights flooded the room, and two footmen appeared in the hallway. The first guests had arrived.

54

THE baroness received them with her customary curt, twinkling delicacy.

"My dear Estelle—you look a child tonight, a mere child!
Where is young Cecil these days—in Havana, you say? Naval
attache? Well, well ... Ah, here is General Edgerton. How distinguished you look tonight, my dear General! Let me introduce
you to Lady Webber.... Merry Christmas, Commander Forbes.
Merry Christmas, my dear Marquis.... Charlotte, I'm charmed
to see you; you look like an angel, a fallen angel! Here, Señor
d'Alvarez, do please have one of these odd American cocktails—
they're made of rum and sherry—or is it gin? I never know...."

The footmen, wearing snow-white gloves, passed among the
guests with trays of cocktails and small, leafy pastries filled with
caviar and anchovies.

Pierre found himself standing between Lady Brooke and
Señor Estrella. He glanced nervously over the gathering. Delia
Potter, he noticed, had not yet arrived.

"I've just returned from Mexico," Señor Estrella was saying,
with a sigh. "Interesting place. But overrated."

"Oh," said Lady Brooke brightly, "did you visit Acapulco?"

Señor Estrella nodded wearily. "Dreadful spot. Not to be
compared with the Riviera."

"Ah," said Lady Brooke sadly. "Don't talk to me of the Riviera. No place in the world can touch the Riviera."

"Quite," nodded Señor Estrella. "Cannes. Antibes. Juan-les-Pins. It's no use looking for that kind of atmosphere in the New World!"

"And don't forget Monte Carlo," said Lady Brooke. "I've spent some of my happiest days in Monte Carlo. It has such a Ruritanian atmosphere, don't you agree?"

"Then of course," said Señor Estrella, "there are other spots too, for the connoisseur. Saint-Tropez has its *vie de bohème*. Villefranche has some specialties of its own. Even Toulon, you know, is not without flavor. And as for Nice ... "

Pierre turned his head. A strange suspense filled his being. He had not yet seen Delia; but he realized, quite suddenly, that she had arrived. He knew that she was standing there, on the right, near the window.

And then he caught sight of her. She was standing near the door. She had just arrived, almost half an hour late, and was smiling apologetically at her hostess, and then walked swiftly toward the center of the room.

She was wearing a long dress of very pale satin, and a diamond in each ear. She looked flushed and glowing. Pierre was filled with astonishment. She looked, at first sight, so much taller and more mature; so altogether different from what he recalled. And then, as he looked a second time, he saw that she was after all the same—it was only something in the attitude, in the expression, that had changed. She greeted the baroness, murmured something with a quick decisive gesture of the hand, and serenely joined the other guests. She moved with the mysterious self-assurance, the God-given poise of the truly beautiful.

She turned her head and their eyes met. There was no change in her expression. He continued to look at her, and she returned his gaze calmly, with a kind of childlike placidity. Then she turned and continued to speak to the naval officer beside her.

At that moment dinner was announced. The doors of the dining room were opened. The guests swept slowly in, an array of tails and silks and discriminating murmurs. Each male guest had been given, in the European manner, a folded card with a plan of the table and the name of his partner on the right. Pierre's partner, he saw, was the Princess Kubinsky. He took her white swollen arm and led her to the table. The sixty candles shone like a sea of ripples over the glasses, the roses, and the six silver pheasants.

55

THE dinner was exquisite. The turtle soup was flawless; the amontillado was superb. There was filet of sole with a light cucumber salad. The goose was crisp and tender, consummately seasoned, and not too fat. There were fine, thick stalks of asparagus with hollandaise sauce. The dessert was an overpowering meringue, two feet high, with a star of gilded marzipan poised on the summit.

Princess Kubinsky, who sat on Pierre's right, leaned over and murmured:

"I'm a great believer in traditions, you know. If we ever stop celebrating Christmas, well then, we might as well abandon the world to chaos. . . . Mind you, not that we always need to have champagne as delicious as this!" She took a sip. "You were born in Paris?"

Pierre nodded. "Yes. In a small gray house with green shutters. I still remember it."

"Ah," said the princess approvingly. "In the Faubourg St.-Germain, I take it."

"In a far less fashionable district, I'm afraid," murmured Pierre.

"Ah," sighed the princess forgivingly. "Still, Paris is Paris. . . . It's my spiritual home!"

Princess Kubinsky had a coarse, disagreeable face, with a heavy jaw and a large thick mouth. Her nose was broad and pink, and there was a faint alcoholic swelling under her eyes. She was dressed in olive-green taffeta with rows of black ribbons; the powder clung to her cheeks in large, perfunctory patches. There was not a trace of distinction in her appearance. Yet, the moment she spoke, this impression was transformed; she had a fine, low, disciplined voice, which suggested endless vistas of past experience.

But Pierre hardly heard what she was saying. His eyes kept wandering down the table. Far below, between a Chinese and a tall, cadaverous Spaniard, shone Delia's lovely profile. It hung suspended beneath the flickering row of candles like a medallion from a chain. He kept waiting for her to look in his direction. But she was listening to Mr. Chang; she smiled serenely, nodded, and lowered her eyes.

"I'm a Russian by birth, of course," the princess was remarking, stirring the froth in her champagne; "but culturally I feel a deep kinship for France. ... I am sure I must have lived there long, long ago. In some previous incarnation. In the age of Louis Quatorze, perhaps. I might have been Molière, I can't help suspecting. Whenever I read him I find such a—how shall I put it?—such a sense of spiritual identification. ... "

She looked past Pierre and smiled; a faintly lurid smile. It occurred to him that she might have been playing a game with him.

"But please," she said, as an afterthought, "don't think I am ashamed of being Russian. As a matter of fact, I am very proud of being Russian! Oh, not because of all these heroic battles and so on. I'm not childish enough at my age, to be impressed by that sort of thing. ... No, I mean"—and she fixed her crafty eyes on Pierre—"the Russian soul. You needn't smile like that, my boy. ... The Russians have the pure, elemental human stature.

That's why no one really understands them nowadays. They are creatures of instinct. They don't believe in reason, like the French. They don't believe in cricket, like the English. Perhaps they don't quite believe in democracy, like the Americans. ... Still, my dear, what other nation could have produced a Tolstoy?"

Suddenly she touched his hand, with a smile, and whispered softly: "Yes. I quite agree. She is breath-taking."

Pierre was startled. "You were saying ... ?"

"She is magnificent. I thoroughly agree with you."

"You mean ... " said Pierre, and paused.

"I mean, my dear boy, the young lady at whom you've been staring." The princess shot a hard, ironical look at Pierre, raised her champagne glass, and turned to the Norwegian chargé d'affaires on her right.

The hostess rose at this moment; dinner was over.

"Will the gentlemen join us ... rather soon?" She looked anxiously at the little ambassador who sat beside her. "We shall all be having our coffee together in the drawing room!"

56

THE conversation over the coffee cups began harmlessly enough. Pierre was sitting in a group with Baron Legué, Lady Webber, Madame Nikolaides, and several others. They were discussing the Germans: a matter on which everyone agreed.

He kept glancing at Delia, who was sitting at the other end of the room, sipping her coffee, between Commander Forbes and the old Marquis del Puente. Her hand was resting on a marble table, lightly touching a small statuette of bronze. A crystal chandelier hung directly above her, and washed her head in a silky brilliance.

As he watched, she slowly raised her hand and placed it against her throat, with the fingers extended. And he had, at that moment, an impression of extreme fragility in her; of a tragic delicacy in her loveliness, like that of a flower transplanted to an arid soil.

"Yes," Lady Webber was saying, "I remember once, some years ago, I was giving a small dinner party in my yacht off Cannes—I think I had the King of Sweden that time; he's a perfect lamb, by the way. He always insisted on calling me '*ma chère cousine*'—no one ever knew why. Well, in any case, I remember saying to Winston, 'Look here, Winston, my dear, you know as well as I what these Teutonic monsters are up to. Another three years and they'll be at our throats. ...' He seemed impressed by what I said; I must say that for him. Though of course I'm just an ordinary person, really quite an ignoramus, with no pretensions except to just a teeny weeny bit of common sense. ... But mind you, *entre nous,* these famous statesmen often know less than you or I. ... "

"That's perfectly true," Señor Estrella chimed in. "Take the case of the Maginot Line, for example. Why, it was common gossip among my friends that it wouldn't hold a week if the Germans attacked; we all knew they could just go around the end of it, if they chose. And lo and behold, that's exactly what happened. But did it occur to the experts, the generals and so on?"

"Scratch a general and you'll find, generally speaking, a nitwit," said Madame de Klopf brightly. "No offense to you, General Edgerton," she added quickly, with a beguiling smile.

"Of course," said Basil Hume, sitting up very straight, "if it hadn't been for France, the war would be over now. Let's face it. It was France and France alone that yielded to the barbarians." He put down his brandy glass with an air of finality.

"What?" cried Baron Legué, in a rage. "France yielded? You must be insane! A few little monkeys yielded, if you please. The rest of France suffered and fought, and fought bitterly!" He was panting with indignation.

"But really, my dear Baron, all these sufferings of France," said Madame de Klopf, rather cynically. "You must admit they're a trifle exaggerated. It was poor little Holland, the symbol of order, which was slashed, bombed, starved, flooded, and stripped of her empire. Don't talk to me about France, please!"

"I am weary," cried Madame Nikolaides, who was sitting beside Pierre, "of hearing lamentations about these fatty empires brought to their knees. I lived in a country which drew its sustenance from the rocks and the sea. We were hard, we were brave, but we had hardly a gun to fight with. And now what do we get? Nothing but ingratitude!"

"Ah," murmured Mr. Chang, in a bright, cultivated chirp. "You Occidentals think you have been suffering. But wait till you have seen the invader's knife at your throat for a decade or more! Patience, infinite patience ... "

"The Chinese," said Lady Brooke frostily, "have no monopoly on patience, Mr. Chang."

"Well," said Wilfred Silliman gallantly, "I absolutely adore England, myself. But what would have become of all that gorgeous pluck and patience, frankly, if America hadn't come to the rescue ... "

But before he could finish several voices rose in an indignant chorus. Basil Hume, Princess Kubinsky, and Baron Legué all began to speak at once.

"Please, please," cried the hostess softly, her finger trembling. "This is Christmas Eve!"

The guests grew silent. "And now," observed the baroness, "I have a small surprise for you." She glanced at the clock; she nodded. "It's almost midnight," she sighed. And she rang a small glass bell.

A footman appeared: the doors of the library swung open. A Christmas tree was revealed, candles burning, tinsel glittering. Peppermint canes and chocolate reindeer, waxen angels and marzipan doves, golden pineapples and silver trumpets, all dangled brightly from the boughs. The little quartet in the corner began to play "Silent Night." One by one, a little shyly, the guests began to sing. Madame de Klopf looked sentimental; Princess Kubinsky wiped away a tear. Wilfred Silliman produced a discreet little smile. Even Basil Hume allowed his features to grow mild and forgiving.

Punch was served from an oblong bowl, which glowed in the candlelight like a colossal ruby. The chairs were cleared away and the lights were lowered, and the smiling musicians started in on a waltz. The dancing began by the light of the Christmas tree.

At last Pierre saw his opportunity. He walked across the room with a beating heart. Delia was standing next to General Edgerton, earnestly listening with her punch glass in her hand.

She turned her head and saw Pierre; a strange expression appeared in her eyes—a spark, he thought, almost of terror. But then she blushed and smiled; and her face was flooded with delight.

57

DELIA looked so extraordinarily lovely as she stood there, in her flowing satin gown and her sparkle of diamonds, that Pierre stood struck with a kind of incredulity; for a moment he was unable to speak.

Then he said: "Will you dance with me, Mrs. Potter?"

She glanced apologetically at General Edgerton. "Do forgive me," she whispered, and nodded softly to Pierre. He placed his arm around her, and they began to move across the floor; he felt her body floating ever so lightly beside him.

For several minutes they did not speak. The great drawing room was dim, only the candles shone with a ceremonious radiance. The music began to sound wonderfully cool and Mozartian. The whole room seemed to sing, to burst into flower.

Then Pierre said: "You did remember me, then?"

Delia nodded. "Oh, surely! I remembered you. But I was afraid ... " She paused.

"You were afraid?" whispered Pierre.

"Ah, nothing," she said, with a smile. "I never thought, you know, that you'd recognize me! It's been so long ... "

"Yes," said Pierre, overcome with joy; "it's been so very long!"

Her slender satin body was hovering in his arm, light as a feather. A wandering light played in her hair, and she seemed so altogether magical that Pierre half expected her to rise, like a mist, and vanish from his arms.

They danced through the twilit room, and to Pierre it seemed they were utterly alone. A waltz began. There was a blossoming swirl of silk and taffeta. Pierre felt himself gliding effortlessly on and on, as though borne on a tropical tide.

He caught sight of himself in a mirror, with Delia in his arms. They turned, her dress flashed brightly, and the image vanished; but he had noticed his own face, bright and handsome, beside hers. And a quick, proud sense of possession passed through him.

They turned at the end of the room. He glanced across the corridor; a small dark room lay beyond, with a single window opening on the night.

"Come," he whispered. "Let's go and look at the stars!"

He drew her urgently across the hall. They entered the deserted music room, and wandered across to the great bow window. There was no moon but the stars were brilliant and innumerable. Their light fell on the piano, on the leopard skin beside it, on the cello in the corner, on the untidy litter of scores. He could read the name of Scarlatti on one of the albums.

Below them lay the park and the curve of the skating pond, abnormally bright for a moonless night. The ice lay black as jet, but the wavering edge of the shore shone like a fine steel ribbon. The lamps in the park were extinguished, only a velvety blue light shone from the hut at the edge of the pond.

"Christmas!" said Pierre. "One can feel it in the air!"

"Yes," said Delia joyfully. "One can see it in the sky, can't one!"

Her dress of pink satin shone with a hidden vitality; the fabric seemed suddenly fragrant, alert. He placed his hand upon hers, ever so lightly. His voice was a burning whisper. "You are lovely! Lovelier than anyone I've ever seen!"

Delia glanced at him with a quick, dissolving look. She drew her hand from his. "Please," she said softly, "it's very late, isn't it? I must be going, I'm afraid. ... "

She turned and was gone. Pierre saw her re-enter the drawing room and disappear among the guests. Through the open door at the end of the hallway he could see the dancers moving. The music sounded faint, but he could hear, with peculiar clarity, the ceaseless rustle of dancing feet. He caught sight of Commander Forbes, in his splendid uniform, sailing past with the Countess Loewenstierna, who was strangled with pearls. He saw Madame Chang, in a sheath of white lamé, smiling graciously at young Señor d'Alvarez; and then a gray mothlike couple floated by— Lady Webber in the arms of Baron Legué.

He felt as though time had been caught on the wing, miraculously transfixed; as though the present moment, in all its transparency, would remain forever unanswered and unfulfilled. In its very suspense, as in a drop about to fall, there was a portent of disorder: a microscopical reflection of tragedy. He stood motionless by the window, agitated and puzzled. He scarcely knew what it was he really felt.

He looked again through the window. Two young skaters had appeared on the ice. They moved dimly across the jet-black mirror of the lake. Slowly the edge of the shore expanded, then fluctuated, vanished. The trees grew thick and towering. He heard the tinkle of a sleigh in the distance, and caught sight of the tiny pavilion on the shore; the firelight was shining on the ruddy faces. He heard once again the laughing voices and the smooth, delightful hiss of the skates. He saw old Marie-Jeanne pouring the chocolate, and old Gaston beating his mittens, and the racing lovers with their floating scarves. They smiled at him gently, and beckoned to him through the darkness. He felt a stab of horror; they were the shapes of the dead.

He turned from the window, crossed the hall, and re-entered the drawing room.

The guests were beginning to leave, in groups of two or three. Princess Kubinsky was kissing the old baroness on both cheeks. "Merry Christmas, dear Gaby!" she cried effusively. "I hope we can all be as brave as you!" Wilfred Silliman and Lady Brooke were likewise departing. Lady Webber stood huddled in a heap of silvery furs.

Pierre looked around the room for Delia; but she was nowhere to be seen.

58

PIERRE spent the following evening with Baron Legué. The next day he lunched with Jonathan and visited a new exhibition of Renoirs. That evening he dined at Mrs. Bellamy Carter's. There he met Lady Webber again, who tapped him lightly on the arm and asked him to a gala performance at the opera, to be given for the benefit of the Russians on the following Friday. Pierre accepted eagerly, with that vague, restless sense of expectation which had haunted him for a week.

Friday arrived; he put on his dinner jacket, combed his hair, and with great care sprayed his handkerchief with cologne, and set forth for the Metropolitan.

The traffic was exceptionally heavy on Fortieth Street, and he stepped from his taxi at the corner of Seventh Avenue. He caught sight of a row of black limousines in front of the marquee, and of a startling array of furs and jewelry.

He paused in front of the florist's shop across the street. The roses and lilies shone through the frosted window, nestling in great basins of moss. A stocky young Italian was selecting an orchid for an elderly gentleman in a top hat. Both were smiling—perhaps at some casual innuendo. Something in the old man's face looked vaguely familiar. He paid the fellow, took his orchid, and left; just as he was about to cross the street he noticed Pierre. He looked at Pierre with sudden interest, in which there was an element of coquetry. Pierre felt a sudden spark of recognition pass between them. He blushed and nodded faintly. The old man replied with a coy little smile, then turned and hurried across the street.

Pierre entered the shop and selected a large white carnation. He slipped it into his lapel and crossed the street toward the opera.

He was just in time. Lady Webber had left his ticket with the doorman. He ran up the broad, red-carpeted stairway and hurried down the corridor to the left. He glanced at himself in the full-length mirror as he passed; he felt pleased with his healthy, well-groomed looks.

An elderly female usher opened the door of the box for him. The music had begun; they were playing the national anthem. Pierre hung his black coat and hat in the small crimson anteroom, then drew aside the curtain and stepped into the box.

The auditorium was dark, and he scarcely recognized the faces in the box. They had all been standing for the anthem. Now they sat down, and Lady Webber, who was sitting in front with Mrs. Clyde and the Countess Pirelli, turned and greeted Pierre with a silent smile. Only two chairs in the box were still empty. He sat down in one of them and looked around.

He was startled to see the elderly gentleman of the flower shop sitting beside him; and he suddenly realized that it was Wilfred Silliman, whom he had already met on several occasions. It was, perhaps, the top hat which had obscured his features. On Wilfred's right sat Baron Legué, dark with illness and exhaustion. Commander Forbes was sitting in the corner, almost invisible.

There was a moment's silence, as the conductor paused to wipe his glasses. At that same moment the door to the box again was opened, and Pierre heard a whisper of apology and a rustle of taffeta. He turned; it was Delia.

She stepped discreetly past the men toward the empty chair, and sat down without a word, and without glancing at Pierre.

The curtain rose. It was the opening scene of *Das Rhein gold.* The watery light from the stage was reflected on the golden tier of boxes; the faces of the audience looked faintly phosphorescent.

The music flowed on. The Rhine maidens hurled their voices into an orgiastic shout of triumph. Then the music grew softer. The motive of the renunciation of love emerged. Pierre kept glancing in Delia's direction; but she did not seem aware of him, and kept her eyes upon the stage with a mild, attentive smile.

Lady Webber sat motionless, with a glazed look, like a doll. The Countess Pirelli looked reflective and austere, while Mrs. Clyde's face was shining with an eager concentration. Pierre could see the three elderly heads in a silhouetted row, one white, one gray, one henna, and all three with brilliantly elaborate coiffures.

The scene ended, the curtain fell, and the lights went on in the auditorium.

59

THE three old ladies turned around in their seats. They began to smile and nod to their acquaintances in the neighboring boxes.

"Well," said Countess Pirelli, with a sigh. "A bit disappointing, don't you think?"

"It was well conducted, at any rate," said Mrs. Clyde. "Holzknecht has been surprisingly good this year."

"I can't bear Wagner," said Lady Webber flatly. "Conducted well or conducted badly. It's all the same to me." She was wearing, Pierre noticed, a pale blue orchid.

"What is the next thing on the program?" inquired Baron Legué, tapping Lady Webber on the shoulder with his pince-nez.

"A scene from *Don Giovanni,* I suspect," said Lady Webber. "With Mazetti conducting. It's a regular hodgepodge, this gala affair. I hope the Russians enjoy it, at least." She glared angrily at one of the center boxes, where the Russian Ambassador was sitting with his wife and a group of attaches.

Delia turned and nodded politely to the ladies, then to the three elderly gentlemen, and then, very casually, to Pierre. She looked, it seemed to Pierre, entirely different tonight; she was wearing a dress of plum-colored taffeta, and there was a richer, deeper color in her face. She drew her fingers lightly along her throat, in a gesture he had noticed once before, and frowned a little as she read the program.

Wilfred had risen and left the box for the intermission, accompanied by Commander Forbes.

"What is wrong with Wilfred these days?" whispered the Countess Pirelli, with a look of concern. "He looks a wee bit gloomy."

"Poor Wilfred," said Lady Webber. "He's having a *crise du coeur.* About that Brattlebury woman. You remember her, don't you? He brought her once for cocktails. She's gone off with some perfectly horrible Venezuelan. He's inconsolable, of course. Wilfred takes such things to heart; he's a man of feeling. He puts women on a pedestal...."

"Oh, there's Susan Wilmerding," remarked Mrs. Clyde. "Do you see her? Over there in Laura Carter's box."

A look of repugnance passed over Lady Webber's features. "So Susan's at large again, is she?"

"I lunched with her yesterday," observed Mrs. Clyde.

"She's a perfect cow," said Lady Webber crisply.

Mrs. Clyde raised her opera glasses to her eyes. "Now really, Estelle," she murmured reproachfully, "you can't truthfully say that Susan Wilmerding is a cow."

"Did I say cow?" snapped Lady Webber. "Pardon me. I meant hippopotamus. I can't help it, but that's what she is. It's no fault of mine. You can imagine my amazement, my dear," she went on ruthlessly, "when I went down to Durand-Ruel's the other day and saw, in front of an especially fine little Renoir, this female hippopotamus, wearing, of course, long black gloves and a pink hat with an aigrette. I finally realized it was none other than Susan Wilmerding. She must have seen my look of surprise. She turned her back on me without a word. *Alors, c'est épatant, vous savez. ...* " She flicked a handkerchief from her bag, gave it a contemptuous whirl, and placed it to her nostrils.

"Poor Susan means well," remarked Mrs. Clyde sadly. "It's just that she lives in the past. Like all the Wilmerdings."

The spectators had returned to their seats, and the lights were lowered. Pierre was leaning over, about to speak to Delia, when Mazetti, the new conductor, flicked his baton.

The curtain rose on a troop of peasants moving merrily across the stage. Don Giovanni appeared, and presently began to sing his great song to Zerlina: *"Là ci darem la mano!"* It was Pinza; he was in exceptionally brilliant form.

Pierre had his eyes fixed on Delia. She was listening carefully, as a child does, with a gentle curiosity rather than with any real perception or sympathy. She was leaning forward, and her hair fell softly upon her fine white shoulders.

Donna Anna and Don Ottavio entered the stage, and the great quartet followed: *"Non ti fidar, o misera, di quel ribaldo cor";* and Donna Anna delivered her terrible, tragic recitative, ending with her mighty aria.

The audience applauded wildly, and after the curtain had fallen Lady Webber declared: "Well, I've never seen Mazetti in such form. He's absolutely perfect for Mozart. Come, Henrietta, let's stretch our legs."

The three old ladies, followed by Delia, rose and stepped into the corridor. They had already disappeared around the curve when Wilfred and Pierre stepped from the box.

Wilfred said in a portentous whisper: "Look! Amy van Twillingen's here tonight!"

Pierre saw a broad, coarsely featured woman slowly approaching, dressed in a vivid Tiepolo red, accompanied by Basil Hume and the Norwegian charge d'affaires. He recognized Mrs. van Twillingen, whom he had met one night at Mrs. Carter's.

Mrs. van Twillingen rose above the arid levels of contemporary society like an obelisk, or a totem pole. Her reputation, like her face, was heavily embossed with legend. Countless drawing-room tales circulated about her whimsicalities, some a shade Rabelaisian, but all of them touched with a kind of awe. This accumulation of anecdotes, combined with her name, her fortune, and her increasingly rare appearances at the opera, had ended by concealing her real nature in a mist of fable. She was engaged, as it were, in the mysterious process of being absorbed into the great American mythology. Aware of this, no doubt, like all dictatorial figures, she had come to behave in a quaint, unpredictable manner. No one, probably, quite understood Mrs. van Twillingen. She was the last of a vanishing tribe; a true baroque. There was something not altogether real about her; something faintly absurd and yet undeniably majestic.

She was laughing in her usual high, salacious tone at something that Basil Hume had said. Then she caught sight of Wilfred Silliman. Her face became sulky, like a child's, until she suddenly spotted Pierre. Her laughter was resumed, identical in tone, but altering its purport from applause to coquetry.

"Ah," she said, drawing closer and tapping Pierre lightly with her fan; "here is one of my ... what shall I call it? ... my handsome young favorites!" She giggled, with a somewhat oracular air, and seemed at a loss for anything further to say.

Wilfred clung busily to the periphery of the group, hanging on Mrs. van Twillingen's words, and on the alert for an opening.

"Can you come to dinner next Thursday, my dear boy?" said Mrs. van Twillingen, fixing her watery eyes upon Pierre.

Pierre smiled apologetically. He didn't quite know what to make of the invitation. "Thank you," he said. "I should love to, but I'm afraid I can't; I'm ... I have already accepted elsewhere."

There was a solemn hush. Wilfred looked appalled; Basil Hume shifted uneasily from one foot to the other.

Mrs. van Twillingen regarded Pierre with a brief, portentous melancholy. Then she passed down the corridor, followed by the Norwegian charge d'affaires.

"Really," murmured Wilfred Silliman, wiping his brow, "you shouldn't have said that. No one ever refuses one of Mrs. van Twillingen's invitations! Never, as far back as I remember, has such a thing occurred!"

"Look," whispered Basil Hume; "there goes Hubert Marsden."

Marsden was a young English poet who had become extremely fashionable in the past two years.

Pierre looked around with interest; he greatly admired Marsden's poetry. A slovenly young man in green tweeds was strolling past. A lilac handkerchief hung from his cuff. He looked ill and irritable, glancing nervously from side to side, blowing endless streams of cigarette smoke from his nostrils. His face looked pale and rather blind, like an albino's. His whole person had an indefinably amphibious quality, as though it had just risen from the depths of the sea, still blinking with the unaccustomed light, and gifted with some rare, subaqueous organs.

He vanished down a stairway. At that moment the warning signal rang, and they all hurried back down the hall to their seats.

The third number began. It was the fourth act of *Carmen*. There was a bright, dusty, animated atmosphere on the stage, with gaily dressed vendors selling water, oranges, and fans outside the bull ring.

"It's Sir Ronald Gower conducting," whispered Mrs. Clyde, in tones of adoration. "There he is! He's absolutely incomparable in *Carmen!*"

Pierre glanced once again at Delia, during the love duet between Escamillo and Carmen: *"Si tu m'aimes, Carmen."* The flavor of foreboding grew more intense; Delia's eyes were shining with excitement.

And at last an inner link was established between Delia, as she listened, and the brilliant, ominous stream of music. Pierre saw the golden tier of boxes, the aging ladies with their furs, even the singers and the orchestra, all fade into the mist of paraphernalia. Only Delia's pure, attentive beauty remained, and seemed in harmony with the operatic music.

Finally Carmen cried to Don José: "You can never again make me love you! No one can make me do anything! Free I was born, free I die. ... "

And at last the curtain fell.

Sir Ronald acknowledged the ovation. The ladies in Pierre's box rose uneasily, gathered their furs, and hastened down the corridor.

60

LADY WEBBER'S long black town car rolled up in front of the marquee, and the three old ladies stepped in, accompanied by Wilfred Silliman. The rest took a taxi.

Commander Forbes got out at the Ritz, and the baron at his flat on Fifty-third Street. Pierre and Delia drove up Fifth Avenue until they reached the park.

"Shall we walk the rest of the way?" said Pierre eagerly. "It's only four blocks. ... Look! See how the snow sparkles!"

Delia turned to him with a wondering look; she hesitated. Then she smiled and nodded. They stepped into the park.

Delia glanced nervously at her satin slippers; but the snow was crisp and dry, it fell from their feet like powder. They wandered slowly among the trees.

There had been a fresh fall of snow that evening. The park was full of a cool white silence. The boughs were laden with clouds of snow, and the paths looked marvelously hushed and inviting. It looked like a scene in the depth of a wood. The snow lay cushioned, caressed with shadows. Nothing stirred. There wasn't a sound.

"How strange it is," said Delia softly. "How fresh and lovely."

And Pierre began to tell her how one winter night he had lost his way in the Haute-Savoie, and had walked for several hours through the white, moonlit trees. Delia listened in silence;

and Pierre had the feeling that she had lost herself in his tale, like a child; and that, unlike most women he knew, and in spite of her astonishing beauty, she was curiously lacking in vanity and self-regard.

They climbed the steps that led from the pond, and silently walked toward a small stone bridge. The ice was covered with a sheet of snow, but beyond, where the ice dissolved in a narrow strip of water, the white gave way abruptly to an equally pure black. Near the street a few walkers passed soundlessly through the snow. Beyond them, deeper in the park, it was completely still and deserted. They stood quietly on the bridge. Everything shone, nothing stirred. There was an air of utter tranquillity. Pierre was filled with a brilliant elation which he did not pause to analyze: it was the lovely night, and the loveliness of his companion; but it was more than that too. It was a deep and sudden sense of harmony.

They wandered back through an aisle of trees. Now and then, as they passed, a twig stirred lightly overhead, and a feather of snow fell to the ground, slow and soundless.

As they approached Fifth Avenue the boughs began to glitter, and the dim blue light of the street began to penetrate. The arch of ice-studded twigs shone like sapphires.

They arrived at Sixty-third Street. Pierre looked at his watch. "It's exactly midnight," he said very quietly.

"Yes, in twenty-four hours," said Delia, smiling, "just think, the new year will be here!"

"Are you going to celebrate?" whispered Pierre.

"No," said Delia, with a touch of regret. "I'll be staying home alone, I'm afraid."

"And your husband?" said Pierre carefully.

"Quincy has been staying over in Washington," said Delia. "He's been working. Frantically ... The war, you know."

"You should celebrate," said Pierre slowly. "You shouldn't be alone."

They had arrived at Delia's house. She ran up the steps, put the key in the lock, and turned around to say good night. Her face had burst into a childish radiance; and Pierre wondered what had brought the rush of joy to her eyes.

"Good night!" she said quickly. "Thank you ever so much!"

Pierre felt he could not leave her. "Wait," he said. "Don't go yet. ... Please."

"I must go," she whispered. "I must, really. ... "

"I shall be in the park tomorrow," said Pierre in a swift, impassioned voice, "at four o'clock. At the bridge where we stood tonight. I must see you! Please! ... I shall be waiting for you!"

He impulsively drew the carnation from his buttonhole, pressed it lightly to his face, and thrust it in her hand with a yearning look.

She looked at him quietly, without answering. The smile slowly vanished; her fingers touched her throat.

"Good night," she said again, in a low, hesitant voice.

"Good night," said Pierre. He watched the door close upon her.

61

DELIA was sitting at the piano. She played a Schubert impromptu, but the notes hung in the air, incoherent and scattered.

She paused, immersed in a sudden daydream. Then, resolutely, she tried a Chopin scherzo; it was useless. The chords fell dead from her fingers.

She allowed her hands to trail over the keys. She turned her head; the bewilderment grew. A cloudiness seemed to come over her senses. The furniture in the drawing room looked strange, eccentric, as though she had never set foot there before. The pattern of the keyboard looked suddenly bizarre. The hands poised on the keys looked lifeless, like ivory, and seemed to be severed entirely from her body.

She raised her head involuntarily. Her eyes fell on the ormolu clock on the mantel. The hands were pointing, as usual, at a quarter to five. Her heart gave a leap. She glanced at her wrist watch. It was twenty-seven minutes to four.

And she said to herself: "No. I shan't go. Why should I go?"

She rose from the piano and walked to the window. She drew the curtain aside, and allowed the faded velvet to rest on her arm. It was beginning to snow again. The garden was lost in a drifting, circulating veil. Small flakes were clinging to the pane and gathering on the icy terrace. There was a statue of a boy beside the birdbath in the corner; a small white cap had settled on his head.

The world was changing; indeed, it had already changed. What had been gray and still was overcome with a white, noiseless agitation. She felt a flash of joy, and then a pang of something resembling dread. The snowflakes outside seemed to stare at her as they passed; something in her body replied, and seemed to grow white and floating. She turned from the window and leaned over the piano. She reached down and played a chord, and then, more softly, another.

The kitten sprang up on the bench beside her, and then leaped upon the keyboard. The piano uttered a weird little cry. The small yellow tigress stiffened her tail; then she arched her back, leaned against Delia's arm, gazed at her languidly, and began to purr.

Delia thought: "He said four o'clock. Beside the bridge. How impudent! What did he mean by it? ... Or was it really impudent? He meant to be cordial; I'm sure of it. ... Just a walk and a friendly chat: like last night. What else could he have meant? ... No, no, he meant nothing, I'm sure. Nothing at all."

And she found her heart beating incomprehensibly. The image of his bright curly head had grown vivid, and the clear and penetrating look in his eyes.

She glanced at her watch. It was eleven minutes to four. She thought: "No, I shan't go. There's no reason why I should go."

And she tried, for some groping, ill-defined reason, to focus the trend of her thoughts on Quincy. She thought: "Quincy will be back from Washington on Tuesday."

But the moment she tried to think of him as a man, his image became nebulous, a small gray shadow.

Suddenly she asked herself: "Do I really love Quincy?"

But the question so startled her, the moment she considered it, that she immediately cast it from her mind. "Of course I do," she vaguely whispered, half aloud.

She drew her fingers along the keys and played another chord; it rang like a bell, clearly and firmly.

The white carnation which lay on the mantel, beside the ormolu clock, caught her eye at that moment. She strolled across the room and looked at it closely; her hand instinctively rose and touched it. It had begun to wilt. She was about to pick it up; she changed her mind and let it lie.

But all the while there was a leaping in her heart, half pleasant and beckoning, half disturbing; yet it scarcely occurred to her to wonder what caused it.

Again she turned toward the window. The snow had ceased falling. It had grown a little lighter, and a hint of sunlight was emerging. The garden outside looked fresh and inviting. And she thought: "The park must be lovely now. White and sparkling."

Her imagination was filled with pleasure at the thought of the park, covered with clean white snow and slowly brightening in the hazy sunlight.

She looked at her watch. It was two minutes past four. And she thought, with a quick little stab of regret: "He'll be gone by the time I arrive. He'll think I'm rude; he'll have gone. ... "

And instantly the vision of Pierre grew clear and urgent. A relationship with him had suddenly, by some obscure device, been established.

"Well, I think I'll take a walk," she said to herself, aloud, firmly. She sighed, as she crossed the room, with a swift, uncomprehended elation. Then she entered the hall and drew her coat from the closet.

62

PIERRE was standing on the stone bridge, waiting. He stared, a bit impatiently, across the frozen pond.

Beyond the pond rose the terraced canyon of Central Park South. The snowfall had ceased, the clouds were parting, and cool areas of light were passing over the giant walls.

He looked at his watch. It was five minutes past four. He had come rather early and had been waiting for half an hour, wondering whether or not she would come.

Below him lay the inlet, all white and frozen except for a rippling crescent where the ducks had gathered: he watched them paddling through the winter sunlight, grunting contentedly.

A feeling of disappointment, even a touch of resentment, began to creep over Pierre. He glanced down the path. Two soldiers were strolling among the trees. One of them stooped to fling a snowball at the other; the other turned, and the snow exploded on his buttocks. They laughed and wandered on, playful as puppies.

He sauntered over the bridge and down the path toward the shore. At that moment he saw Delia. She was walking lightly, crisply, through the trees, and turned up the path that led to the bridge. She was wearing a dark fur coat and a small red hat with a golden buckle. His heart leaped with relief, and a throb of triumph.

He walked casually toward her.

She smiled when she saw him. "It's turning into a heavenly day, isn't it?" she said, in a low cool voice. "I couldn't resist coming out!"

She stared at the sky with a look of wonder. The area of blue was rapidly expanding.

"I've been watching the ducks," he said with a smile. They were standing by the shore. Then he added quietly: "I'm happy you came. So very happy."

Her eyes brightened. She leaned down by the water's edge and held out her hand. Several ducks turned their heads and looked at her drowsily. One, and then two or three more, came floating toward her with an inquisitive air. They drew a row of fine, rippling arrows on the water.

She drew off her glove and dipped her finger in the water. "It's really icy!" she exclaimed. "How can the poor little things bear it?" She touched the sheet of ice at the very edge, where it lay thin and brittle. It was sharp as a knife. She gave a cry and drew her hand from the water: a drop of blood was gathering on her forefinger. She turned her head and looked with surprise at Pierre.

Pierre caught his breath: her face, at that moment, looked almost incredible. Her lips were parted, and the great blue zones of her eyes lay extended. Pierre again had a sense of deep, utter vulnerability.

"How stupid of me," she murmured, and placed the finger to her lips. She smiled. "You know, I never thought the ice could be so sharp!"

"Wait, don't put on your glove," said Pierre. "Let it dry in the sunlight.... There, we'll go now."

He took her by the arm and she rose again; he held her wounded finger and watched the dark, clinging drop. He continued to hold her arm as they strolled up the steps. They paused, then started up toward the driveway.

They crossed the drive, and entered the broad flat promenade—the Mall. It lay white and smooth as a sheet. The rows of benches were tufted with parallel stripes of snow. The statues of Burns and Scott, the one with his hound, the other with his scroll, were spotted with snow; helmets, mittens, buckles, and epaulets of snow flashed in the sunlight. The sun now covered the park. The whole sky was a limitless blue. The world seemed transformed into something light and liberated, marvelously airy and spacious. The towers along the park looked like floating cathedrals.

Pierre felt that he and Delia were now utterly alone in the world; that the city had vanished and time ceased to pass. A blazing stillness filled the afternoon.

Delia leaned back her head and stared straight into the sky. Her face was radiant, smiling with pleasure. Two dark birds were playing in the sunlight overhead. She watched them spinning, wheeling, cavorting.

Then she turned and looked at Pierre with a kind of astonishment, and a glance of happiness so swift and carefree that he felt a sting of guilt.

Then he felt something strangely sweet and soothing pass through him. A dark little man with a merry look wandered past them; some schoolboys in the distance had begun to build a snow man. The two dark birds shot past, one after the other, quick as arrows. And he quietly wondered: "Can this be happiness, after all?"

"Can you skate?" he said in a low voice. "And please, may I call you Delia?"

"Oh yes, I can, a little," she said, and blushed faintly. "Well, yes, if you wish ... "

"We must come and skate together someday, Delia!"

"Yes!" she said joyfully. "We can skate down in Rockefeller Plaza, you know; the ice there isn't too bad, really. ... " A shadow passed over her face. "Quincy never skates," she added softly.

"You should see the Bois de Boulogne in the winter," said Pierre, with sudden enthusiasm. He took her by the arm. "Have you done any skiing?"

Delia shook her head rather humbly.

"It's quite wonderful," he said in a low, tense voice. "Wonderful. Up in the Alps. Mégève. Sestrières. Davos. It's like being in heaven. One is afraid of nothing! Absolutely nothing!"

The snow looked so blindingly white, the sky so very blue, the air so brilliant, the city so legendary, that he felt transported to another hemisphere. He glanced at Delia. Her cheeks had grown rosy, her eyes were intensely blue and alive; and she too seemed no longer a part of the city, but something fresh, wild, and intoxicating.

A sudden laughter filled them both. They leaned down and filled their hands with the fresh, clean snow, and rolled it into snowballs. Pierre pretended to throw his; she ducked and cast one of her own balls at him. He dodged; it flew past him through the still blue air, and burst on a bench. He bent down and began to toss soft little snowballs at her until her coat was covered with flakes, and she cried for him to stop. Her face was wet and sparkling. He took her arm and gently wiped the drops from her face with his handkerchief.

He felt, at that moment, that they were lovers already.

The sun was about to sink. The white flash of the snow was beginning to yield to a rich, meandering gold. They walked down the path toward Sixty-third Street. They had ceased laughing; there was a stillness, a kind of solemnity in their eyes.

They wandered past the Zoo. Most of the animals were indoors, hiding from the winter cold. But the sea lions were splashing exuberantly in the pool, and the polar bear, with icicles sparkling on his belly, was snorting and pawing delightedly at the snow. Two silver foxes lay curled in their cage, and two raccoons, cozy in their winter fur, were rolling around together like a soft brown cushion.

The streets were in shadow when they reached Pierre's house.

He took her hand and said softly: "Will you come in with me, Delia?"

She looked quietly down the long gray street; and then, slowly, she nodded her head.

63

IT WAS night. The room was dark; but the stars were uncannily brilliant, and cast a pale blue light over the bed.

Pierre sat up and leaned over her. He felt a glow of surprise; it was almost incredulity. She lay motionless beneath him, her eyes closed and her lips parted, her slumbering figure lost in the shadows. The faint, youthful fragrance of her body reached him. He drew closer; he felt her warmth. He could hear her breathing. He saw, in her smooth white throat, the rhythmical throbbing of her pulse.

A shaft of light entered the window—perhaps some curtain across the way momentarily parted. The ray of yellow light passed over her body, carving away the shadow as though it were some shielding membrane, and exposing for an instant each separate detail, vibrant and feathery as in an etching—the golden hood of hair, the shell of her ear, the cool curving neck, the slope of her breasts, the sudden indentation of her thighs, the lingering shadow of her legs, and the faint, expressive gleam of her toenails; each detail presented a brief message of its own, shy, sensual, or ironical, and then was lost again in the tissues of shadow. The light fell away. He felt a rush of compassion, touched with awe, the full significance of which eluded him.

He bent down and kissed her throat. She seemed to stir in her half sleep, and without opening her eyes she reached up, touched his shoulders, and folded her arms around him.

She sighed, and whispered his name, "Pierre. Pierre."

He drew the palm of his hand tenderly over her forehead.

She whispered: "It's growing awfully late, isn't it, darling?"

"Yes," he said. "You've been sleeping. Are you hungry, my sweet?"

She opened her eyes and smiled. "I've been sleeping? Really? ... How long have I been lying here?"

"For hours and hours," he said softly. "It's almost midnight."

She drew herself up on her elbows. She glanced toward the great black window, with its impressionistic panel of towers and stars.

"Almost midnight?" she said hazily. She seemed to meditate. Then suddenly she whispered his name again, ardently: "Pierre! Oh, Pierre!"

He nodded. "Are you happy?"

She looked at him earnestly. "I've never, never been so happy!"

Pierre felt again that faint, transitory pang which bordered on guilt; a feeling brought on by the innocence and pathos, the whole crystal clarity of her surrender.

He said to her suddenly: "You aren't afraid, Delia?"

She shook her head with a smile. "Afraid? Why should I be afraid?" She took his fingers in hers. "I'll never be afraid, Pierre, my dear, while you're with me."

There was a distant ringing of bells; and then more and more bells began to ring, until the whole city shook with a wild exulting clamor of bells, horns, whistles, trumpets, and sirens.

Pierre rose and looked into the street. Automobiles were passing, blowing their horns, bright with streamers. Hilarious groups were filling the avenue, laughing and singing and waving their arms.

Delia came over and stood at his side; he drew her body to his, and kissed her eyelids. He whispered: "The new year has begun, darling. For some of us. For you and me."

She smiled and nodded; a breathless feeling of festivity passed through him. When he looked at her again he saw that her eyes were filled with tears. An expression he had never seen before clouded her face, giving it a new dignity, and a new secrecy.

64

DELIA walked slowly through the drawing room. She looked
at the rows of Whittier, Longfellow, and Lowell; at the black
marble fireplace, the old plush hangings, and the porcelain poodles on the mantel. It all appeared, not odd and alien as yesterday, but utterly stale and irrelevant. She suddenly realized that
this room, and indeed the whole house, had no longer anything
whatever to do with her.

It was a quarter to five. For once the ormolu clock happened, for several moments, to be right. She had been sleeping
all morning. She had been asked to an eggnog party at Kitty van
Lennep's, but called up at noon and said she was unwell. Oleanda,
the Negro maid, brought her lunch on a tray. She had spent the
afternoon making phone calls, writing letters, and daydreaming.

She could not shake off a feeling of unreality. It was as though
she had just emerged from a chrysalis: the light, the colors, the
sounds had acquired a new texture. The objects, the letters and
the telephone calls were discarded fragments of her old self. They
had nothing at all to do with the new.

She sat down on the sofa and rang a bell that hung from the
wall.

The Negro maid appeared from the kitchen. "Would you
bring me some tea, please, Oleanda?"

She then picked up a book which lay on the table beside her. It was *Sense and Sensibility.* She leafed absently through the pages. She had been reading in it only two days ago; but now she remembered nothing of the plot, and the names of the characters looked quite unfamiliar.

Oleanda appeared with the tea and some muffins and honey. She leaned over, with a look of love, and poured a cup of tea for Delia. Agatha, the kitten, strolled in from the hall; she leaped with a purr on the sofa beside Delia; and then fell gradually asleep, still purring.

Delia continued to read in the small green book. She forced herself to concentrate. At one moment the events in the novel seemed astonishingly real, as though she herself were the central character, and every phrase had a startling relevance to her own situation; then the focus changed. The style became stilted, the scenes grew blurred, and a shadowy presence outside the book drew closer, like a great ponderous animal.

Her heart began to pound, an insistent sweetness tugged within her. Her eyes left the page and she wondered: "What is wrong? What does this mean? Surely life is the same as before—the room, the curtains, the piano are the same. What has happened?"

But she knew only too well what had happened, though she did not dare yet to put it into words. She allowed the unworded knowledge of it to flood her heart and body. The book dropped among the cushions. The kitten woke up; she stretched her legs, yawned daintily, gave a petulant mew, and curled back into sleep.

Delia abandoned herself to her fancies. She allowed the scattered fragments of the night before to reappear, one by one, until the breathless, incredible vision was complete. The rest of the world fell away like a shell. Only the core of darkness, of sweetness, remained.

She remembered once again the ducks in the pond, and the drop of blood, and the flying snowballs; she remembered again the twilit studio, and the sudden ringing of bells at midnight. She remembered the hoarse low sound of his voice, and she remembered the touch of his curls on her finger tips.

And at last she could no longer contain herself. Little by little the staggering meaning of the night grew clear to her; her body was flooded with joy and terror. She sank back upon the sofa, pressed her face into the cushions, and burst into a silent fit of tears.

The evening passed and the room grew darker.

It was almost six o'clock when she heard the telephone ringing on the Sheraton table beside the sofa. She had fallen into a kind of dazed slumber. The sound of the bell shot through her dreams like a needle. She took the receiver from the hook; her hand was shaking.

"Hello? ... Yes, it's Delia. ... I've been sleeping. ... No, I haven't been out. ... This evening? Oh, yes, Pierre. ... Yes, yes, I do!"

She turned her head; footsteps had entered the drawing room behind her.

"Go ahead, my dear! Don't mind me," said a crisp, competent voice. "I just thought I'd drop in to say Happy New Year. ... Goodness, it's dark in this room!"

It was Mrs. Mannering.

65

ON THE afternoon following New Year's Day Jonathan went strolling down Fifth Avenue. It was a dull gray day, a bit warmer than usual. Tiny rivulets were crawling through the icy hillocks along the curb.

Jonathan's life, the last few days, had been calm and unadventurous. He spent Christmas Day with his mother. During the following week he went to several concerts, revisited some of the galleries, listened to *Orpheus* and *The Magic Flute*. He failed to see Quincy, who had left Washington only for a day. Mrs. Mannering he saw only once, at a dinner at the Van Lenneps'. He had tea with his old aunt Lucy one afternoon at the Ritz; he met Pierre at a cocktail party at Mrs. Clyde's; and he ran into Horace Hayden at lunch in the Plaza bar. His mornings he spent reading Lady Murasaki. He played squash at the Yale Club in the afternoons, and dinner he usually had at Gramercy Park with his mother. And so he waited, with a kind of placid dejection, for his furlough to come to an early end.

He had not laid eyes on Lydia again. She had, with odd finality, disappeared from his mind as well as his daily life.

And instead, a new, more delicately grained yearning began to appear in his daydreams. More and more frequently, ever since their meeting on Fifth Avenue, his thoughts strayed back to the image of Delia; his fancy kept playing with the sound of her voice and the glow of her eyes, the whole freshness and elation of her person. But something restrained him. A barrier of shyness, a sense of family taboos, a kind of loyalty to Quincy perhaps, a lingering romantic inertia—all combined to hold him back. He never quite dared to call her.

He wandered along the avenue. The traffic was rather thin, and the pedestrians were surprisingly few. A post-holiday bleakness hung in the atmosphere; the shops had a drained, dejected look.

He arrived at Rockefeller Center, and paused in front of one of the entrances. Above him rose a Negroid Atlas supporting a wiry sphere; it was an oddly depressing statue. The surrounding walls had a flat and sterile coloration. It was like the entrance to a penitentiary. Only one thing caught his eye: the massive panes of glass above the doorway had captured, by some stroke of felicity, the subtly distorted reflection of St. Patrick's Cathedral across the way. It was the one flash of imagination, the single fresh, original touch.

He wandered on, and entered the sloping promenade. He passed the row of little French and English shops, and arrived at the Plaza. A row of spectators had gathered along the balustrade. The terrace below lay covered with artificial ice, and the skaters went gliding around, clockwise, to the lilting rhythm of an Offenbach waltz.

A gigantic Christmas tree rose above the golden Prometheus, with brightly hued balls nestling among its boughs. It was surely the largest Christmas tree in the world; yet, set in that staggering arena, it looked like a miniature, a bit incongruous.

Jonathan paused. His eye took in the theatrical sweep of the buildings. He had never seen them look quite so vast, so barren, so wholly unmodified by sunlight or shadow. They were tremendously imposing; but it was the power of a monstrous, smoothly calculated machine. Real grandeur there was none. The sense of magnificence, of human aspiration, lay devoured in the savage upward rush. They rose like great sea-gazing cliffs, but deprived of the casual elegance of nature. Not a glimmer of real creativeness emerged; not a touch of devotion, of grace, or exultation; only the blinding appetite for convenience and profit. Human dignity had perished in a towering utilitarian chaos.

He glanced down again at the skaters. And instantly the sense of warmth, of delight, of human triviality, returned. There were several lusty Dutch sailors darting about, two dignified young ensigns, a Canadian or two. Three pretty girls in pink did a dazzling series of pirouettes. Jonathan felt a rush of pleasure, in response to the glow of well-being which radiated from the happy skaters.

But then, quite suddenly, a kind of numbness seized him. He felt weirdly poised between pain and delight. The sensation was so instinctive, so startling, that for a moment he hardly knew what had brought it on. He looked again. Below, gliding along in the current of skaters, he caught sight of Delia and Pierre, arm in arm.

Jonathan watched them for several minutes, with a growing pang of curiosity, an undercurrent of pleasure which only intensified his sense of loss. Their faces looked unbelievably happy; the spark of exhilaration flickered about them.

And as he watched, the full meaning of their happiness grew clear to him. They were easily the most beautiful couple on the ice; Pierre had never looked so fresh and lively, Delia was like a flower that had burst into bloom. They were lovers; it was instantly, utterly evident.

Yet a strange kind of pathos hovered about them. They were lost in each other; they saw no one else. An ecstatic blindness shone in their eyes. They turned and passed below him, lips parted and eyes shining. And a subtle recognition came over Jonathan, a sense of something pitiful and potentially tragic. He almost forgot, for a moment, his own feeling of loss.

The music ceased. A uniformed attendant appeared and waved his hand. The skaters turned and started skating in the opposite direction; counterclockwise. Pierre paused and whispered something in Delia's ear. Her cheeks grew pink with a flush of shyness. They left the ice, arm in arm, and stepped into the café together.

Jonathan turned and walked slowly back to Fifth Avenue.

66

HE RETURNED to the Devonshire. He strolled through the lobby, and was about to enter the elevator when he heard a familiar voice calling softly: "Jonathan! Wait a moment!"

He turned and saw a small gray shape wandering through the marble columns; it was his mother. She smiled anxiously as she approached, and held out her arm. She looked, now that he saw her in this unfamiliar setting, appallingly frail.

He went to meet her. She made her way timidly through the maze of mirrors and marble columns. Her eyes were fixed upon him, gently but resolutely. A happy smile appeared in her eyes.

"Jonathan, my dear!"

"Mother, what are you doing here?"

She smiled apologetically. "I knew I'd find you here, if I waited a bit. I had nothing else to do … so, well, I came and waited for you!"

"You shouldn't have come," said Jonathan gently. They wandered into a small blue lounge below the lobby, and sat down on a couch between two lamps.

"I was uneasy, a little," she sighed. "You'll be going again so soon. I want to see all I can of you, dear boy."

There was something white and chilly in the effect of the lamplight on his mother's features. Gradually a feeling of suspense began to rise in Jonathan. He felt again, as he had felt an hour ago, that some painful secret had been withheld from him. He watched her carefully.

"You look tired, Mother."

"Do I?" She smiled again. "I've just been at the Frick. They were having an afternoon concert."

He nodded. "You enjoyed it?"

"They played a delightful quartet by Schumann." She placed her hand on his, very lightly.

"You looked at the paintings?"

She nodded vaguely. "I was looking for you, really. I had an idea you might be there. I scarcely noticed the paintings. There was a lovely Turner. And a charming Gainsborough."

She drew a deep breath. "Oh, I've had such a busy morning. I wrote again to Norah; I called up Lucy. Then Dr. Leveridge came to look at me."

"Yes?"

"I had lunch sent to my room; it's simpler. Then I took a little nap. I couldn't sleep, of course. Your aunt Pauline—I always think of her as Mrs. Mannering, I'm afraid—dropped in for a few minutes. Then I read a bit."

"What did you read?"

"Oh, something I read as a girl. *Fathers and Sons.* I love Turgeneff; I read him when I was twelve, even before I started on Scott and Thackeray. I found his books in Aunt Hilda's library. He's such a gentle, comforting writer."

She turned and looked at his forehead. "Do you mind if I ask you something, my dear?"

Jonathan looked at her calmly. "No. What is it?"

"Is there..." She grew shy. "Is anything troubling you, Jonathan?"

He hesitated. "I think not, Mother. Why?"

She looked away again, and watched the shadows on the ceiling. "My imagination, perhaps. You look preoccupied. I wondered ... " She paused.

"Yes?"

"Is there anything to do with a woman, dear?"

"I have no idea what you mean, Mother."

"A Russian dancer? Something of the sort?"

"What on earth ... Has Aunt Pauline been talking nonsense?"

Mrs. Ely placed her hand on his arm. "I just wanted to feel sure," she whispered. "I knew there was nothing. Forgive me, dear. It was stupid to mention it. ... You're having dinner with me tonight?"

"Yes. I'll come down with you now, if you like."

As they rose, she turned and faced him, and looked at him quietly. "There is something else, too, Jonathan."

The light shone softly on her face. Her eyes were glowing with a strong and resolute composure. Jonathan felt a wave of tenderness pass through him, but with that a new undercurrent of anxiety. He did not know why; but something had frightened him.

"Yes? What is it, Mother?"

"Nothing unusual, dear. Dr. Leveridge said I must be careful."

Jonathan took her arm and they walked together through the lobby.

"Tell me, Mother," he said softly. "Is it serious? Tell me."

She shook her head casually. "Not really. I'm sure, dear."

They entered the street and he called a taxi. Night had fallen already, and the ice had hardened again.

As she sat beside him in the darkness, she looked through the window and murmured: "I feel I've been a very lucky woman,

Jonathan. My life, I suppose, has been far from flawless. ... Still, I wouldn't really have wished it otherwise. It hasn't always been happy; but I can't say fate has been unfair. It's been a blessing to be alive. That's what I've taught myself to feel."

She turned and smiled at him. But then he saw, through the darkness in the taxi, that her mild little face had suddenly turned pale; the smiling features were frozen with pain.

Jonathan felt, at last, a stab of real terror.

67

QUINCY POTTER returned from Washington the following day and went straight to his office on Fifth Avenue. He had been working very hard. There had been disagreements and quarrels in his Washington office. The head had resigned; his assistant was threatening to resign. The morale was thoroughly bad. Everything was in a state of bureaucratic delay, jealousy, and confusion. Quincy felt what he felt very rarely—depression and fatigue.

Delia was not at home when he phoned from the office at four o'clock. At a quarter to five he stepped across the street to the St. Regis for a drink. He ran into Pauline Mannering in the lobby. She looked bright and smart in her new mink coat.

"Oh, Quincy! So you're back for a visit to New York. . . . It was horrid of you to desert us during the holidays!"

He smiled at her rather grimly. "Well, you know . . . "

She interrupted him: "You do look tired, dear. Well, so am I. I've just been having tea with Laura Carter; it's a strain, you know." She smiled. There was a sudden, rather unusual intensity in her voice. "You're heading for the bar? Come, let's have a drink together," she said brightly. "It will cheer us up."

They entered the warm, crowded barroom and sat down at a table near the door. They ordered their drinks: a bacardi and a whisky and soda.

"Oh, there's Charlie Holliday," said Quincy, as he surveyed the row of men at the bar. "Excuse me a moment." He rose and chatted with Charlie Holliday, an old fraternity brother of his, now a flourishing architect, and jotted down his new telephone number in a small green book. Then he rejoined Mrs. Mannering.

She was gazing at him in a cool, helpful way.

"Really, you need a rest, Quincy. Why don't you and Delia go to Florida for a month?"

"Florida for a month?" Quincy smiled dourly. "There's a rather nasty war on, Aunt Pauline."

Mrs. Mannering sipped patiently at her whisky and soda. "Must you call me Aunt Pauline, dear? It sounds so octogenarian. Why don't you just call me Pauline?"

"I shall," muttered Quincy, without expression. "Excuse me a moment," and rose to his feet. "I forgot to phone Jack van Lennep to call off my squash game."

He disappeared in the telephone booth to the right of the bar. Presently he emerged again, wiping his brow.

"I'm too tired to play today," he sighed, as he sat down again. "I put it off till Friday."

"You know," said Mrs. Mannering, with a careful, sympathetic glance, "I've never seen you like this, Quincy. You've been overworking; that's all there's to it."

Quincy had been staring listlessly at the ceiling. But something in Mrs. Mannering's voice seemed a little odd. She was staring at him with a frozen expression. She had changed, he realized, in the past two years; something in her had crystallized. Her face had the expensive, stereotyped look of Fifth Avenue; the arch of surprise in the eyebrows, the pinch of discontent in the mouth, the hard glaze of the eyes, the overmanipulated cheeks and chin—it was all part of a pattern. He wondered vaguely how old she was; forty-five, possibly?

"Really," said Mrs. Mannering after a pause, more firmly, "you and Delia should leave town for a while. You need a rest. . . . So does she."

"Delia?" said Quincy blandly. "You think she needs a rest?"

"She needs a change," observed Mrs. Mannering softly.

"Well, I've asked if she'd care to spend a week with her family in Philadelphia; I don't think she does."

Mrs. Mannering drew out her golden cigarette case, pressed the sapphire button, and took out a cork-tipped cigarette. Quincy reached over and lit it for her. She cast a swift, icy look at him. Her voice grew very casual.

"When did you get back, dear? From Washington?"

"This afternoon," said Quincy wearily. "At three o'clock."

"You haven't seen Delia yet?"

"I phoned. She wasn't home."

"Listen, Quincy," said Mrs. Mannering, drawing a deep breath and gazing at Quincy with a clear, straightforward look, "I know it's none of my business. I know you'll curse me for telling you this. But there's such a thing as friendship. I feel there's something you should know."

Quincy put down his highball and looked at her with a glazed expression. Her tapering hands caught his eye. The scarlet fingernails shone brightly; the skin was ivory-colored, unnaturally glossy.

"Yes? What is it?"

"Delia's been feeling rather upset lately, you know."

"Upset?" Quincy took off his glasses and laid them on the table.

He caught sight at that moment of his own face in a distant mirror. He was slightly myopic; the face was blurred, watery. It had lost all trace of shape or color or intelligence. A current of chilling depression passed through him.

Mrs. Mannering lit a cigarette with deliberation. "You remember Pierre Maillard," she murmured, "don't you?"

Quincy continued to stare at the mirror.

"He's been making love to Delia," said Mrs. Mannering calmly.

Quincy's expression did not change. He kept watching the mirror. His smooth pink face had an air of complete passivity.

"You needn't believe me, of course," added Mrs. Mannering rather dryly. "If it makes you happier not to."

For a moment neither said a word. Then Quincy said in a calm voice: "I don't." He turned slowly and beckoned to the waiter for the check.

68

QUINCY walked slowly up Fifth Avenue, from the St. Regis to his house on Sixty-third Street. He was trying to soothe and gather his thoughts; to recover that brisk, superficial composure which he had built up, over the years, and which was his only defense against life.

He covered the eight short blocks in fifteen minutes. It was a shining winter's day, and a long delicate cloud hung over Harlem, like a feather. Everything seemed normal, familiar, well-disciplined.

Fifth Avenue was filled with its usual five o'clock crowds. The shops were shaking off their Christmas displays and sinking into a kind of prosaic torpor.

Quincy took out his handkerchief and blew his nose. He had caught a slight chill on the train from Washington.

He reached Fifty-ninth Street and paused for a moment. The golden head of General Sherman shone brilliantly against the azure sky. A small victoria was rattling past, and the old black horse's breath was steaming.

He found that he was beginning to feel rather odd. There was an incessant ringing in his ears, and every time he shook his head, the surrounding walls seemed to shudder and burst into fragments.

"I'll have to go to the oculist's tomorrow," he muttered, half aloud.

Quincy's understanding of human nature was honest but limited. He had never in his life been acutely unhappy; he had never known defeat, in any form that he could recognize. If he had been more astute he might have dismissed Mrs. Mannering's little interview as an evidence of envy, malice, or frustration. But this did not occur to him; nor did he feel she might be lying. His conclusion was, quite simply, that she had been misinformed.

But the sickening uneasiness continued. His last two weeks in Washington had disconcerted and unnerved him.

He thought: "Perhaps she's right about one thing. A rest might do us both good."

And for the first time since his school days at St. Paul's, he felt a hint of something totally alien to his nature; a touch of the sinister, of the uncontrollable. There was a queer, faintly disgusting flavor about things; there was an odd little scent in the air, like ammonia. And a deeply repressed feeling of inadequacy, a sense of impotence at the root of his mind, sprang into life again. He felt his lips twitching slightly.

He heard his name whispered behind him, very softly; or so he thought. He turned quickly. But no one appeared to notice him.

A long black car drove past him as he crossed Sixty-third Street. A tiny bald man with dark glasses sat inside. Quincy began, for no clear reason, to feel distinctly uneasy.

"It's the war," he decided. "It's crept into my nerves. The feeling of uncertainty; nothing you can count on, quite. It's bound to tell. ... "

And he suddenly felt overwhelmingly tired. He could hardly bring himself to walk the remaining block.

He was approaching his house when he saw his own front door flung open and a tall young man hurrying down the steps with his hat in his hand. Quincy paused and stared at the blond head with bewilderment. At first he did not recognize him; he supposed there was some sort of mistake. Then he saw who it was.

It was Pierre Maillard. He looked extremely handsome and intensely happy. He almost ran into Quincy. Instantly he stopped short, stared at Quincy with surprise, and blushed.

"Well, you've come back, I see," he began, and caught himself. He continued: "Good evening, Mr. Potter." But he obviously realized that he had made a blunder.

Quincy stood motionless and stared at him without a word.

"I just," stammered Pierre, "stopped to leave a small package for . . . for Mrs. Potter."

Quincy nodded and looked past him with a kind of child-like anguish.

Pierre recovered his self-possession, bowed to Quincy with studied politeness, and walked swiftly in the direction of Madison Avenue.

Quincy looked after him for a moment. Then he coughed faintly, scowled a little, took out his handkerchief again, and climbed the steps to his own front door.

69

QUINCY unlocked the door, entered the hall, hung his hat on the usual hook, and walked slowly into the library.

This was a room he rarely used. It was dark and rather stuffy. The best-looking books had all been placed in the drawing room. The books in the library were rather dowdy, ill-proportioned volumes, ancient sets of the *Atlantic Monthly,* and *Godey's Lady's Book.*

He drew aside a curtain and sat down at the desk. A cold winter light fell over the blotter, the silver pens, and the round crystal paperweight. On one side of the desk lay a bronze calendar, and the red leather case Delia had given him for Christmas. He touched it lightly with his forefinger, with a gingerly, puzzled air.

He took off his glasses and laid them in front of him. Then he picked up a pen and pressed it vertically against his chin, taking the end of it between his teeth.

He sat like this for ten or twelve minutes. A kind of milky blue haze crept over his eyes. The room grew dim, and he saw nothing clearly.

A touch of panic came over him at this point; he coughed, and tapped briskly on the desk with his pen. He looked around the room, with a sudden air of determination. He picked up the crystal sphere and held it cupped in his hand: it hung there, like a part of his body, strangely heavy, alive. And a sense of reality, of self-confidence, returned.

He laid down the crystal and picked up a silver paper knife. He regarded it with curiosity, and turned it slowly around. Then he laid it against his cheek; it felt surprisingly cool and soothing.

Then he took out his handkerchief again, wiped his forehead, blew his nose, and walked to the door. He called, "Oleanda!"

The maid appeared from the pantry. She looked surprised, and a little sullen, when she recognized Quincy.

"Is Mrs. Potter at home?" demanded Quincy, in a thin, flute-like tone.

Oleanda shook her head, then nodded, then shook her head with indecision. "I don't know, sir. I can go and look upstairs, sir."

"Would you tell her," said Quincy, "that I'm in the library and would like to see her?"

The maid cast a furtive look at him and began to climb the stairs.

He drew himself up a little, put on his glasses again, straightened his tie, and wandered quietly toward the window.

The street outside was swiftly darkening. There was no snow on the pavement, but a sheath of ice still clung to the edge of the sidewalk. He noticed the delicate frost which his breath had cast on the windowpane. He raised his finger and drew, with care, a small neat pattern in the frosted area: the back of a cat, a circle with two ears and a tail, a design he had learned to draw on the blackboard at school.

He heard footsteps in the hall, and turned. He saw Delia standing in the doorway.

"Come in, please," he began, in an impersonal tone, as though he were addressing a committee meeting. "Won't you sit down, Delia?"

An immediate transformation passed over her face. Her cool, indifferent air gave way to a sudden flush of color, her eyes grew very bright, and her lips began to tremble.

She walked quietly across the room and sat down in an armchair under the lamp. He returned to his chair behind the desk.

He cleared his throat and picked up the silver paper knife. For a moment neither of them spoke.

Then he said, without looking at her: "Have you been happy with me, Delia?"

She looked at him silently for several moments, and then said in a soft, breathless tone: "I don't quite understand, Quincy."

His voice was perfectly calm. "I am wondering whether you have been happy with me. I thought you had been, of course. Was I wrong, perhaps?"

Delia stared at him and said nothing. Her face remained composed, the only sign of distress was in her gentle, vulnerable eyes, and a moment later, in the hand that rose and rested on her throat.

Quincy glanced at her, noticing every detail in her expression, and looked away again immediately.

"Something curious has just happened to me," he said, with an air of precision. "I don't wish to be unfair to anyone. I don't wish to make it any harder for either of us than strictly necessary."

He paused, and felt a kind of revulsion at the words he had just uttered. He heard them echo in his mind: they seemed pompous, ridiculous.

She continued to look at him with the same gentle fascination. She said nothing.

And he felt that everything he had said was ludicrously clumsy and ineffectual.

He looked at her quietly and said, in a voice much softer than usual, and almost feminine: "Is it true that you've been seeing Pierre Maillard?"

Delia's features had grown firm and controlled. She said, "Yes," in a cool clear voice, and pressed her hands together in her lap.

Their eyes met. And Quincy felt, for the first time since his marriage, that he was looking at an absolute stranger. Delia's bright, spectacular beauty struck him suddenly anew; as though he had never set eyes on her before. He saw the fine rich curve of the lips, the coldness in her eyes, the patrician composure. He felt a twinge of desperation, and a moment later a sense of emptiness, of worthlessness, of futility. He felt, at that moment, a new kind of love for her; a new perception of her quality as a strange, secret being.

There was a moment's pause.

Then Quincy said gently: "Do you love him, Delia?"

Delia hesitated. Then she turned her head and looked with intensity at the door. "I can't help it," she said in a rapid, impatient tone. Then she added: "I don't know. I don't know." A fit of agitation had come over her.

Quincy rose. He uttered a deep, uncontrollable sigh, drew out his handkerchief, and slowly wiped his forehead. He felt dizzy and ill. "We'll talk it over later," he said, in a tone which for the first time bordered on hysteria.

Delia rose, walked silently from the room, and disappeared.

Quincy returned to his chair and sat there for a long time. The room was quite dark. The street lamp outside shed an icy glow through its dark blue coating. The pens, the paper knife, and the crystal paperweight shone faintly on the desk, like fine surgical instruments; everything else was lost in shadow.

Quincy felt as though some hideous little operation were being performed on his brain. A long steel needle seemed to be piercing his skull, again and again, more and more deeply. The world around him sank into fog, then grew feverishly sharp: swarming and palpitating with detail.

Then the needle seemed to pass lower and lower—along the nape of his neck, through his chest, through his lungs. He felt that some frightful misunderstanding had occurred; that he would suddenly awake and find his life exactly as before.

The needle moved slowly downward through his abdomen; he felt frozen to his chair. The whole room grew cold and rigid. He felt that if he moved he would burst into splinters. The knife, the pen, and the crystal looked like plummets of ice.

Then a kind of gentleness began to glide through him. His body was flooded with a healing coolness. He sighed and wiped his brow. He blew his nose again, twice.

Then he rose and climbed the stairs to his room.

70

DELIA returned to her room, flung herself on her bed, and stared motionlessly at the ceiling for a long time. The room grew dark. The clock beside her bed was ticking softly. But time had ceased to pass and she heard nothing at all until, presently, she grew aware of a light knock on the door. Oleanda stepped cautiously into the room.

"Shall I bring your dinner on a tray, ma'am?"

Delia raised her head, and looked at Oleanda silently.

Oleanda was wearing her vermilion turban and a bright blue apron. The light from the hall fell on her broad, heavy silhouette. She looked back at Delia with a deep animal glow, a loving tenderness and concern.

"Aren't you well, ma'am?"

"I'm a bit tired," said Delia softly.

"Shall I bring your dinner to your room, ma'am?" repeated the maid.

"Please, Oleanda."

The door closed. Delia rose, turned on the light, and walked to the dressing table. A cool pearly light fell on the array of boxes and bottles. She sat down and stared at her face in the mirror.

Oleanda presently appeared with the tray, and placed it quietly on the table. "Good night, ma'am," she whispered. "I hope you're better in the mornin'.'" She closed the door noiselessly behind her.

Delia glanced vaguely at the dinner tray, with its cup of tomato soup and bowl of green salad. But she did not touch it.

She drew her fingers through her hair, which shone like satin under the light. She felt it rippling through her fingers, and watched it dance about her neck. It quivered as she touched it: supple, animally alive. Her face had changed; a new suggestive depth, an unusual luster had appeared. She sat staring at her face until, at last, it took on a weird, frozen look. She felt it was the face of another woman.

She drew off her clothes absent-mindedly, and tossed them one by one on the chair. Then she wandered across to the bathroom door, and stood naked before the full-length mirror. Her body, too, had altered. It had fallen, by some mysterious process, into more subtle, more eloquent lines. Every part of it had acquired a new life, a new and thrilling susceptibility.

She put on a light blue dressing gown, lay down on the bed, and turned off the light. She could hear the mutter of traffic in the distance, and the sound of voices in the house across the street.

Her thoughts returned to Quincy. But only for a moment. She saw his pale, kindly, and utterly meaningless face as he sat behind the desk and tapped his knuckles with the paper knife. She dismissed the image instantly; it disturbed her; it bored her.

An electrical tension lay coiled in her body. A new fear had arisen in her, only remotely linked with Quincy's presence. A shaggy presence seemed to materialize in the darkness; she felt a thick, hot breath pass over her checks. Far below, on the stairway, she heard the stealthy creak of footsteps.

But she cast aside this inexplicable fear, as she had cast aside the thought of Quincy, and surrendered herself to her new, sweet, overpowering daydream: the vision of Pierre.

She thought, as she lay there, of his calm bright face, his laughing eyes, and his warm low voice. She felt herself smiling as a wave of happiness swept over her. She pressed her face into the pillow, and kissed the cool white fabric.

She lay like this, immersed in her reverie, for perhaps half an hour. Then, at some imperceptible signal, her mind grew alert. She sat up in her bed and gazed with sudden desperation into the night. The stars were shining above the roofs across the way.

She walked to the window. Her room was on the fourth floor of the house. She opened the casement and leaned over the street; she could scarcely see Pierre's bedroom window, one flight lower than her own, and some distance away. But she saw a faint strand of light shining there, and she knew that he was waiting for her.

She stood there a moment longer, leaning over the street. It was empty and still; not a car was passing. The haze of the dim-out looked calm and reassuring.

And then, that same instant, a leap of horror was upon her. The street had vanished. All was in darkness. She felt the crouching shadow behind her; the hairy, unutterable monstrosity. She grew dizzy with nausea, then altogether limp. She felt a blinding desire to leap through the window and escape into the darkness outside. For a moment she felt herself glide across the sill, hover on the edge, then silently fall.

A car passed below. The beam of light flowed over the pavement, like a thin blue wave.

She took a deep breath and placed her fingers on the sill; she stood upright. "There," she whispered. "It's nothing. Nothing at all."

She closed the window, sprang across the room, and turned on the light; she glanced about instinctively: there was nothing, of course. Then she breathlessly began to dress. Her heart was pounding and her hands were trembling. She could hardly button her gown as she sat on the edge of the bed; she leaned over, with her blond hair falling around her face like a little shawl, and grew almost frantic when she could not find one of her slippers.

She found it, rushed to the mirror, smoothed her hair into place, and then turned out the lights. Without pausing she ran down the three flights of stairs.

71

PIERRE opened the door and folded her in his arms. They crossed the studio and sat down on the broad, deep cushions of the window sill.

"Well," he said quietly. "What has happened?"

She grasped his two arms vehemently and laid her face upon his shoulder. For several minutes she said nothing. He began very gently to stroke her hair.

Then she raised her face and looked at him with fervor. "I don't know," she whispered. "Quincy spoke to me. He knows ... " She hesitated.

"Yes?" said Pierre.

"He asked me if I love you."

"And what did you say?" asked Pierre very softly.

She did not seem to understand. He repeated the question, and she whispered passionately: "I don't know. I've forgotten. ... Perhaps I told him I love you. I've forgotten."

"And that's all?"

She nodded. "I left the room. And that's all. ... I haven't seen him since. I stayed in my bedroom."

Again she buried her face in his shoulder. He leaned over and kissed the top of her head, again and again, until at last she grew calm. Then they rose, walked back through the darkened room, and lay down side by side on the little couch.

Presently he said: "Do you think you could ever be happy with Quincy?"

She shook her head and gazed at the ceiling. "I don't care what happens to Quincy." She drew a deep breath. "I don't ever want to see Quincy again."

"We must try to think clearly," said Pierre, after a moment.

She placed her right hand across his neck. Then she began to speak very swiftly and earnestly, as though she were reciting a piece she had learned.

"My darling, don't you see, the rest of the world no longer matters! You understand me, don't you? Everything has changed. The way I lived has grown dreadfully unreal. Like dust. It has all blown away. ... Only one thing is left."

He listened silently; he held her left hand in his own, and raised it lovingly to his lips, his cheek, and his brow.

"Oh, Pierre," she whispered in a quick, nervous tone, "I see you shining like a great light, my darling, and all the rest of the world is dark. I don't see anything but you." Then she added ardently: "Without you, Pierre, I would be lost. I would die, I think."

He leaned over her, drew her body to his, and kissed her impulsively. She began to smile. His face hovered tenderly above her own. In the faint blue light she looked inexpressibly lovely, her features melting with love, her eyes alive with a sudden hope.

"I shall never, never leave you," he said. "Don't be afraid."

"I am not afraid," she said. "How can I be afraid?"

She looked up at his eyes; she saw them stir in the darkness, look down at the floor, and rise toward the window. For an instant, by some swift and remorseless intuition, she caught sight of the hidden doubt in his mind. And she felt, for one moment, overcome with panic. But the moment passed; its meaning was too elusive, too deep and painful for her to grasp.

He looked down again and smiled. His face melted as she watched it, and he pressed his lips once more to her own.

And her fever melted away in the warm, clear rush of his passion. Her misgivings vanished; the shape of her dread dissolved. The world fell miraculously into harmony once more.

It was almost one o'clock when she finally arose, slipped into her clothes, and whispered good night.

72

THE house was dark when she returned. The light in the hall had been turned out. Sturgis, she knew, had gone to bed; Oleanda must have gone home long ago. She closed the door behind her very softly, and tiptoed into the drawing room.

She paused near the door and drew a deep breath. The faded gentility of the room enclosed her. She could smell the old leather, the velvet and taffeta. The invisible spirit of the room seemed alive; to be lying in wait for her, calculating, pleading.

A marvelous feeling of liberation had sprung up in her; every trace of fear had vanished. She felt like a traveler gazing at some dreary landscape which he is about to leave forever. Everything in the house seemed dead, or dying. She crossed the room toward the window and drew aside the velvet curtain.

A half-moon had appeared. The garden shone; thin shells of ice, shed by the branches, lay glistening on the flagstones. A disk of ice lay in the birdbath, and caught the pale blue shape of the room.

It was scarcely ten days ago that she had stood here, and had watched the snowflakes silently falling. In those ten days her life, her nature, the world, all had utterly, irrevocably changed. She touched the curtain dreamily. And she wondered what would have happened if she had stayed at home that snowy afternoon: nothing at all, perhaps, until the day of her death.

She turned. The ivory keys of the piano shone in the moonlight, faded for an instant as a cloud crossed the moon, and then were brilliant again.

Suddenly she grew alert. There was a sound of footsteps on the stairway. Her hands clung to the velvet curtain, and her body grew tense. She stared breathlessly into the hall.

For another minute or two she saw nothing. She heard the slow, groping sound of footsteps on the stairs. She did not recognize the tread; it was too heavy for Sturgis, and far too faltering for Quincy.

She did not feel afraid. She felt a ripple of suspense; a tingling; that was all. The velvet curtain brushed her cheek. She waited, motionless.

She heard a faint click, and a yellow light filled the hall. Then she saw a shadow moving, and a tall, gaunt shape appeared in the hallway, staring vacuously ahead, with one hand extended. It was Quincy. He hesitated, and came to a halt; he drew his hand across his forehead in a somnambulistic gesture, then turned and wandered slowly into the library.

Delia stood beside the window for another ten minutes. She felt tense and curious, but entirely calm. She kept wondering what Quincy was doing in the library; and at the same time she felt a strange, almost contemptuous indifference. At one moment she felt that he must have gone mad. A moment later his behavior seemed normal and commonplace.

She crossed the room, swiftly and silently, and peered into the hall. The library door was ajar. She took another step, and leaned forward. The green, overarching desk lamp had been lit, and cast a pyramid of light above the desk. She could see the crystal paperweight shining brightly. Quincy was sitting motionless behind the desk, his arms folded on the blotter, his face buried in his arms. The glare of the lamp fell on his dimly colored hair. She noticed the crimson portfolio beside the lamp, and the glint of the silver paper knife.

A flush of distaste, of revulsion, passed through her. The knife lay shining on the red stain of leather; there was something paralyzed and cold in Quincy's posture.

And a startling conjecture shot through her mind.

Then he stirred, and seemed to cough a little. She realized that he was sobbing. Her sense of utter indifference returned.

She continued to watch him for several minutes. Then she stepped through the doorway, boldly crossed the hall, and climbed the stairs in a calm, unhurried tread.

73

WHEN Jonathan returned to his hotel after lunch the following day, the door captain stopped him and said:

"I believe there's an urgent message for you, sir."

Jonathan stepped to the desk and gave his name. The girl handed him a small white envelope which had been placed in his box.

It was a telephone message from the Doctors' Hospital. It read: "Please come to the hospital immediately. Your mother is gravely ill. Room 212. Dr. Leveridge."

Jonathan hurried back into the street, called a taxi, and drove to the hospital.

He entered the glass door. And instantly the familiar scent of hospitals enclosed him—the flavor of disinfectant, rubber, and linen. He felt a flash of alarm, and then a sudden calm, a sense of fatality. He took the elevator, walked down the white, noiseless corridor, and knocked at the door of Room 212.

A low voice said: "Come in."

He entered. His mother lay with her head supported on several pillows, at a curious angle, and did not see him at first. Her face looked dark and drawn. She was staring at the ceiling with dazed, expressionless eyes.

He approached the bed. She closed her eyes at that moment. The odor of camphor and iodine filled the room. A bowl of lilacs stood on the white dresser, and their fragrance mingled with the scent of medicaments. Dr. Leveridge, a tall, angular man, was standing at the foot of the bed. He nodded to Jonathan, beckoned him to the window, spoke to him in a whisper, and left the room. An elderly nurse remained sitting by the bed.

Jonathan sat down at the other side of the bed and looked at his mother's face. It had utterly changed.

She opened her eyes. A light of recognition appeared there. They were the only part of her body that had not been shattered by her illness. They gazed at him mutely, laden with expression. The lines in her face expressed nothing but pain, but her eyes expressed the simplicity and innocence which pain could not alter.

He reached over and took her hand in his. He felt a shock; her hand had the texture and temperature of a lifeless object.

Her eyes grew calm and stern, and a look of concentration appeared in them. She opened her lips in a taut, unnatural way. He realized that she was trying to say something. He could hardly hear, but by instinct he knew that she had said, "Dear child." She paused, and again her lips moved apart. He could hear, or rather feel, that she was trying to say: "Don't feel upset, dear boy."

He sat beside her for two hours. He finally left her in the late afternoon.

He leaned over her to say good-by. She had fallen asleep. A sudden exhaustion had seized her face, and her mouth had opened, as though the jaw had fallen from sheer weariness. He bent over, kissed her forehead, and left the room.

The city, as he stepped out of doors, looked wholly unfamiliar. The buildings rose through the evening light, washed in a hovering oyster gray, edged with gold, minutely shadowed with a rising tide of blue, and imperceptibly merging, in the southern distance, with the scattered hues of the evening itself. It was the moment, immediately preceding a bright wintry sunset, when New York becomes indescribably stately. The city has a power of evoking, during this one moment, an infinite spaciousness and timelessness; it takes on the air of some great Asiatic city, the majesty of a vanished civilization. The sounds are absorbed in a deeper soundlessness, and the colors are stained with a sudden antiquity. This magical effect reached a climax, as Jonathan watched, so brief as to be scarcely perceptible. The light sprang from wall to wall, from summit to summit. The clouds were outlined with a fine, fluctuating strand of fire. The structures hung pale and dematerialized, like phantoms.

Jonathan stood watching in the street, deeply excited. He felt the kind of awe he had felt in Sicily once, and in Rome. Some vast, prehistorical presence was stirring. With a single gesture it had reduced the walls to the cool, smooth stillness of a desert. The human elements lay buried, like vanishing footprints. Old age, sickness, solitude, hysteria lay cooled in a single devouring shadow.

The moment passed. The light grew cool. The suggestion of depth and tranquillity vanished. Again the sharp, characteristic light of New York fell on the buildings, flattening them against the sky, so that they and all that they contained appeared terribly cold, hard, and barren.

Jonathan turned and wandered down Eighty-sixth Street until he reached the entrance to the subway station.

74

HE REMAINED in the subway long after he had passed his own station. The car was packed, but he sat in a daze, no longer aware of where he was going. Suddenly he found that the train had arrived at Fourteenth Street. He hurried out, wandered vaguely up the stairs, and found himself on the windy street corner.

He looked around, faintly surprised; he recognized the corner. He had stood there once, in the rain, arm in arm with Lydia. It occurred to him that Lydia's house was only five minutes away.

And her image sprang back upon him with a shock. She was no longer quite a person to him; not quite a living woman. Her character had taken on a new and subtler meaning: she had gradually become, in his mind, a kind of animated essence, a sexual and psychic distillation of the city. He had never really expected to see her again. And he knew that it was wiser not to see her. But he was filled at that moment with an irresistible curiosity.

He found himself wandering down toward Tenth Street. It was growing darker. The place had that furtive, lingering hush which hangs about the Village. Several dim, disheartened creatures were wandering through the dusk. There was something absent-minded, a little trancelike, in the setting. Soon he arrived at Lydia's house. It seemed quite empty. He entered, climbed the stairs, and knocked at her door. No one answered.

He waited for two or three minutes. His heart was pounding. He felt, somehow, that he was on the verge of solving an enigma.

He turned the knob and the door opened. The room was empty. It looked exactly as it had long ago, on the night when he had waited for her so feverishly. Only now, instead of fading gradually into dawn, it was rapidly darkening into dusk. He turned on the switch; the light did not work. He walked slowly across the room and lit a small red candle which stood on the bookshelf. The light fell gently on the studio couch and the books. There were bits of her luggage still strewn about. The blue-and-yellow portrait by Van Gogh still hung on the wall. Only one thing had been added: a large, dark portrait of Lydia herself which he recalled having seen, while it still was being painted, in Sebastian's studio.

He picked up the candle and held it under the painting. It had been finished, presumably, but there was still an incomplete look, a kind of indecision, about the work. There was a certain anonymity and rawness in the face. It hung suspended against a fierce magenta background, nervously defined, and stared past him with hollow, timorous eyes. He would never have guessed that it was Lydia, whose eyes were so expressive and bold.

Yet something of her character had been captured; an aspect of it which he had rarely seen, and had largely guessed at—the quality of obsession.

And he felt the shadow of her personality fill the room. Everything—the books, the walls, the luggage—reflected her haunted, nomadic air. He felt that he was being watched surreptitiously. Quietly he placed the candle back on the shelf.

He remembered the candlelight, one evening, as it fell on the bottle of wine and the silvery slices of Camembert; and the tongue-like caress of the light on her body as she did an arabesque in front of the mirror.

He hesitated. For a moment he thought of waiting for her. He remembered then how he had waited once before, frantically, hour after hour, and the dazzling moment of her arrival.

He decided to go. But a fit of reminiscence, tinged with yearning, held him a moment longer. He strolled to the window for a final glance at the darkening street.

As he leaned from the window he heard, indistinctly, the sound of voices and footsteps on the stairway. They came to a halt on the landing, and paused for a moment in front of Lydia's door. He felt himself blushing; it was too late to leave. He turned and gazed helplessly at the door.

The door was flung open, and three excited faces, brightened by the leap of the candlelight, stared in surprise across the room.

75

GOOD HEAVENS!" cried Lydia. "It's Jonathan, of all people! I thought we were being robbed, or caught in a trap, or something. ... Well, well!"

She glanced at him with a certain caution; she was obviously wondering why he had come. She took off her coat and black astrakhan cap and tossed them carelessly on the couch. Her two companions took off their coats. One was a dark young sailor, the other a large, black-eyed woman; both were strangers to Jonathan.

Lydia leaned over and gave a twist to the bulb in the reading lamp. A clear, penetrating light filled the room. The two strangers kept staring suspiciously at Jonathan. Lydia introduced them; a little too casually, perhaps.

"This is Corporal Ely—this is Olga Bunin. And this is Tom ..." She hesitated. The sailor murmured his name. She repeated it haltingly: "Tom Zambarelli."

They all sat down, Jonathan on a chair, the two strangers on the couch, and Lydia on the edge of the dresser.

Lydia seemed overexcited, ill at ease.

"Come," she said, "let's have something to drink. I have a bottle of bourbon. Ghastly stuff, but it's better than nothing!"

She slipped into the bathroom, rinsed several glasses at the sink, and returned with a half-empty bottle of bourbon. She poured out the drinks—very liberally—and placed a glass in Jonathan's hand. He sipped it; there was a lingering flavor of tooth paste.

Lydia gazed intimately at Jonathan, and proceeded to ignore the other two.

"Why haven't you been to see me, darling?" she cried, in an unnatural tone. "What have you been doing? Where on earth have you been hiding? I phoned you several times at the Devonshire, but of course you're always out. ... "

Jonathan could see that she was abnormally nervous. Something was troubling her; she was playing for time.

She continued to talk in her high, excited voice.

"And now your furlough's almost over! Where are you going next? Are they going to send you to Europe? Oh dear, I hope not. ... I shudder to think what will happen when they start that big invasion. Do you think they ever will? Peter Sebastian says no. Nickie Dimitroff says yes. One doesn't know whom to believe. ... Have you been to the ballet lately? ... Only once? What did you think of *Aleko?* It's not the thing for Simonova, of course. She can hardly put one foot in front of the other, poor creature. ... Did you hear about Valdez? He got into a jam with the police. Down in the Bowery; you can imagine the kind of spot. He's been going berserk. We bailed him out, of course. Still, it's not exactly inspiring. ... Janet Bloom, by the way, had an awful fight with Myrtle Hemingway. With slaps and scratches, and pulling of hair. All about Janet being late for rehearsal. You knew, I suppose, about Myrtle and Janet. There's a dreadful spirit creeping into the company. ... "

She cast a sidelong glance at the couple on the couch. The woman was a blooming, heavy-breasted brunette, with expressionless black eyes; she was chewing gum. The sailor had dropped his cap on the floor, and sat indolently on the bed with his legs spread apart, his eyes half closed, and his thumbs tucked between his trouser buttons. He had oily black hair and a sensual, pockmarked face. He too was chewing gum. Both had emptied their glasses, and Lydia rose to fill them again.

Jonathan surveyed the room. He recognized the frayed spot in the rug, the nail marks in the wall, and the chrysanthemum-shaped stain on the ceiling. He recognized the familiar scent of coffee grounds and mingled ointments. He glanced at the bookshelf: noticed a book by Kafka, whose vogue, it appeared, had penetrated even the ballet; and beside it, a copy of *Alice in Wonderland.*

He looked again at the portrait. He could see it more clearly. There was something forced and derivative in the manner; but the colors were brilliant, and the expression in the face was rich and revealing. Under the rosy smoothness of feature the artist had discovered, and exposed, the darkening rush of her mind.

"You like it?" said Lydia, with sudden vivacity. "Peter says he's not satisfied with it. God knows why not. He merely says those things, you know, as a kind of self-defense. If anyone else makes the slightest criticism, of course ... Well, anyway, I can't say that it flatters me. But then, one doesn't expect modern portraits to look pretty. Look at Picasso. Look at Modigliani. If we really looked like that, we'd all be throwing ourselves in the river. ... Here, let me pour you another drink, Tom. How about you, Olga? Have you a cigarette, darling? ... Thanks. Heavens, it's cold in this room. ... "

She rose, raised her fingers to her cheek, and walked thoughtfully toward the window.

The couple on the couch had begun to make love. The sailor was making crude, alcoholic passes at the brunette; she continued to parry them absent-mindedly. An idiotic smile lay frozen on her lips. There was a look of boredom and contempt in the sailor's face.

Jonathan rose discreetly to say good-by.

Lydia took his hand and held it tenderly. She gazed at him with affectionate concern.

"Must you really go, Jonathan? ... Well, it was lovely to see you. ... Don't forget, I'm doing *Spectre* tomorrow night. Promise you'll come. ... Well, it was lovely to see you, dear!"

And he felt, as she closed the door behind him, that she was both intensely relieved and desperately uneasy at his going.

76

JONATHAN arrived at the hospital early the following morning. Dr. Leveridge met him outside the door. There was a moment's silence as the doctor looked gravely past Jonathan. Then he placed his hand on Jonathan's shoulder and said in his deep, deliberate voice:

"There is very little hope. Try and prepare yourself, my boy."

Jonathan entered. The room was filled with the scent of ammonia.

The early sun was oblique and golden, and drew a bright screen across the wall which faced the window. The bowl of lilacs was dipped in an amber essence, and seemed to shed an unhealthy radiance. Mrs. Ely lay silently, without moving, her eyes fixed on a point on the wall directly above the flowers. Her face was darker, more drawn than yesterday.

He leaned over and kissed her. He could see that she recognized him, and was trying to twist her face into something resembling a smile.

Mrs. Ely's sister, old Mrs. Westover, had arrived and was sitting beside the bed; her hand was resting lightly on the coverlet. Her face was averted, and when she turned to look at her sister, it assumed a curiously masklike expression, intended to hide her grief as much from herself as from the woman who was lying on the bed.

No one spoke. A hideous, indefinable feeling of guilt passed through Jonathan.

He left the room toward noon, and returned an hour later.

The curtains had been drawn across the window, and the room was lost in a sea-green haze. At first he saw only the usual shapes in the room.

Then he looked at the bed. A small, dark creature lay crouched among the tangled sheets, her knees drawn up, her hair wet and matted, her features flushed and distorted with pain. There wasn't a sound; no one was stirring. It was with a sense of nightmare that he grasped, finally, the simple fact that this was his mother, and that she was dying.

He drew close, leaned quietly down, and kissed her. She was beginning to moan with pain, but for a moment she recognized him. A rapid movement passed through her body, a ripple of extreme physical suffering coupled with some last, violent effort of the mind. She had become, on the brink of death, a creature infinitely complex and mysterious. She opened her eyes again. The paroxysm had passed. A look of exhaustion appeared on her face.

She lay back once more; she sighed with relief, and her body fell into lines of relaxation. Her features grew gradually gentler and paler. He watched her with a kind of frenzied concentration. He saw the ignobility of bodily pain fading from her face and a cool, delicate composure reappear.

The curtain stirred gently. The nausea of grief in Jonathan gave way, for a moment, to an overpowering sense of awe. Something savage, something monumental, was occurring. It was not only his own protective pattern, his link with his ancestors, which was being consumed. A whole system of humanity, a whole tradition of love, was hovering on the verge of extinction.

All of life, henceforth, would be a little colder, a little lonelier. Again the curtain stirred. A breath of air passed through the room.

There was a sigh, ever so slight, from the direction of the bed; a faint stirring, it seemed; and then complete silence.

The nurse approached quietly and leaned over the bed. Mrs. Westover hid her face in her hands. Dr. Leveridge took a deep breath and cleared his throat, then walked to the window and raised the curtain. A cold, clinical light, horrifying in its whiteness, swept over the bed and flooded the room.

PART THREE: 1945

77

PEACE had returned. And already, within a month, the whole aspect of New York had experienced a subtle change.

The flavor of victory, from the very first, was slightly disturbing. There had been the usual speeches, parades here and there, a popping of champagne bottles, a rain of confetti. But a curious irritability soon became evident. An inner disunity, astutely drugged during the war, burst out like a rash within a month of the victory. The old and the young; the rich and the poor; ambitious, discontented wives and the armies of occupation; all joined in the clamor. It was faintly macabre. Opportunism; instability; disintegration within. The perilous cycle had begun.

But only within, for the time being. Without, by early autumn, the city was showered with wealth and abundance. The lights along Broadway grew more and more brilliant. The traffic grew steadily more intense. Enormous town cars emerged from their wartime hibernation; an endless column of Lincolns and Cadillacs began to flow along Park Avenue. A torrent of dazzling gowns, satin slippers, precious furs, an endless cataract of chocolates, cheeses, and fruits flooded the shopwindows along Fifth Avenue. The oily shimmer of luxury was spreading. Elderly ladies drenched in sequins and prosperous gentlemen in black ties arrived each night, in growing numbers, at the doors of El Morocco and the Waldorf.

In other ways, too, the city's atmosphere was changing. There was a growing stream of returning soldiers and sailors, with the flush of variegated adventures still on them, and a rather ominous glint in their eyes. Welcoming hordes from the entire country came to greet them. A hegira of eager wives, parents, and children was flooding the apartments and hotels. No rooms were to be had; the restaurants were packed; the theaters were sold out for weeks ahead. There was a sense of inexhaustible cash, of almost hysterical voracity.

And another, more wistful migration had begun as well. The accent of exile had grown more and more infrequent; the nomads were pulling up their tents, one by one. The mingled spice of Dutch, French, British, Polish, Canadian uniforms was rapidly vanishing from Broadway. An air of nostalgia, of coming disintegration pervaded the European cliques.

The Countess Pirelli, in spite of her asthmatic condition, had already departed for Rome. The Baroness Landau was packing her Boudins and Cousinets, and was planning to return to Paris in October. Lady Temperly had already shipped her books back to London; she was waiting for a passage on the first possible boat.

A prosaic, faintly bitter tang was in the air. The sinister little picnic had come to an end. The suspense, the sacrifice, the spectacle had dissolved. Young men were no longer dying on the fields of battle. The headlines were smaller; the newsreels were duller. The crisis had begun to turn quietly inward, and was burrowing toward the darker regions of the human soul.

78

JONATHAN was on his way to the Yale Club, where he was lunching with Horace Hayden.

He had just returned to New York, after several months in a camp in Alabama. He had at last been discharged from the Army, and felt his tweeds hanging on him with an odd, delightful looseness. He already felt his stride and his expression changing. Everything looked a bit more casual, more accessible. The little shopwindows along Madison Avenue looked intimate and inviting. He felt himself gliding, with astonishing ease, into the wayward rhythm of civilian life.

He entered the lobby of the club. "How are you, Mr. Ely?" said the door captain affably. "Nice to see you back, sir. You've been gone quite a while, haven't you? ... Mr. Hayden is waiting for you in the taproom."

He found Horace sitting in a huge leather armchair, reading a paper and sipping a cocktail.

"Ah, there you are!" he said brightly. "My dear Jonathan, you look simply bursting with health! It's so restful to see you. ..."

He slapped Jonathan affectionately on the forearm and ordered another bacardi.

Horace had changed. He had grown considerably stouter, his eyes protruded more than usual, and there was a bald spot on top of his head. He had shed his bohemian ways with a vengeance: he was wearing a pin-stripe suit with a white shirt and a dark tie. He sat a little straighter than formerly, his remaining hair was oiled and tidily combed, and his fingernails were a smooth, well-manicured pink. Even his way of talking had changed; it was crisp and fastidious. There was just a trace of an English accent.

"Well, do tell me about yourself," he said affably. "What are you planning to do now? Take up architecture again?"

"Yes," said Jonathan, with a curious feeling of dejection. "I suppose so. I'm seeing Charlie Holliday tomorrow morning. There's a chance he may have an opening for me, one of these days. ... "

He looked around the room. He recognized every detail—the red leather armchairs, the buffalo head on the wall, the smell of heavily waxed walnut. In a distant corner he caught sight of two old classmates of his, playing checkers.

Nothing in the room had changed. But Jonathan detected for the first time a touch of falseness, of sterility, in the atmosphere. The semi-genteel masculinity was unconvincing. There was a touch of staleness in the air.

Horace proceeded to talk of his own projects. He was publishing a book of poems; and he explained all about it. Several of these poems had already appeared in certain *avant-garde* quarterlies, others he had read aloud to his friends, who found them fashionable and obscure. The idea grew up that Horace had a real gift, which it would be criminal to conceal any longer. He had approached several publishers. They all inquired, in cautious tones, whether he was contemplating a novel. He sighed, and left their offices in a state of indignation. Finally he found a small, experimental firm which was willing to do the book. Horace gallantly offered to help with the finances. Great care was being taken with the format and the binding. He hoped to persuade Otto Baum to do some rather Freudian illustrations.

"Have you chosen the title?" asked Jonathan tactfully.

Horace explained that he was hesitating between several. His publisher was in favor of *I Sing of America*, which had a spacious, patriotic ring, and a journalistic snap as well. But Horace felt it was a bit vulgar, somehow. One of his left-wing friends had suggested *Manifesto to a Dead Comrade,* but this, Horace felt, might make unnecessary enemies; besides, it was hopelessly outmoded. Otto Baum, who was a surrealist, had thought of *The Amphibious Pony.* Horace himself was inclined toward *Apperceptions*, which he felt was a cool, cerebral kind of title, and not the sort of thing that the critics could afford to sneer at.

"Have you seen Hubert Marsden's new book, by the way?" he asked Jonathan.

Jonathan shook his head. "I'm afraid not."

"Well, you should," said Horace breathlessly. "It shows a new facet to his genius. He has become a great mystical poet. The book is full of references to Plotinus, Kierkegaard, and the rest. I'll send you a copy tomorrow, definitely!"

The waiter approached to take their order. They both ordered cold salmon with mayonnaise. Horace, in a fit of hospitality, ordered a carafe of white wine.

He then began to discuss his social existence.

"I lunched at Amy van Twillingen's the other day," he remarked casually. "I'm devoted to Amy. She has a heart of gold. I've been seeing quite a lot of her lately, as a matter of fact. ... "

Jonathan felt somewhat surprised. He remembered how, four years before, Horace used to denounce the very circles Mrs. van Twillingen personified. Perhaps the higher society, as well as Horace, had been growing more receptive of late.

"I had dinner the other night at Estelle Webber's," he continued rapidly. "Estelle's a dear, really. I don't care what others may say. She has imagination. That's what matters. And, you know, these people have more culture than is generally supposed. I find Estelle's judgments on painting remarkably astute...."

"By the way," he went on, reaching into his pocket. "Can you use a ticket for the ballet tonight? Kirillova's dancing, I believe. I'll be brokenhearted to miss her, but Estelle has asked me to dinner tonight; I can't disappoint her."

"Thank you very much," said Jonathan. He took the ticket and slipped it into his pocket, with a faint sensation of distaste.

A brightness appeared in Horace's eyes. He stared across the room with sudden interest. "I think I see a friend of yours," he murmured.

Jonathan turned. Sitting at a corner table he saw, to his great surprise, Pierre Maillard, in the company of Wilfred Silliman and a tall military person of high rank.

"Who is the man in the uniform?" inquired Jonathan.

"Oh, that's General Edgerton," said Horace. "A classmate, I believe, of that old snob, Wilfred Silliman." He took a sip of wine; he seemed suddenly in a bad humor.

"You've heard what that good-looking French friend of yours has been up to?" he went on.

"You mean, as a painter?" said Jonathan circumspectly.

"Oh, he's had a brilliant exhibition at Wildenstein's," said Horace coldly. "And another at Knoedler's. He's definitely a success.... But, well, there's been a bit of talk." He paused significantly.

"Yes?" said Jonathan, with misgiving.

"You haven't heard? I'm surprised. Well, your poor old cousin Quincy has been left in the lurch. His wife is carrying on a mad affair with this young Maillard, and it's the talk of the town. Rather shameless, the whole business. They're seen together everywhere. Quincy's living alone, of course. There's talk of a divorce. ... "

Jonathan felt deeply shocked; not at the facts, which he had already guessed, but at Horace's manner of portraying them, which cast a false and heartless light on Delia. He felt that something brutally unjust was being done to her; and he began, for the first time, really to dislike Horace.

They finished their coffee in a somewhat disconcerted mood, and presently rose.

Jonathan walked across the room and greeted Pierre. Pierre got up, blushed a little, shook his hand, and smiled with pleasure.

"So you're back! And a free man! That's wonderful news. ... Won't you join us for a bit of brandy?"

"I'm afraid I can't," said Jonathan. He shook Wilfred's hand and was introduced to General Edgerton.

Then he looked at Pierre again: he had aged a little, and had lost his radiant color, his youthful luster. There was a new maturity and firmness, a touch of belligerence in his face. There was a hard little glint of success in his eyes. But he was still amazingly handsome; he still had his old, adventurous charm.

Jonathan felt there was a trace of uneasiness in his manner. "Let's meet soon," Pierre said eagerly, as they parted. "Let's have one of our old talks again. It will do me good! You really must go? ... Well, good-by, Jonathan. ... "

79

JONATHAN strolled over to Fifth Avenue. It was a hot, sultry day, and he decided to take an open-air bus to the Frick Museum. He wanted to cast off the indefinable feeling of alarm which his visit to the Yale Club had left with him.

A delightful coolness greeted him as he entered the museum. There was a sound of water and a scent of greenery in the marble patio. The place was almost empty. Two guards were wandering through the adjoining hall.

He stepped among the Old Masters; and instantly a sense of calm, a sense of lucidity came over him. He felt suddenly at peace again, and secure.

He paused in front of the mighty Rembrandt self-portrait. The face which before had seemed swollen with suffering now looked at him with a warm, glowing equanimity. He was unexpectedly reminded of Beethoven. A note of triumph had been woven into the texture of despair; not deliberately, nor merely for the sake of compensation, but as though in the very nature of suffering one could find, if one looked far enough, the inevitable element of redemption.

He passed into another room, and gazed at the El Greco over the fireplace. It was an old, white-headed man in a rose-colored robe. The cloth was smooth and luminous, but the face looked shattered, consumed. The withered features and the long white beard had a rigid, mineral sheen; petrified by decades of anguish and self-denial. The fine suggestion in the skin of arteries and creases had the quality of a mountainside hacked by estuaries and torrents. Yet this frozen, fanatical face of St. Jerome, which once had seemed so horrifying, now was lit by a miraculous beauty, and Jonathan felt strangely elated as he left the room.

He entered an airy chamber filled with huge Fragonards. The room seemed flooded with an evening sunlight. Everything was hovering and floating, delicately poised in mid-air. The smooth young lovers with their opened lips, the fat, smiling cupids, the sensual elegance of the trees—all breathed of a world where pain did not exist. Yet once again, as Jonathan stood there, the paintings deepened and expanded. And what he saw then was no longer an exquisite caprice but the great autumnal lament of a civilization at its peak, balanced on the edge of its decline and dissolution.

He re-entered the patio and sat down on a marble bench. The sound of a Bach *chaconne* rose from the hall beyond. He closed his eyes and listened. And his discovery, as he listened, grew gradually clearer. The highest art, it appeared, whatever its nature, contains in itself its own complement and contradiction. The more passionate it grows, the deeper its inherent calm; the more flawless its composure, the more piercing is the inner turbulence. And this aesthetic paradox reflected, with ceaseless variety and subtlety, the tragic enigma of humanity itself.

The music ceased. He opened his eyes and rose. When he entered the street again, he felt wonderfully fortified, refreshed. New York seemed casual and benevolent once more; it had an air of intimacy, or humanity.

80

WHEN Jonathan arrived at the opera house that night the performance had already begun. He hurried down the corridor to one of the side entrances. The faint, familiar strains of Tchaikovsky's music could be heard. He entered and crept toward his seat, which was at the very end of the tenth row, and presented an oblique, imperfect view of the stage.

The first number was *Aurora's Wedding.* He was just in time to see the Blue Bird enter the stage. The dancer, whom Jonathan recognized as Valdez, appeared from the left and did a series of leaps. Then a female dancer appeared from the opposite side. For a moment Jonathan thought it was Lydia. He leaned down and peered at the program. It was not Lydia; it was a dancer named Christine Cordoba.

The ballet continued. The stage grew more crowded. The King and Queen sat impassively on their thrones, and the Majordomo stood pompously beside them. There was a continual swirl of silks and satins, a flutter of capes, ruffles, and periwigs. Even the music sounded inflated and tedious; Jonathan began to feel a little bored.

Then the Rose Adagio began. He realized, with an indifference which surprised him, that Lydia had entered the stage. She was doing the famous adagio with Dimitroff. Her costume was dazzling; she looked superb, until he began to notice that she was dancing very badly. She seemed listless and weary. There was a falsity in her acting, a kind of deliberate overemphasis. He detected a touch of cynicism in her manner. The audience remained cool and unimpressed throughout the dance.

But then, at a certain turn of her head, a tremor of recognition passed through him. She was now no longer merely a dancer; a host of memories intervened. Some shadow of his earlier feeling for her swept over him: a mingling of curiosity, premonition, and tenderness. He wondered if, possibly, she might have seen him. But no, of course not, he then reflected. The adagio came to an end. There was almost no applause. Lydia and Dimitroff disappeared from the stage, and Jonathan thought he saw a look of anger in Dimitroff's face.

In the intermission he walked restlessly down the corridor to the foyer. He caught sight of several familiar faces in the distance: Peter Sebastian wearing a dark green shirt, Wilfred Silliman in evening attire. But he preferred not to meet them, and slipped back into the crowd. He crept down the stairway again, found his seat, and waited for the curtain to rise.

The second number was a *Pas de Quatre,* with a pale, simple backdrop. The curtain rose on four ballerinas frozen in an architectural pose. They continued to hover for several moments, poised on the brink of motion. They looked cool and impersonal, their faces averted, like a group of porcelain figures in a glass cabinet.

Then the ballet began; they melted into movement. And instantly he recognized them, as their faces caught the light. They were Sheila, Natalia, Lydia, and Kirillova.

The dance struck him, at first, as purely technical and meaningless. Then, little by little, he found that he was touched; he began to respond to its antiquated charm. It was a ballet characterized by an extreme, almost excessive graciousness of manner, on the part of the dancers toward one another as well as toward the audience. The whole tone was that of an exquisite desire to please, decorously blended with reserve. And the effect, as the dance progressed, grew to be one of a curious purity and pathos.

After Sheila's highly traditional solo, Natalia stepped forth and did a crisp little waltz, spontaneous and extremely direct in its appeal. Jonathan had forgotten how extraordinary she was. Her cool, clear splendor completely dominated the stage.

Then it was Lydia's turn. She was far less stately than Natalia, and really less beautiful; and there was, for a minute or two, a disappointing air of technicality. But then she gained control of the dance. It was, Jonathan realized, incomparably the most difficult. There was a series of sharp pirouettes, and then a series of high beaten cabrioles. Gradually, through some secret of her own, she created an air of great precision and power.

And again her physical magnetism rose before him, not immediate but slow and sullen, as once before, long ago. He was struck with the arrogance of her profile, the sensual mouth, and the clean, hard, Slavonic chin. She created, once again, an illusion of depth; an illusion of melancholy loveliness.

Then, as the audience grew intensely still, Kirillova stepped forth. The other three dancers remained motionless in the background.

She started very slowly; the change from immobility to motion was scarcely perceptible. She posed *en arabesque*, a long easy line, creating an effect of complete repose in the air, like a wave about to break, then slowly breaking. The impression she conveyed, during these opening moments, was extremely subdued and almost colorless. There was a peculiar stiffness in her movements. Her technique, it seemed to Jonathan, had begun to decline. Her face looked worn. Her arms and legs were too thin. The effect was too angular; she looked almost brittle.

"Look!" whispered the elderly woman beside him. "Isn't she incredible?"

An electrical current seemed to pass through the audience. And instantly, to Jonathan as well, the miracle of her dancing grew apparent. The muscular mechanism which in the other dancers shone like an ornament, was in Kirillova invisible. She was devoid of virtuosity. Not only was there no trace of effort, but even the dance itself seemed expressionless and impersonal. And similarly, the emotional effect which she wished to convey remained almost hidden, and was scarcely hinted at; it emerged imperceptibly, like an ambience, a mood; a sense of indefinable solitude. And Jonathan felt a sudden breath-taking chill, a signal which he felt very rarely and which told him that he was in the presence of perfection. Kirillova's dancing was now so cool, so mathematical, so wholly given to the pure, unbroken surface of the movements, that he grew oblivious to the presence of the dancer herself. Her dancing was not, as with the others, a lovely garment presenting a concrete human image. It was like water or light, transparent, elemental.

Her solo came to an end. The element of time, which she seemed to have conquered, again sprang into being. The four dancers joined gracefully for the finale. They did a *bourrée* in a circle, and then the waltz theme began. The dancers on the side started slowly toward each other, merged in a sudden rush of movement, then passed and yielded to the other two. They did a second *bourrée,* back to back in a circle, holding hands, and doing a series of *relevées sur le point.* Soon the ballet was over. There was a rush of applause. The dancers did their curtain calls with a quaint, fastidious grace. Then the curtain fell and the lights went on.

Jonathan rose, with his heart beating violently, and walked quickly down the corridor on the left, which led backstage.

81

HE CAME to a green metal door, beside which sat a stout man in a derby.

"Where's your pass?" he muttered gloomily.

"Pass?" said Jonathan.

"You've got to have a pass, you know."

"Well, I'd like to see ... " began Jonathan, frowning. Then he lied. "I have to see Mr. Lochwitzky."

The man in the derby peered at him suspiciously. "You're sure?"

"Sure? ... Certainly!"

"Is it urgent?"

"Absolutely!"

The man in the derby looked wearily past him. "Go ahead," he muttered. "Up that stairway on the right."

Jonathan ran up the stairway, passing a group of men who were deep in an argument. One of them, he noticed guiltily, was the *régisseur,* Lochwitzky. He hurried on. He passed a little alcove, at the end of which he saw a door slightly ajar. He turned in, and saw that it was Kirillova's dressing room. He glanced through the opening. There was nothing but confusion—a litter of clothes, flowers, pasteboard boxes, and make-up cases, all of them battered and discolored. Kirillova herself, streaming with sweat and painfully homely in her make-up, was leaning against the dressing table. Several young men were gesturing effusively. An old man with a red beard was shaking his head gravely. Behind him, dressed in black, stood a gaunt, forbidding woman who was evidently Kirillova's mother.

Jonathan followed the narrow, dusty corridor. Everywhere there were trunks and suitcases, and various stage properties such as banjos, urns, torches, and a throne. Three pairs of wet scarlet tights were hanging on a radiator to dry. There was a stale, sour smell, and an atmosphere of anarchy. Members of the *corps de ballet*, half clad and perspiring, were hurriedly tripping in and out of one another's rooms. They kept peering at Jonathan as they passed; the girls with an air of cool disparagement, the boys with a look of casual coquetry.

He glanced into several dressing rooms, but without finding Lydia. In one of them he came upon Valdez, completely naked except for a tall crimson hat.

"Come in, Jonathan!" he shouted. "Don't be shy! It's only me!"

The dressing table was littered with an array of pastes, lotions, creams, powders, pencils, and tufts of hair. There was a smell of wet rubber and bodily exertion.

Valdez was daubing his face with a thick yellow cream. He had lost his looks; his features had sharpened. But the light in his eyes had grown mellower, more detached.

He looked at Jonathan with a friendly twinkle in his eyes. "Well, well, so you're with us again! Healthier looking than ever! How did the war treat you?"

"Oh, rather easily, I'm afraid," said Jonathan, in an offhand way. "I wasn't sent overseas, as it happened."

He caught sight of a dark, shining face in the mirror, black-haired, eyes glittering. He felt faintly shocked: it was his own. Small drops of moisture hung from his forehead.

"You've seen Lydia?" said Valdez, fastening a large mustache to his upper lip.

"Not yet. I'm on my way."

"Poor girl," said Valdez coldly. "She's been dancing atrociously. She's made new enemies, as usual. Now it's Kirillova. Kirillova won't speak to her. And Janet Bloom refuses to dance in the same ballet with her. There was a horrid little scene."

"Why? What happened?"

"Insults!" said Valdez with relish. "Insults, my dear! Lydia hasn't learned to hold her tongue. ... She tells Janet to go back to her farm in Oklahoma. That's no way to talk to a girl who hopes to be a ballerina. She tells Kirillova that she looks like an ostrich. What can one do? She's cutting her own throat!"

He rose, slipped on a supporter, and began to dress; it was a brilliantly colored Russian peasant costume.

"Can't you talk to her?" said Jonathan, in a worried tone.

Valdez shrugged his shoulders. "She's like a child. She'd merely think I've joined the great conspiracy against her. ... No, she's hopeless. Hopeless." He smiled playfully at Jonathan. "Well, anyway," he said, "don't say I didn't warn you!" He turned to the mirror and drew a thick black line across his forehead.

Jonathan hurried on. Presently he came to a door on which was scrawled in white chalk: "Petrova. Ivanova. Doyle."

He listened for a moment. He heard nothing, and paused. The door was ajar; the dressing room appeared to be empty. He felt unaccountably flushed and expectant. He opened the door a bit farther, and peered through the opening.

Lydia was sitting alone in front of her mirror. She was wearing a shabby, maroon-colored dressing robe, and was languidly smoking a cigarette. She was lightly scratching the little mole on her chin.

Instantly Jonathan recognized the strange, sulky flavor which hung about her.

He crept softly behind her and placed his hands over her eyes.

"Who is it?" he whispered. "Can you guess?"

She placed her own hands over his, and held them there for a moment. The touch of her palms shot through him like an electric current.

Then she drew his hands away, gently and firmly, and gazed at his face reflected above her own in the mirror.

"Jonathan." She sighed deeply. He wasn't sure she had guessed it. "At last. At last ... "

She turned around and smiled. Her hair was a wilderness of curls, and her face was weirdly disfigured with make-up. Her eyelids were huge and a bluish black; the rest of her face was white and flat. A layer of unguents hid the familiar features. It was as though she were wearing a kind of sexual, ceremonial mask; yet, to Jonathan, it was curiously moving to see her like this.

"Come closer. Let me look at you." She drew his hands toward her. Then she looked at him with her glittering, absent-minded smile. The whole enigma of her personality came to a point in that smile: he hadn't the faintest idea what it implied. Yet he felt his body fill with a familiar yearning as he watched it.

Then the smile slowly vanished; the mask grew impersonal once more. The shadeless bulb which hung from the ceiling cast a bleak, hard light on her features. She gazed at him silently. There was something hypnotic in the slope of her eyes.

"Wasn't Kirillova superb?" she said suddenly. "I've never seen her in better form."

Jonathan nodded vaguely. "Yes, I agree. She was wonderful."

"This is her greatest season," Lydia went on. "She's never been like this. After this, I'm afraid, she'll be heading downhill. ... Soon she'll have to start writing her memoirs, poor dear."

Jonathan glanced with curiosity around the dressing room. It was even more untidy than Kirillova's. The embroidered costume for *Aurora's Wedding* hung over a chair, moist, disillusioning. A layer of dust and oil covered everything. There was an aroma of cold cream and talcum. Lydia was watching him carefully with her great brown eyes.

"There, turn your head a little," she said. She flicked the ash from her cigarette and smiled. "Yes, your chin is a bit heavier. And you've lost just a teeny-weeny bit of hair, haven't you, dear? Soon you'll be middle-aged. ... What are you doing after the show tonight?"

"Nothing," murmured Jonathan earnestly. "I'd love to see you, Lydia."

"Can you wait for me at McCarthy's?"

Jonathan hesitated. Then he asked softly: "Would you like to come to my hotel?"

She shrugged her shoulders, and closed her eyes for a moment. "You'd rather?"

"Yes. The Devonshire, as usual. Room 612, this time. ... When will you be there?"

"Oh, midnight or so." She looked back into the mirror, and drew her two forefingers over her eyebrows. "Oh, by the way, dear ... "

"Yes?"

She smiled rather wearily. "You'll have some drinks waiting for me? I'm simply dying of thirst."

"Anything special you'd like?"

"Well, gin is my drink, you know. . . . There's the second bell, dear; I've got to rush."

She leaped to her feet and snatched a bright red costume from the hanger. Another dancer entered the room at that moment, dressed in a long black robe, with a mask and a hood of black silk.

The last number on the program was a fantasy called *Russian Soldier*, with music by Prokofieff and choreography by Fokine. But before it was over Jonathan left his seat, crept out of the opera house, and walked swiftly up Broadway.

82

JONATHAN sat by his window and looked into the darkness. He glanced at his watch again. It was almost midnight. The ice, the gin, and the ginger ale were standing on the walnut dresser.

He kept wondering: Would she come? And he began to wonder: Did he really wish her to come?

He remembered how once he had waited for her, in her own room, and she had finally returned. He recaptured the moment when he had leaned from the window, and she had crept up behind him, and had taken him in her arms. And again, even now, the rush of magic did not fail him.

And suddenly he wondered: Was he falling in love with her again?

A photograph of his mother stood behind the two bottles on the dresser. He rose, leaned over and stared at it, examining each feature.

Her large, unusually gentle eyes looked back at him. Her soft pale hair looked faintly unreal, like a coronet of mist. The lines in her face had been smoothed and dulled by the photographer. The longer Jonathan stared, the more wraithlike she appeared.

He closed his eyes for a moment; and instantly the reality was upon him. He saw her again, more clearly than ever before, and his mind absorbed the full flavor of her character—its simplicity and patience, its cool, humble tenderness; and behind these, the latent force of her passion.

He opened his eyes again; the image was gone. The photograph stood on the dresser in front of him, alien and lifeless.

He walked slowly to the window. At that moment the door opened, without a preliminary knock, and Lydia entered the room.

She looked flushed and rather mischievous. The mask of make-up had been washed from her face, leaving it soft and pearly. She was wearing a blue pull-over and a gray flannel skirt; she had shed her glamour.

She stood in the doorway a moment. "You look surprised!" she said softly, with a smile. "You thought I wouldn't come?"

"I was sure you'd come, Lydia. ... Look, even your drink is waiting for you!"

She sank into the armchair. There were drops of moisture on her forehead. "Darling, is there ice?" She sighed with fatigue, and drew the palms of her hands across her head.

He brought her the drink, and she lit a cigarette.

"Well, I had a hideous fight with Lochwitzky after the performance was over. That's why I'm late."

"What was wrong?" said Jonathan gently. "He looks like a harmless sort of fellow."

"The man's an idiot!" snapped Lydia furiously. "He wanted me to change and dance one of the village maidens in the last scene of *Russian Soldier,* to take Rosalie's place. Rosalie wasn't quite up to it—well, you know; the usual thing. I refused, of course. I'm sick of being the scapegoat. I've taken enough from that dreadful man. ... " She was trembling with indignation.

Suddenly she grew quite calm. She turned to him and said: "Did I dance well tonight, Jonathan?"

Jonathan nodded with conviction. "You were absolutely splendid in the *Pas de Quatre*. ... I'm no judge, of course. But you did those pirouettes brilliantly."

She gazed dreamily in front of her. "I was in good form," she murmured. "I think I knew, somehow, that you were watching. ... Was my make-up all right?"

"Oh, excellent, I thought."

"Not too white, possibly?"

"Not at all. Just right."

She smiled, and sipped at her drink. "Well, you know, I'm thinking seriously of leaving the company. The Monte Carlo people are dying to have me. So is that other group—what do they call it? The American Ballet or something. I wouldn't dream of joining them, naturally." She sighed again. "Oh, I'm so tired of that dreary *Russian Soldier.* It's so passé already. I do wish they'd drop it. ... I think I'll speak to Sevastopoulos about it tomorrow." A glitter came into her eyes. "I'll tell him what I really think of it. He needs a good dressing down. He's been making a perfect fool of himself. What with Janet Bloom and so on. It will do him good. ... "

He watched her carefully. A peculiar glaze had passed over her features—a familiar but heightened, almost trancelike petulance. There was something faintly alarming in the low, hostile monotone of her voice.

She smiled and gazed sweetly at Jonathan. "Well, why don't you say something, Jonathan?"

"I was thinking," he said softly, "of what you were just saying."

"You agree, don't you, darling?"

"Of course," he said meekly. "You're absolutely right. There's no doubt about it."

"Of course I'm right," she declared. Then she added dreamily: "Why don't you really do something, Jonathan? Now that you're out of the Army? I mean, really achieve something?"

"Such as what, for example?"

"Well, after all, you have a certain intelligence. You could become famous, if you really wanted, I'm sure. You might be a great architect. Design skyscrapers and so on. You could make loads of money. . . . You're lazy, that's the trouble."

"And what would I do with the money, once I have it?"

"Oh, darling, don't be ridiculous; we could buy a villa in Palm Beach, and have a yacht, and three Cadillacs, and give the maddest parties!" She rose and poured herself another drink; then she turned and gazed at him mildly. "Life," she murmured, "could be so lovely. So amusing."

Her voice was quite calm as she continued: "I'm sure we could be happy together. I feel you'd be good for me. You're not glamorous, but you're cozy, darling. I really need you, somehow. . . . You know, if I ever found you really caring for another woman—well, I'd do something rather frightful, I think. Yes, really. . . . "

She leaned against the dresser and looked at him with sudden gravity. He was sitting on the bed. There was, for several moments, an electrical silence. At last she said rather slowly: "Do you still love me, Jonathan?"

He looked at her without answering. Her voice had changed. Her face was melting, and her lips began to tremble. Something in her was about to break.

Suddenly she threw herself on the bed beside him and buried her head in the pillow. Her body was shaking with violent sobs.

He leaned over her gently, and drew his hand over her curly head.

"Don't cry, Lydia. Please. Don't cry, darling."

She sat up and gazed at him with a blind, broken look. Her face was pink and glimmering with tears. "Jonathan," she whispered hoarsely. "It hasn't been easy. Really, it's been hard. ... I've been so frightened. So terrified."

He put his arm around her without a word, and drew her head upon his shoulder. A feeling of deep compassion filled him. For a moment she had yielded; she had shown him a glimpse of her real self, of her hopeless and devouring sense of insecurity. Her head lay limply on his shoulder. He held her hand; it was damp and cold.

Suddenly she drew herself together. She sat up and stared into the mirror. Then she rose.

She stepped into the bathroom to wash her face. When she reappeared she murmured: "I'm going to leave you now, dear. Do you mind?"

"You'd rather not stay?"

"I think not, Jonathan. I feel weak. I want to be alone. I need a good night's rest."

He rose and put his arms affectionately around her.

"Just as you say, Lydia. ... A bit of sleep will do you good." He kissed her lightly on the forehead.

She moved away, with the faintest touch of impatience, and slowly opened the door. "Well, good night, my dear. ... Will you phone me soon? Please?"

He nodded quietly. "Good night, Lydia."

"Good night," she whispered again, and closed the door softly behind her. He could hear the swift rustle of her footsteps down the hall.

83

ON THE following morning the sky was gray and gloomy. In the middle of the morning there was a vigorous shower. But when Jonathan looked out of his window at eleven, he saw that it had suddenly cleared. The sun was shining, the clouds were dissolving, and the sky above the park was a deep rich blue.

He was sitting by the window in his red silk dressing gown, with the breakfast tray on the desk beside him—an empty teapot, the shell of an egg, a withered triangle of toast.

He had finished reading the morning paper; he tossed it aside, lit a cigarette, and began to leaf idly through Marsden's new book of poems, which Horace had just sent by messenger. He found it a bit depressing. Lines which had pleased him three years ago now seemed modish and contrived. His attention wandered; he picked up the telephone.

He called Lydia's flat to ask her to lunch with him. The telephone kept ringing; no one answered. He called the theater. Lochwitzky answered the phone, and angrily announced that Lydia had failed to appear for the rehearsal that morning.

He thought for a moment of calling Quincy. But he felt, somehow, not quite in the mood to see Quincy.

He tried to call Charlie Holliday's office, but was told that Mr. Holliday had been called to Boston for three days.

He phoned Mrs. Mannering at Wyndham Park; she was at the hairdresser's, but had left a message inviting Jonathan for dinner the following day. Then he called Mrs. Westover. But the maid explained that she was having an interview with her doctor.

Finally he called Pierre at his studio. There was no answer.

Jonathan, with a feeling that something had gone wrong, decided to take a stroll in the park and then lunch at the Zoo. He put on a blue shirt and a gray flannel suit, took his hat in his hand, and left the hotel.

It was a brilliant autumn day, and the streets were still sparkling with the morning shower. The naked lady in the Plaza shone like fresh lacquer. The taxis and busses, the street lamps, the shopwindows, the plots of grass surrounding the Plaza, all were twinkling in the sunlight. It was almost one o'clock. Fifth Avenue was full of people hurrying to lunch with their habitual glassy, faraway stare.

Jonathan turned into the park at Sixty-first Street and strolled toward the Zoo. A group of little girls, all in bright blue dresses, rode past in the pony cart. Two old ladies in lace caps, apparently twins, were feeding a swarm of pigeons. A fat little schoolteacher was telling his pupils about the aoudad. Two Catholic priests were staring rather bitterly at the llama.

He turned left and followed the row of cages. He passed the Himalayan yak, the European red deer, the African giraffe, and the hippopotamus. The hippopotamus seemed to regard him with an air of cynical recognition.

He walked up a curving path and strolled among the trees. Groups of people were sitting on the benches, on the stones, on the grass. They had a swarthy, Mediterranean look, most of them. Beyond rose the staggering array of towers, brilliant and golden in the pitiless sea-light. And once again Jonathan was reminded of Venice—the bright, rich Venice of Carpaccio and Veronese. There was the same sense of intermingling races, of maritime activity, of profit and wealth; and something of the same flamboyance and glitter. Only, instead of velvet doublets and brocades, there were smartly tailored dresses and tight-fitting uniforms. Instead of canals mirroring the great *palazzi*, a flood of green rolled past the Pierre, the Sherry-Netherland, and the Plaza.

The park looked alive, eruptive, agitated, as it extended to the north and west, blazing with autumnal colors. He wandered on a little farther. One tiny landscape followed another, each hewn from the hard volcanic rock, each molded from a different pattern. There was a feeling of Europe in miniature; a wistful assortment of flavors. He saw a hint of the Italian lakes, a shadowy glimpse of Somerset, the moist, rich greenery of Touraine, the rocks and crags of Scandinavia. Once there was even a trace of Attica, and once the gray, barren tinge of Castile. And scattered among these nooks and crannies he could hear the mingling of tongues—French, Russian, Yiddish, German, Spanish, Italian, even Chinese. He had a sense of swarming, freshly co-ordinated energy; of a world still fluid, the murmur and unfurling of history.

He wandered still farther, and came to a small, sudden precipice which overhung a stream. It was entirely secluded here, and almost soundless. At last he felt himself standing in the pure, uninvaded presence of America. The colors were strong and distinct, but nowhere luxuriant. It was a small, savage continent complete in itself; an essence, a distillation of the New World. He felt he had entered some unexplored region: a raw, prehistoric smell rose from the water. Smooth, gray stones had broken through the sward, like arrowheads. There was a rustle of furtive wilderness. The trees above the gully resembled more the trees of Africa than those of Shropshire, say, or Burgundy. They lacked the pruned and traditional, the unmistakably human touch, the individuality of curves and arches. They stood symmetrical and light and spare, so that in the breeze each leaf shook separately, and the place took on a hazy vibration, the electrical uneasiness of the jungle.

He walked back along the edge of a flat brown meadow, down a wooded slope, past the black bears and polar bears, and presently arrived at the café terrace.

Around the pool below the terrace a group of sailors with their girls had gathered to watch the sea lions. It was their feeding hour; there was a sense of drama. The guard was hurling slender blue fish over the railing. They flashed in mid-air, one by one, like stilettos, and lit unerringly in the sleek, resilient snouts of the sea lions.

And suddenly, with a shock of surprise, he saw a familiar figure at the opposite end of the pool, intently watching the sea lions. It was Delia.

84

JONATHAN walked around the pool to the other side; he walked very slowly, almost reluctantly. His eagerness was coupled with a curious discomfort. He drew out his handkerchief and wiped his forehead.

Delia had not yet seen him. She was wearing a dress of a beautiful pearl gray, and a black tam-o'-shanter. He could see, at a glance, that she had learned to dress far more smartly.

"How nice to see you again, Jonathan," she said, in her vague, lovely voice. "I just heard you were back. Pierre told me he'd seen you. You look ... " She hesitated.

"Yes?" She was going to say he looked older, he felt, but a feminine tact restrained her.

Instead she said, very gently: "You look a bit thinner."

"Perhaps," said Jonathan, "I am, a little!"

"But you look splendid, all the same," she added vaguely. "Are you going to stay in New York now?"

Jonathan nodded. "I think so. I hope to join Charlie Holliday's office before long."

"So you're going to be an architect," she murmured thoughtfully. "That will be lovely, Jonathan."

They stood side by side, their fingers resting lightly on the iron railing. The sea lions had finished their lunch and were lolling in the sun.

He watched her face carefully. She had scarcely changed. She seemed as fresh and serene as always; a bit firmer, perhaps, more mature and composed. Her face shone like crystal in the bright autumn air. Her skin still retained its luminous transparency, and her hair hung to her shoulders like amber silk. He felt a yearning to touch it very lightly. And he realized, again, how intensely beautiful she was. He could tell, as he looked at her skin and her hair, that they had been touched—perhaps only half an hour ago—by the kiss of a lover. He wasn't sure how he knew this; but the impression was immediate and unmistakable.

They wandered past the leopards and the slumbering pumas toward a row of benches, and sat down. He placed his hat on the seat beside him, and leaned forward, with his elbows resting on his kness.

She looked at her watch and said quietly: "I'm meeting Pierre for lunch." Then she added dreamily: "At one-fifteen." Her voice gave the words an odd, emotional shade.

"Oh." Jonathan nodded. "Yes, of course."

She turned and looked at him. A touch of defiance, of intensity, entered her eyes when she mentioned Pierre's name. She had built a protective barrier around herself; yet he felt that she was longing to confide in him.

"What are you thinking, Jonathan?"

"I was thinking of Pierre," said Jonathan.

"You haven't talked to him yet?" She was watching him carefully.

"Well, only for a moment. At the club, yesterday."

"Oh, of course. He told me. I wonder ... "

She hesitated. There was a touch of anxiety, almost of pain, in her voice.

"Yes?" said Jonathan softly.

"I wonder whether you'll think he has changed."

Her voice was quite calm again. She looked casually toward the leopards' cage.

"He may have changed, a little," said Jonathan. "New York changes everyone. ... And then, you know, he was always an unpredictable fellow."

"Ah, you think so?" She looked at him with sudden curiosity.

For several minutes they sat in silence. He stole a covert glance at her. She looked like a child. Her face shone with the glow, the inviolable secrecy of a child; and a child's dangerous susceptibility as well.

But the expression changed. Her brows contracted. She looked more feminine, suddenly, and very much older.

He felt the presence of a deep, painful struggle in her. Her lips parted; she blushed; she seemed about to speak. But then she gazed at the sky with a look of sudden yearning, and said nothing.

The leopard's body flowed rhythmically behind the bars. He halted for a moment and fixed his eyes on Delia; a lustrous, unappeasable gaze.

There was a pause. Then Jonathan asked very gently: "Do you still see Quincy occasionally, Delia?" He picked up a maple twig from the ground and bent it slowly.

"Quincy?" She seemed startled. "No, I never see Quincy. I never even think of Quincy any more."

"I saw him," said Jonathan, "just before I left last time. Over a year ago. I just wondered ... "

She said nothing, and gazed steadily at the clouds.

"He looked ill." Jonathan tapped the ground with his maple twig; he drew a spiral in the sand, very carefully.

"You mean, he looked unhappy," said Delia slowly.

Jonathan was shocked by the cold, ruthless tone of her voice. "Well," he began, "Quincy was always ... "

She looked at him with a sudden bitterness. "Listen, Jonathan," she put in. "Quincy never dreamed what love is. Nor did I, while I was with him. He's unhappy. But why? Because his vanity was hurt. Because his smug, wearisome routine was interrupted. That is all." There was a tone of contempt, almost hatred, in her voice.

"Are you sure, Delia?"

She shrugged her shoulders. "Certainly."

He was astonished at the sudden change in her expression. The look in her eyes was quite unlike her, hard, almost cynical. For the first time Jonathan noticed the sensuality in her lips, and a touch of obstinacy. Only one thing, it seemed, now really concerned her. On all other matters she was cold, indifferent, and selfish.

And yet he felt, oddly enough, that she was a truer and finer, more harmonious character than before. The shadow of imperfection had given her depth.

"I never want to see Quincy again," she said softly.

He watched her face. It grew sullen as she spoke of Quincy. The experience of pain had begun to touch her beauty, troubling its lucidity, assailing its bloom.

And then her expression changed once more. It grew charged with sadness; her beauty returned, but graver, more suggestive than he had ever seen it.

She said softly: "It's been full of dark moments, Jonathan. ... It hasn't been easy."

He felt deeply moved; for he realized, more by her voice than her words, that she was speaking now of her love for Pierre. Yet there was something faintly familiar in her words, a dark, little echo; and then he realized that Lydia had spoken those same words the night before.

There was a deep, accumulating roar. Jonathan turned: it rose from the house of the lions. It spread, gathering power; it unfurled like a cataract. It seemed to penetrate the streets, the apartment houses. It wasn't the sound of hunger, it was a cry of boredom, of a long and terrible ennui.

He broke the maple twig in two and cast it aside.

"Delia," he began in a low, urgent voice, "what I say can't matter to you now, I suppose. But someday you might think of it. I want you to know that I always ... "

But it was too late. He could not bring himself to say it.

She looked at him sweetly, and waited. "Yes?" Then she glanced at her watch. "Oh, it's almost a quarter past!"

She leaped to her feet. "I don't want to be late," she murmured, with a flash of desperate delight in her eyes. And she hurried away, vanishing among the cages.

85

DELIA and Pierre had lunch at a smart Belgian restaurant on Sixty-third Street. After lunch they wandered down Fifth Avenue and looked at the shops. They entered a flower shop, and she bought him a red carnation. They strolled into a bookshop; he glanced at the novels, while she leafed through an album of Botticelli prints. Then they walked into a Russian shop and looked at the Fabergé boxes, the delicate embroideries, the czarist silverware.

Finally they wandered arm in arm into the park. Their exhilaration had vanished, and they walked along silently, not quite knowing what was wrong.

It was just three o'clock. The sun was hot and heavy after the early rain. Rich, spicy odors rose from the ground. The vast sensuality of nature was beginning to wither away into the dryness of autumn, dead flowers, dark leaves, quivering insects. Migratory birds were settling in the twigs. The slopes of grass looked brown and dying. Only in the shadows there was still the lingering smell of rain and the dark, soft glitter of raindrops.

And Delia felt something in this thin autumn landscape which echoed a presentiment in the back of her mind: a sense of things passing, of a vanishing sweetness and a relentless, gathering desuetude.

After the painful crisis of her relations with Quincy, with his family, and with society at large, Delia had swiftly adapted herself to a new way of living. She had deliberately ceased seeing her old friends—women like the Wilmerding sisters, Kitty van Lennep, and Janet Hall; friends who had gone to school with her in Bryn Mawr, or had known her family, or Quincy's family. Instead, she resolutely set about making friends with Pierre's friends, and people who she imagined might become friends of Pierre's: Europeans, chiefly artists, journalists, and idlers. She grew to know people like the Countess Pirelli, Baron Legué, and Maxim de la Tour.

She had taken a small, agreeable room at the Shropshire, with a kitchenette attached. She cooked her own breakfast, lunched with Pierre or one of his friends, had a group of young Frenchmen occasionally for cocktails, and then dined with Pierre at one of the small French restaurants. She gave up her membership in the Junior League and the Colony Club, and joined the Museum of Modern Art and the Alliance Française. She had an annual income of forty-five hundred a year; it wasn't very much, but it was adequate. She bought some smart new dresses, under Maxim's impeccable guidance. She picked up a small Pissarro at Knoedler's as well as a beautiful Forain etching; and she hung one of Pierre's recent sketches over the bed. It was a casual, provisional kind of life; stimulating and airy but faintly unreal.

She began to take an interest in contemporary painting. She visited all the museums, and attended the openings on Fifty-seventh Street. She read Pierre's favorite writers—Anatole France, Flaubert, Constant.

She even read, now and then, something which the Baron Legué lent her, and which Pierre had not read; a new volume by Aragon, perhaps, or Sartre. It didn't occur to her to wonder whether she enjoyed these books. They fascinated her because, subtly involved in every page, lay the ceaseless necessity of her love. She spent her hours in weaving, assiduously, ingeniously, a web of life which hung suspended from Pierre, and Pierre alone.

She found solace in persuading herself that society was changing, and that its rules of conduct were altering. Quincy was part of a puritan past; Pierre was part of an international future. This crisp little formula was sufficient for her. And she gradually began to feel a new kind of happiness, fanatical, irresponsible, and tender. Her love for Pierre steadily deepened and widened. His presence was sweet to her continually. She explored each trait in him, and found each one worthy of love. He seemed to her miraculously gifted, well-mannered, and quick-witted. Every opinion he uttered, every glance, every gesture shone with a unique and many-sided brightness. There were times when she felt alarmed at her constant need of his nearness. Each hint of ennui in him terrified her. Any mention of another woman filled her with a strange, angular pain, which she never quite admitted to herself might be jealousy. Nor was it merely jealousy. It was partly that, but it was also the cloak which hid a deeper foreboding that she dared not contemplate.

86

THEY wandered on to the pavilion where the rowboats were for hire; there they took a small blue boat and rowed to the middle of the lake.

Pierre took off his coat, rolled up his shirt sleeves, and braced his feet against the crossbeam. The sun was hot and rather heavy. Soon his face and arms were dripping wet.

"Take off your shirt, why don't you, dear?" said Delia; and he did. He rolled it into a ball and tossed it to her, and she held it in her lap, feeling the faint exhalation of moisture against her palms.

The marshy smell of the water played around them and mingled with the smell of tar and sun-soaked wood. She listened to the rhythmic squeak of the oars and the plashing of wavelets under the prow.

She leaned over the side, and dipped two fingers in the water. "How lovely!" she cried; the sunlight cast a row of knives across the long green ripples. And suddenly she felt lighthearted again.

They came to a halt in a small sheltered cove. They had brought two bottles of beer; Pierre opened them against the oarlocks, and the foam shot forth and spattered his forearm. They laughed, and raised the bottles to their lips.

"Do you feel happy, darling?" whispered Pierre.

She smiled lovingly and nodded. Her heart was full. He looked very beautiful to her as he sat there, casual and manly, with his blond hair ruffled by the breeze, and his great ironical smile.

The lake was sprinkled with little rowboats. Pierre recognized someone that passed near by, and waved his hand casually.

Delia turned to look. She saw a heavy-set man in a dark shirt and a pale, slender girl with a mass of brown curls. They were sitting in a freshly painted yellow boat.

"Who is that?" she asked softly.

"A painter. Peter Sebastian. I hardly know him."

"Who is the girl with him?" said Delia, very calmly watching Pierre.

"I don't know." Pierre shrugged his shoulders. "She's rather striking, don't you think?"

Delia did not reply; her smile had vanished.

Presently she said: "I didn't know you cared for curly-headed brunettes."

He smiled at her rather quizzically and said nothing.

They cast their bottles into the water, and watched them bubble and descend. Delia gradually began to feel happy again, as she watched Pierre leaning over the edge of the boat and gazing intently at the water, like a little boy.

They were floating lazily in the middle of the lake; the oars were drifting. Delia felt an impulse suddenly to pour out her heart, to cast aside all trace of misgiving. She leaned sideways and stared at the snakelike ripples.

"Please, darling," she began, in a low, rapid voice, "don't think it's been difficult for me. Giving up that drab old life, I mean. With the Potters and Mannerings and the rest. It was terribly dull, really! I'm glad to be rid of it. For the first time in my life I can do as I please. ... Thank God, darling, I never had a child with Quincy! ... Yes, from now on I want to move in your own circle, completely. I want to be friends with all of your friends. They're so much more stimulating. So much more real. You can't think how dismal Quincy's Yale friends could be. They all dressed alike, thought alike, talked alike, walked alike. It was too, too dreary. ... "

Pierre had begun to row again. They were passing under a bridge. "Pierre, darling, we'll go abroad together before long, won't we? I'll want to see the Louvre and the Luxembourg, of course. Really thoroughly, mind you; not just with a guidebook. You've really taught me to appreciate painting, you know! We'll visit Venice and Lake Como. Mightn't we take a tiny villa in Capri? I'd love to visit Morocco with you, and Egypt. ... We could be so free, so terribly happy; I want to be far, far away from New York. ... "

He didn't seem to be listening. He was gazing across the lake, and his bare, moist chest was shining in the afternoon light.

She was overcome at that moment, with a feeling which almost stunned her. It was like a dark wave passing over her, blinding and overpowering her. She longed to fling herself at Pierre's feet, put her arms around him, and cover him with kisses.

The moment passed, leaving her empty and melancholy.

She stared back at the bridge. Her voice grew sullen. "Why is it, Pierre? You never speak to me seriously. You don't seem to think that I have a mind."

"You have charm. You have beauty," said Pierre lightly. "Those are much more important to me, you know!" He was smiling in his ironical way.

"There you are! Is it that you don't want a woman to be intelligent? Is that the French idea?"

"French? Not at all. In France we want women to be intelligent, but in a different way from men! In human matters, in emotions!"

"You'd like a woman to be mere decoration?"

"We want a woman to be womanly. So that a man can be manly."

"You sound very condescending," she said bitterly. "Very old-fashioned as well."

He did not reply. He was no longer smiling. His features grew set and hard; it was a look she had seen before, which she had learned to interpret, and which filled her with dread.

The boat turned a corner; they passed an overhanging willow tree. The yellow leaves spun in the air, like tassels. She watched their shadow flow over Pierre, caressing his face and naked shoulders. A twig brushed her forehead, like a little whip. And suddenly she felt like bursting into tears.

Two minutes later they were back at the landing. Pierre put on his shirt and coat with a sullen air, and they started silently up the path.

At that moment it began to rain a little.

"Shall I call a taxi?" said Pierre coldly. They were standing beside the drive, near Seventy-second Street.

A victoria drawn by a chestnut mare was passing. Pierre hailed it, and it came to a halt. They entered.

The raindrops fell on the roof of the carriage, and sounded like a small hammer beating above their heads. They breathed the smell of moist old cushions and of warm, weatherbeaten leather. They caught a whiff of the damp, healthy mare.

Delia leaned over and looked desperately into his eyes.

"Something has happened to us," she whispered. "What is it? What is it, darling?"

"Nothing," said Pierre, putting his arm casually over her shoulder. "But you must learn to be reasonable, Delia. I really can't ... " He hesitated.

"Yes?"

But he did not finish the sentence.

Delia began to feel a little calmer. But something in her, a residue of worry, drove her on. She longed to ask only a single, simple question: "Do you still love me as much as ever?" It was the only question which mattered at all.

But instead she said: "Something has been poisoned in us, Pierre. Something is wrong, awfully wrong. What is it? We no longer trust each other." The words startled and disturbed her the moment she uttered them.

Pierre looked at her gravely. He shook his head. "I don't understand your whims, Delia."

She leaned back, and suddenly the passion in her rose to the surface; she could no longer contain herself. Her lips began to tremble. And the passion in him replied. He drew her head close to his without a word, and looked into her eyes with a blending of pity, anger, and desire. Then he kissed her lips with a loving tenderness.

She yielded silently and closed her eyes. For a moment she felt completely calm; the anxiety vanished; she saw her plight with detachment. And she tried to understand what was happening.

She was struggling to find her way in a labyrinth. She was seeking to destroy the monster who divided and threatened them. But it cast up a sheet of mist the moment she approached it, and its features remained enigmatic, unseen. And the farther she wandered, the more she felt lost, darkened, endangered, until gradually a terrible fear came upon her: that the monster who was threatening her was not some outside power, but something in the very essence of her love.

She opened her eyes again. They were approaching the Plaza. The gilded statue of General Sherman rose in front of them.

Pierre dropped her at her hotel, the Shropshire, a block or two from the Plaza. It was just after five. He kissed her lightly on the cheek, paid the coachman, and walked back to the Plaza, where he had been invited to tea by Lady Temperly.

87

LADY TEMPERLY was just pouring the tea when Pierre entered the drawing room.

"Ah, here is our brilliant young painter!" she cried gaily, her eyes sparkling. "I am delighted, my dear, that you could join us. Here, sit down on the couch beside me. . . . You know Lady Brooke, of course? And you've met Horace Hayden, haven't you?"

Pierre had not seen Lady Temperly for several months. She had been dividing her summer between Mrs. Carter, at Southampton, and Mrs. Clyde, at Newport; she had returned to her rooms in the Plaza only ten days ago.

She had aged, Pierre noticed instantly. Her hair was tinged with a cool dead blue, and her face was more like a mask than ever. But her eyes retained their nervous sparkle. She kept glancing, almost feverishly, from one face to another, never allowing the conversation to lapse for a single instant.

"We've just been discussing Henry James!" she explained. "Everyone is reading Henry James all of a sudden. Even my *femme de chambre*. I used to enjoy his books, rather, but this new vogue I find a trifle disconcerting, I must say."

"I myself," declared Basil Hume, "care only for his late novels. Books like *The Ambassadors* and *The Golden Bowl*. The early works, you know, were merely finger exercises. Caprices. Ballet sketches. It's in those labyrinthine later works that one must look for his real genius!"

The debate continued. Horace Hayden sided ardently with the Late Jamesians, Dr. Cavanaugh sardonically supported the Early Jamesians. Pierre had read only *The Turn of the Screw,* and remained discreetly silent.

He glanced around the room; it looked surprisingly barren, almost desolate. All the books had been removed. The pictures—the Augustus John, the Félicien Rops—had gone, leaving a faint gray stain on the wall. Several large brown crates were standing in the hallway, and there was a scent of raw wood and sawdust. Even the tea service was no longer Lady Temperly's own. but bore the insignia of the hotel.

And somehow, the air of coming departure touched even the voices, the nods, the tinkling teacups. Everything seemed autumnal, ready to drift away. Pierre felt that he too was troubled by a restless feeling, a sense of impending, inevitable change. His afternoon with Delia had left him puzzled and depressed. Her presence hung over the drawing room like a cloud, and Lady Temperly's guests, with their rustle and chatter, seemed as insubstantial as autumn leaves.

"Apropos of Henry James," Lady Temperly was saying, "I remember a dinner party in London years ago. Henry James was sitting directly opposite me, near the end of the table. He talked for forty minutes on end, one interminable sentence. It lasted from the hors d'oeuvres all the way to the souffle. No one, of course, had the faintest inkling of what he was saying. It was like trying to find your way through a jungle. He sat absolutely still the rest of the evening, like a Chinese Buddha. There was something rather oriental about dear old Henry James, I'm afraid."

Mrs. Bellamy Carter arrived at this moment. She was wearing a stunning tweed suit with a bright red scarf, which exactly matched the glowing color of her cheeks. She looked as though she had just taken a long walk over a wind-swept moor; and, as always, she looked staggeringly lovely.

"Dear Clarissa," she murmured, in apologetic tones, "do forgive me! I just returned from the country five seconds ago; I didn't have time to change. It's too indecent of me, I know. ... "

"You look divine as always, Laura, my dear," said Lady Temperly. "You are—what shall I say? The Récamier, the Montespan, the Du Deffand of New York!"

"Well, you," said Wilfred gallantly, "are certainly New York's Rambouillet, my dear Clarissa!"

The evening light sprang through the window, gliding over the rug, the empty teacups, and the cold, barren walls. It looked like a golden vine which had suddenly cast its fiery tendrils across the room.

"Basil," pleaded Lady Temperly, "do go and draw the shade. That dreadful sunlight ... "

She herself rose and rang the service bell, her mothlike shape floating noiselessly through the darkened room. The waiter appeared and removed the dishes. As he did so the china teapot began to tremble on the tray, then fell and broke on the tiles in front of the fireplace.

A painful silence filled the room. The waiter gathered the fragments and quickly departed. Lady Temperly sighed. "We are still," she said softly, "at the mercy of the barbarians!"

Wilfred made a gallant effort to restore the conversation to a literary level. "I've just reread *The Egoist*," he observed. "A masterpiece. I simply adored it. But who reads Meredith nowadays? I feel too *démodé* for words. ... "

"Still, say what you will," retorted Lady Temperly, "poor old Meredith was never altogether a gentleman, in the strictest sense. I remember meeting him at a tennis party at Lady Lamprey's. I was only a schoolgirl, of course. ... "

She gazed reminiscently at the ceiling. In the gathering twilight her features took on a peaked, birdlike quality; her bluish hair quivered, like the crest of a cockatoo. Only through the glittering crevices of her eyes shone the remnants of a rich and passionate, hopelessly buried character.

Wilfred Silliman rose to leave. After he had gone Laura Carter inquired, with some concern: "Wilfred's been looking rather pale lately, I've noticed. Is he ill?"

"Haven't you heard?" said Lady Temperly sadly. "After Wilfred's dreadful experience with that Brattlebury woman, who left him for a young Bolivian, or Uruguayan, or something of the sort, he had a relapse; and then he fell madly in love with Kitty de Montfleury. You must have heard about it, Laura! We all breathed a sigh of relief. Kitty, after all, is a mature, fully developed type of woman, not given to flights of fancy. Mind you, I don't say she's past her bloom. She's still in the flush of womanhood, by French standards. She can't be a day over forty, or forty-five. It was a restful period for Wilfred, we all agreed. And now she's planning to go back to Paris. Which leaves poor Wilfred, as usual, high and dry. There you are. Love, for a man of Wilfred's sensibilities, is always a gamble. He's wasting away, I'm afraid."

Pierre could not be sure how much of this digression was intended as irony; Lady Temperly stared into space with a solicitous air.

And it occurred to Pierre that the whole tea party, in fact, was an elaborate little game. Its vivacity, its very existence sprang from its opportunities for disguise. Its whole flavor was that of a flight from reality, of a slightly feverish masquerade. And against this background of vanishing pastels, his scene with Delia appeared somber and disturbing. The airy gestures, the tinkling spoons were like a quaint little undertone to a grave and tragic theme.

There was a brisk double knock on the door.

"Please!" cried Lady Temperly. "Do come in, won't you?"

88

THE door opened, and two stout and rather bustling ladies in black gloves entered the room.

"Oh, I'm delighted you could come!" exclaimed Lady Temperly. "Sit down, May. Sit down, Susan. Would you like some tea? It will only take a moment. Or a glass of sherry, perhaps? ... No? You're sure?"

She introduced the Wilmerding sisters to the rest of her guests.

The Misses Wilmerding had been patrons of the arts for over a generation. But unlike certain other ladies, they were austere and circumspect in their appraisals. They were experienced huntsmen, out for big, well-authenticated game. Most of their protégés were gentlemen in their seventies. They would have no traffic with the ballet or the theater, or with any advanced tendencies in poetry or painting, all of which they associated with equivocal morals. May was the sturdier, the more resolute of the two. She was plump and short, wore suits of peppered tweed, and had a shrewd, uncompromising glitter in her eyes. Susan was the frailer, the more susceptible and dreamy. She dressed more daintily than her sister, with fruits and feathers quivering lightly on her hat. Once, thirty years ago, she had been engaged to a Spanish marquis, whom she had met in Granada. The affair had ended in a betrayal, a flood of tears, and a nervous collapse.

She had retired to Aix-les-Bains with her sister. Never, during her subsequent voyages to Europe, had she ventured near the Mediterranean. Both May and Susan had acquired, in the course of their long, determined challenge to the onrush of fashion, a certain rocklike impassivity. They almost never went out in public, except on behalf of some charity, such as the Polish Relief. Lately they had begun to take a philanthropical interest in politics.

The conversation swung to Russia.

"We may as well face the facts," declared Basil Hume acidly. "It's only a question of time before we come to blows with Russia. They're intoxicated with their power. They've made up their minds to rule the world. It's no longer a question of communism with them; it's sheer unadulterated megalomania."

"The peace, I'm afraid," remarked May Wilmerding pointedly, flicking off her black gloves, "has not solved the really big, the really disturbing problems."

"It has only made them look still bigger, and still more disturbing," sighed Susan, placing a handkerchief below her nose.

"Sometimes I almost wonder," whispered May, "well, whether we really were wise, after all ... " Her voice trailed off discreetly.

"Yes," put in Susan: "whether we really were altogether far-sighted in crushing ... you know ... those Teutonic elements." She coughed a little.

Lady Brooke and Dr. Cavanaugh rose to go. It was six-thirty; the tea party was beginning to break up.

"Well, I think we should try to understand Russia," announced Horace Hayden, who was clearly determined to stay till the end. "After all, Russians are just the same as Americans, basically."

"I'm afraid that's only too true," retorted Basil, with a prophetic air. "Russia and America. The two great dinosaur powers, physically vast, spiritually minute, rising like monsters above the ancient cultures, waiting to cast their machinelike equalitarianism over the world ... "

"Please!" interrupted May Wilmerding, with fury. "Say what you wish about Russia, but don't compare it with America, if you please! Dinosaurs! Well, really, Mr. Hume!"

"Well, in any case, Europe is finished," said Basil caustically. "It's a museum, that's all. Full of shattered odds and ends."

"Don't talk like an imbecile, Basil!" snapped Lady Temperly. "Europe finished, indeed! Europe a museum! Are you mad?"

"And please remember," put in Horace Hayden, "Americans are growing rather weary of coming to Europe's rescue, and receiving nothing but sneers in return. After all, you can't deny it, America is the land of the future!"

Basil's face grew purple with anger. A real quarrel was taking shape, and this time not about Henry James or George Meredith. The Americans, still divided between Horace Hayden on the left and the Misses Wilmerding on the right, were lining up against the Europeans, who themselves were similarly divided.

"Land of the future!" exclaimed Baron Legué, who had been sitting in silence. "You dance attendance on French fashions, French painting, French film directors. All you have is gold, oceans of gold. ... "

"America," admitted Horace Hayden, "is still groping for her spiritual identity."

"Yes!" snapped Basil. "Groping for it among the pocketbooks and profit columns!"

"I did not come here," said May Wilmerding, rising, with a strange pallor on her face, "to hear my country insulted. I can't help feeling that foreigners had best stay at home if they don't care for our customs. Come, Susan, I think we'd better leave." The two sisters swept from the room.

"America and Europe," sighed Lady Temperly, "will never quite see eye to eye, I'm afraid. ... There's more than just an ocean dividing them!"

"Americans are childishly oversensitive," said Basil Hume. "When they go to Europe, they feel at perfect liberty to sneer. But the moment a European utters a peep over here, they lose their tempers. ... "

"Everyone is rude in New York," agreed Baron Legué. "One can't buy a newspaper without risking an insult. One can't enter a restaurant without being terrorized by the waiters. If that's what democracy finally comes to ... "

"Would you prefer concentration camps?" said Horace Hayden, his eyes bulging.

"I think not," murmured the baron, rising. "Nor would I prefer the Black Hole of Calcutta."

"Please, please," cried Lady Temperly in a strange, high voice. "Let us stop quarreling! Let us stop quarreling!"

The drawing room had grown dark and rather cool. An evening wind was stirring the thin lace curtains. Pierre rose to leave; Lady Temperly smiled as he thanked her, but it was a dry, frozen smile.

89

JONATHAN arrived at Wyndham Park late the following afternoon. It was his first visit since Mr. Mannering's death.

Avery met him at the door.

"Mrs. Mannering will be down in half an hour, sir."

"Am I the first guest, Avery?"

Avery nodded discreetly. "The first for a long time, sir. ... "

Jonathan walked across the oak-paneled drawing room. It was the same as always, but there was a musty smell hovering about. His footsteps had a hollow sound as he crossed the floor.

He entered the library. It was empty and dark. The curtains had been drawn; a layer of dust covered the furniture. Jonathan drew a curtain to one side, and a haze of sunlight filtered through the dusty panes.

Through the window he could see the great feather-shaped elms outside, faintly gilded with autumn. The lawn was thick and tufted, and the tennis court beyond was spotted with weeds.

Jonathan turned to look at the books. There were large gaps in the shelves where the more precious volumes, such as *Adonais* and *Vanity Fair,* had been removed for sale at auction shortly after Mr. Mannering's death. The framed manuscripts had also gone, leaving pale rectangles on the wall behind them. A film of deterioration hung over the rows of morocco; the leather and gilt had lost their sheen. The whole delicate structure of Mr.

Mannering's collection, all his obsession with rarities and variations, had quietly collapsed. The books looked as dry and lifeless as insects.

Jonathan opened the door into the garden, and slowly crossed the lawn. His footsteps made no sound; the grass gave like a cushion. The distant elms dropped plummets of shadow on the grass. The air was utterly still, and the boughs were leaning toward the source of brightness; their leaves hung unnaturally stiff and shining.

There was something disquieting in this hush and dereliction. Jonathan felt that the spirit of the place had died, and a new antagonistic presence had come to take its place. There was a sound of unfamiliar voices in the distance. He had a feeling that he was being observed. He wondered whether he had lost his way into a neighboring estate.

But as he turned he saw the familiar house behind him and, advancing silently across the lawn, the tall pale shape of Mrs. Mannering.

She greeted him, and he saw in her eyes the same cool curiosity that he himself was feeling.

"Jonathan, my dear! You haven't changed a bit! Well, you look more solid, of course. A little more mature ... How does it feel to be a civilian again?"

"I've almost forgotten I was ever in the Army," said Jonathan, smiling. "Everything is exactly the same as before. Only perhaps a little more ... " He hesitated.

"Yes?" said Mrs. Mannering, watching him shrewdly. "A little more desolate, perhaps?"

They were standing under a large elm; small yellow leaves fell past them slowly. Jonathan glanced at Mrs. Mannering with a certain surprise.

He had not seen her for four years. She had grown bland and matronly. Her hair was not quite gray, and had been frozen by the hairdresser into rows of tiny curls. She was still very smart; her figure was still shapely. But the tension had gone out of her. Her face had shed its crispness, and her eyes were apathetic. Her movements were slower, her voice was a little thinner.

They walked together down the path that led to the shore.

"I'm so happy you could come, dear. Life's been so dull lately," she said rather resentfully. "Everyone's away. Ever since the war ended people seem too busy to call on their friends!"

The path turned. They could see the smooth gray water of the Sound below them. It was altogether still and deserted here.

"I've asked Delia to come out for dinner," Mrs. Mannering observed casually. "Poor Delia. She's cut herself off from her old friends. It's been months since I've laid eyes on her. It's so disastrous, what she's doing! I'm worried to death about Delia." She sighed.

"I met her at the Zoo the other day," said Jonathan carefully.

"Oh, you did?" Mrs. Mannering glanced at him swiftly.

"For several minutes."

"How did she look?"

"Lovely. As always."

Mrs. Mannering coughed slightly. "Well, Delia used to be perfectly lovely, of course, in a dull kind of way. But Kitty van Lennep says she's coarsened a bit. Well, it was bound to happen. That whole affair has been a calamity. And then, poor Quincy ... "

They approached the shore. "It's always a ghastly mistake," she continued, "to mix nationalities. At least with the French. They are so calculating. One can never be sure of their motives."

"Pierre," said Jonathan somewhat guiltily, "is a good sort. I've known him for years. He's an excellent character."

"Perhaps," said Mrs. Mannering tartly. "I wouldn't trust him an inch, myself."

"What is Delia planning to do?" asked Jonathan, after a moment. "Is she ... arranging for a divorce?"

Mrs. Mannering raised her eyebrows. "Well, I'm sure Pierre isn't seriously thinking of marrying her."

Jonathan was startled. "What makes you think so?"

"I know him pretty well, you know," said Mrs. Mannering, in a delicate tone. "Perhaps I know a thing or two that even Delia doesn't know."

Again Jonathan had the sense of some hostile influence in the air; a stirring in the leaves, a shadow across the grass.

"I hope," he said with sudden fervor, "that they will stay together!"

Mrs. Mannering looked at him with frozen lips. Then she said: "Please be careful, Jonathan. Remember, you are Quincy's cousin."

Jonathan felt a moment of penetrating disgust. He felt that Wyndham Park, the house, the garden, the spirit of the place, was touched with some withering kind of acid.

He said quietly: "I hope that Delia will be happy."

"She has dug her own grave," said Mrs. Mannering very softly.

The path turned again. They heard the sound of laughter beyond the leaves. Through the trunks they could see the shallows of a cove, and the tawny eel grass moving softly. A rowboat lay fastened to a rotting pier, and two naked youths were standing astride it, boisterously rocking it to and fro. They began to wrestle. Their wet bare skin shone in the sunlight. The younger one rose suddenly, flushed and excited, stood poised on the edge of the boat, and dived into the water. The other, the darker and more heavily muscled, sprang after him and they began to race through the water, followed by the leaping sparkle of drops.

Jonathan glanced at Mrs. Mannering. She had turned quite pale; her lips had tightened.

"Come," she said in a thin, harsh voice. "I don't care to see this kind of thing."

They followed the path back to the house in silence.

90

TWO tall candles were burning on the dining-room table, leaving the rest of the room abnormally dark. The only other guests, aside from Delia, were old Lucy Westover, and of course Wilfred Silliman.

The dinner itself was silent and uneventful. Jonathan told a few trivial anecdotes of Army life in Alabama. Mrs. Westover spoke of the great days of tennis, when manners on the court were still impeccable. Mr. Silliman spoke of the decay of social standards, which permitted parvenus like Horace Hayden to burst into the better drawing rooms. Mrs. Mannering spoke of her committee work for the Junior League and the Vassar alumnae.

Jonathan kept glancing at Delia at the other end of the table. She looked calm and composed; but she hardly seemed to be listening. She was dressed in black crepe, and looked paler than usual.

After dinner they strolled into the living room for their coffee and a rubber of bridge.

Mrs. Westover took out her knitting and kept up an accompaniment of small talk, while Delia and Jonathan played as partners against Mrs. Mannering and Wilfred.

Avery passed behind them, pouring out the cointreau into tapering Swedish glasses.

"Well, it's restful," murmured Mrs. Westover, "to have you back with us, Jonathan. I like to see the family stick together. You're finally turning into a real Mannering, I can't help noticing. Those worried lines on your forehead, and the square jaw, just like your uncle Winthrop's. ... I only met your father twice, my boy, but he struck me as an eccentric, I'm afraid. An idealist. A dreamer. Frankly, I never understood why your dear mother married him. Grace always had her whims. You're different, thank the Lord. Solid and dependable. Well ... "

"What do you bid, Wilfred?" demanded Mrs. Mannering.

"Two hearts," said Wilfred blandly.

"Two spades," said Jonathan cautiously.

"Three hearts," declared Mrs. Mannering.

"Three no-trump," murmured Delia.

Wilfred quietly doubled.

Delia looked startled, almost panic-stricken. "Am I playing the hand?" she murmured.

She glanced swiftly at Jonathan, for the first time in the evening. Her blue eyes had darkened; there was a momentary look of appeal, an almost imperceptible flicker in her pupils. The barrier of reserve between her and Jonathan seemed to waver.

"How is Quincy, by the way?" inquired Mrs. Westover cheerfully. "Doing well in his new office, I hope. That war work was never the right thing for him. He took it much too seriously. By the way, my dear, I don't wish to bring in politics, but since we're on the subject of Quincy, I hear his behavior has been distinctly bohemian. Didn't you tell me he'd voted for Roosevelt, Pauline? It's the first time a Potter or a Mannering has ever been so careless, I must say. Whom can one trust nowadays? Here is a man of breeding, a member of the Racquet Club, educated at St. Paul's and Yale, a friend of the Van Lenneps and the Wilmerdings, and suddenly he turns his back on it all. ... It's been a blow to me, frankly."

Delia went down four tricks. Both Wilfred and Mrs. Mannering were very experienced players.

"I'm terribly sorry," she murmured, without glancing at Jonathan.

Jonathan dealt and bid. "One diamond."

"Two clubs," said Mrs. Mannering.

"Three diamonds," said Delia faintly, after a pause.

"Four clubs," said Wilfred, delicately raising his brows.

"Five diamonds," said Jonathan rather hesitantly.

"I think I'll double," stated Mrs. Mannering.

Jonathan played his hand as well as he could, but he went down three tricks. Delia's hand turned out considerably weaker than he expected. Wilfred's face was inscrutable; Mrs. Mannering looked unconcerned.

Mrs. Westover gathered her knitting and bid them all good night.

The curtains in front of the window began to stir; a wind was rising.

And Jonathan grew aware of a subtle heightening of the atmosphere. The only light in the room was the orange glow of the bridge lamp, which shone on the faces, the hands, and the square of green baize. For a moment no one stirred; they all seemed to be waiting.

"I think we're in for a storm," said Wilfred, glancing at the window. "The weather's been a trifle bizarre all day."

"It's been disgustingly hot," agreed Mrs. Mannering. "A bit of rain will do us good. I dealt, didn't I? ... Two hearts."

"Bye," said Delia. She had hardly spoken all evening; her voice was mild and indifferent.

Again she glanced at Jonathan, but instantly lowered her eyes. She looked tense and self-absorbed. The slant of the lamplight cast a shadow below each eye, and a restless blue line across her forehead. She looked a little feverish; perhaps it was the glow of the lamp.

Avery appeared with a highball tray, which he placed on the small glass wagon beside Jonathan.

"Won't you pour out the drinks, dear?" said Mrs. Mannering blithely.

"Three hearts," said Wilfred, with a touch of austerity.

Jonathan went bye, and began pouring the drinks.

"Four hearts," said Mrs. Mannering. "No more bids? I'm playing the hand, it seems. Your lead, Jonathan. ... Splendid, Wilfred. Thank you! Well, I'm afraid I'll have to trump that. ... I'm relieved that Lucy has gone to bed. I was growing a bit nervous when she went on like that about Quincy. You don't mind my talking frankly, do you, Delia? After all, we're among friends here. ... What are you putting on, Jonathan? ... Splendid. That's my fourth lucky finesse tonight. ... Well, as I was saying, I thought of asking Pierre out today, but you can't be sure about Lucy; she can be so tactless. God knows what she may have heard. ... It's you, Delia. You're playing the queen? Well, well, I'll have to put on my king, I'm afraid. ... I'm fond of Pierre, myself. He has charm. Too much for his own good. He's been spoiled by women. And he's extremely good-looking, of course. Still, one should never trust beauty in a man. Beauty should be reserved for women. ... There, I think I'll do it this way. Good. I'm lucky tonight. Well, that's game. You're dealing, I believe, Delia. ... A beautiful man can never be trusted. Above all, a beautiful Frenchman. Don't think for a moment, Delia, that I think you've done anything wrong. After all, we've passed the age of puritanism! It's merely a matter of practical common sense. ... You went bye, Wilfred? Well, I'll say two hearts. ... I was lunching with Estelle Webber at the Colony yesterday. She tells me some rather odd stories have been going around about Pierre. I shouldn't say this, I know, but it's for your own good, Delia. Not that I expect you to take my advice. Still, there it is. ... You said two no-trump, Wilfred? I'll go three. ... Well, one might as well face it, these foreigners are not our sort. They have a streak of corruption in them. It would be silly to expect Pierre to be faithful to any woman; he's just not built that way. Mind you, I don't say he's not perfectly manly. ... Oh, a brilliant hand, Wilfred! Thank you again. You're an absolute angel. ... No, I think the sooner these foreigners go back to Europe, the better for all of us. ... Your lead, Jonathan. ... Why, Delia, dear, what's the matter?"

Delia had risen from the bridge table. She looked extremely pale. Her hand lay pressed against her throat in a swift, uneasy gesture. She glanced quickly around the room.

"I'm afraid I'm not well," she said softly and rapidly. "I must be going back. Do forgive me, please. ... "

Mrs. Mannering looked at her with concern.

"Certainly, dear. If you think you'd better go. I noticed you hadn't been looking well. Wilfred, do ask Avery to order the car. I'm too upset about it, darling. A good night's rest, that's what you need."

Wilfred and Jonathan had also risen. Wilfred rang the bell and spoke discreetly to Avery. Delia walked into the hall, with a light quick tread, swiftly drew on her coat, and slipped into the night.

91

THE chauffeur dropped Delia in front of her hotel on Sixtieth Street, but instead of going in she walked swiftly up Fifth Avenue to Sixty-third Street, and entered the house where Pierre lived.

She rang his bell in the entrance hall. There was no answer. She waited breathlessly, and rang again, and then a third time.

Then she stepped into the street again and looked at his two windows. Both were open, and she saw the curtains stirring in the darkness.

She called softly, "Pierre!" No one answered; the windows remained dark, and she knew that he was out. But for some uncertain reason she called again, and then once more.

Her heart was pounding violently and her hands were trembling. The night was dead and sultry, but she felt a sudden chill in her arms. There had been a hint of a thunderstorm in the air; but the storm had not come, and a thickness hung in the atmosphere.

She glanced down the street. On the ground floor of a neighboring house a light was shining brightly. She watched the rays fall on the pavement, and then she realized that they shone from her own former home, in which she had not set foot for a year. She felt a twinge of something which resembled loneliness, but was darker and more engulfing than loneliness. The pale, sloping light suggested all that had vanished, the years of boredom and waste, the life she had scorned and cast aside. Yet the sight of it in the darkness consoled her for a moment. And then, a moment later, it left her more disturbed than ever. It symbolized the life of security which she once possessed but discarded, which she loathed but still intensely needed, and which she now felt was forbidden her.

She wandered on a few steps, until she stood directly outside the window.

It was the central window of the drawing room. She recognized the lace curtains, and behind them the curtains of green velvet. She could just see the old ormolu clock on the mantel, and the head of a small porcelain dog.

And the whole, dense aroma of the room sprang to life again, penetrating the barrier of glass and stone. For the first time she felt the full impact of its flavor, and grasped the true meaning of each detail—the books, the rugs, the rosewood console. It was a frail and obsolete little fortress: a last defense against the powers of darkness.

At first she noticed no one in the room. Then she saw that a man was sitting on the couch, with his back turned, reading a book and smoking. She saw the little plume of cigarette smoke drifting past the lamp. The head stirred; she recognized the lusterless, thinning hair, and the slightly egglike shape of the skull.

As she watched, he rose and walked slowly across the room. She could now see his face and the upper part of his body. She could tell by his expression that he was alone. He stood at the farther end of the room, facing the window which gave on the garden. His hand was resting on the piano. Now his face was turned away, and there was something pitiful in the shape of his dull, unimaginative back. Then he turned and stood in front of the fireplace, and stared vacantly at the clock. Now she saw his face clearly.

And all the bitterness, the resentment which had been gathering in her for weeks came to a head at that moment and were focused on Quincy. She felt obscurely that he was to blame for the feeling of waste, the sense of insecurity which began to obsess her. His face revealed nothing but passivity and pathos; yet this only sharpened her antagonism. She was about to leave.

Quincy's face seemed to break. He leaned forward against the marble mantel, from which his hands were hanging limply, and placed his forehead against his hands. His face was now in shadow, but she guessed precisely what the expression must be, and the peculiar, desolate nature of his suffering.

Yet this realization, which came to her instantly and unmistakably, left her completely unmoved. She felt no trace of pity for Quincy, and not the slightest concern. She no longer felt any contact with his presence beyond the window.

She continued to watch, but the scene in the room was like a scene in a dream. Every strand of emotion in her was in a state of tension, and her normal feelings and faculties were almost numb. Everything in her was pointed toward Pierre and Pierre alone; and toward the rest of the world she felt nothing but an utter estrangement, touched with loathing.

Quincy raised his head again and glanced toward the street. A change of expression passed over his face. His eyes seemed to sharpen, as though something had occurred to him. He crossed the room again, with the air of a sleepwalker, and came to a halt directly in front of the window where Delia was standing.

Quickly she moved away, and hurried down Sixty-third Street.

92

DELIA arrived in her hotel room in a state of exhaustion. She turned on the light and stood by the door, faintly surprised.

For a moment she felt that she must have entered the wrong room. It seemed wholly unfamiliar, peculiarly bleak and ugly. The furniture looked drab, the colors in the rug were garish.

Then she caught sight of herself in the full-length mirror. Again she was startled; it was a stranger she saw. The figure which faced her, dressed in black crepe, looked intensely pale and rather ill; the eyes were bloodshot, and the face was lined with fatigue. With a tremor of disgust she recognized who it was.

She closed her eyes for a moment, then crossed the room swiftly. She sat down at the desk and immediately tried to call Pierre's studio. There was no answer. "Please try again," she told the operator in a faint, thin voice. "It's rather urgent. You may have dialed the wrong number." But again there was no answer. She stared at the black receiver in her hand, and hung it cautiously back on the hook.

She lay down on the bed. She had opened the window, and a warm restless breeze was ruffling the curtains.

She drew her finger tips across her eyes and tried to think.

Something appalling was happening; of that she felt certain; something she was utterly unable to control. A swift, invisible decay was at work in the love between her and Pierre.

Her own love was no longer sweet and resilient. It was studded with misgivings, splinters of bitterness; even the moments of bodily passion were no longer consoling.

She reached up, found the switch, and turned off the light. And as she lay in the darkness, she tried to force her thoughts into some sort of order. She tried to grasp the reasons for her growing uneasiness. Mrs. Mannering's phrases came back to her, one by one. Each had its own insidious little sting.

"You can't expect him to be faithful." "Some rather odd stories have been going around." What did it all mean? There was something in the very vagueness of these hints which haunted and sickened her.

But she knew, as she reflected on these things, that they did not lie at the core of her agitation. The real poison lay deeper. She felt, with a touch of anguish, that there was a subtler energy at work, something self-destructive in the very nature of their love and the world surrounding it; something for which there was no cure, from which flight was impossible, and from which disaster was bound to flow. She tried to visualize a state of happiness ahead: it refused, obstinately, to cohere. Yet she saw no reason for all this, it was an irrational fear; and this only added to her sense of terrifying helplessness.

She turned on the light again, rose, and for the third time tried to phone his studio. Her fingers trembled as she waited. But again there was no answer.

She picked up a book from the mirror-topped table beside the armchair. But she did not even open it; she dropped it again, and began to walk swiftly up and down the room. She could think of only one thing; only one thing mattered: Was Pierre, after all, still in love with her?

She paused in front of the open window and looked out. She took a deep breath; there was a fragrance in the air, an autumnal scent which rose not from the trees, but from the withering vitality in the street itself—the nervous rustle of the traffic, the diminuendo of a thousand footsteps. There was something consoling, something resembling an opiate, in the hot and quivering, anonymous night.

She turned; her hand fell instinctively on the telephone, and swiftly recoiled. She pressed her hands together and walked rapidly across the room.

She sat down again, lit a cigarette, and picked up the book. It was Conrad's *Typhoon.* She opened it calmly, but her eyes wandered instantly from the page. She stared in front of her, and a single question repeated itself over and over, in a constantly varying rhythm.

The telephone rang. Her heart leaped violently, and she had to pause for a moment to collect her nerves. Slowly, with a sort of fright, she touched the receiver.

"Hello? ... Yes, dear. ... Yes, I came home earlier than I expected. ... No, I'm quite alone. ... Please do. ... How long will you be? ... Fifteen minutes? ... Good-by, dear."

Her voice had been light and casual. But her heart was pounding uncontrollably. She had succumbed to a mingling of hope, panic, and ungovernable joy.

The window was open. Her sense of isolation had dissolved, and the feeling of delight that swept over her now seemed, somehow, to renew her link with the world outside. She leaned out of the window and felt the heavy air flow past her. The street far below was teeming with life; with a life which now was filled with warmth, intimacy, and hope. She thought wildly: "I am happy again. If I could only die at this moment, while I still am happy ... "

She turned away from the window. The appearance of the room had changed utterly; it looked gentle and protective. The light shed a warm yellow glow on the rug, the rosy curtains, and the chenille coverlet.

She decided to lie down for several minutes. Her heart was beating at a feverish pace. She closed her eyes; little by little she forced her body into discipline.

Then she rose and sat down in front of the mirror. She was astonished when she looked at her face. Her freshness and luster had returned. Her eyes looked back at her with a heightened intensity, a desperate exultation. She continued to sit and gaze at her face, with a novel kind of pleasure and curiosity.

Then she looked at her watch. Twenty-five minutes had passed. A hideous little fear was beginning to return. She rose and walked slowly back toward the window, as though drawn by a magnet, and pulled aside the curtain.

There was a knock on the door.

"Yes?" she cried. "Is it you, Pierre?"

93

PIERRE entered. She smiled at him lightly, and ran her hand carelessly through her hair.

Instantly the magic of his physical vitality filled the room. Everything in the room—the light, the objects, her own being—reflected the glow cast out by his presence.

His face was shining with pleasure. And yet, mysteriously, instead of reassuring her, this expression suddenly confused and even antagonized her.

He leaned over and kissed her. He seemed to notice immediately that something was wrong.

"Aren't you well, Delia?"

She glanced at him rather indulgently, and smiled. And it occurred to her that during these last few days she had begun to practice a ceaseless dissimulation with him.

"You're late," she said softly.

"Am I?" he said, and pressed her hand affectionately. "I was out with Maxim de la Tour. He's going back to Paris next month. I envy him, I must say!"

Delia's heart sank once more. "Would you like to be going too?" she said, with indifference.

"Certainly!" His voice was still exuberant. "But I can't afford it, of course. Two exhibitions during the next two months, and besides . . . " He stood in front of her as she sat there, leaned over, placed his hands on her cheeks, and tilted her head. "You wouldn't be able to go with me yet. And I don't want to leave you. Not even for a month," he said softly, and kissed her forehead.

A wave of hope stirred in her; but only for a moment.

"Was there," she murmured, "anyone else with you?"

"Oh, a new girl of Maxim's. A Chilean girl."

Delia felt herself instantly on the alert. "How was she?" she inquired casually.

"Dull. Stupid," said Pierre. "She sat and looked at Maxim with huge adoring black eyes. That was all. She didn't say a single word all evening."

Delia felt an irrepressible spirit of combat rising in her. "Well, did she look at you too? You're better-looking than Maxim, you know."

Pierre laughed lightheartedly. He sat down on the window sill, sideways, with one foot resting on the sill. "By the way," he said, in a more sober tone, "I shan't be lunching with you tomorrow. Do you mind, Delia?"

"Not at all," said Delia very softly.

"Mr. Prendergast, who practically runs the new museum, has asked me to come. I can't really refuse."

"Certainly not," whispered Delia. "I quite understand."

Pierre looked at her contritely. "Are you angry, darling?"

She shook her head. "I don't expect you to keep your promises to me," she said, in an unnatural tone.

His face grew more solemn. She could see the line of his lips hardening, and a small dark furrow between his brows; she felt a stab of fear.

Her voice grew submissive. "If it's really important for you, dear," she added. "Only ... "

He was watching her coldly. One hand lay flat upon his knee, the other was resting on the window sill.

"Well, it doesn't matter," she went on quickly. "I can find someone else, I suppose. It's just that I like to keep to my plans. I like to feel that I can depend on ... my friends."

Pierre turned his head and looked into the night. He said nothing.

His face was in darkness as he stared at the sky, but the back of his head, with its tight little curls, shone softly. There was something innocent and lovable in the way his hair curled above the back of his neck; and Delia, as she watched him silently, felt her familiar tenderness return.

He lit a cigarette. The lines of his face and the curve of his hand grew bright in the match light; he looked cold, incomprehensible. And a feeling of hopeless isolation swept over Delia once again.

A twinge of bitterness, almost of hatred, shot through her tenderness. The two emotions seemed to fuse and to feed upon each other. A sudden maniacal little vision occurred to her; he sat so lightly, so helplessly on the edge of the sill. She drew a deep breath and drew her hand across her forehead.

She said, in a changed voice: "I think I know what you are feeling."

Pierre turned around. His eyes were bright and angry. "Why are you so odd tonight, Delia? What on earth has happened? What is wrong?"

"You feel chained," said Delia in a low, stubborn tone. Then she said very slowly: "You are tired of me."

She regretted having said this the moment she uttered the words; but she went on. "You want a change. Shall we stop seeing each other? For a month or two? Is that what you wish?"

Pierre's face remained bright and hard. She glanced at him with a pang of misery. "It's too late," she thought; "there's no hope. Everything is over. Everything." And she thought of trying one last dramatic gesture; hurling herself on the floor in front of him, bursting into a frenzy of tears.

Then she thought: "Am I going mad?" She saw, in a flash of lucidity, the whole situation as it really was: trivial and petulant. But somehow this only added to her sense of hopelessness.

"I don't care to discuss it," said Pierre in a low voice.

Then his expression changed again, as he stood and looked at her; his face melted, and a look of pity appeared.

He sat down on the arm of her chair and looked into her eyes. Then he kissed her, at first gently, then firmly and passionately.

And the tension was released, with almost painful abruptness, and her body melted into his arms. She burst into sobs, and as he drew her closer, his lips began to move tenderly over her eyes, her cheeks, and her shoulders. The whole world was transfigured as she felt his hands move across her. All other feelings dissolved, and were transformed into love.

"I felt frightened," she whispered. "That was all. That was all."

94

ON THE following day Jonathan received a card which read: "Mrs. Clyde. Sutton Place. Thursday, September 13, 5:30 to 7:00." Across the top of the card was written, in blue ink: "To say good-by to Lady Temperly."

Jonathan had never met Lady Temperly, but he knew Mrs. Clyde, who was a close friend of the Westovers and the Wilmerdings.

On Thursday morning he received two phone calls.

The first was from Prince Sharavaji, whom he had not seen since his ballet party four years ago. Jonathan immediately recognized his tinkling, sparrowlike voice.

"Jonathan? Well, well! Can you guess who this is? ... Perfect! You are a genius, my dear. Come for tea with me this afternoon. ... At five? ... That will be delicious. Good-by. ... "

The second was from Quincy. His voice sounded flat and apologetic.

"I've been wanting to see you, Jonathan. How about a bit of squash this afternoon, old fellow? I've booked a court at four. ... Oh, don't worry, I've hardly touched a racket myself for months. I'll be seeing you at four then? So long. ... "

When Jonathan arrived at the club he found Quincy waiting for him in the locker room, already dressed for the game. Jonathan borrowed a pair of white shorts and a freshly strung racket, and began to undress.

A distinct change had come over Quincy. He had gained weight perceptibly, and his hair had receded farther. The skin on his face was pink and shining; an antiseptic scent rose from his person. He kept coughing a little, placing two perpendicular fingers over his lips each time, and stared at Jonathan with a glazed, preoccupied look.

"Well, I suppose you're glad to be back in New York?"

Jonathan nodded. "It's livelier than Alabama, at any rate." He stepped into the white shorts.

"You're pretty fit, I see," muttered Quincy. "How do you keep your weight down?"

"Oh, life's been fairly simple in Alabama, you know," said Jonathan, tying his shoelaces. "Not much to get fat on.... Well, shall we start? Have you a ball?"

They entered the squash court and began to play. It was a warm day, and soon they were sweating heavily. Quincy was not a very good player, but today he was distinctly worse than usual. He was listless and slow on his feet, and was continually forgetting the score. They played five games, which lasted twenty-five minutes.

"Well, I'm sorry I didn't give you a better game, old man," he said wearily, as they left the court. "I'll have to get old Danny to give me a few lessons; I've lost my form entirely."

"Your eye," admitted Jonathan, "was just a bit off."

They sat down on a bamboo couch and ordered two highballs.

Quincy sat in silence; he looked pale with exhaustion, and his jersey was dripping.

He wiped his face with a towel, leaned back, and said: "I've been thinking of going South this winter. For a change of air. I haven't been well, you know. Sinus. Insomnia. A constant headache all summer ... What would you think of a trip to Mexico?

I hear it's been tidied up a bit. Of course, I can always stay with the Barclay Potters, down in Palm Beach." He sighed, and kept running his finger tips along the bamboo arms. There was not a trace of his old briskness and enthusiasm.

He turned to Jonathan and said softly: "Have you seen Delia since you're back?"

"I saw her last Sunday," said Jonathan. "Out at Wyndham Park."

Quincy raised his glass, looked at the ceiling with his luster-less eyes, and put the glass down again without drinking.

"I hope she's well," he said in an unnatural tone. "How did she seem?"

"Rather quiet," said Jonathan discreetly. "Beautiful as always, of course."

Quincy shot a strange look at him. "Yes," he muttered. "She was beautiful, wasn't she?" He coughed a little, and pressed his fingers more firmly along the bamboo.

For several minutes they sat in silence. Quincy lit a cigarette.

"You're my oldest friend, Jonathan," he said in a dull tone, and coughed again. "What do you think? I can't help worrying. I hear she's changed. Of course, if she really wants a divorce ... "

There was something weak and helpless in Quincy's whole manner. Jonathan felt thoroughly ill at ease; he felt, to his own surprise, almost no sympathy for Quincy. He could think of nothing at all to say.

Quincy's voice grew thin and painful. "I wish I knew what to do, Jonathan. I haven't seen her for months. I don't dare call her up. I'm at a loss, absolutely. ... "

He raised his glass again. This time he pressed it to his lips; but again he put it down without actually drinking.

He stared vacuously toward the locker room. His smooth pink face seemed to swell a little; there was something rather dreadful in its egglike serenity, utterly unlined by pain or passion. His misery was shapeless and coreless, and a little repulsive.

His expression changed. An unusual light came to his face, and he looked at Jonathan with bleak, distended eyes. "I'm at a loss," he repeated hoarsely. "I'm at an absolute loss! What is wrong? Life seems to have shriveled away! Nothing seems real any longer! Everything is gray and meaningless. I miss Delia, of course, but, well, it's more than that. I used to feel bright and fresh when I came to the office every morning. I used to feel ambitious. I used to enjoy seeing my friends, playing squash, eating dinner. ... Now it's all completely stale. Dull, gray, empty. I don't want to see anyone. I don't feel like doing anything. ... "

He picked up the towel and ran it over his forehead.

"You need a rest," said Jonathan gently. "You need a change, Quincy."

Quincy stared vacantly at the ceiling. "Sometimes," he said slowly, "I feel that everything I've worked for, and believed in all my life, is nothing but thin air. ... Nothing at all, nothing."

They sat silently for several minutes, sipping their drinks. A group of young players had just returned from the squash courts, cheerful and dripping, and were arguing playfully about the matches.

Jonathan looked at his watch. "Excuse me, Quincy," he murmured. "I'll have to rush!" And he hurried off to the shower room; he was due in twenty minutes at Prince Sharavaji's.

95

PRINCE SHARAVAJI'S SUITE in the Sherry-Netherland was almost unrecognizable. Instead of the Dresden figurines and Sheraton chairs there now were Polynesian masks on the wall, and chairs of plastic and chromium.

The prince welcomed Jonathan with his usual melancholy delight. His golden bracelets tinkled as he waved his arms in welcome. He had grown somewhat stouter, in the oriental manner, with dark circles around his eyes and a bluish withering of the hands. He was wearing a shirt of pale green silk, a brown pin-striped suit, and brown suède sandals.

"Yes," he said slyly, as they sat down, "I heard you were back! Dear, dear, you look dreadfully healthy, my dear Jonathan. Not like the rest of us lascivious, dissipated New Yorkers. Ah, what a strain it is, this New York! ... I have tea, you see, the way I used to at Balliol. It gives a moment of Old World repose. ... Cream, my dear? Sugar?"

He poured a cup for Jonathan. A plate of small French cakes was brought in by a Negro butler, together with a jar of honey and a white covered dish.

"Scones! Crumpets!" cried Prince Sharavaji, lifting the cover from the dish. "And honey for tea! ... Such is my longing," he explained sadly, "for the English customs." He sighed and sipped daintily at his tea.

Presently he said, raising his brows: "I see you've noticed my new paintings. Well, do you like them?"

"They're quite a change," observed Jonathan tactfully, "from the Boucher and the Fragonard that used to hang there."

"Boucher! Fragonard!" Prince Sharavaji smiled condescendingly. "Ah, Jonathan, they were just a phase. Just a bagatelle. I was still groping for my true discriminations!"

He pointed to a large, geometrical painting beside the fireplace. "That one is a new Duchêne. He is a Non-Objectivist. He doesn't paint mere objects, you understand, such as flowers or cows. There's nothing sentimental about him; just a kind of cerebral essence. ... He is dreadfully fashionable this year!"

He pointed toward another—a scene of starving refugees crossing a frozen cataract. "That is a new Karnilowski," he explained. "Full of pain. Full of political awareness. The artist, Jonathan, must learn to face modern realities! ... Another cup, my dear? Another crumpet?"

"You have become," Jonathan ventured, "a real New Yorker,

it seems!"

The little potentate beamed with gratification. His lips curved into an uncontrollable smile. "I have a sentiment of ease here," he admitted. "Of culture. Of sophistication."

"Do you sometimes feel homesick for India, perhaps? Now and then?"

"Oh mercy!" cried the prince uneasily. "You joke, Jonathan. That crude amorphous land! No, no. Civilization has moved westward!"

But in spite of his naïveté, something in Prince Sharavaji had changed and deteriorated. His childlike enthusiasm had been replaced by a nervous glibness; his refreshing bad taste had given way to mimicry and modishness. He looked a bit worn, and rather miserable.

He smiled at Jonathan mischievously. "We have a mutual friend, my dear. Can you guess?"

"Man or woman?" inquired Jonathan affably. "Old or young?"

"Oh, young! A lady! Very pretty! Very talented...."

Jonathan shook his head. "I can't imagine."

"Try and guess," said the prince playfully. "She does something with her toes."

"With her toes?" said Jonathan rather nervously.

"In the ballet!" exclaimed Prince Sharavaji, with a salacious air. "She has curly brown hair and a little mole on her chin.... Can you guess?" He sounded a bit breathless. His eyes were shining—with pride, it appeared.

Jonathan nodded thoughtfully. "I think I can guess," he murmured.

"She is a brilliant woman, Jonathan! A very sensitive soul. I feel she understands me. We have become very intimate. She knows"—he leaned forward and whispered—"all that a woman needs to know."

And he grew confidential. "Ah, Jonathan," he presently exclaimed, in lyrical tones, "New York is a great Babylon! The minute I step into the street my heart begins to flutter! Wherever I look, I see nothing but temptations! Masses and masses! The most delicious varieties! Fifth Avenue, Broadway, Forty-second Street..." A meditative look appeared on his round, iridescent face. "It all reminds me of those wicked sculptures in Madras. Or the fall of Rome... Where will it end?

"Tell me," he continued, in somber tones, fixing his coal-black eyes on Jonathan, "do you feel that the world is doomed, Jonathan?"

"Doomed?" said Jonathan cautiously.

"I have visions," declared the prince. "I see mountains of flame. Skyscrapers crumbling. Floods of disaster ... I see the end of modern civilization! And do you know why, Jonathan? Listen. I shall tell you. Because of fear. The world is swarming with fear, like a swamp full of mosquitoes." He leaned closer to Jonathan. "All night long," he whispered, "I hear them buzzing. ... "

"Yes," said Jonathan thoughtfully. "I see what you mean, I think."

It was almost six. Jonathan rose and thanked his host.

"Again soon, Jonathan! We must exchange gossips!" He waved his tiny blue hand as Jonathan hurried down the corridor.

A golden-gray mist hung over the city. Jonathan took a bus across Fifty-seventh Street toward Sutton Place, where Mrs. Clyde resided. The bus was very crowded, the atmosphere was suffocating; he got out at Third Avenue and walked the rest of the way.

The air was quivering with heat, like a huge gray jelly, and the scent of humidity hung everywhere. The asphalt was soft: a faint smell of tar mingled with the acrid flavor of carbon and oil. Small mirages, like rivulets of oil, lay trembling on the levels of First Avenue.

He arrived at Mrs. Clyde's just as a tall, familiar figure, with a condescending flourish, stepped from the taxi. He turned and smiled at Jonathan; it was Wilfred Silliman.

96

WILFRED rang the doorbell. It was a crucial moment for him.

Wilfred Silliman, all things considered, was the archetype of snob. He had lost none of his hair, which was an undulating pearly gray. He was wearing a wing collar, a gray Charvet cravat, a heavy golden watch chain, and oyster-hued spats. He might, except for the trace of coyness and anxiety in his eyes, have passed as a diplomat—a charge d'affaires, perhaps. His manners were flawless, if a trifle ornate: his voice was thin, gentle, tremulous. His face, almost morbidly well preserved, was pink and soft, a little amorphous. His native habitat nowadays was New York, and at the height of the season, Newport; and he was thoroughly familiar with the genealogical intricacies of both centers. Dust had gathered upon them, possibly, but to him they still were vital and august. He knew the precise relation borne by the Clydes of Boston to the Clydes of Sutton Place; he knew the subtle distinctions to be drawn between the Westovers of Philadelphia and the Westovers of Newport. He knew every vicissitude of Mrs. van Twillingen's tastes in the opera, Mrs. Carter's adventures among the couturiers, and the Misses Wilmerding's feelings on politics. He also knew what was to be known in the line of scandal. He was a receptacle for the most delicate feminine confidence, an expert in every nuance of gossip. He had been adequately educated, at Groton and Harvard, but his intellect remained on a purely digressive level; his culture provided a kind of protective coloration, like his spats. He had, when he was younger, lived for some years in London, and subsequently, off and on, in Paris. For several years he had kept a villa in Cap d'Antibes. But Wilfred's excursions among the European aristocracy had not, all told, affected his habits. For the last six years he had clung to New York, where he had acted as a zealous intermediary among three different groups—the exiled circles of Lady Temperly and Baroness Landau, the smart coteries of Mrs. Carter and Mrs. Clyde, and the old New York families such as the Wilmerdings and Westovers. He had become, imperceptibly, a figure of some prestige.

The footman took his hat, and Wilfred passed into the drawing room. A second footman called his name as he crossed the room and entered the garden. He blushed, raised his eyebrows, smiled very faintly. It was, perhaps, not entirely a fatuous social ambition that set his heart beating; it was a pathetic, almost feverish yearning for elegance, a compensatory romanticism which bordered on despair. Wilfred, left alone with his own mind and heart, would have been a shattered man.

Mrs. Clyde's drawing room was dramatically handsome. The walls were of a cool blue-gray, and covered with paintings by Guardi, Longhi, and Canaletto. Every possible detail was in keeping with the Venetian atmosphere. The great arched doors that gave on the garden had been flung open, joining the room and garden into a broad, resplendent terrace. The East River lay directly below, and it had, seen through Mrs. Clyde's adroitly placed shrubbery and statuary, something of the air of the Grand Canal.

The garden was full of guests; there might have been seventy or eighty. Three long tables had been set up near the garden wall, decked with canapés, hors d'oeuvres, and a variety of pastries. Tremendous bowls of roses stood at intervals among the dishes. Along the balustrade a small rococo bar had been erected, and here three elderly butlers were gathering the drinks on silver trays.

Wilfred glanced over the assembly with a practiced eye. Instantly he realized, by a quickening of his pulse, that the party was of an exceptional brilliance. He could tell it by the dazzle of hats and gowns, by the battalion of fashionable ladies, by the elaborate and costly décor, but most of all by a certain electrical awareness and heightened vivacity that hung over the gathering. All the ladies had made a point of being at their very best. It was the first really momentous postwar party.

After this swift preliminary survey, Wilfred caught sight of Mrs. van Twillingen, in a turquoise dress, wandering disconsolately among the shrubs; he hurried down to join her.

"Ah, Wilfred," she sighed, clinging to his arm. "How restful to see you! I've hardly dared go out since I returned from Southampton. Tell me, who are all these people? New York has become a potpourri! One sees nothing but ... well, these eccentric parvenus!"

"You're utterly right, my dear Amy," admitted Wilfred mournfully. "Society these days is just a hodgepodge, I'm afraid."

"Why, even five years ago," said Mrs. van Twillingen, waving her fingers, "one could at least go out to lunch without drifting into all this flotsam and jetsam. Who are they? Where do they come from? What do they want, my dear?"

She looked around the garden with deep anxiety. Many of the guests were Europeans; others were writers, editors, painters, musicians, and what was generally known as cafe society.

"Well," sighed Mrs. van Twillingen, shaking her head, "as Alice said, it all grows curiouser and curiouser. Mind you, everything in *Alice in Wonderland* is still true today. It was a deeply prophetic book. ... " She suddenly sneezed, and her features dissolved in a web of fine, oriental wrinkles.

Suddenly she said, in a vehement whisper: "Look, Wilfred. Whom do I see? Don't tell me Laura Carter has been invited!"

Mrs. Carter came strolling across the lawn, arm in arm with Señor Estrella, and laughing gaily. She looked particularly smart today, in a trim little suit of dove gray, rather pensive, yet touched with a certain piquancy in the form of a row of animals down the front—a golden boar, an elephant, a unicorn—and a dazzling hat of red velvet studded with the signs of the zodiac.

A waiter approached with a tray of cocktails.

"Non, merci," said Señor Estrella. *"Je déteste les cocktails."* He lit a cigarette and gazed toward the water.

There was a perceptible tension in the air. Mrs. van Twillingen greeted Mrs. Carter with an icy nod.

"What an amusing suit, my dear Laura," said Wilfred nervously. "And where did you find those *outré* little animals?"

"Oh," said Mrs. Carter, "they're just something I picked up in Rome before the war; they're wicked little rascals, aren't they?" She touched the animals with her finger tips. "I've given them names—Fifi, Baba, and Coco ... Oh, there's Maxim de la Tour. I must dash over and speak to him." She hurried away.

Mrs. van Twillingen watched her departing figure with ill-concealed repugnance. "Really," she said, "how can Henrietta have those *déclassés* persons about? Things have come to a pretty pass. And those preposterous clothes she's been wearing ... Fifi and Coco, indeed!"

Wilfred nodded sadly. "You're too, too depressingly right, my dear," he murmured. "I can't think what's come over Henrietta of late. ..."

But in actual fact, Wilfred was feeling intensely happy; his face was beaming with gratification. This was, indisputably, the brightest party in months. It really had something of the prewar glamour, he felt, in spite of some rather debatable elements that had forced their way in. And even they, he reflected, added a certain spice; he had just caught sight of a well-known actress and a handsome young baritone.

More and more guests were arriving. He saw Sir Ronald Gower, with his gray goatee, talking solemnly to old Mrs. Westover, who was carrying a green parasol. He glanced around for Lady Temperly; she had not yet arrived. Countess Loewenstierna, in all her Scandinavian splendor, seemed to be flirting lightly with Baron Legué. Kirillova, dressed in ivory white, entered the garden with the Marquis del Puente; and directly behind her came Dr. Cavanaugh, engaged in an animated discourse with May Wilmerding. Lady Brooke was wearing a hat of sky-blue tulle, almost two feet high—one of the new Parisian models. Even the Princess Kubinsky, he noticed, looked relatively chic today, in a spangled bolero and a black toreador hat. They strolled to and fro through the sunlit garden, forming a brilliant and, to Wilfred, an inexhaustibly fascinating pattern.

He continued to watch, noting each little nod, smile, and separation. There was nothing that escaped him. He was like a great choreographer, extracting an emotional spark from the slightest gesture and encounter. He noticed that May Wilmerding had cut Kitty de Montfleury; he saw Princess Kubinsky discreetly ignoring Kirillova, Lady Webber blowing a kiss at Baron Legué, and Señor d'Alvarez making a beeline for Commander Forbes.

And a kind of sadness began to creep into his soul; a sense of things uncapturable, of the evanescence of human contacts.

Suddenly he grew alert. A cautious, catlike glaze passed over his eyes. Someone had entered the garden who interested him even more, perhaps, than the others: a slender young man in a blue pin-striped suit, with a red carnation in his buttonhole.

For a moment Wilfred remained uncertain. The young man turned and smiled at Lady Webber, who was darting toward him with sudden animation.

Then Wilfred recognized him; it was Pierre Maillard.

97

PIERRE stepped into the garden and glanced around rather irritably. He had been feeling more than usually nervous all day. Delia had called up in the morning and, in a casual tone, explained that she could not meet him for lunch.

And he felt, as he had once or twice before, a twinge of resentment and alarm. Something was wrong. A hint of decay had entered their relationship. The freshness, the mutual delight were dying.

Yet this flavor of discord, for the time being, only accentuated the subtlety, the inexhaustible sexual magnetism of their love. The spice of pain, bitterness, suspicion had intensified its flavor; the very process of disintegration was somehow deepening its power.

He looked across the garden; Delia had not arrived. He caught sight of Jonathan in the distance, and began to wander slowly toward him.

He was intercepted, almost instantly, by Lady Webber. She peered at him playfully.

"My dear boy!" she exclaimed, placing her hand on Pierre's arm. "So you're still in town? Tell me, are you going back to Paris soon? I'm simply ill with nostalgia for Paris.... The light, the noises, the queer little smells!"

It occurred to Pierre that Lady Webber, some four years previously, had pitilessly condemned "the rot, the spiritual decadence" of France.

She smiled at him demurely. The brilliant sunlight flooded her features, illuminating them like a finely etched map; the withered delta of the eyes, the crimson promontory of the lips, all the lines of ambition, cunning, tenacity were ruthlessly exposed.

She continued reminiscently. "I once had a tiny flat on the Ile St.-Louis—that was before you were born, I'm afraid! Never, my dear, shall I forget those lovely plane trees along the quay, and the smell of freshly baked brioches, and those dear little victorias rumbling over the cobblestones! The real heart of France, I always knew, was invincible. I'll be returning in March, myself. ... "

They were standing beside one of the refreshment tables. Pierre picked up a shrimp on a toothpick, and dipped it casually in the mayonnaise.

At this point he noticed a middle-aged gentleman making a series of sweeping bows to the left and the right, always bringing his feet neatly together, and producing an air of regal formality. It was Monsieur Semenoff, the new second secretary in the Russian Embassy, who had just arrived from Moscow. He was followed by a young attaché, who introduced him to Lady Webber.

"I only visited Russia once, I'm afraid," said Lady Webber, in sprightly tones. "Back in 1911. I didn't see very much of it, I must confess. We stayed on our yacht most of the time. We were cruising through the Black Sea that year—Cecil was dying to see Trebizond. Of course, that was before you had your revolution. But even from our yacht, I seem to recall, we could already see unmistakable signs of social unrest. Still, we couldn't help feeling a shade upset when the revolution came with all that shooting. You do understand that, don't you, Monsieur Semenoff?"

Monsieur Semenoff regarded her coldly. "Well," he murmured, in a pronounced accent, "I hope you have been able to resign yourself to it, madame!"

A butler passed with a tray of drinks. Monsieur Semenoff contemplated the glasses with evident suspicion, and finally, with strange reluctance, chose a martini.

Pierre excused himself, and sauntered across the lawn to greet his hostess, Mrs. Clyde.

She was standing at the end of the garden beside the fountain, welcoming her guests, one by one, with a curt little nod. She was dressed ascetically, as always, in a long gray dress devoid of ornament. She looked like a priestess, a presiding sibyl.

Henrietta Clyde's position in New York society was unique. She was a symbol of impartiality, and rose in solitary grandeur, untouched by the cliques, fads, and shams of the city. She was a tiny woman with kind, attentive eyes, a bun of gray hair, and a limitless memory for detail. She had been at Bryn Mawr; and she still retained something of its crisp, asexual, neo-Hellenic flavor. It was she, more than anyone, more than even Wilfred Silliman, who kept the austerity of New York's social hierarchy from falling into dereliction and decay. Like Wilfred, she was sadly aware that new blood was needed, that the world of the Wilmerdings and Westovers was falling behind the times. Her task was to fuse the old and dusty, the indigenous, with the new, the gaudy, the cosmopolitan, yet without ever jeopardizing her own superb neutrality. Specimens of every faction met under her roof; her Friday Evenings were justifiably famous. Chinese statesmen, Greek scholars, French novelists, Peruvian archaeologists lectured wittily to groups, which included Lady Webber and Mrs.

van Twillingen, on the finer points of Menander, Machiavelli, and Mallarmé.

At the end of each lecture she usually contrived, with the most delicate humility, to correct some obscure error on the part of the speaker—a painting erroneously dated, a line of Dante misquoted. She straddled, like the Colossus of Rhodes, the best the Old and New World had to offer. And like the Sphinx of Egypt, she steadily maintained, even in moments of alarm, an air of luminous inscrutability.

She greeted Pierre with an archaic little smile. They happened, for a moment, to be standing alone. "I've tried a rather dangerous experiment today," she whispered cautiously. "I've invited every possible type of person—artists and bankers, curators, ballerinas. I've asked people who've been enemies for years. I've even asked, as a kind of gesture, two or three of the Russians. Not without misgivings, mind you. Will it work out smoothly? After all, we stand at the beginning of a terrifying era, Monsieur Maillard, and we must learn to get along, even if it means certain sacrifices. ... "

More guests were arriving, and Pierre wandered toward the edge of the garden, which was flanked by a balustrade. He suddenly caught sight of Delia. She had just arrived. He saw her walk toward Mrs. Clyde with a calm, firm step and a shining smile. He saw how in one swift glance she surveyed the garden, appraised the assembly of guests, and instantly noticed his presence.

She left Mrs. Clyde to join a near-by group of guests, and began to talk to Mrs. Carter in an animated manner.

And seeing her like this, at a distance and among strangers, Pierre was once again astonished by her extreme loveliness. For an instant he felt that he had never really seen her before. He saw a novel quality in her face, a deep, searching expression which gave a new and subtler tone to her beauty. She was wearing a dress of steel blue, which accentuated her golden coloring. He noticed, for the first time, that she had grown a little thinner.

He watched her for several minutes. He observed every change of expression in her face; he was waiting for the moment when she would turn at last and look at him, smile perhaps, and begin to walk toward him.

And he felt a wave of sudden joy pass through him; because he was near her once again, and because he felt the thread between them growing tense and electrical.

Lady Brooke and Basil Hume happened to be passing at that moment, with bright red cocktail glasses in their hands.

"Tell me, Basil," Lady Brooke was saying, "who is that lovely creature talking to Laura Carter?"

"That blond girl?" murmured Basil. "Delia Potter, I believe. I met her one evening at Gaby Landau's."

"I must say, she is dazzling," said Lady Brooke, peering through her lorgnette.

Basil Hume pursed his lips. "She makes one realize, I'm afraid, how rarely one sees a beautiful woman."

Lady Brooke shrugged her shoulders. "How right you are," she said frostily. "The glamorous Mrs. Carter had better look to her laurels, don't you think?"

They wandered on; and were presently joined by Commander Forbes and Señor d'Alvarez.

Pierre's eyes kept following Delia. She was acquiring a new kind of magnetism as he watched her. He knew that she was aware of him; yet she remained strange and distant, like a figure in a pantomime. She was listening quietly to a bald, elderly man, who was shaking his finger excitedly, and then bowed, kissed her hand, and hurried away. A lady in a crimson turban approached, paused significantly, and smiled discreetly at Delia. Delia nodded rather coldly, and then greeted a man with a monocle, Señor Estrella, and his companion, a small trim woman in aquamarine.

And somehow, beside Delia, all the other guests looked unreal. They faded into stray flakes of light and color; their voices merged in a dull, metallic chatter. Everything about them seemed insipid beyond words. Delia's face, framed in her glowing hair, shone among all the rest; it alone had the authentic luster, like a golden coin among chips of celluloid.

And slowly, as he watched, his elation deserted him, and a feeling of suspense absorbed him once more. She was smiling at something Señor Estrella had said; her eyes lit on Pierre and passed casually on. Then at last a stab of real pain shot through him, and he could hardly keep from walking up and taking her in his arms.

He stood motionless beside the balustrade, with his cocktail glass in his hand. He raised it to his lips, and found it was empty. His heart was in a state of curious confusion. His yearning had sharpened; he loved her in a new, violently possessive way. And yet this only intensified his resentment, his latent hostility and anger.

And then a moment later, quite unaccountably, a wave of passionate, imploring tenderness passed through him.

He waited another minute or two. Then he placed his glass on an empty tray and started across the lawn toward Delia.

He heard his name spoken, and turned. Maxim de la Tour was approaching, accompanied by a vivacious, dark-eyed girl in a vermilion dress.

"Pierre," he said, with a smile, "I want you to meet a friend of mine. A charming young dancer. Lydia Ivanova."

98

LYDIA had arrived at the party with Nicholas Dimitroff, the dancer, whom Mrs. Clyde had recently taken under her wing. She had never been at quite this type of gathering before; but she felt at ease instantly. She recognized several familiar faces—Horace Hayden, Kirillova, Princess Kubinsky. Several others—Mrs. Carter, Mrs. van Twillingen—she recognized by repute. But most of the guests were unknown to her; she felt the *frisson* of exploration. It was one of her good days. She looked witty and charming, her eyes glittered, and her poise was flawless.

The moment she arrived, Maxim de la Tour came up to her. He had met her once at Prince Sharavaji's. Dimitroff drifted away toward the cocktail table.

"What a relief to see you here," said Maxim in a low voice. He was a tall, angular, intensely nervous man. "It's a horrifying party!"

"Horrifying?" said Lydia eagerly. "Why? What has happened?"

"Nothing yet," said Maxim grimly. "But there's trouble in the air. I can feel it. Everyone's in a perfectly vile humor!"

"Except you and I, perhaps?" said Lydia softly. She glanced ironically at Maxim.

She was about to say something more when she saw a rather ornate gentleman, with a faintly familiar bearing, approaching with two decrepit old ladies; one with a prim gray dress that reached to her ankles, the other youthfully gowned in cherry-hued taffeta. Maxim introduced her to Mrs. Westover and Lady Webber, and then to Wilfred Silliman.

"Lady Webber," declared Wilfred, "like myself, is a great balletomane. She's quite an admirer of your dancing!" He smiled coquettishly at Lydia.

"Ah!" said Mrs. Westover. "So you dance in the ballet! How courageous of you. I am told it's the most exhausting of all sports. Even more than tennis. Aren't you afraid of straining your heart, my dear?"

"Dancers," murmured Lydia, "develop rather strong hearts, as time goes on."

Mrs. Westover watched her with bright, malicious eyes. She was wearing a shawl of gray lace, and a large gray hat covered with violets. "Still, accidents do happen!" she declared. "I once saw Isadora Duncan in Paris. She slipped and fell headlong on the floor, poor girl. But she was mad, of course; just a wee bit mad." She raised her cocktail glass to her lips. Her voice was beginning to quaver.

"And then there was poor Nijinsky," said Wilfred, leering faintly. "There must be something about dancing, I'm afraid ... "

He took out a lemon-hued handkerchief and coughed. Lydia had a distinct impression of having seen him before.

"I remember," put in Lady Webber, with a gleam in her eyes, "a little party I gave at Cannes, ages ago, for Pavlova. Nijinsky was there too, and that old monster Diaghileff. It was just an informal little dinner, mind you; just potluck; not one of my really big things. Betty Londonderry was there, and dear old Tony Westmoreland. We had Annushka—she always insisted that I call her Annushka—do *The Dying Swan* in the garden by moonlight. The Mediterranean was twinkling down below. It was breath-taking, my dear.... "

"We'll never," said Wilfred in elegiac tones, "have parties like that again, I'm afraid!"

Lydia looked at him astutely. Suddenly she recalled where she had seen him, and smiled faintly. Wilfred, with his antenna-like social instinct, seemed instantly aware of her glance, and its ironical import. He coughed again, faintly, and gazed intently across the garden.

Lydia felt a surge of excitement; she scented the possibility of drama. The garden was flooded with life and color. The party had reached its peak, that indefinable moment when all alertness comes to a crest, like a wave about to break, before subsiding into a kind of lingering undulation.

Wilfred drifted away again, arm in arm with Mrs. Westover. Lady Webber darted off toward the Marquis del Puente.

Maxim smiled wearily at Lydia. "I don't suppose there's anyone you'd care to meet particularly?"

"I should doubt it," said Lydia. "Who's that eerie, frightened little man with the moustache?"

"Mendoza, the painter. And that's his wife, pursuing him."

Lydia nodded. "And the young man standing alone there? In blue?"

Maxim hesitated. A faint glaze appeared in his eyes. "A friend of mine," he said carelessly. "Pierre Maillard."

Lydia's face remained expressionless. "Come," she said. "Introduce me to him, please."

Maxim led her across the lawn without a word, and introduced her. She took Pierre's hand and smiled at him brilliantly.

"You are," she said lightly, "almost exactly what I expected!"

"Expected?" said Pierre, blushing faintly.

"I've heard so much about you," murmured Lydia.

Pierre smiled somewhat nervously. "Thank you," he said. "I feel honored."

"I'd heard you were clever, of course." She gazed at him calmly. "And frightfully good-looking."

He blushed again; he seemed slightly disturbed. "Has Maxim been talking nonsense, as usual?"

"No, no," she said, with a penetrating look. "Not only Maxim. You're a friend of Jonathan Ely's. And you know José Valdez, I think . . . ."

Pierre's face remained casual. "Oh yes, of course. Now I remember. I think I've heard about you too, possibly!"

Their eyes met: there was a mingling of mutual attraction, curiosity, and antagonism.

"We must meet again, soon," said Lydia softly. "Just the two of us."

Pierre nodded politely. "That will be a pleasure."

"I hope so!" whispered Lydia, with an electrical smile. She added dreamily: "We have such a lot to talk about."

For a moment they stood together in silence. There was a momentary lull. A heaviness had come into the sky, and a torpid breeze had arisen. The cloth on the table beside them was rippling; the foliage grew restless in the evening light.

Lydia looked across the garden. Long plum-colored shadows were moving over the grass, and the dresses were washed in a sloping haze. The last fringe of sunlight was approaching the river.

Kirillova was saying good-by to Mrs. Clyde. A tall dark Spaniard and a stalwart British officer were standing at the end of the garden, deep in a tête-à-tête. Mrs. van Twillingen was listening, with an air of petulance, to a stout old lady in emerald green.

She glanced again at Pierre. The sunlight drew a fine cop-
pery line along his profile, emphasizing its firm, rather insolent
sensuality. It was more than his beauty that attracted her: it was
a quality faintly kindred to her own, a predatory luster, a sexual
duplicity which gave him subtlety and charm.

He turned at that instant and looked across the garden, at
a very blond young woman in blue. Lydia felt a stab of hostility; she saw the exceptional beauty in the woman's face; a type
of beauty so finely grained, so far removed from her own. And
this was followed by a curious pang of misery, when she saw the
woman turn and gaze, for the merest instant, at Pierre. Lydia
immediately perceived, in that one glance, that they were lovers.
Their eyes glowed; their faces grew radiant and secretive. The
spark of passion was unmistakable.

And a kind of desolation came over Lydia; a sense of defeat
she herself could scarcely have explained. A moment before she
had felt vital, triumphant. Now she felt bitter and rather empty.
She drew her fingers along the edge of the table, and wearily put
down her glass. She decided to leave.

At that moment she caught sight of Jonathan, who had been
talking to a group of people in the drawing room. She saw him
entering the garden, and strolling across the lawn toward the
woman in blue. She immediately detected the expression on
his face, and understood precisely its meaning: she knew that
Jonathan, too, was in love.

A tremor sprang from her heart out to her finger tips.
Everything in the garden—the hats and glasses, the gowns, the
statuettes—grew lithe and sparkling.

It was not jealousy, precisely, that she felt; it was more nearly
a mingling of humiliation and fear. Jonathan represented to her,
still, the world of decency and innocence; the world of conscience,

in a sense; and an abandonment which she would have accepted from another man as a part of the game was, in the case of Jonathan, painful and infuriating.

She turned slowly to Pierre, and smiled impulsively.

"Come," she whispered, "let's go and join your friends. Won't you introduce me to the young lady in blue?"

She took his arm and drew him gently across the lawn. "May I?" she said; and plucked the red carnation from his buttonhole. She tucked it into her hair, with a mischievous little smile, as they wandered over the grass toward Delia.

99

DELIA stood alone for a moment after Señor Estrella had departed. Then she saw two tall women, both in black, languidly wandering toward her: Princess Kubinsky and Kitty de Montfleury.

She felt tense and overexcited. This was her first real party, her first excursion into "society" in several months. She had come out of bravado, and because she knew Pierre was coming. And for the first time she witnessed her old, abandoned world—the world of the Wilmerdings and Westovers—mingling with her new, adopted society: the circle of Pierre, Maxim, and Kitty. She felt acutely nervous, and began to wish she hadn't come. The women around her looked like tropical birds, with their crested hats, their beady eyes, their implacable self-assurance. She glanced in Pierre's direction with a sudden rush of yearning.

He was leaning against the balustrade, with a cocktail glass in his hand. He looked grave and preoccupied; he drew his thumb along the marble. Then he raised his hand and lightly touched his carnation. Her yearning dissolved in a new, inexplicable fit of estrangement. And quite suddenly, without knowing why, she desperately desired to hurt him.

At that moment she noticed Maxim de la Tour near the bar, accompanied by a young woman in vermilion; and a moment later they were joined by Lady Webber, Mrs. Westover, and

Wilfred Silliman. Behind them rose an armless Apollo, lost in a creeping triangle of shadow. They stood in a circle, glancing about, like a group of conspirators on an operatic stage.

Kitty de Montfleury and Princess Kubinsky came up and greeted her. Kitty pressed her arm affectionately. She was an extremely narrow, sinuous person, with an aqueous glint in her pale gray eyes.

"Do forgive me, darling, for not coming up to you before," she said, smiling adroitly. "I noticed you were chatting with Laura Carter. I've been trying, rather frantically, to avoid dear Laura."

"Poor Laura," said Princess Kubinsky, in her low, hoarse voice. "She has built this marvelous façade. But behind it hides a broken heart."

Kitty looked faintly fatigued. "Really, Olga. Broken heart! Laura Carter has no heart. Only a bit of chiffon, I should think, daubed with Chanel Number Five. ... "

"She is a great beauty," said Princess Kubinsky. "She shines and tinkles, like a Chinese pagoda."

"Pagoda!" snapped Kitty. "Well, in point of antiquity, perhaps. But the style, my dear, you must agree, is inferior."

"You are cruel today, Kitty," said the princess funereally. "Laura Carter has never in her life hurt a fly. ... She lives in a dreamworld. She has, *au fond,* the soul of a wood nymph."

Kitty glared with indignation. "And the morals as well," she said bitterly. "From what I've been hearing!"

Princess Kubinsky peered through her lorgnette with sudden interest. "Who is that girl," she murmured, "talking with Pierre Maillard?"

Kitty glanced across the garden. "Oh, that!" she said brightly. "That's the little ballet dancer Prince Shabby-wabby has taken up with. Pretty, isn't she, dear?" She winked slyly at the princess.

"In a cold, hard way," said the princess dourly. "I can see she's the type that has no soul, no *délicatesse*. ... Only a ravenous appetite."

"Look at poor Lady Temperly over there," said Kitty pensively. "The party's been given for her, but she's just arrived this moment, naturally, when everyone else is ready to leave. No one's paying the slightest attention to her; except, of course, the dear old Marquis del Puente, who has one foot in the grave. Now that she's sailing at last, no one feels she's worth troubling about. ... It's a wicked world, isn't it?"

"Well, I must be going," said the princess, in her usual portentous tone. She glanced at her watch. "It's a quarter to seven already."

"Dear, dear!" cried Kitty. "I promised Mimi Suarez to drop in on her for a minute. She's sailing for Genoa on Monday, poor angel. She's having a party too; just a teeny, cozy one. You're going there too? ... No? You hate cocktail parties? How wise of you! They're a waste of time, I utterly agree. Between you and me, darling, I'd rather bury myself in the country with a lot of books, and not see a soul. Well, I must rush. Ta-ta!"

She pressed Delia's hand, slid through the garden like an eel, and vanished into the drawing room.

For a moment Delia was alone again. She immediately turned, and looked across the garden for Pierre. She could not find him; her heart began to tighten.

She saw three elderly ladies standing in a group near the fountain. Lady Webber was chatting lightly with May Wilmerding and Mrs. Westover. Delia caught them glancing in her direction, and felt obscurely troubled.

Then she saw Pierre. He was standing alone, near the fountain, with the slender girl in vermilion, engrossed in conversation;

she saw the woman smiling softly, and a flush appearing on Pierre's face.

And instantly a stab of fear shot through her. The restless pattern of gowns, the voices weaving through the garden took on an air of stealthy antagonism. Quick glances were being exchanged; stray whispers were passing. Even the shrubs, she felt, exuded an odor of malice.

Pierre turned his head; their eyes met suddenly. And all her fears and misgivings, all her grievances dissolved. She saw the hard thin glow in his eyes, the familiar, knifelike look of desire. And a flood of happiness shot through her.

She turned again, and saw Jonathan wandering toward her, with his usual shy and preoccupied air.

He took her hand, with a rather hesitant smile. "Delia," he said quietly; "I hoped I'd find you here!"

Something in his voice was instantly comforting to Delia. She felt the presence of a sane and reassuring influence. And for the first time since she knew him, she felt a kind of tenderness, an intuition of something deeper and stronger than friendliness.

"I'm glad you've come, Jonathan," she whispered. "So very glad. ... "

He looked at her with his slow, warm, searching eyes, and a puzzled expression appeared on his face. He seemed about to say something, but hesitated; and then he stared past her, with a sudden look of incredulity.

She turned her head and saw Pierre approaching; the girl in red was smiling and clinging to his arm.

And an incomprehensible dread came over her. She stood silently beside Jonathan; her heart was beating uncontrollably.

Pierre came up; he looked at her rather curiously. Then he said very crisply: "Delia, I'd like you to meet Miss Ivanova. Miss

Ivanova, this is Mrs. Potter. Jonathan, you already know Miss Ivanova, I believe.... " His voice was hard and cold; an angry look shone in his eyes.

There was a moment's pause. They looked at one another, all four of them, with a flash of bewilderment. Jonathan looked worried, Pierre was frowning, Lydia was smiling expectantly.

And Delia felt suddenly that a point of crisis had arrived; that an instant of revelation was at hand. She drew her fingers across her throat and smiled casually at Lydia.

She noticed Lydia's witty eyes and rich, domineering chin. She raised her eyes imperceptibly; and saw Pierre's carnation nestling among the chestnut curls.

For a moment Delia felt blinded with suspense. Then she turned to Jonathan.

100

JONATHAN looked up at the sky. A sultry breeze had arisen; a slate-colored cloud was crawling above the river, darkening and dilating as it went. The sun hid for an instant, then briefly reappeared, then vanished. The garden was now completely in shadow.

Ever since his arrival at Mrs. Clyde's he had felt rather odd. It was partly the heat; the listless, irritable migraine which precedes a cloudburst. Everything shone with a distended luster. No one seemed to be quite at ease.

He had paused in the drawing room to talk to Mrs. Westover, and then to Kitty van Lennep, whom he hadn't seen for several years. When he finally entered the garden he saw, to his surprise, that Delia had arrived. She was standing alone in a distant corner, looking unusually pale and grave.

He walked up to her; and a moment later he was once again surprised. He had scarcely greeted Delia when he saw, slowly wandering across the lawn, two intensely familiar faces: Pierre and Lydia. It was like a moment in a dream; the juxtaposition was so odd, so unexpected, and so entirely casual.

He glanced at Lydia. She was wearing a smart and beautifully tailored gown of brilliant red; and he noticed with surprise a golden bracelet on her arm, studded with large, oval-shaped rubies.

She looked remarkably well, her manner was easy and self-assured. Only in her eyes, beneath the look of casual mockery, he instantly recognized the hint of torment; that sheen of a black, impenetrable cistern in the soul.

"It's always exciting," she was saying to Delia, "to meet people one has heard about!"

"Oh," said Delia shyly, "you've heard about me? How very odd ... "

Lydia smiled flatteringly. "Odd? Not at all, Mrs. Potter! You deserve ... well, to be talked about."

Delia was blushing painfully; and Pierre, for the first time since Jonathan knew him, looked patently nervous and disconcerted.

"You are a dancer," said Delia softly, "Miss Ivanova, aren't you?"

"Of sorts!" said Lydia carelessly. "It's not the career I'd choose a second time. ... " She paused, and looked carefully at Delia. "Well," she added, with an engaging little look, "I really must be off! I'm delighted I finally met you, Mrs. Potter!"

"Oh, you're leaving?" said Delia involuntarily. "Already?"

"It's almost seven," said Lydia, with a touch of regret, as she took Delia's hand. "But I do hope I'll meet you again! Before long!" She turned to Jonathan. "Good-by, Jonathan. ... And do give me a ring, won't you?"

And then she turned to Pierre, with a swift, sinuous motion. She smiled at him with a startling intensity. "And you too, my dear," she said, in hardly more than a whisper. "Remember your promise! A heart-to-heart talk, just the two of us. I have so much to say to you. ... "

She held his hand a moment longer, her eyes fixed on his. Then she cast a final penetrating glance at Delia and Jonathan, and hurried across the garden toward the drawing room.

Delia and Pierre stood silently side by side. Then Delia turned to Jonathan with a white, frozen look. "It's late. I'll have to go too, I think," she murmured. She touched Jonathan's hand lightly, and walked swiftly across the lawn.

Jonathan saw her approach the drawing room and pause to greet Mrs. Westover and May Wilmerding. Miss Wilmerding nodded to her rather coldly, and Mrs. Westover, without speaking, glared at her bitterly and turned her back. Delia blushed violently, hesitated, and disappeared into the drawing room.

Pierre had been watching; he immediately followed Delia. Jonathan, left alone, wandered down to the edge of the terrace.

The sunlight vanished, and the sky hung veiled. An unmitigated bleakness seized the scene. A scent of phosphorus hung in the air, and Jonathan realized that the storm was about to break.

He stood there another minute or two, his elbows resting on the balustrade. There was something unusual in the atmosphere: it seemed to envelop, to saturate the whole landscape. It exposed innumerable little lights and shadows, minute crevices among the rocks and the buildings.

He grew thoughtful. The crisis had come and gone. All four of them had finally met: and nothing, nothing at all, had happened. Nothing, it seemed, except the infinitesimal thrust of a needle, the injection of a tiny drop of poison. Or was it his imagination? Perhaps it was. He saw Lydia at last in a cool, flat light. Her fascination had vanished; and instead he saw merely her weakness, her vulgarity, her restless and omnivorous vanity. Nothing but a feeling of indifference remained; that, and a lingering sense of waste.

He wandered back to the house. He looked for Pierre but he had gone. The party was rapidly breaking up. The last of the guests were strolling toward the drawing room, and saying good-by to Mrs. Clyde and Lady Temperly. The stormy light enveloped them all as they moved toward the entrance, gesticulating and bowing; the powdered faces and withered hands, the trembling gloves, the twinkling glasses.

Jonathan followed the rest into the drawing room. Just as he was entering the hallway, Horace Hayden took him jovially by the arm.

"Isn't it a tragedy," he murmured, "about Clarissa leaving us?"

"I really didn't know Lady Temperly," said Jonathan politely.

"Well," sighed Horace, "we'll miss her dreadfully. No one can take her place. Her departure is a blow, a real blow to the intellectual life of New York."

He drained his cocktail glass. His eyes were watering slightly. "Well, good-by, Jonathan. I'd love to go and have a drink with you. But I have to slip into a dinner jacket this very instant!"

"You're off to dine with some duchess or marquise, I suppose," observed Jonathan.

Horace was flattered. "Oh, it's only Gaby Landau," he said lightly. "I'm devoted to Gaby. She's so sweet and unassuming."

He hurried across the entrance hall, waving intimate little good-bys as he passed.

Jonathan cast a final look into the garden. It was entirely deserted. It shone, a deep tempestuous green, through the great arched doors of the drawing room. The butlers were scurrying back to the pantry with trays of empty plates and glasses. The statues had turned a leaden color. Mrs. Clyde and Lady Temperly were standing alone on the edge of the terrace, glancing nervously at the sky, waiting for the downpour.

101

JONATHAN found Pierre waiting for him in the street, in front of Mrs. Clyde's. He looked flushed and rather troubled.

"What's become of Delia?" asked Jonathan.

"She insisted on going alone," said Pierre in a low, tense voice. Then he added slowly: "She was very upset."

They walked silently to the corner. "You should have gone with her," said Jonathan gently.

Pierre took a deep breath. "Come," he said. "Let's have a drink."

It was beginning to rain. There was a dull roar of thunder. Everything grew dark, and the air was filled with lilac drops.

They jumped into a taxi and drove to the Plaza. The downpour reached its peak as they drew up at the entrance. Pierre paid the driver and they ran up the steps, trying to dodge the avalanche of raindrops.

They walked into the dark-paneled room and ordered their drinks.

"There's something queer in the air today," muttered Pierre. He drew out a cigarette. "What is it? ... I feel caught in a whirlpool."

Jonathan nodded. "Yes. I know what you mean."

"The war's over," said Pierre grimly. "And what has it given us? Fear. Callousness. Irritability. ... We've all been the losers, it seems!"

"The losers? You too, Pierre?" Jonathan peered at him ironically.

Pierre seemed about to say something; his face grew tense; he paused.

The waiter placed their highball glasses in front of them, with a bowl of pistachios. The room was dark and restful; there was something protective in the great leather armchairs and the ponderous, illuminated carvings on the wall. The nervous tension of the city was out of sight and out of hearing.

Jonathan watched Pierre's face. Pierre sat with his eyes lowered, staring at his fingers extended on the table. His features had sharpened; the inexorable imprint of character had begun. The lines of pride, promiscuity, calculation were emerging.

"You're growing older, Pierre," he said gently. "Like the rest of us."

Pierre looked at him rather oddly. "You think," he said in a casual tone, "that I've hardened?"

"Possibly."

Pierre's face grew sullen for a moment. Then he said: "And you, Jonathan?"

"Yes?" said Jonathan. "Have I changed too?"

"Just a bit," said Pierre, with a smile. "You're a little gentler, A little calmer. A little sadder. That's all!"

He glanced at Jonathan with a flash of intimacy; a playful glitter returned to his eyes.

And Jonathan's feeling toward him immediately grew warmer. He realized how radically different from himself Pierre was. It was not that Pierre was complex. It was that he possessed, in spite of all his waywardness and egotism, a secret stability; a sense, somehow or other, of permanence.

Yet he was dimly aware that his feeling toward Pierre had been tainted. He didn't know why; but he knew it could never again be natural.

"What's been happening to us all?" exclaimed Pierre, with sudden intensity. "What is it that draws us deeper and deeper into unreality?" He turned his highball glass slowly in his fingers. "Pleasure and pain. Love. Anxiety—they're all beginning to fall into patterns. With a background of music. Like the gestures in a *scène de ballet* ... Look around at our friends. Men becoming mere masks, mere mannequins—that's what I find so horrifying! Men frozen by society into a state of hallucination. It happened deliberately in Germany. But it's happening elsewhere as well. In a gentler, subtler, less controlled way. ... "

Pierre offered his cigarette case to Jonathan; Jonathan took one and lit it. "You've turned into a pessimist, Pierre. You spoke very differently five years ago!"

Pierre looked at him sharply. "You feel I ought to go back?"

Jonathan hesitated. Then he said, "Perhaps. I don't know."

Pierre glanced across the room; he looked troubled. Then he shrugged his shoulders.

"Going back doesn't help. The tradition of Europe; the culture of the individual; they're dying away. To remain an individual nowadays, to fight the mechanical Colossus, is too exhausting. So we become Orientals. We slide into the easiest category; into a labor-saving, pain-killing, well-upholstered routine. We accept the clothes, the ideas, even the gestures and appetites, of a group. ... "

Jonathan tapped his cigarette and looked wistfully at the ceiling. "And how can we be saved? Fly to Capri? Or Madagascar?"

"Saved?" Pierre smiled. "We all want to be saved! But from what? A hidden danger! And for what? An invisible happiness. ... No, Jonathan, it isn't so easy. Only one thing I'm sure of. We have to struggle to discover our nature, and then keep struggling to be true to it. The real defeat, the real nausea, springs from self-betrayal. Turn traitor, and the other vices follow in turn. Fame, power, wealth, beauty—they only hasten the decay. We've all seen it happen, haven't we? Again and again?"

"True to our nature?" said Jonathan gently. "What is our nature?"

"Well," said Pierre, with impatience, "call it our capacity to feel. And we've been losing it! The city's draining it out of us! We're being anesthetized! The real, the actual pains are being washed away. Only the ache of hollowness remains! And grows like a tumor. ... "

Jonathan turned around in his chair and looked through the distant window. The flurry of rain had passed, and the stains were fading from the asphalt. The day was coming to an end. The street was full of pedestrians rushing through the dusk. They fluttered past like autumn leaves; crisp and aimless, dejected.

He looked again at Pierre—at Pierre's fine, sparkling eyes, his firm lips and bright hair, and the strong, leisurely movement of his hands. He felt a sudden excitement pass through his body, a conflict of feeling unlike what he had ever felt.

"Pierre," he said softly, leaning forward, "do you really love Delia?"

Pierre sat back in his chair and stared gloomily at the table. He ran his finger along the edge of the glass.

"Life would be simple," he said quietly, "if we could always answer questions like that!"

Jonathan felt the conflict in himself growing painful and mysterious. It was not only a struggle between his affection for Pierre and his jealousy, between his love for Delia and his sense of defeat, between his pity for Lydia and his disgust. It was linked with something very much deeper—the sense of an insoluble crisis approaching; of a chaos of mutual misunderstandings.

"Well," he said very softly, "our lives are changing, Pierre. We used to feel the sunlight around us."

"And now," said Pierre, "we've entered the labyrinth!"

"And the darkness keeps growing," said Jonathan thoughtfully.

"And words," said Pierre, "mean less and less. They end by drawing a veil over the reality. A part of us remains bestial. In all of us there's a tiny cave, where the uncontrollable monster still lurks!"

He raised his brows; he looked toward the window. "Here we live," he went on calmly, "in a city which is the apex of human calculation. A miracle of scientific reason. A dazzling triumph over the unknown. And yet ... human nature seems more helpless than ever; lost in a jungle of uncertainties!"

For several minutes they sat in silence.

Jonathan finished his drink and rose. He pressed Pierre's hand.

"Well, I must be going, I suppose. ... Good-by, Pierre."

He hesitated; there was something else he longed to say. Then he added softly: "You really should have gone with Delia!"

He made his way through the bar, and picked up his hat in the lobby.

102

PIERRE stepped into the lobby soon after Jonathan left him, and tried to phone Delia; but her room did not answer.

He returned to the Oak Room, had a light dinner, and then phoned Delia a second time. Again there was no answer.

He walked slowly through the lobby and out on Central Park South.

It was almost ten o'clock. The heat had returned; even worse, if anything, than before. A moist, overladen breath was flowing through the city. It prowled along the edge of the park, past the hideous little gingko trees, and drew forth a bittersweet smell from the shrubbery. Middle-aged men and women in light, wrinkled clothes were sitting motionless on the benches. Sailors in white were sauntering among the trees, and weary horses drew their victorias along the winding asphalt. A furtive languor stole over the city; a deeper, shadier aspect of its character emerged.

He strolled over to the Shropshire, where Delia lived, and called her from the lobby.

"Hello?" Her voice sounded thin and strained.

"Delia! Where on earth have you been?"

"Oh, it's you," she said, in an unnatural tone. "I had dinner downstairs. There was a message that you'd called."

"May I come up?"

For a moment there was no answer. Then she said: "Yes. If you wish."

He found her standing by the window in a light blue dressing gown. He walked across the room without a word, drew her in his arms, and kissed her on the mouth. She drew back, without responding.

"You were wearing that blue robe the first time I ever saw you," he whispered. "You were sitting in your garden. Oleanda was bringing you a pot of tea."

She looked listlessly past him at the door. Then she turned her head and looked through the window with expressionless eyes.

"Delia," he said softly.

She did not reply, and seemed to avoid meeting his glance.

He looked at her with anxiety, and a slight twinge of guilt.

For the first time he noticed that she was growing older; her beauty was darkening; she was losing her bloom. He could see it in the light from the lamp beside her, which created faint shadows below her eyes.

"What is the matter, Delia?" he said very softly. "You've been crying."

She turned and glanced at him with defiance. Then she shrugged her shoulders and walked over to the chair. She sat down and folded her arms, and looked at him with a cold, pale stare.

"Why do you ask?" she demanded. She began to speak in a quick, even tone. "You know perfectly well. I never want to see those people again. Any of them. Ever. I want to leave New York. ... And I shall never come back!"

She grew silent, and stared fixedly at the wall behind him.

"Don't mind them, darling," he said gently. "Don't let them hurt you."

He felt there was something she longed to say; a question she desperately needed to ask.

But all she could bring herself to say was: "I want to go. And never come back again!"

He sat down on the arm of the chair and softly stroked the back of her head. "Don't feel upset, darling. Don't let it matter to you."

"I knew I should never have gone to the party," whispered Delia.

His hand came to rest on the back of her neck. He leaned down and kissed the top of her head. The sweet fresh odor of her hair somehow calmed him, and restored his self-assurance.

"Forget about it, darling," he murmured. "You'll have your divorce soon. Soon you'll be free of it all. Soon … " He did not finish the sentence.

"Everything in New York seems hateful to me now," she said, after a moment. "Hateful and horrible. I want to leave. But where can I go?"

"We'll see," he said soothingly. "Perhaps Bermuda. Or Mexico. Don't worry. We'll see."

There was a painful silence. Then she said, in a slow, abnormal tone: "I don't want you to marry me, Pierre, if you're not sure of yourself."

"Sure of myself?"

"Sure of your love," she said, after a moment's pause.

"I love you, Delia," he whispered. "Why do you keep doubting it?"

"I don't know," she said slowly. Her voice grew very quiet. "Something frightens me. Something keeps rising between us. Will you love me, Pierre, a year from now?" She sighed; and her voice grew hard again. "No, you don't really love me. I can feel it."

He felt his lips tighten; a familiar irritability was coming over him.

She seemed to notice this instantly. Her blue eyes sharpened. He could feel her whole body growing tense and rebellious. "I shall never marry you, Pierre," she said in a proud, hostile tone, "until I am sure you will always love me!"

He did not reply. There was another silence.

She leaned back her head and looked up at him. Her eyes were wet with tears. There was something utterly pitiful in her face, which was still as lovely and delicate as a child's, yet tainted with anxiety as with a kind of disease.

And as he leaned down to kiss her, he felt that his love likewise had lost its freshness, and was stained with a feeling of pity and remorse.

He sat down on the floor at her feet, and laid his head on her lap. Her hand moved dreamily through his hair as she spoke, and gradually her voice grew soft and yielding.

"Why am I so afraid, Pierre? What is it I'm afraid of? I no longer feel calm, or natural, or safe. I hear whispers at night. I have frightening dreams. What is it?"

"You need a rest," said Pierre. "We all feel these things now and then, darling."

"No," she said in the same expressionless voice. "It's something else. I feel I've done something wrong; dreadfully wrong. And that I'll suffer for it."

"What have you done that is wrong?" asked Pierre, turning his head and looking up at her.

"We should never have met," she said. "I should never have fallen in love with you. When you gave me that flower—that started it all. The chain of evil."

"There was nothing evil in what we did," said Pierre.

"But it brought us evil," said Delia rapidly. Her voice had grown thin and excited again. "Evil and pain. It grows and grows. I feel there's no end to it." She pressed her fingers together.

"Would you return to your earlier life?" said Pierre, after a moment. "If you could?"

"I don't know," muttered Delia. "But I can never go back to it. . . . I don't know what to do. I just don't know."

They both remained silent. They sat for a long time without moving; he with his blond head buried in her lap, she with her fingers resting on his hair.

Pierre closed his eyes. For a moment he fell asleep. Among the liquid succession of images, one grew vivid and poignant. He found himself lost in a forest at night, deep in the Alps, with the snow falling softly.

Then he woke up again, and slowly raised his head. Delia was staring at him with a new, piercing intensity; her eyes looked abnormally dark and brilliant.

"Pierre," she said quietly, "do you mind if I say good night? Will you understand?"

He nodded and rose. She turned her head toward the window.

"Good night, Delia." He kissed her tenderly on the cheek.

"Good night, Pierre." She stood motionless, and continued to look toward the window.

He stepped into the hall and closed the door softly behind him.

103

DELIA, as she was going out the following morning, heard the telephone ringing. It was Jonathan. He asked whether she was free for dinner that night.

"Tonight?" she said, faintly surprised. "Wait a moment." She tried to remember whether Pierre had offered to meet her. Then she said: "Yes, Jonathan. I think I'll be free."

"May I call for you at seven?" said Jonathan.

"At seven," she said. "Good. I'll look forward to it, Jonathan." As she put down the receiver she felt an unexpected relief. Something in Jonathan's voice had pleased and vaguely reassured her.

She went out and lunched with Baron Legué and an elderly friend of his, Madame Petra, at a small Belgian restaurant on Sixty-third Street. After lunch she went to the hairdresser, bought some handkerchiefs, and returned to the Shropshire.

There was a phone message awaiting her, saying that Pierre Maillard had called.

She phoned his studio immediately.

He answered, in an exuberant voice: "Darling, I have wonderful news! The Modern Museum is buying my new picture. Mr. Prendergast arranged it. At a splendid price. Shall we celebrate? Are you free for dinner tonight?"

"Tonight?" Delia remembered, for an instant, her engagement with Jonathan. Then she murmured, "Yes, I'm free."

"Come to Voisin's at seven, darling, will you?"

"Seven o'clock, then," said Delia; and her heart began to pound once more in its strange, painful, uncontrollable way.

She wrote an apologetic note to Jonathan, breaking her engagement, and had it sent to the Devonshire by a messenger. Then she lay down to rest. At five-thirty she rose and wrote two letters; one to a cousin stationed in Guam, the other to an aunt who was living in Buffalo.

Then she took her bath, slipped into a new, very simple but beautiful dress of a deep silvery lavender, put on her little hat, cast a fox fur over her shoulders, and started off to Voisin's.

It was a minute or two past seven when she arrived. She looked for Pierre in the bar on the left, but did not see him. She sat down in the corner and ordered a cocktail, and began to observe the neighboring guests.

It was refreshingly cool. The bar was not crowded. In the opposite corner two dark young ensigns were sitting with two rather corpulent blondes, and at another table two gray-haired men were conversing in animated Italian.

She could see the agreeable blue-and-gray patterns of the dining room. Everything was soft and quiet, and rather old-fashioned. The silver wagons filled with hors d'oeuvres and pastries were being rolled about on velvety wheels.

Over each window hung a cage with a canary. One of them uttered a shrill, rhapsodic note. Another replied, and then the rest; the room was filled with a dizzy twitter.

She heard a quick, tripping sound of footsteps, and turned around nervously. But it was only the headwaiter beckoning to the two Italians.

But already a grain of misgiving had entered her. There was something odd, something furtive, about the place.

The waiter brought her cocktail. She raised the glass to her lips. The taste was peculiar, a little acrid.

A very smart young couple had just arrived. They sat down at the next table and ordered their drinks. The woman glanced inquiringly at Delia, as though in recognition, and began to smile. Then she leaned over and whispered to her companion.

Delia glanced at her watch. It was a quarter past seven.

And the familiar wave of pain, fear, and anger rose up in her. It was as though a kind of poison had begun to operate, spreading through her system, infecting every thought. Her imagination was feverishly at work; and again, for the twentieth time, she repeated in her mind Lydia's words to Pierre: "You too, my dear... Remember your promise... Just the two of us..."

And it occurred to her, in a flash of panic, that he might be with Lydia at this very moment, and that this might be the reason for his delay.

She saw again Lydia's broad, sensual face, the smile on her lips, and her dark, provocative glance. A sickening little tremor passed through her; she was filled with a loathing which was closer to fear than to hatred. She saw again the swift supple twist of Lydia's body, and the penetrating look she cast at Pierre. Everything about her grew equivocal and suggestive. Perhaps, she thought wildly, Pierre at that very moment was drawing her into his arms, whispering to her, and kissing her. The image shot through her mind like a flame.

She tried to cast it aside; but it left her breathless with misery. She kept repeating: "No. It's absurd. It's impossible. I must be sensible."

The dining room looked a little misty. The waiters kept darting nervously about, and the caged canaries were twittering incessantly.

She raised her glass and held it poised against the light. A fine ruby glow hung trembling in the center.

She put down the glass again, suddenly alert. A shadow had moved across her line of vision. A tall, elderly woman in black passed her table, bearing a heap of silvery furs in her arm. She was about to call "Kitty!" Then she realized it wasn't Kitty. The woman vanished into the powder room.

The couple beside her were still whispering and smiling. And the impression returned instantly: that they knew who she was, and were talking about her. She felt herself blushing with humiliation, and immediately turned and looked away. She was filled with an acute sense of isolation; and a moment later, with a confused but violent feeling of bitterness.

Strange thoughts were beginning to pass through her mind. A terrifying scene, distinct in every detail, gradually took shape in her imagination. Her heart beat wildly as it crystallized before her, more and more clearly and powerfully. And she realized then that what she really desired, above all other things, was to make Pierre suffer; to score one last triumph by causing him pain.

She noticed that her hands had begun to tremble, and were moving across the table in a curious, independent rhythm.

At that moment Pierre entered. He strode up to her table with a gleaming irresistible smile.

104

JONATHAN was walking back to his hotel. It was shortly after five. He was walking with a light, springing step; he felt happy.

He had just been to see Charlie Holliday in his office, and had made the last arrangements for joining the firm. He was to start work there the following Monday; he felt, following his visit, full of vigor and optimism. And the prospect of dining with Delia filled him with pleasure.

He paused at his favorite spot near the Plaza, and sat down on a marble bench in front of the hotel. Near him an old lady was casting yellow seeds to a flock of pigeons. Several sparrows had come, and were darting in and out, cleverly stealing the tiny seeds. Two boys were sailing a paper boat in the fountain; a white-headed nurse was rolling a blue perambulator. A young Negro walked past with a large bouquet of roses, paused beside the fountain, then hurried on.

Everything looked so bright and pleasant, and Jonathan found himself in such a happy mood, that all his grievances against New York dissolved. He suddenly found the city extraordinarily charming.

He rose, returned to his hotel, and found a note from Delia waiting for him:

Dear Jonathan:

I'm so sorry I can't have dinner with you tonight. Please forgive me. Thank you again. Yours, Delia.

He stared blankly at the note, puzzled and disconcerted. Then he read it a second time, and tried to decipher some meaning behind it. He glanced at the heading, printed in fine Gothic letters: "The Shropshire. Central Park South. New York City." When he raised the paper to his face, he detected a faint aroma. He stared at the handwriting—it looked crisp and determined; not at all the script he would have imagined from Delia.

His feeling of pleasure and vitality vanished. He returned to his room with a sense of aimlessness and futility.

He lay down on his bed and lit a cigarette. Then he picked up Delia's note and read it a third time. He felt utterly depressed; he felt that now, once and for all, she had hopelessly eluded him. Something alarming was about to happen; but there was nothing he could do; nothing.

Shreds of twilight were filtering through the blinds. A sea-like passivity stole over the room. It was the climate of a dream: the air of crisis and urgency, accompanied by a gently gathering paralysis.

It was growing dark when he went out again to have dinner alone. He strolled over to the little restaurant where he and Lydia used to go. He entered, hung his hat on a hook, and saw to his surprise Peter Sebastian sitting alone at a table, wearing a red-checkered shirt.

Sebastian instantly recognized Jonathan, and beckoned to him gloomily.

"Well, it's years since I saw you!" he exclaimed, swallowing Jonathan's hand in his own huge, hairy paw. His tiny black eyes looked sharply at Jonathan. "Sit down. I've just begun. Try one of these omelets, they're a specialty here. Well, well."

"And how is your work?" asked Jonathan rather meekly.

Sebastian nodded with an oracular air. "Coming along. Coming along. And you?"

"I'm joining an architect's office," said Jonathan. "Next Monday."

"Have you seen Lydia lately?" muttered Sebastian, lowering his eyes.

"I saw her yesterday," said Jonathan. "But only for a moment. At a party."

Sebastian nodded again rather cynically. "She's out for big game these days," he grunted. "God knows where it will end."

The change in Sebastian was not at first evident, because of his size and eccentric attire. But he had changed considerably. He had grown even stouter, and had lost much of his hair; and he wore, in compensation, his remaining hair much longer. But the real, the disturbing change was in the eyes; they were those of a broken, nauseated man.

He had obviously been drinking heavily. An empty bottle of claret stood on the table beside him.

He laid his tremendous hands flat on the table and shot a piercing look at Jonathan; he seemed to swell a little, and said: "Sometimes I can hardly stand it."

Jonathan listened sympathetically.

"The hideousness of it," Sebastian continued. "It's like a cancer. It nibbles and nibbles away." He looked as though he were about to explode. "Sometimes I feel myself falling into thousands of little pieces."

Jonathan didn't know quite what Sebastian meant; he found no point of contact with Sebastian's temperament, and felt ill at ease.

"They keep talking about the greatness of man!" shouted Sebastian, in a voice that went thundering across the room. "Yes, great in thinking up new kinds of corruption! Swine! Swine! That's all they are. Let them grovel in their own filth! Let them wallow in their own decay! From the moment they're born they do nothing but rot, rot, rot. Look around. What do you see? Endless rows of machines, with hordes of stinking little chimpanzees running them. That's our great civilization! I've had enough of it. I'm going."

"Going?" said Jonathan gently. He looked up at Sebastian's swollen face. He seemed ready to burst into tears; it was the face of an enormous, miserable child. Jonathan grew aware of the pitiful weakness of spirit within that huge ill-co-ordinated body. "Where," he asked patiently, "are you going?"

Sebastian didn't answer. They finished their coffee in silence, then rose.

"Come," whispered Sebastian, taking Jonathan anxiously by the arm. "Let's go for a little stroll in the park."

They entered the park opposite the St. Moritz, walked down several steps, and entered a small secluded valley. A blanket of heat coiled about them instantly. They walked slowly and silently along the edge of the pond.

"Did you ever understand her?" said Sebastian, lighting his pipe.

"Understand her?" repeated Jonathan cautiously.

"She's a terrifying woman," said Sebastian. "I don't like to think of her."

"Were you very fond of her?"

Sebastian looked down at his feet; he muttered: "I was insanely in love with her."

They walked along silently. Sebastian kept puffing at his pipe.

Then Sebastian added: "And I'm still in love with her."

"What," said Jonathan after a moment, "do you think she is looking for?"

Sebastian walked on a few steps, belching a little. Then he came to a halt, stared at the water, and said: "Power. Power."

"Well, I suppose so," said Jonathan. "Power for what?"

"For destruction," muttered Sebastian, kicking a small black stone. "That's all. The power to corrupt. That's what her sexual promiscuity springs from. Not from the body but from the mind. That's her only way of gaining power. Of feeding her horrible, bottomless vanity."

"And yet," said Jonathan thoughtfully, "I think she's afraid. She needs a sense of power, perhaps, because she's afraid."

"Afraid?" said Sebastian. He snorted. "Afraid of what?"

"Who knows?" said Jonathan. "Of loneliness. Or failure. Of growing old. Of something in herself; a kind of illness. Who knows?"

"Perhaps," muttered Sebastian. "Perhaps ... Who knows?"

"Still," said Jonathan rather dreamily, "she had her points. She had courage. She had imagination. She was tremendously alive."

"It was exactly those," said Sebastian slowly, "which made her so dangerous."

"What will happen to her," said Jonathan, "do you suppose?"

"She is clever," said Sebastian, with a little sneer. "She'll find her final victim." He paused, and blew his nose. Then he said, in a tone of sudden self-pity: "I wonder where she is now? I kept waiting for her. But she didn't come."

"Was she to meet you at the café?" asked Jonathan sympathetically.

Sebastian didn't reply. He knocked his pipe against the iron railing.

Suddenly he turned; he seized Jonathan's hand, pressed it with terrifying vehemence, and hurried down the path.

105

DELIA entered the dining room with Pierre behind her. The headwaiter led them to a banquette table on the left, facing the entrance. He placed two large menu cards in front of them; another waiter came up to take their order. Then Pierre called to the wine waiter and ordered a bottle of champagne.

Delia had forced herself into a state of composure when Pierre entered the bar. Now she turned to him and said: "You were late, Pierre."

He smiled casually. "Yes. Didn't you get my message?"

"What message?"

"I phoned the hotel at half-past six. I asked them to tell you I'd be late. I couldn't help it."

"Why not?" said Delia calmly.

"Maxim took me to see Mrs. Vredenhuvsen. I couldn't leave any earlier."

"Who on earth," said Delia sullenly, "is Mrs. Vredenhuysen?"

"Oh, one of these fabulously rich dowagers," said Pierre, in a lighthearted tone. "She wants her portrait done."

The waiter brought on the smoked salmon. The champagne arrived in a silver cooler.

"Must you meddle with all those people?" said Delia, frowning. "Those ridiculous old ladies?"

Pierre glanced at her swiftly; a faint flush sprang to his face. He seemed about to say something, but then, apparently, thought better of it. He quickly picked up his fork and knife.

She stared across the room. She felt a demon rising in her.

"Those people have nothing to offer you," she said slowly. "I hate to see you sliding into that cheap, fashionable kind of career."

Pierre glanced at her again rather quizzically.

She found herself saying calmly and distinctly: "I hate to see you becoming an opportunist, Pierre. I hate to see you thinking of nothing but success."

Instantly she knew she should not have said it. With alarm she saw the hardening of his jaw, the color in his face, and the hard, cold look in his eyes.

For a minute or two there was silence. Then he said in a low, considered voice, "I'm very sorry, Delia, if you don't approve of me.

The coldness that had risen between them now terrified her. Pierre was staring impassively toward the bar. His profile was turned; with a pang of yearning she noticed each familiar feature—the bright crisp lock above the forehead, the arrogant, faintly Negroid lips, the full and oversensual chin. The youth, the fragrant touch of adventure were going; the stubborn, egotistical lines of maturity emerged.

For an instant her passion reached a horrifying peak. She almost burst into a cry of desperation. She longed to fling aside the curtain and say the one, the only thing that was in her heart: that her love for him was more than she could bear.

But she could not bring herself to say those simple words. Instead she said in a low, indifferent tone:

"New York is changing you. It is killing the best part of you." Her voice grew tense. "You should leave! Quickly! Before it's too late. ... "

The main dish had arrived at this moment, and the wine waiter opened the champagne. Pierre raised his glass, looked at Delia very earnestly, and suddenly smiled. He took her hand under the table, pressed it, and whispered: "Let's forget our troubles! Let's drink to each other, darling!"

When she saw the look in his eyes, her heart was flooded with joy; all feeling of recrimination vanished, and the world seemed brilliant and secure again. She raised her glass, and they drank.

Their waiter was a small tense man who looked like Napoleon. He carved the lamb, flourishing the knife ceremoniously, and placed their plates in front of them with religious solemnity. Several other waiters were flying past at full speed, one with a tray of hors d'oeuvres, one with a towering souffle, a third with a tin of hot rolls and muffins.

Delia remained happy for about twenty minutes. Pierre told her, very wittily, about his interview with Mr. Prendergast. She told him, rather wistfully, about her luncheon with the Baron and Madame Petra. He smiled, picked up her hand, and kissed it. Everything seemed delightful again.

But when the dessert arrived, something began to trouble her; at first she didn't know quite what it was.

Then she knew. Pierre had noticed a dark, frozen-looking woman at another table. She turned her doll-like face to him and smiled. He nodded politely.

"Who is that?" said Delia tensely.

"Anne de Bettancour," said Pierre. "I knew her brother in Paris."

"Do you know her well?"

"I scarcely recognized her," said Pierre, shrugging his shoulders.

"She looked … " began Delia; she hesitated.

"Yes?"

"Never mind," said Delia, in a strange low voice.

She had a feeling that all her own beauty had dissolved, and that her face looked hideously artificial; and that something in her character as well had shriveled; her charm was gone; she felt bleak and hateful.

A current of pain spread through her forehead. She longed intensely to burst into tears.

The dessert wagon was rolled up, full of glitter and color. There were shining éclairs, a chocolate pudding, bowls of plums and peaches, a caramel custard.

Delia stared at them coldly. They looked oddly unreal to her; like objects of glass or celluloid.

"No, thanks," she murmured. "I'll have some coffee."

"And brandy?" said Pierre.

She hesitated; her eyes were flashing. She drew the palm of her hand across her forehead. Then she said, with intensity: "No. I think not."

He had noticed something ominous in her tone, and grew silent. And again the strange, implacable yearning for strife rose up in her.

The canary overhead had been chirping intermittently. Now he sprang to a sudden, hysterical falsetto. Delia's fingers toyed nervously with the silver fox which lay beside her.

She turned casually to Pierre and said: "Have you been seeing that ballet dancer?"

He looked a little puzzled. "Which ballet dancer?"

With her heightened perceptions she had noticed him blush, and an evasive glint appear in his eyes; and her worst suspicions seemed to be appallingly confirmed. A blinding rush of despair tore through her, and it was only by a violent effort that she kept her outward calm.

"The one at Mrs. Clyde's yesterday," she said lightly, with a touch of sarcasm. "She wasn't bad-looking. Don't tell me, my dear, that you've forgotten her!"

Pierre looked rather relieved. A strange twinkle appeared in his eyes. "Yes, I'd quite forgotten her. What was her name?"

"Ivanova. Something of the sort." Delia's voice grew piercingly casual.

"Ivanova," said Pierre, in an offhand way. "Quite. Why in the world should I be seeing her?"

"Didn't she say something about a tête-à-tête you promised her? Something like that?"

Pierre raised his brows. "Tête-à-tête? God knows what she said. I never expect to see her again."

He seemed perfectly sincere. But instead of feeling reassured, her suspicions only grew still more insidious. She sipped at her coffee; she felt ill and feverish. The dining room seemed to be quivering with light, like an aquarium. She heard nothing but the senseless twittering of the canaries. And the feeling of an evil conspiracy against her, a conspiracy involving the entire world and even those who once had loved her, grew all-enveloping.

She turned her hot, desperate face to him and said: "Why aren't you honest with me, Pierre?" She paused; then she added in a high, tense voice: "You gave her your flower! Didn't you?" He sipped at his brandy and looked across the room; there was a nervous movement in the muscles of his jaw.

"You are no longer in love with me!" she suddenly burst out. For an instant she saw an abyss yawning beneath her. She grew frightened and stepped back. But her fury drove her on. She was beside herself. "You no longer need me! You no longer want me! You have fallen in love with someone else!"

He turned and stared at her without replying. She saw a cold and alien light in his eyes, and grew sick at heart when she guessed its meaning. And she thought, "It is true. Everything is over. He has actually begun to hate me."

And the anguish of this thought was so overwhelming that she felt her heart and mind grow completely inert. The room seemed utterly still. A wave of darkness crossed the walls. All power of thought or speech deserted her. She wanted only one thing; to be left alone.

She leaned over, gathered her furs, and rose. He looked at her calmly, and shrugged his shoulders. "Well?" he said. There was something hard and contemptuous, she thought, in his eyes.

"I'm not well," she murmured. "I'm going to leave you."

Without another word, she walked through the dining room, which seemed uncannily still and empty, and stepped through the hall into Fifty-third Street.

106

SHE walked a few steps, after leaving the restaurant, and found herself on the corner of Park Avenue. She glanced around. The street looked wholly unfamiliar. Then she turned and recognized the brightly lit marquee of the restaurant.

She drew the silver fox a little closer around her neck; and although the night was intensely hot, she found herself shivering. Her fingers kept plucking at the tiny fox paws.

Her mind was totally numb. She could not remember what had happened in the restaurant, why she had left, or why she was standing here alone. All she knew was that a strange, dark lull filled her body, and that the world had utterly changed. She felt completely removed from the city around her, the lights and the noise, the hissing taxis.

She stepped into the street. A car veered and squealed; it had barely missed her. She ran to the next corner.

She turned and saw the spire of Grand Central Terminal, darkly looming above the traffic. It seemed to quiver as she watched; to rear on its coils, like a cobra.

A young sailor approached, hesitated, and spoke to her. "Can you tell me the way to Forty-second Street, lady?" His voice was gentle and humble; he looked a little drunk.

She pointed vaguely southward. "Down there," she muttered, and turned her back to him. It was an effort even to speak.

A tall, dark lieutenant with a mustache was standing at the corner. He watched her for a minute or two with an air of curiosity. Then he came up and said: "Could I help you, miss?"

She turned her head without answering and walked down the street a few steps. She was filled with a detestation of everyone who passed her. "What is wrong with them?" she thought. "Why can't they leave me alone?"

She made an effort to collect her thoughts, and to review what had just happened. She recalled the twittering canaries, and the light of the chandeliers. Then she remembered Pierre sitting calmly beside her, and the cold, impatient light in his eyes. And instantly a needling pain shot through her.

She thought: "He no longer loves me. He hates the sight of me.... He would have followed me if he still loved me."

She turned and watched the door of the restaurant, which shone vividly beyond the light hanging under the marquee. At that moment the doorman nodded politely and a young man, with his hat in his hand, came striding through the entrance. It was Pierre. He stepped into a cab which was parked beside the entrance, banged the door behind him, and vanished down the street. He was gone before she grasped what was happening.

She began to walk rapidly up Park Avenue. She turned left on Fifty-seventh Street and hurried toward Madison Avenue.

She began almost to run. And she said to herself: "Why hurry? There is nothing to be done.... Everything is over. Nothing can be done, nothing."

She forced herself to walk very slowly. Through the darkened show windows of the galleries she could see small paintings, chinaware, and *objets d'art*. She paused in front of one of the displays. In the center stood a painting of some peasants in a hay wagon. On the left was a porcelain rococo shepherdess. On the right stood a bronze figure; a naked boy with a bow and arrow.

She turned and gazed at the illuminated masses of stone above her, and saw the mountainous twinkle of Radio City in the distance. The great towers seemed suspended in the air, tremulous, destructible.

And in a flash she saw everything in a new, clear light. The torrent of human blindness and violence seemed to shine, to burst into flame, like sunlight on the sea.

She drew her fingers across her eyes. "I am going mad," she thought. "I am going mad."

At that moment she heard her name spoken in a woman's voice. She looked around. A tall, flat-faced woman in a dark suit was smiling at her. It was Janet Hall, an old friend of hers from Philadelphia who had been at school with her ten or twelve years ago.

"Delia! I thought it was you, my dear!"

Delia could not bring herself to smile; she saw Janet Hall's face through a kind of haze. Her features looked peculiarly coarse and hard, and there was something in her glance which seemed odious and unnatural.

"I haven't seen you for months, darling!" said Janet in her strident, overemphatic voice. "I didn't even know you were in town! Were you there all summer? I've been up at Cape Cod. I've only been back a few days. . . . You're looking splendid, my dear. Perfectly splendid!"

Delia scarcely listened. She felt nothing but a passionate desire to be alone. Janet's brisk, efficient manner seemed suddenly repulsive.

She said in a dull tone: "Well, good night, Janet. I'm in a hurry, I'm afraid."

Janet looked at her with surprise, and a touch of annoyance. Delia turned and left her without another word.

She turned right at Madison Avenue, then turned again at Fifty-ninth Street. She passed a cigar store, a newspaper stand, a toy and confectionery shop. She glanced through the window. The place was brilliantly lit: china dolls, tiny monkeys and elephants of glass, and a horde of giant pandas were crouching among the candies.

She crossed Fifth Avenue, passed the Plaza, and paused for a moment at the subway entrance. She looked across at the park; she felt she had forgotten something. She touched her furs very lightly. Then she hurried on.

She arrived at her hotel, swiftly crossed the lobby, and walked up to the reception desk.

"Has anyone tried to phone me?"

The clerk glanced casually at her mailbox.

"No, ma'am. There's no message."

Delia closed her eyes for a moment, and then strolled quietly to the elevator.

"Fifteenth floor, please," she murmured. The metal door closed. There were no other passengers in the elevator. She felt herself soaring, floor after floor, enclosed in a prison of iron and steel. She felt suddenly that she was about to scream.

She closed her eyes, clenched her fists, and dug her nails into the flesh. The sense of self-mastery returned. And her heart leaped furiously, half in triumph, half in nausea, at the thought of what was about to happen.

The elevator came to a halt and the door slid open; she stepped into the hollow twilight of the corridor. She felt a bit dizzy, and paused for an instant. Then she hurried breathlessly to her room.

107

PIERRE had taken a taxi to the flat of Baron Legué. He arrived there in a state of nervous exhaustion.

The baron was rather surprised to see him. "What has happened?" he exclaimed, as he opened the door. "You look upset, my boy!"

Pierre shook his head gloomily. "Nothing. A quarrel. I don't know."

The baron knew almost everything about Pierre; he understood him and loved him. "With Delia?" he said quietly.

Pierre nodded, and stared sullenly at the floor. For several minutes they sat in silence.

Pierre was in a state of mingled anger, bewilderment, and fear that bordered on desperation. His instinct scented the true nature of his crisis with Delia; but his reason rejected it. It did not make sense. He felt his body still sweating with excitement. But gradually, as he sat with the baron, he began to feel a little calmer.

The baron said: "Would you care for a bit of brandy?"

Pierre looked up at him wearily. "Well, perhaps," he said. "A little."

The baron rang a bell; a young Filipino butler appeared. "Bring us the brandy, please. And two round glasses," said the baron, with a curving, cuplike gesture of the hand. He sat down and waited for the drinks to arrive before he spoke.

Pierre glanced at the old man crouching deep in his chair. A set of chess figures lay in a box at his side; the baron had picked up an ivory knight, and was turning it slowly in his fingers. Pierre was suddenly shocked by the old man's face, which was accentuated by the oblique light of the reading lamp; it seemed reduced to pure bone. His age and illness had taken on an almost ravenous intensity.

"You've made your plans about returning?" said Pierre presently, raising his brandy glass.

"To France?" said the baron. He smiled; an appalling little smile. "Ah, Pierre; will I ever return? I'm not well, you know. Not at all well ... " He shrugged his shoulders. He extended his bony fingers, and held the ivory knight under the yellow lamplight, turning the figure slowly around.

"We've been living in our own little Europe," said Pierre. "We've hardly seen the real America."

"Hardly at all," said the baron in his beautiful slow voice. "We've lived in a nomad's tent. With our eyes fixed on a mirage. ... And now it's all over. The tents are being gathered. The nomads are on the march. ... But I'm too old; I shall stay behind."

He shook his head slowly; his huge red eyes shone gently at Pierre. And he began to speak of his beloved Touraine, with its poplar-lined streams and its fragrant meadows. His two favorite phrases recurred: *toujours la proportion; les choses bien balancées.* "One feels so safe there," he murmured. "The landscape is so small. So human." He raised his thin little hands and made the shape of a square with four outstretched fingers.

For several minutes they sat in silence. Some new, nostalgic reality had been created between them. It hung in the air, vibrating faintly, like the sound of a flute or a violin. Pierre closed his eyes. The French landscape gathered around him, more radiantly and irresistibly than ever before. He saw the cattle wandering at dusk past the willow trees; the light appearing lazily in the distant village, and the village steeple glowing, a brilliant crimson, like a cockscomb; he saw the harvesters cycling homeward down the lane, and the girl with the hazel twig herding the geese; he heard the voices in the arbor, and the tinkle of glasses, and the sound of singing among the hills; the gust of the land came over him again, the smell of the hay and the rain-drenched furrows, and the marvelous scent of the casserole in the kitchen, flowing forth with all the grace of a serenade. Scent, sound, and sight mingled in a fit of violent yearning. And he felt that his years in America had been a mirage; a terrible series of self-deceptions.

He opened his eyes. The baron sat motionless, fingers pressed into a triangle, watching him with a sly, pale, tender look.

The baron was a collector of old glassware. Behind him stood a cabinet filled with rows of old wineglasses which he had picked up, one by one, in the antique shops of New York; fine Venetian, Bohemian, Jacobite goblets, touched with the iridescence of age. The lamplight fell on their delicate curves and tall, spiraling stems. One breath of air, it seemed, and they would fall into fragments. And the baron himself, with his frail, tapering mind, looked as brittle as his glasses; he seemed about to collapse.

"We've tried to build our own little Europe over here," he continued in his weary, melodious voice. "We built our pathetic replicas of Paris and Brussels, and tried to protect them from the hurricane." He fixed his bloodshot eyes on Pierre with sudden animation. "But now the war is over. Listen, my boy. The war was not precisely pleasant, but it was only a hint, a prelude to the approaching melodrama. The world has grown too small for our machinery, and too big for our hearts. All we see is stone, metal, paper, numbers, names; they've fallen like a curtain over the shape of man. We'll have an era of weird little cults, I suppose, a hysterical hodgepodge of panaceas. But they'll be useless, one and all. Just a kind of lurid rhetoric. The great new pestilence will continue.... Millions of little people are swarming in the streets outside. But they're turning into ghosts. Their capacity for freedom is dying."

He paused; a thin dry smile appeared on his lips. "Shall I give you my philosophy in a nutshell, my boy? Very well. Here it is. It's rather unfashionable, I suppose. Freedom, I've learned, is a rare and fragile article. Like these wineglasses. It can't be produced by machines. Man seeks his freedom and identity nowadays in a monstrous tangle of machinery. And he is defeated; there is no freedom or identity without faith in man's dignity, man's uniqueness, man's inner and eternal right to tragedy. Without this faith all common ground for understanding vanishes; the higher authority has perished. And men are reduced to a poisonous loneliness." He sighed and closed his eyes. "I feel like one of these wineglasses. I feel dusty, unreal. I'm afraid I've become an anachronism."

He smiled again. He spread his fingers, with a kind of exquisite fatigue, around the gleaming brandy glass. "And you, Pierre? You're staying here?" He gazed at the ceiling.

Pierre had been troubled by a strange, irrational suspense; a small black shadow was hovering in the back of his consciousness. He took a deep breath.

"I've decided to go back to Paris," he said quietly. His voice grew sharper. "As soon as possible."

The baron raised his brows equivocally, and shot a quick look at him. Pierre turned and fixed his eyes on the slender glasses in the cabinet: they shone like icicles, ready to dissolve.

"And what about ... the young lady?" said the baron.

Pierre shook his head. "I'll never be able to make her happy. It's better if I leave. I don't, I can't, I'll never belong here. ... "

The baron watched him without speaking. For several minutes they sat in silence. Then the baron said: "I think I understand, Pierre. Perhaps you're wrong; perhaps you're right. But anyway, go back. Before it's too late."

Pierre felt that he had suddenly grown very much older; an era of his existence had passed. He drained his brandy glass and rose.

"Good night, my friend," he said affectionately, and took the old man's hand in his own. "Thank you. You've helped me! For a while, at least ... "

"Good night, my boy," said the baron. He rose and led Pierre to the door. He stood for a moment beside the elevator. "Don't be frightened," he whispered. "There are things in life that one cannot help." He looked sharply at Pierre. "Whatever happens, don't be frightened. ... Be brave. Be yourself."

Pierre stepped into the night, on his way to the Shropshire. An electrical fragrance filled the air. The city was filled with a subtle vibration, like the fluttering of a million tiny wings.

108

JONATHAN, after Sebastian had left him, continued slowly down the path. An intense silence now filled the park. The locusts and willows hung their boughs over the water; not a leaf, not a blade of grass was stirring.

He walked up a slope and crossed a meadow. There was an illusion of pure rural solitude. He almost expected to hear the tinkle of a sheep bell, and to see a flock of sheep wandering over the hillside. A single glowworm was circling through the shrubbery, flashing his torch as he sailed along.

He remembered having walked here with Lydia long ago. Everything seemed the same, only darker, more derelict. The freshness and animation were gone; the air was muted and elegiac. Two or three young soldiers were strolling about. They all were waiting for something to happen, it seemed—the trees, the soldiers, the invisible sheep; waiting for a climax, waiting for a vision.

But nothing happened. The suspense continued: not the suspense of human drama, but of a new, incalculable core of violence.

He turned and wandered down toward the Zoo. He stopped at a fountain to drink, and could hear the wild beasts stirring in their cages.

He paused beside the pool and saw the sea lions, inert on their pedestals, black and glossy. They were rolling their eyes, unable to sleep. The cockatoos huddled in the near-by cages, with their crested heads tucked under their wings. Their colors looked cold and phosphorescent in the lamplight.

Jonathan sat down on a bench below the terrace. The scent of wild animals filled the night. He recognized the strong, spicy odor of the foxes, and the rancid, penetrating smell of the bears. He caught sight of a black bear, like a velvet cushion among the rocks; and of a great sleepless polar bear, climbing from the pool with his wet fur sparkling. And he noticed a curious little tremor behind the bars, as though the rocks were coming to life: rats, dozens of them, had appeared from the crevices and were rippling daintily over the stones.

He reached into his pocket and drew out Delia's letter. A faint scent of lilac rose from the paper. The script looked odd, indecipherable, in the darkness. And her character, once so simple and transparent, now so deceptive and obscure, closed in on him slowly; he felt her presence as never before.

One of the animals in the lion house began to roar. It started slowly, gathering volume and passion, until the leaves in the trees and even the water in the pool seemed to quiver.

He kept staring at the dark hieroglyphic pattern on the page. He knew the words by heart; but the inner message remained hidden. What did she really mean? What had happened, what was happening?

And a flock of memories stole through his mind. He leaned back on the bench, with his arms extended, until he saw nothing but the stars in the sky. He thought of his summers in Maine, and the constellations over the lake; the swarms of gnats above the water, the leap of a fish and the lingering ripples; the scent of pine, and the scent of dew on the sun-soaked rowboat.

Orion, the Pleiades. Their pattern had endured. And what had happened to him in the meantime? A search for love; a search for permanence; and finally, an acceptance of his solitude. He saw the relationship among Delia, Lydia, Pierre, and himself, a fragile pattern against the vast impersonality of the city: he saw the pattern join and slowly gather meaning, then suddenly break apart and dissolve. The fruit of human contact had never ripened. The climate was too tempestuous, too arid.

A second roar emerged from the lion house, higher, more penetrating than the first: a tigress, perhaps, or a young lioness. The cockatoos ruffled their feathers in reply. The sea lion coughed and rolled on his back. There was a scuffling and hissing among the raccoons, and then a piercing cry; the yelp of a coyote.

Jonathan felt his body tingling: the whole Zoo was on the alert. A jungle crisis had sprung up suddenly. The imprisoned birds, the beasts, and the reptiles were weaving a web of invisible passions in the darkness. Strands of fear, hatred, rebellion, and perhaps of subtle sympathy, were moving mysteriously from pool to pool, from cage to cage.

Then, for no perceptible reason, the tension was broken. The crisis passed. The silence returned. There was one last shudder of alarm among the foxes, and the sense of slumber began to spread.

Jonathan wandered back through the park. The night lay tranquil and human; until, at a sudden turn of the path, the entire city rose above him.

He paused on the bridge. Beyond the lake rose the Pierre and the Plaza, like trees in full bloom, casting their spectacular blaze of petals into the pool below.

And still beyond, like a terrible cathedral, rose the dim gray rectangle of Radio City. A copper haze hung over the summit. The walls shone softly, like a volcano's.

109

DELIA arrived in her room and turned on the light; she cast her fur and her hat on the velvet armchair.

Then she threw herself on the bed, ran her hand across her forehead, and carefully lit a cigarette. But the taste of the tobacco seemed stale and disgusting; she killed the cigarette and tossed it through the window.

She rose and walked to the desk, and stood beside it for a minute, with her finger tips beating lightly on the chair. Her whole body seemed to converge in a single rhythm. She grew aware of a violent throbbing in her temples; not actually painful, merely peculiar—a furious desiccated sound like the sound of a rattle.

Her hands sprang into motion. The left one seized a sheet of paper, the right one reached for the pen and lightly stabbed the inkwell; and then moved with a crouching intensity as it wrote:

Pierre—I must see you. Phone me the minute you come in. Please. I am terrified. D.

She slipped the note into a pale blue envelope, which she addressed to Pierre in a clear, decisive hand. Then she stood for several minutes with her palms on the desk, and the envelope resting lightly between her fingers. The pen rolled from the desk, and fell on the floor beside her, with a tiny spattering of drops. She let it lie.

Again her fingers grew alive. They trembled lightly, like a cat about to spring. She dropped the envelope on the desk, quickly crossed the room, and sat down in front of the dressing table.

She continued to stare at herself in the mirror; she was shocked at the thing she saw in her face. The eyes looked huge and expressionless, and there was a deep blue shadow beneath the eyes.

"Do I really look like that?" she wondered, with a pang of despair. Her hand moved instinctively toward the powder box; but it paused in mid-air. Instead of picking up the powder puff she calmly reached down and opened one of the enameled drawers.

A small photograph album, bound in maroon, lay in the drawer. She took it out and laid it before her, beside the warm pink boudoir light. Listlessly she began to turn the pages. They were photographs of her childhood in Philadelphia. She had planned a fortnight ago to show them to Pierre, but at first had forgotten, then had deliberately refrained.

There were two or three photographs of herself as a baby. Then there was one in which she wore a white lace dress, and was sitting on the lawn with her older sister; she must have been four or five, and her head was covered with curls. There was one taken on her seventh birthday, squinting in the sunlight and holding a doll: she was wearing a bright new polka-dotted dress. Then there were several of herself and her friends at school; she remembered their names—June, Agnes, Lucille.

The last photograph in the album was taken when she was fifteen, sitting in a hammock under an apple tree. In this her own features had emerged quite clearly. She stared at it closely, with sudden fascination: and a momentary pang of delight swept through her.

She looked again at her face in the mirror, and the feeling of desolation returned; this time, however, not acute and stabbing, but encircling, profound, and almost hypnotic.

She sat like this, in a kind of torpor, for ten or fifteen minutes. The album slid and fell to the floor. She sprang to her feet, crossed the room, and picked up the telephone.

"Has anyone tried to phone me?" she said, in a thin staccato voice. "Mrs. Potter. Room 1503."

"Mrs. Potter?" said the operator. "Fifteen-three? Just a moment." Delia waited; her fingers drummed feverishly on the edge of the bed.

"Hello? No, there've been no calls for you, madam. . . . Thank you. Good night."

"Good night," said Delia. Her voice had fallen to a whisper. She stood absolutely motionless for several minutes, her mind drained of all reaction or plan. The rattle in her temples grew a little sharper.

Then she heard something else—a kind of bubbling noise. She looked down: the receiver was still in her hand.

She placed it carefully back on the hook. Then she strode across the room, locked the door, and turned out both of the bedroom lights. Slowly, softly, she walked to the window.

She caught sight of the envelope lying on the desk: the sight of Pierre's name was almost unbearable. She picked it up, tore it methodically, and dropped the fragments through the open window. She leaned over the sill and watched them pirouetting, like flakes of snow, through the towering darkness.

Far below dark shapes were moving along the street; they looked like little insects, faceless, unfathomable. She felt severed, at last, from the life of men.

She looked at the sky. The stars were as brilliant, as innumerable as she had ever seen them. They seemed to watch her with a warm, intimate tranquillity. There was something strangely personal, like the look of a face, in their pattern.

A cry pierced the hot, nervous silence behind her. Her senses were galvanized; she clutched at the sill. It was like the scream of a captured animal—a shrill and defiant plea for mercy.

Then it sprang forth again; a delirious little echo. It was, she realized, the telephone ringing. And instinctively a spasm of hope welled up in her. She suppressed it immediately. The phone kept ringing.

Then it ceased, and the silence flowed back through the room.

She grew aware of a strange, sweating turbulence in the night. A strand of hair blew over her face, caressing her cheeks and eyelids.

There was an infinitesimal click: the sound of a doorknob furtively turning. And the bedroom behind her sprang into life, filled with some wild, unutterable presence. She turned. The whole room looked shaggy and cavernous; the walls, the furniture were beginning to stir.

"No, no," she whispered. For a moment there was silence. Then she heard a sound of footsteps hurrying down the corridor.

A stinging sensation rose from her heart, and hung uneasily suspended in her throat. She drew her fingers across her neck very lightly. "There ... there ... " she murmured; and her courage returned.

She drew her legs onto the sill and looked down. She saw nothing at all; or almost nothing. The lights were extinguished and the traffic had vanished; only a soundless, boundless vacuum remained. She leaned out farther. The air from the park flowed past her, bearing a scent of withering foliage.

There was a quick little knock on the door; and a moment later, the violent rattle of the doorknob. A voice cried "Delia!" And a wave of triumph leaped within her, a final and desperate exultation.

She clung for one last moment to the window sill. All things grew suddenly clear and comprehensible, and a marvelous lucidity flowed through her mind. She opened her hands, bowed her head, and leaned forward.

And simultaneously, like lightning, a flash of regret pierced her body. The world shot apart; she uttered a cry. The sky rushed down like a blazing torrent and enclosed her in everlasting darkness.